FIREBIRD

THE SOVEREIGNTY WARS

MICHAEL COLE

SEVERED PRESS
HOBART TASMANIA

FIREBIRD

CHAPTER 1

2137
Somewhere in northeast United States ruins
Border between Laferrier Territory and Rhino Territory

Her knees pressed down against the shards of shattered cement and gravel as Dr. Saegusa knelt low. She was encompassed by the huge shadow of the remaining section of bridge that still stood in the ruins of a once busy city. Beyond that shadow were the ashes of an old playground. Seeing the charred segments of metal slides, support beams, hoses, and other mechanics, she determined it was likely an outdoor waterpark. She had heard of such recreations, though she would never know what it was like. Huddled on the ground, she envisioned children playing with their friends and parents, free from the horrors of the impending future. Generations ago, the city was vibrant, as was the rest of the world. But it ended in a flash. A literal flash, one of a hundred that consumed the world. In man's attempt to battle his brother, he had destroyed himself. The bridge, the few segments that still stood, was among the last of the structures which had withstood the nuclear blast. The earth shook each day with the aftershock from another collapse. The major cities were vacant, except from a few stragglers who had no allegiance to any territory. There weren't many resources that could be mined from the cities nowadays.

Saegusa squinted from the flashes from overhead. Blue-white streaks of radiation lightning ripped across the maroon sky. They stretched far in bent, crippling bands, as though the Earth herself was angered. They were brighter at night than during the day, and the permanent radioactive glow of the atmosphere was a daily reminder of the mistakes of mankind's past.

It seems some lessons are never learned.

She could hear the whining of engines, followed by the downward gust of wind generated by the turbines of a patrolling Harrier. Thirty feet long, armed with plasma cannons on each wing, the aircraft patrolled slowly. She could see it after it passed over the edge of the bridge. Its metal hull, originally bright silver, was now a dull grey, symptomatic of its heavy use. Plasma turrets under the rim of its wings rotated, the targeting sensors scanning for anything its pilot believed to be enemy forces. Elevators under the wings kept the vehicle airborne, while rear thrusters pushed it ahead.

Rhino's military knew she was here somewhere, and they would not stop until they had captured her.

Saegusa huddled down and watched. Across the charred playground were the ruins of collapsed apartment complexes, shops, parks, and other features of a world lost. Green flashes ripped between the ruins, accompanied by the crackling echoes of gunshots. Fire and smoke swirled several hundred yards out.

"Damn it!" Saegusa glanced to her right, seeing the scarred face of Commander Mick Parker. He bared cracked teeth as he watched the atrocities, his muscular body tensing up with anger. More Harriers joined in the distance, firing green plasma bullets downward onto a target visually obscured from the team's view. The gunshots resumed, but quickly dwindled in frequency. Now the air was full of the echoes of explosions and pained screams. Commander Parker hit the ground with his fist then glanced behind him at the fifteen men who crouched near the cement pillar. "The bastards! They found Charlie Team."

A young soldier sprang to his feet, his uniform tattered, smoke covered, and torn in numerous places. "Then let's go! We gotta help them!"

"Shh!" Another soldier hissed, while a third stepped up and cupped his hand over the eager man's mouth and pulled him back down.

"Keep it quiet!" Parker hissed. He held up a hand and crouched, his eyes aimed up at the sky as they heard the engines of another Harrier craft passing by. Dust and gravel swirled beneath it and swept over the squad of LaFerrier Territory troops. The hums grew faint as the Harrier continued its sweep. Parker slowly exhaled and maintained a calm appearance. "They're gone. There's nothing we can do." The squad remined in position, forced to watch the horrid flashes of green plasma charges in the distance. Soon the cracking of rifles came to an end, while the firing of plasma weapons continued. Rhino soldiers enjoyed the harm they inflicted, and they did a thorough job of making sure there were no survivors.

Parker leaned down toward Dr. Saegusa. Her black hair was almost grey with the accumulation of grit. Her tan trousers and black long-sleeved shirt were weathered, as was the large leather pouch she carried over her shoulder.

"Doc, I hope you got all the samples you needed," he said.

"I do. I promise," she said. Her voice was apologetic. With an escort from LaFerrier Territory, the bio-chemist had traveled across the northeast border in search of samples from a rare species of flower known as the Radialem. It had come into existence after the war, despite nuclear contamination. Whether it was a new form of evolution, or just the earth flipping the bird to nuclear fallout, these plants provided a sap that could treat radiation sickness. Labs had synthesized many of the properties and used it to create treatment pods. Once a week, people would have to spend thirty minutes in a treatment pod to eradicate the radiation in their bodies.

However, the synthesized solution made from the sap was growing more difficult to produce. Labs in every territory were growing full of people awaiting their turn for treatment. It was a process which grew increasingly problematic. Saegusa, the leading authority in medicine and bio-engineering, along with several medical specialists in her home territory of Espinosa, believed they could conjure up a solution. They would continue her father's research and develop a serum to combat cancer cells and eradicate the looming threat that plagued the population. It seemed to be a plan that could help everybody. But there were those that wanted her research for themselves, such as the Rhino and Sovereignty Territories. These territories were considered the superpowers of the western continent and had a harsh distain for each other. But they never engaged in war with each other, as the conflict would be so destructive, that even the winning side would be crippled for decades to come.

Unless one of them could get their hands onto Dr. Saegusa's research and reverse bio-engineer it. Spies and recon units had received word that both territories were in search for Dr. Saegusa and her findings. In the wrong hands, her knowledge and research could be used as a deadly bio-weapon, a new form of poison acid gas that could plague an entire countryside. Only Saegusa knew the specific components needed for the weapon, as well as the counter-weapon used to eradicate the gas itself. Once utilized, the acid gas could be designed to eradicate an enemy force. Afterwards, the counter-weapon would be deployed, which would dissolve the acid gas and make the territory hospitable once more. A bio-degradable, eco-friendly weapon of mass destruction.

The superpowers would do anything to get their hands on such research.

Saegusa opened her pouch again to check on the various samples collected in glass vials, then closed it back up.

"Of course, that damned plant couldn't grow in any area other than the freaking border," Parker remarked.

"It does...all the way near the west coast. Two-thousand miles away," she said.

"Well, *that's* helpful," he remarked.

"If we can get this to the lab and add the compounds and engineer this medicine, we won't have to use those damn pods anymore," she said. She sighed and watched the skies once more. They were so damn close to getting back. Then again, it probably wouldn't have mattered. Rhino was always looking for a reason to extend into LaFerrier's region. It was just a matter of time before a full-on invasion would take place. Espinosa had little in the way of military resources and had to rely on their ally, LaFerrier, for an armed escort. But their forces were meager compared to Rhino's. The superpower was already armed with advanced plasma weaponry, while LaFerrier was limited to old-fashioned cartridge rounds.

Parker watched as the group of Harriers broke off and began circling the city. Rhino knew Saegusa was somewhere in the area and would stop at nothing to seize her and her research.

"We can't hide forever. They'll find us eventually," he said.

"Then there's no choice," Saegusa said. "I have to make a radio call for pickup."

"Their pilots will pick up on that transmission and zero in on our location," Parker said.

"There's no other choice," Saegusa said. She clutched her automatic rifle and checked the thirty-round magazine. "We can't fight our way out of this."

"No, but we might be able to help you get away," Parker said.

"What are you talking about?"

"I might be able to distract them long enough for you to make a run for it," he said. "Take one of the Jeeps and high-tail it to the south-west. The Journey Road isn't far from here. Once you're on that, you can floor the pedal all the way to Fort Bowman. It we hit them hard enough in the meantime, they won't notice you."

"Commander," Saegusa had to strain herself from raising her voice. "That's a suicide mission. You'll never make it out alive."

"Let's face it. We're not making it out alive anyway. But they won't kill you. They need you, so even if they do track you, they won't fire upon you."

"Yeah, but…"

"No arguing!" Parker ordered. He turned around to face his men. "The doc's right. Now that Alpha, Charlie, and Delta teams are gone, we're outgunned and outnumbered. But we can't let them get the doc. We have only one tactic: Attack and divert. As your commander, I'm obligated to tell you that nobody will come out of this alive. So, I'll only take volunteers. You have sixty seconds to step up."

It only took a moment for the group to stand up and assemble. The men double checked their armaments and stood in position of attention, ready to receive orders. Saegusa stared at them with wide eyes.

"Commander, you don't have to do this…"

"Yes, we do. If they capture you, they'll download your neurological implants and get the data you've collected. If they use your research to develop superweapons, then LaFerrier won't be long for this world anyway. You can bet that they'll test their chemical agents on our Territory, then move on to Espinosa before turning south and engaging the Sovereignty."

"But…"

"I said, no arguing," he said. He took her by the arm and led her past the squad to one of the Jeeps they had parked. There was no windshield or windows. The frame was nothing but jagged metal sustained from years of abuse. But despite the rugged appearance, the engine ran well and the Jeep could zip up to a hundred miles per hour. Soldiers climbed over the rear to disconnect the turret and ammo chain. After all, she wouldn't be needing it.

Saegusa climbed over the enormous tires into the driver's seat. She set her bag aside and looked back down at Parker.

"Don't start the engine yet. Wait till we've engaged the Harriers."

"Okay," she said. Her heart was drumming in her chest. It intensified after they felt the droning sound of engines passing overhead. The squad remained silent and waited for the Harrier to gain distance. They were still undetected. Parker watched the Harrier carefully. It was completing another pass over what used to be a park. In about two minutes, it would circle back.

"Okay, now's the time," he said. "Men, get those RPGs. We will take position on the ridge near that slump of concrete over on the right." He looked to his men and pointed. "Rowley! Brown! Take the other Jeep. After we engage the first Harrier, floor it and light the rest of them up. Let's draw them to us and away from the doc. Ronald! Carey! Set up the fifty-cal over by the slab." He pointed to a section of collapsed bridge fifty yards to the left. "The birds will converge on the RPGs. We'll lead them into a crossfire, and you guys will light 'em up. After we hit them, I want the mobile unit to floor it and divert their attention. Everyone else, on me." He glanced back to Saegusa. "When Rowley and Brown take off, that's when you hightail. Understand?"

"Y-yes," Saegusa said.

"Good. And Doc?" He waited to make sure she could hear him loud and clear. She perked up and nodded. "Don't fall into their hands. Under any circumstances."

Saegusa nodded again. "Yes, Commander."

Parker turned to face his men. "Okay boys, it's been an honor serving with you. I'm glad to see you're not gonna go out like a bunch of pussies. In honor of LaFerrier, move out!"

The men scattered and diverted to their assigned locations. Four men with RPGs moved along under the bridge to a mound of uprooted cement and rubble and awaited the Harrier. The unit with the turret mounted machine gun moved under the slab of thick bridge that sloped at a forty-five-degree angle from the pillar to the ground. The legs of the turret mount scraped the concrete beneath their feet as they set up a firing position.

Parker led several men right, passing the RPG units along the way. They followed a curved path, with a man taking a firing position every few meters. Parker arrived at the end of the standing bridge section and took cover behind the thick pillar. Huge shards of concrete stuck out of the ground like knives, providing ample cover for him while he observed the Harriers with his binoculars.

Several of them spaced off about five hundred meters to the north, while the nearest one was slowly angling back toward the bridge. They moved across the red sky like silver fire flies, weaving between the ravaged foundations of building structures. He could hear the clicking of scanners as they searched for movement. Occasionally the air flashed green as they blasted away at potential hideouts in hopes of luring their prize out into the open.

"Okay, stand by," he called out to the RPG unit. He spoke audibly and with purpose, intending to attract the interest of the pilot. The audio scanners picked up on his voice and the pilot descended to twenty meters above the ground. The Harrier approached the bridge, its dirty hull dripping condensation from the air circulation unit. Parker could see the cockpit and the white uniform and mask of the Rhino Trooper at the controls. The vehicle angled down to allow scans of under the bridge. The elevators spiraled at the center of each wing, kicking up large gusts of dust. The windshield had a red tint to it as it reflected the radiated sky. Lightning slashed the atmosphere, flashing white over the city as the pilot slowly neared the Harrier to the bridge.

Parker could see the goggled eyes of the pilot mask as he stared the trooper in the face. He stood up in the space between cement slabs. His scarred face creased as he smiled at the pilot.

Here I am, motherfucker.

"Now!" he shouted.

Sparks flared from under the bridge, as two rocket-propelled grenades ripped out from under the bridge. They spiraled several times along their paths until they both struck the starboard side of the cockpit. The shot placement was perfect. The front of the Harrier exploded into chunks of flesh, glass, and metal. Smoke and fire flared several meters high as it spiraled. The engines sputtered and died, sending the ship smashing hard into the ground like a metal meteor.

Parker and his men ducked behind cover as shards of hot metal soared through the air. The ship erupted into a hot ball of blue and orange fire as the reactor core burst from within.

Parker covered his face and peeked out once again, straining through the intense heat as he tried to get a visual on the other crafts. They were already moving in with great speed, growing larger as they approached.

The men grew antsy. The Harriers were in attack formation. There were at least five of them. Knees wavered back and forth as the soldiers felt the urge to spring from their crouched postures.

"Hold position," Parker said to the men. His voice was firm, lacking any sense of urgency. Beneath that composure was a man who knew he was minutes away from entering the next realm, whether that be Heaven, Hell, or just blackness six feet under the ground.

The Harriers began to spread out.

"Rifle units, scatter. RPGs, stand by to fire."

The command barely left his lips as streams of green plasma pulses began to bombard the bridge. The ground sparked as energy bullets struck down between the moving bodies. The riflemen ran back under the bridge, zagging hastily between streams of plasma and the numerous explosions they created. Chunks of concrete rained down from the road structure above as other Harriers blasted it from above.

One tenacious soldier, intent on fighting back instead of running, sprayed several rounds into the cockpit of the nearest aircraft. The bullets bounced off the windshield, forming numerous cracks in the glass. The pilot elevated the ship and aimed the starboard turret down. Red crosshairs targeted the rifleman on the cockpit computer. With a squeeze of the trigger, the pilot sent a dozen plasma blasts ripping down at the base of the bridge. The first several energy bullets struck the cement barrier, blowing it to dust as those that followed hit the soldier. They exploded on impact, sending charred body parts flying through the dust bank.

Two other Harrier pilots steadied their vehicles. With the soldiers under the bridge, the pilots focused the targeting systems on the pillars, with the intent to collapse the bridge on top of the squad. It was the exact move that Parker was anticipating.

"RPGs fire!"

Four rocket propelled grenades struck at once, each strategically striking the wing of one of the Harriers. Explosions of fire, plasma, and metal ripped out from both sides of each aircraft, sending both of them plummeting hard into the ground.

At that moment, the fifty-caliber opened fire on the other Harriers. Bullets struck hard against the hull, shredding the outer layer of metal. The aircraft split, firing plasma wildly at the enemy location.

"Mobile unit, you're a-go!"

The engine roared as Rowley stomped on the accelerator. Tires kicked up a mix of gravel as the Jeep sped out from under the bridge to the clearing between the crashed Harriers. Brown, the turret gunner, immediately opened fire, sending white streaks through the air. Rowley floored the gas pedal, racing beneath the other aircraft.

"Woohoo!" he screamed, throwing a fist high over his head. The vehicle bounced over various debris as it raced across the park and into the city. The Harriers rotated and began pursuit. Rear thrusters flashed bright orange, sending the two aircrafts chasing the Jeep like rockets.

"Come get some!" Brown shouted. He tilted the turret upward, placing several rounds into the belly of the pursuing Harriers. Engines screamed as the aircraft gave chase. Plasma turrets aimed down and sprayed, flashing the night air in bursts of green. The driver veered right and left to avoid the onslaught. The ground erupted in flashy explosions of energy and grit, dirtying the air with smoke.

The other Harriers opened fire. They zigzagged between the jagged edges of buildings, blowing portions of metal to bits with artillery.

Parker watched as the mobile unit disappeared behind smoke and rubble, with the Harriers zooming above it. They continued to fire, stirring up more smoke around the ruins. The Commander could hear the screeching of tires and the rattling of the fifty-cal. The plan had worked.

"Now's your chance, Doc! Good luck!"

Saegusa gave Parker one final glance. She could see the Commander standing in front of a wall of flame. He was shouting orders to his men. He didn't look back, as his attention was focused on the enemy. There would be more Harriers coming shortly, in addition to drop ships.

She floored the pedal. Tires marked the pavement as the Jeep tore out from under the bridge. Saegusa grunted and cursed under her breath as she bounced in her seat. Like a surfer on raging water, the Jeep rebounded from riding over two football fields of uneven ground. Brick crumbled beneath the tires, the residue blackening the ground beneath it in ash.

The doc clung tight to the steering wheel. With no seatbelt, it was all she had to hold herself in place.

"Shit!" She turned hard to the left, avoiding a pile of ruins in her path. The steel beams scraped the rim of her tires. She took in a breath of relief only to yell out again. "SHIT!" A huge cement block laid directly in her path. The doctor veered to the right. She passed within inches of the huge block, smashing the left mirror against its edge.

Finally, she found herself on level ground. She was on the main road, headed southeast. At top speed, she would be at Fort Bowman in ten minutes. The troops stationed there were already geared for possible conflict with invading Rhino forces. Once she reached the fort, she would have a strong line of defense that would slow down the Rhinos.

She just needed to get there, fast and silent. Ten minutes, and she would be in the clear. Rhino wouldn't even know she left the area...

The air suddenly swirled around her, throwing her hair across her face. Bright white lights shined down over the frame of the Jeep, blinding her. Squinting, she looked up. A Harrier, a Model-15, hovered directly over her. It was twice the size of the standard Harriers, armed with rockets in addition to plasma turrets. The aircraft traveled parallel to her Jeep, gradually descending.

No...

What she feared had come true. The very fact that it hadn't fired on her made it clear that she had been identified. Though she couldn't see or hear the pilot, she could envision him radioing the rest of the battalion.

It couldn't end like this. She endured through all kinds of hell to save mankind, not make weapons to destroy the rest of it. She yanked the Jeep to the left, screeching the tires over the foundation of a flattened building. Directly ahead was the base of another structure, forcing her to turn violently. The Jeep fishtailed, completing a full spin before the tires regained their traction. She floored the pedal again, redirecting southeast once again.

Plasma rounds struck the ground several yards ahead of her engine, a strategic move by the pilot to force her to stop. She continued through the residual cloud of smoke.

Above her, the pilot grew frustrated. The doctor was wise to his intentions. It was clear she would not fall for the intimidation tactic. He would have to do something a little more drastic.

The thrusters flashed bright orange, driving the Harrier further ahead of its target. The pilot scanned the various structures in search of something large enough to obstruct the Jeep's path. The screen on the control console flashed with a red grid on the screen, displaying the remains of what used to be a tower. Only the bottom four stories remained. From high above, the inside appeared black, as though the opening led to a deep dark pit. The south wall was bent inward at the base, possibly due to the original collapse. Now, it was just a rigid piece of metal, standing forty feet high like an icicle.

The pilot fired his heavy blasters at the foot of the building. The energy beams seared through the metal, toppling the chunk of metal like a tree in the woods.

Saegusa screamed as she saw the forty-foot section smash down twenty feet ahead of her. She stomped on the brakes and spun the wheel to the right. The Jeep fishtailed again, rotating to the right until it was parallel to the obstacle. The Jeep struck hard, indenting the whole side a foot inward. The engine smoked and sputtered, while the vehicle rocked back and forth.

Saegusa sat for a moment, stunned by the impact. In moments, the smoke around began to twist as though it were a tornado. It broke apart into thin black sections of air as the Harrier lowered itself to the ground. The turbines whined loudly, while the turrets rotated back and forth in search of LaFerrier fighters.

Saegusa shook her head as the wind from the turbines assaulted her face. She tried pulling herself out from the seat, but her leg was pinned. Suddenly, the pain registered from where the door had folded down over her foot. She reached for her M16 rifle, but it had fallen out of reach. Not that it would do her much good anyway.

There was only one other option. Beneath the center console was the portable radio unit. She leaned down and snatched it up. With the antenna fully extended, she pressed the transmitter and screamed into the mic.

"Emergency! J-C-1-0-1, calling Bowman Command! Over!"

"Bowman Operations, we read you. What's your location?"

"Nine clicks northeast from rendezvous point. I'm pinned. Got a fifteen over me!"

She looked up again at the Harrier. It set down several feet behind the Jeep, crushing anything underneath it. The turbines powered down, allowing the smoke to float freely overhead. It trailed high into the red sky, blending into the clouds.

Within the smoke, another aircraft glided silently, its engines hardly making a sound. Unbeknownst to the warring territories below, a third party monitored the scenario. High above the warzone, a reflective device shimmered as it reset its system, keeping the advanced-tech aircraft hidden from view.

****

The inside of the cockpit was chilly. The operator liked it that way. Somehow, he felt it made him more alert. That, and he didn't like to sweat. Moisture always felt weird over his mechanical components.

Metal fingers tapped the dashboard to the beat of an old rock song while he listened to the radio chatter.

"Nine clicks northeast from rendezvous point. I'm pinned. Got a fifteen over me!"

"Bowman Operations, we read you. Sending fighter units your way. Just hang on!"

There was a mechanical whining sound from the receiver as one of the parties involved switched frequencies.

"Units Four, Seven, Eight, and Twelve, get out there and retrieve the doc! On the double! We cannot let the doc fall into their hands."

As the operator listened, he smiled casually at another transmitter unit to his right. It was a computer screen with a microphone near the keyboard. A single light formed a green dot at the center of the screen. It flashed repeatedly, with pixelized words assembling underneath it.

Incoming message.

"Do you not plan on responding?"

The operator turned in his seat, looking back at Stuart. The re-programed refinery droid walked on its six spider legs, its angular head held up on a crane-like neck that protruded from its box-shaped body.

"I'm gonna let them sweat it a little longer," the operator responded. "That's what they get for wanting to play it cheap."

He knew the client was picking up on the transmissions as well. Spy drones were always flying in the clouds, recording unsecure radio frequencies and taking photographs of potential targets and P.O.I's.

The droid, Stuart, backed back into the fuselage. Before disappearing behind the door, he rotated his head to look back into the cockpit. The operator looked back, staring at those red squares on the cone-shaped head that were intended to resemble eyes. Of course, they weren't really eyes, but apparently somebody decided during the manufacturing process that it would make it easier for people to interact with droids if they had a 'face'.

"You sure you want to do that? They might take it personally," Stuart asked with its mechanical voice.

The operator raised his hands over his eye and mimicked a scrubbing motion.

"Wahhh," he muttered. He lowered his hands, his metallic left arm closing into a fist. "They can reap what they sow. Don't care what territory or clan they're from."

"Consider this: if we fail to secure the doctor, then they might retaliate."

"If Rhino Territory gets the doctor, then Leader Cornelius will have bigger fish to fry." The operator's voice was void of concern. If anything, he was amused by the misery he was inflicting. He glanced back at the *incoming transmission* alert. He debated whether he wanted the job to begin with. It was clear to him why the client wanted a mercenary to conduct this operation rather than send in a task force. Messing with Rhino Territory would bring serious consequences, even for this client. Watching the message beep, he could envision the radio operator sweating in his seat. The doctor would soon be secured by the Rhino Clan, which would end all hopes of securing her knowledge.

"Unit Four en-route!"

"Unit Twelve en-route! E.T.A—three minutes!"

"Unit Seven and Eight! Right behind you, Twelve!"

"Another minute," he said out loud.

****

Commander Parker listened to the radio traffic on his portable. The shock was plain on his face as he heard Saegusa explain the situation. As he feared, there were other Harriers monitoring the area beyond his range of sight, and they detected the escape attempt.

Parker looked to the southeast, seeing the distant flares from the Harrier-15's thrusters. They dimmed down as the elevators lowered the sixty-foot craft to the ground. The ramps would open in seconds to deploy ground troops.

The strike teams would not get there in time. There was only one other chance.

Parker snatched his transmitter off his belt and raised it to his lips.

"Mobile unit! Change course and engage the fifteen near Main Street!"

"On our way!" Rowley responded. Gone was the enthusiastic tone in his voice, now replaced by a sense of urgency. The mission, which seemed to be going well, was suddenly on the brink of failure. The driver veered sharply to the left, avoiding plasma fire from the Harriers above. The green energy bullets missed narrowly, some singeing the edges of the Jeep. The tires skidded against brick and mortar as the Jeep spun and curved its path to the left. The gunner continued his suppressive fire on the aircraft, the bullets doing minimal damage to the hull. The recoil from the turret reverberated under his feet and through his hands, numbing his fingers as they grasped the butterfly grip.

Rowley kept the wheel turned until the Jeep was pointed southwest. He found a portion of level ground and straightened the course. His eyes opened wide as he recognized the wall of debris in their path.

"Holy--!"

Tires screeched as he spun the wheel to the right, scraping the whole side of the Jeep against a section of brick. The new path led him over a rough trail of wreckage, causing the Jeep to jolt every few feet of distance. He was driving over what was a busy section of the city, which had been flattened in the war. He couldn't keep a straight line for more than a few meters, otherwise he would crash into an obstacle. The continuous plasma fire from above only made matters more difficult. Rowley turned the wheel to the left, then right, then left again.

He had no sense of direction now. All he could see was rubble, smoke, and green bullets exploding all around. The driver grew desperate, knowing that he had to get to the doctor immediately.

As he approached another obstacle, he took a sharp turn to the left. Brown held tight, keeping his hands on the weapon to keep him from leaning too far. He looked up through the iron sights, carefully focusing on the Harrier. Green plasma exploded around him, catching a part of the guardrail.

Ignoring the flashes, he carefully aimed for the turbines. He moved the barrel further up a bit to account for speed and direction. He discharged the weapon, sending a three-round burst fifty feet high. A metallic scream escaped the turbine as several sparks ripped from the elevators. Trailing smoke, the Harrier broke off its pursuit, leaving only one other.

"HA! How you like that!"

"You got 'em?!" Rowley called back. Without waiting for a response, he glanced back, seeing the Harrier moving off into the distance. Suddenly, the daredevil enthusiasm returned. "A-HA-HA!"

The laughter was short lived. Rowley redirected his attention forward just in time to witness the flash of energy engulf the hood. The engine exploded in a fiery display, throwing metallic components through the air like meteors. The Jeep spun wildly before rolling onto its left side, flinging the gunner off the turret mount.

Rowley gripped the wheel firmly as the Jeep skidded for several yards. It came to a stop at the edge of what appeared to be a junk pile. He immediately felt the pain in his left shoulder, which had scraped along the ground the entire distance. Grimacing in pain, he turned onto his stomach and began crawling out the skylight. He was only halfway out when he heard the sound of tank tracks approaching.

He looked up and saw the twenty-ton armored vehicle approaching. It was a large steel platform with tracks on each side. Rotating along the middle were twin plasma cannons.

The screams of the gunner drew his gaze downward. Rowley gasped as he saw his teammate just a few feet ahead of the tracks. His right leg was bent out of proportion, clearly broken in several locations. Brown yelled desperately, crawling backward on his hands as the portside tracks grew nearer. The Rhino military always took pleasure in the pain they inflicted on their enemies.

The tracks cleared the distance. Brown screamed as the tracks came over his feet, crushing the bone to dust. The screams diminished to horrid gargles then silence as the tracks crushed his midsection, chest, and head. The tank came to a stop, with the crushed corpse trapped beneath it.

Rowley pushed himself onto his feet. Before he could turn away and run, the cannons aimed down at him. The muzzles turned hot red like dragon eyes. In the blink of an eye, they fired over a dozen plasma pulses. Hot energy struck his center mass, exploding his body into a red mist, out of which a hundred unrecognizable scraps soared through the air. The following blasts passed through the mist and struck the Jeep, consuming it in a fiery blast.

Parker directed his men away from the bridge and stopped, witnessing the tank massacre the mobile unit. Rescue for the doctor was impossible. The Jeep was reduced to a pile of scrap metal, smothered in blackened human remains. The tank redirected its position and started treading toward their location. He noticed several bodies moving alongside it. A dropship had set down beyond the range of the RPGs and deployed ground troops. They darted along the desolated landscape like white ants, each armed to the teeth with plasma rifles.

The smoke trailing high above it swooshed as Harriers soared through the sky toward the bridge. Parker held his rifle tight. Their numbers and position were compromised. Retreat would only result in pointless death. All they could do was make a last stand against the enemy forces and hold them away from Saegusa's rescue team as long as possible.

At best, it would be a few seconds.

"Take firing positions!" he yelled. "Hold them back! Don't give any ground—"

Parker's commands came to a sharp end as a blast from the tank engulfed him. His command position was eaten by a huge blast that tore him into shreds. All eyes looked back, each sharing the same confusion. It took a few moments for everyone to realize their commander was dead.

"Light 'em up!" another soldier yelled. He fired his rifle, while his comrades set up the fifty-caliber. Plasma blasts rained down on the group, scattering the men. Those at the front of the defense position were blown to chunks of meat as the Harriers rained plasma down on them.

Beneath them, ground troops rushed the defenses. Rhino soldiers, dressed in grey Kevlar uniforms and face-masks, stormed the LaFerrier squad with plasma rifles fixed with bayonets.

The fifty-cal opened fire. Only a dozen rounds escaped the muzzle as return fire punched through the gunner's torso. The soldier next to him reached down to take over, only to be hit in both arms. He stood up, both forearms blown free of the elbows. He staggered in shock. The Rhinos, sick as they were, didn't kill him yet. He was forced to watch, helpless as the rest of his squad got massacred.

Soldiers scattered back under the bridge. Two of the men holding the RPGs took firing positions, only to be consumed by a haze of plasma fire. Blood and tissue streaked through the air until one blast hit one of the RPGs, triggering it and engulfing their corpses in a thunderous blast.

The Rhino troops swarmed the remaining defenses, quickly overwhelming the six remaining troops. Lead and plasma crossed paths, with the waves of green quickly engulfing the bridge area. Heavy blasts peppered the surrounding area, keeping any stragglers from escaping. Explosions ripped upward as a heavy blast desolated the fifty caliber, throwing the injured soldier to the ground.

He tried to crawl away, his brain not detecting the loss of his limbs. All around him, he watched as plasma bullets punched through his friends, dropping them one-by-one. Boots hit the ground on both sides of him. Rhino troops engulfed the area, bayoneting any injured troops that lay in the rubble.

The Rhino Troopers saved him for last. A group of a dozen or so surrounded him and joked about his injuries. They bantered to each other on who would kill him, and how they would do it.

Then at once, they raised their rifles high over their heads and impaled him with bayonets. Twelve-inch blades ripped through bone and tissue, spraying blood from the incisions as the soldiers yanked them free and plunged again, bringing the soldier's misery to a horrendous end.

The soldiers laughed to themselves. Wearing the same masks and uniforms, there was no identification. They were one legion, working for the same Supreme Commander. And they shared the same joy, as they were near to the ultimate goal of gaining superiority over the only other Territory that matched their ferocity. Sovereignty.

They marched under the bridge, while the assault vehicles rolled on to engage the rescue squad closing in on the Harrier-15.

CHAPTER 2

High above the city, the stealth bird continued to circle the skies, while the operator observed the events taking place beneath. He watched as several dozen troops deployed from the Harrier-15. Like little white dots on the monitor, they surrounded Saegusa's vehicle to secure the area. To the northeast, the Rhinos had eliminated the last of her escort unit and were moving in to join the fray. His scanners picked up at least three Ridley tanks, roughly a hundred-and-fifty Rhino troops on foot, and four standard-class Harriers. In the southwest, several LaFerrier mobile units were moving in from Fort Bowman, armed with artillery and heavy machine guns.

On the next monitor over, the *incoming message* alert continued to flash. The operator gave one last lookover on the conflict taking place below. Believing he had stalled long enough, he pressed a finger to the touchscreen.

The monitor flashed blue as it connected the call. It displayed a large room, lit with green overhead lights and a vast assortment of what appeared to be storage pods. In the center of the screen was the caller. He was a man of forty-five, his face wrinkled from strain. His skin was pale, and through the screen, the operator noticed a glint of sweat on his brow. The caller was doing his best to maintain a commanding presence but had failed right off the bat. He knew the drill: If he failed to secure this negotiation, he would undoubtedly lose his head.

He spoke as soon as he appeared on the screen.

"Firebird!"

The operator grinned, amused at the attempt to sound authoritative beneath a shaky nervousness.

"That's me," he said.

"Let's cut the bullshit! We're short on time! You must secure the package for us!"

"There's no *must*." Firebird stood up. He lifted his mechanical left arm, making a fist with the metallic fingers. Around the forearm was a large gauntlet, at the top of which was a rectangular compartment as long as the arm itself. The caller couldn't help but glance at it, particularly the open port at the wrist-end of the compartment, then back at the eyepatch covering Firebird's left eye. The skin around that patch was grey, the aftermath of getting hit with a flamethrower. "No *must* for me. I ordered a hundred-thousand in gold coin. Half up front. Apparently, that was too much. You made your own bed, now you must lie in it." Firebird reached for the keyboard, acting as though he were about to kill the transmission. Then, he stopped and glanced back at the screen. "Unless you get the money right this time."

"Done!" the caller nearly yelled, slamming a hand to the table. Now, his face was dripping with sweat. "We have payment prepared upon delivery of the target.'

"Ha!" Firebird laughed. He glanced back to Stuart. The spider shaped droid came in to see what the ruckus was about. "He thinks the price hasn't gone up!"

Stuart tapped each of his six legs to the floor and angled his head down, mimicking intense laughter.

"Guy has both oars on the same side of the boat," he said.

"With that hair, I can't be surprised," Firebird cackled.

The caller's serious demeanor had faded completely, descending into sheer panic.

"Firebird! Time is running out! The Rhinos have almost secured the target! You must..."

"There he goes with that *must* again," Firebird said.

"What do you want?" the caller said, slamming a fist on the console.

"Your delay has cost you," Firebird said. "The price has doubled. Two-hundred thousand. All gold coins. I expect payment upon the minute I touch down in your sector."

The caller immediately had a look of relief.

"Two-hundred thousand, it is." He looked away, observing something on a different monitor off screen. Firebird knew he was watching the surveillance drone feed above Rhino-LaFerrier airspace. Glancing at his own feed, he saw that the Rhino soldiers were pulling the doctor out of the crashed Jeep. The caller looked back to Firebird, his face animated with urgency. "Now go! GO!"

"Don't get your knickers in a twist," Firebird said. He switched off the screen and moved to the center of the cockpit console. He tapped several keys, bringing the weapons system online. Several controls lit up along the console, while the monitor brought up a selection of options. "Stuart, man the throttle. We're gonna have to move fast."

"That's what you get for stalling," Stuart said as he climbed into the seat. Two small ports opened up along the platform of his body. Small mechanical arms extended from each of them. He grasped the joystick with one, while another reached out to operate some of the secondary controls.

"After I hit *Big Bird*, we're gonna sweep east and lay down a surprise for LaFerrier. Are the mist bombs loaded and ready?"

"Affirmative," Stuart answered.

"Excellent." Firebird brought up the targeting panel. With the touchscreen, he placed digital red crosshairs over the Harrier-15. "Activate rocket launchers."

Stuart tapped a few keys. "Armed and ready."

"Locking on to target..." He pressed the trigger of the joystick and cocked a finger pistol with his left hand. "Phew!"

Two rockets burst from their ports beneath port and starboard wings. Five feet in length, they each contained two-hundred pounds of HDRMs (High-Density Reactive Materials). Propelled by high-intensity thrusters, they ripped down through the sky to their target, warheads primed for detonation upon impact.

****

"NO!" Saegusa yelled as a dozen soldiers flooded onto the Jeep. With superior strength from the nano-enhancers injected into their bloodstream, they ripped the door away with the ease of peeling an onion. The doctor reached for her holster, yanking her revolver free. She extended it through the empty windshield, placing the muzzle directly against the forehead of a trooper. She could see his eyes widening through the black goggles as she squeezed the trigger. An instant later, his helmet opened along with his skull, spraying the hood of the vehicle with blood and brains.

Saegusa swayed to her left to shoot at the other troopers. Before her finger could squeeze the trigger, she felt the butt of a rifle strike the side of her head, driving her down into the passenger seat. The digital vision from her bionic eye fizzed, and her mind was lost in a daze. Her temples throbbed and blood leaked from her nose and mouth. She felt several hands grab her by the shoulders and lift her up out of the Jeep. Limp and near to losing consciousness, she floundered as they dragged her toward the Harrier.

They only completed a few steps when the squad all stopped at once. All eyes looked to the sky as a hot screeching noise pierced the air. Saegusa looked up, watching the red sky with flickering vision. She could see the flares of a thruster growing larger and larger in the span of a moment, trailing a thin trace of smoke behind it. A torpedo-shaped object came into view, followed immediately by another.

They struck down on the Harrier's cockpit, detonating the warhead on contact. A bright flash followed before a shockwave ripped through the ground. Metal and fire expanded from the decimated aircraft, sending shrapnel trailing over a hundred meters overhead. The Rhinos scattered into a disorganized frenzy. Frantic chatter swept their radio channels. Nobody could trace the source of the rockets.

****

The Ash-Cloud was a top-of-the-line stealth vehicle. Modified from the body of a top-secret raid bomber, its engines left little-emissions in its wake. The advanced mechanics allowed it to stay low enough to avoid breaking the sound barrier, except when entering combat.

It didn't come cheap to Firebird. Rather, it didn't come at any financial price at all. After all, it was originally used to track him. The problem with that scenario was that the previous operators succeeded in finding him and were foolish enough to engage him on foot instead of bombing him from the air.

"Bring us a-hundred-and-fifty yards over the LaFerrier squads," Firebird said. He watched the Jeeps racing along the road on his screen. Each was armed with an M60 or a fifty-caliber machine gun. By the looks of it, one of them had a mounted grenade launcher. Pity. That was the closest thing LaFerrier's forces would have to an armored division. Only two Territories had access to the good stuff, and both of them acted like bullies, pushing the smaller territories around.

In the span of a moment, Firebird contemplated the tactic to neutralize the rescue team. He would want to save his rockets for the bigger fish. The Ridley-tanks moving in from the opposite side would not be so easy to take down. Their armored plating could only be penetrated by pure force. The electrified vapor generated by the mist-foggers would not fry the engines as they would lighter vehicles.

Stuart steered the Ash-Cloud into position. The stealth reflectors along the underside of its hull kept its presence invisible to those riding the vehicles. Firebird armed the launchers and tracked the trajectory of the four Jeeps. Red dots marked the target zones, several meters ahead of the trajected path. Four grenade-shaped bombs shot from the turret mounted under the nose of the ship. They hit the ground below in five seconds.

Several dozen screams echoed at once from the LaFerrier troops as the bombs erupted into a vast grey mist that expanded for several meters. Blue streams of electricity streamed through the electrified mist, surging through the vehicles as they pierced the cloud. Electric currents flared like lightning through the vapor, immediately frying the engines as soon as the Jeeps entered the cloud. Tires skidded as all four Jeeps came to a sudden stop. The soldiers hollered in pain and frustration as the electric currents zapped their skin. They scrambled out of the disabled vehicles, jolting every few moments from intense electric shocks. They scattered helplessly, over two miles away from the target location, oblivious to the invisible Ash-Cloud as it flew northeast.

"Those guys were in for a shock," Stuart joked as he watched the viewing screen.

"How original," Firebird said. "You think I would've programmed a more unique sense of humor into your computer chip."

"It's only as good as yours," Stuart said. "You said it yourself, you programmed it."

"Don't remind me. Instead, arm missile pods two, four, and five," Firebird said.

"Already done."

With the tactical computer, Firebird conducted a scan near the bridge, targeting the three Ridley tanks. He locked onto the starboard side treads of each one, as the platforms would likely withstand the blasts.

"Oh, say can you see...." He discharged the first missile and watched it sail through the air at its target. The missile struck just under the top side of the tank's starboard tread. The vehicle rocked heavily to its right as the links came apart and the wheels detached. The platoon of soldiers scattered as they witnessed a second missile spiraling into the next tank. It struck in the same location, severing the tread and immobilizing the vehicle. Chaos ensued, as soldiers caught in the blast ran amok, covered in flame. Others flailed on the ground, having lost a leg or an arm in the explosion.

Firebird laughed out loud as he zoomed in on a trooper who had been impaled with a metal fragment. It had pierced his chest like a spear and came out the back. The sides clunked against other panicking soldiers as they ran past him, knocking some of them to the ground.

"...Over the land of the free..." he continued singing. He clutched the firing mechanism and placed his finger on the trigger. *"And the home of the brave!"*

"Sir, it's 'o'er', not 'over'," Stuart said.

"Oh, whatever!" Firebird launched the third missile and watched it smash into the third tank, immobilizing it. The explosion burst from the side of the tank like a huge orange bubble. Soldiers unfortunate enough... or unintelligent enough…to be standing nearby were thrown through the air, trailing a mix of blood and smoke before landing.

"That's the last of the heavy missiles," Stuart said.

"I can count," Firebird said. He marched into the cabin and opened the portside fuselage door. Stuart looked back, seeing him arming the Plasma minigun through the door. He strapped himself into the mount and clutched the controls. Beneath him, the four standard-class Harriers hovered over the wrecked model-15. The rest of the platoon was in shambles. The soldiers had scattered in disorganized fashion. They were slightly less than a mile off, with no vehicle to help them close the distance. As long as the job didn't take much longer, he would be done before they could close the distance.

"I need some music," Firebird said.

"Long Tall Sally?" Stuart asked.

"Nah, did that last time. Something simpler," Firebird said.

"Since we're gonna perform the circling shark maneuver, how 'bout the *Jaws* theme?"

"Perfect. Better yet…do the heavy metal version. Take it away, you bucket of bolts," Firebird said. The droid started the theme. The first two cords hummed through the speakers as the Ash-Cloud began to circle the wreckage of the Harrier-15. They were about a hundred feet above the other Harriers as they began to spread out in a defensive formation.

"The plan worked, sir. They think LaFerrier fired the missiles," Stuart said.

"It's always helpful to exploit one's stupidity," Firebird said. He watched the bright shimmering along the side of the hull as the ship powered down from stealth mode. The aircraft was visible now, its hull marked heavily from over a hundred combat missions. The elevators increased rotation, blowing hot air under the wings.

The famous double tonic intensified over the speakers.

"Dun-dun-dun-dun," Firebird hummed with the beat, watching several soldiers yelling and pointing up at his location. He gripped the butterfly grip and aimed at the center Harrier. "You're gonna need a bigger army."

He discharged the weapon, sending a massive stream of blue plasma bullets raining into the Harrier. The energy, hot as the sun, punched effortlessly through the steel hull, frying the inner components, as well as the unlucky soldiers inside.

The Harrier spiraled out of control, whipping sharply to starboard. Its portside turbine exploded, the internal blast rupturing the power cell. A dull cracking sounded from inside its hull, followed immediately by the aircraft blowing completely apart from within.

Saegusa's senses all returned as she watched the orange and blue plume of light erupt several yards above her. Through her bionic eye, she watched as huge chunks of hull rained down on the squad of Rhino soldiers.

There was another craft circling over them. The design looked familiar, though it wasn't something that was commonly used in warfare. It was not LaFerrier, and it was definitely not Rhino Clan. Sovereignty, maybe? Seemed unlikely that they would risk all-out war with Rhino.

Extending from its portside was a huge minigun, firing blue streams of plasma into one of the other Harriers as it tried to engage. The energy concentration was intense, letting off an extreme heat that even she could feel. The vehicle completed its turn, only to catch several steaming hot rounds through the cockpit, exploding the pilot into red mush. The Harrier spiraled wildly then smashed down hard into the dirt, breaking into huge chunks as it bounced.

The soldiers ran amok, many of them firing wildly at the sky. The two remaining Harriers blasted their main thrusters to increase altitude. Stuart throttled accordingly, keeping the Ash-Cloud in its tight circular pattern.

Wind assaulted the mercenary's face as he continued gunning. The Harriers returned fire, sending numerous green energy bullets zooming past the hull, nearly grazing the turret. Stuart banked left, angling the turret directly at the Harrier.

The mount shook from the recoil as a hundred blue plasma bullets ripped from the six-muzzle minigun. They peppered the Harrier's hull, each ringing with a loud firecracker sound as they punched through the cockpit. The nose of the aircraft exploded into several twisted pieces of metal and body parts, which rained down to the ground. The main body of the Harrier, engulfed in blue flame, followed it down and smashed into the remains of a large building.

The final Harrier sidewinded then sped in a semi-circle around the stern of the Ash-Cloud.

"Hold tight," Stuart called from the helm. He cocked the lever to activate the afterburners, accelerating the Ash-Cloud into high velocity. The Ash-Cloud soared high in the sky, avoiding the range of the last remaining Harrier. Green plasma bullets zipped by, scattering as they traveled further into the atmosphere.

Firebird jolted against the arm rail as Stuart disengaged the afterburners. He angled the ship downward again, letting it freefall. He re-engaged the cloaking device, giving the hull a glassy appearance as the reflectors mimicked the elements around it. Firebird retracted the minigun and shut the fuselage door, the outer steel completing the camouflage encasement. He hurried back to the cockpit and took a seat beside Stuart.

Through the viewing screen, he watched as the Harrier circled aimlessly. The pilot had lost track of them and judging by the rapid movements and rotations, he was clearly growing nervous.

"This almost seems mean," Firebird joked. He activated the forward cannons, located on both sides of the nose.

Stuart mimicked a shrug by arching his legs and scrunching his neck. "If you are feeling compassionate, you could aim for the wing and disable the engines. The safety measures would likely prevent the pilot from…"

Firebird locked on and squeezed the trigger, sending several rounds ripping into the windshield. The front half of the Rhino aircraft broke into several fragments, while the stern spiraled repeatedly until smashing nearly a kilometer to the south.

Stuart shrugged again. "Or, you could just do that. That works too." The droid brought the Ash-Cloud down near the objective. There were at least twenty

Rhino soldiers still near the Jeep, many of them dispersed to avoid the debris and plasma fire.

"Let's wrap this up," Firebird said. "Take us for another round trip so I can take out the perimeter soldiers."

"What about those closer to the Jeep?"

"I'll have to go on foot. I'll blow up enough debris with the minigun to generate a smoke cloud for cover. Once I'm down there, they won't know me from a hole in the ground...like the ones they'll be buried in."

"Actually, I believe the Rhino Clan cremates their dead..."

"Quit sabotaging my one-liners, you junkyard reject," Firebird said. The mercenary returned to the cockpit and accessed the armory. He opened the door to a large metal compartment. On the inside was a rifle rack, containing five Predator-Rifles. He grabbed one by the barrel and slammed in a fresh magazine containing fifty rounds of explosive tip rounds. Like miniature warheads, they would explode upon impact. Those unfortunate enough to be hit by one of these rounds almost never lived to tell about it.

After strapping the rifle over his shoulder, Firebird double checked the thirty-round magazine in his Gravestone auto-pistol. Though not as devastating as the explosive rounds of the Predator Rifle, the armor-piercing bullets would have no trouble punching through the Rhino Troopers' Kevlar vests.

Cross-strapped on his belt was his secondary handgun, an old-fashioned Smith & Wesson Model 67 revolver. It was his favorite relic from an age long gone. Though heavily scraped and battered from its use over the years, it worked as well as the day it came out of the manufacturer, having been maintained by Firebird's father, and his father before him.

For the final checkup, Firebird raised his left fist and slammed his other hand into the gauntlet's underside. From the large shaft on top, a silver blade protruded twelve inches from his wrist. It was the fourth blade to be installed in the gauntlet. In time, it would chip or break, as the previous three had. No big deal. Firebird worked often, a perk of being in high-demand. The craft often brought a lot of wear and tear to his tools.

He retracted the blade and returned to the minigun mount. He slid the door open again. Fifty feet below him, Rhino troops moved in mass panic, some of them firing wildly in the air in hopes of a lucky hit. All eyes turned toward him as the camouflage faded. Stuart initiated another shark circle maneuver.

"Where shall I begin?" Firebird said to himself as he watched the pathetic troops pointing up at him with their rifles. They were clearly in a state of hysteria after witnessing their air units get decimated. He listened to their chatter echoing from the radio scanner.

"There it is! Five o'clock!"

"Where's the armored division?"

"Get your acts together and shoot that son of a bitch!"

Firebird smiled at that last comment. Watching the soldiers moving around like termites on a log, he noticed one of them pointing and directing others. His guess, that was the leading officer.

The commander pointed at a group of three...

"Group two, take position up on the hill to the north! Group three…" the figure turned around, getting the attention of four troops huddling near a broken wall. *"Stop your cowardice and advance south. Use your grenade launcher as the bastard passes low again!"*

"Hmm, might wanna start with them first," Firebird mumbled.

As the commander began to bark orders to the dozen or so troops guarding Saegusa, Firebird aimed the muzzle down at the four men. He could see the large round muzzle of the grenade launcher, held by the troop on the farthest left. He was the first to start moving to the designated location.

"Perfect!" Firebird aimed the barrel down and began blasting away. Blue plasma bullets pelted away, hitting the soldier center mass and peeling him to shreds. All Firebird had to do was aim the barrel up and keep the barrels spiraling. The stream of bullets consumed soldiers, exploding them one after another in clouds of red. It was target shooting that even an amateur could pull off. The last one at least showed some sense of bravery. He stood his ground and aimed his plasma rifle high at the aircraft. But before he could pull the trigger, Firebird moved the stream of bullets up like the flame of a welding torch. The chest and belly exploded into chunks. Both arms launched out to the sides like bottle rockets, trailing thin lines of blood before hitting the dirt.

"Should've moved," Firebird said. The Rhinos would say the soldier was brave. Firebird had a different word: Stupid.

"Go! Go! Move out!"

The commander's voice on the scanner was growing annoying. Firebird considered having Stuart switch it off.

Better idea.

He aimed the barrels at the tall, broad-shouldered trooper, who was moving to-and-fro as he prepared his men to take defensive position.

"Get down low! He'll pass again, and then you'll…"

The words ended abruptly as blue plasma struck his face, rippling the mask… and his skull, clear from his shoulders.

"You're getting better at this, sir," Stuart remarked.

"It is getting a little too easy," Firebird said. "Add power to thrusters to quicken the pace. I'll pick off a few more, then handle the rest on foot. Can't shoot too close to the damn Jeep without risking the prize." Stuart followed his instructions. The world below seemed to spin as though on a disk as they orbited the crash site at greater speed. Running to the north was the group of three. Group Two, as the commander referred to them.

They ran, one ahead of the other two. The soldier in the lead, tenacious and rambunctious, shouted many obscenities to the gunner above him. They approached the small hill that led up to an old crumbled church near the main road. Firebird waited until they reached the foot of the structure to open up on them. The next obscenity ended in mid-sentence as plasma blasts carved him open from the shoulders to the hips. The head flew from his torso, which ripped into a cloud of guts. The two other soldiers stopped on their heels, unclear whether to turn and run back, or split up. Their hesitation proved to be their last, as the barrage of plasma engulfed each of them in a fiery haze. Bodies blew apart, their remains instantly covered by the huge dust cloud generating from the onslaught created by the minigun's punishment to the ground below. Each bullet that smacked down created a huge burst of smoke, which combined with other bodies of smoke generated by the hundreds of other plasma projectiles into one huge mushroom cloud.

Firebird continued firing around the Jeep, throwing the surviving troops into a continued state of chaos and confusion. The smoke and dust continued to accumulate, obscuring the entire area. And of course, he managed to pick off a few more unlucky troops along the way.

****

Saegusa jolted as the petrified soldiers yanked her away from the nearest barrage of plasma fire. Seven troops gathered by her, many of them firing back at the vessel. Their shots were small and puny. Even if they could hit the hull through the vortex of dust, they would not penetrate the hull.

Saegusa put her mechanical eye to use and switched to infrared vision. The landscape turned blue, with several orange figures moving about around her. Then, like a torrential downpour limited to a width of roughly five feet, a huge onslaught of orange hit the ground thirty feet ahead of her. She could see the body signatures of three other soldiers approaching the Jeep, only to be engulfed in the gunner's sights. The figures vanished into fog-like clouds of orange which quickly spaced apart and faded. The endless plasma fire moved off, ripping into another straggler to the northeast. She heard his rifle discharge repeatedly, then a brief scream, which concluded with a sound that resembled a grapefruit being smashed with a sledgehammer.

"ALERT! ALERT! What's the ETA for backup?!" one soldier shouted through the microphone.

"We have air units five minutes out! Hold position! They're after the doctor! They will not use heavy weaponry near her!"

"Understood!" the soldier answered. Saegusa felt him grab her by the back of her neck, thrusting her back into the Jeep. "Everyone get closer! Don't spread out! This fool is trying to get us to disperse!"

The men gathered near the Jeep and crouched low, not one of them saying a word as they attempted to trace the sounds of the Ash-Cloud. The air grew thick. So thick, they could hardly see a foot in front of their faces.

Saegusa watched with her infrared. The plasma firing had ceased, bringing the area to absolute silence. The group could still hear the elevators, though the swirling dust cloud kept the ship invisible to them. But the doctor could see the heat emissions left over by the turbines. She tried not to stare too hard, as she didn't want to inadvertently give away its position.

The aircraft was lowering to the ground, the downdraft from the elevators adding more dust to the huge cloud. Staring through the scorched soil flying through the air, she watched as a human signature appeared in the open fuselage doors, and quickly descended to the ground. It was clear what the combatant had planned.

Still, she didn't know who he was, or why he was rescuing her from the Rhino Clan. But she knew one thing: she had heard of only one man known for piloting the rare Ash-Cloud stealth plane. Nobody knew his real name. The ones who saw him referred to him as Firebird. He was a mercenary with no allegiance to any territory. From what she had heard, he was the best there was. Pay him enough, and he would move mountains to get the job done. Screw him over, and there would be no fortress strong enough to keep you away from his vengeance. He would always find his target.

Espinosa! she thought. *They must have sent him! It had to be them!*

There was one other thing she was certain of: The Rhino troops would not risk shooting her. Perhaps she could make things a little easier on her mysterious rescuer. She glanced up at the nearest trooper. He stood just a couple of feet away from the Jeep, his rifle aimed out in search of any enemy figures. The others formed a tight ring around the Jeep, with at least three standing by the passenger side and one at the front and back. Only one other troop stood at the driver's side, and his attention was fixed to his left. The only troop directly in her way was the one outside the door space.

The opportunity was now. Saegusa sprang from her seat and thrust her left foot down behind the troop's knee, bending it forward all the way to the dirt. The soldier rotated his hips to the left, instinctively bringing his rifle around. Saegusa grabbed it under the barrel and thrust her arm forward, clunking the weapon hard against the trooper's face. His head snapped back hard from the impact, loosening his grip. Throwing her body weight against his, she shoved the rifle vertically against his chest, pointing the muzzle directly under his chin. With her other hand, she lunged for the grip and slipped her thumb into the trigger guard. She pressed down.

A burst of plasma ripped upward, splitting the mask and face from the rest of the soldier's skull. The lifeless body rocked for a moment, its face nothing but a blank red scab. She yanked the rifle from his dead hands and turned on her heels, firing wildly into the confused group of soldiers. They dispersed, dodging the searing hot streaks of green plasma.

Saegusa took off in a mad dash, disappearing within the tornado of dust. She glanced back with her thermal vision, seeing six red figures starting to give chase. Judging by the way the orange heat signatures were spreading out, they had already lost sight of her, giving her the advantage of escape.

She held her breath as long as she could to keep from inhaling the toxic mixture of smoke and dust. She looked ahead in search of the mercenary. She could not pick up his signature through the thickening cloud. Nor could she find the ship. Her infrared vision flickered like a TV losing its signal. The infrared fizzled as the surrounding heat interfered with her systems. There was no sign of the ship either. Running forward as fast as she could, she was as blind as the troops chasing her.

Pushing off with her left foot, she moved right, hoping to find the edge of this suffocating cloud. Her lungs were starting to ache from holding her breath. She had no mask to filter, unlike the soldiers. She was already feeling woozy. But she had to not breathe. If she breathed, it would be over. Her lungs would fry from the chemicals floating in the air. Though it would not result in death, it would trigger uncontrollable gagging, giving her location away to the troops. She held the rifle close to her chest and looked back. The infrared worked for a moment, allowing her to see her pursuers. The troops had completely separated.

Two of them searched almost a hundred meters directly behind her, following the path she previously was going. Two others lagged behind, staying close together, possibly suspecting she would try and double back.

But where were the last two? Where was the merc?

She felt herself losing balance. She needed air, and she needed it bad. Her biological function was overpowering her discipline. Being practically blind wasn't helping. She couldn't be sure how far she had to go to get out of this cloud.

She took another step back. Her foot moved a couple of inches then hit solid granite. Tripping over the chunk of debris, she yelled out, losing her grip on the rifle. It flung from her grip, disappearing inside the thick dune around her. Whatever it was that she tripped over, it was part of a larger pile. She knew this instantly, as when she twisted to catch herself, her stomach came down on the edge of what felt like a cement block. What little air was left in her lungs blew out through her mouth in a pained yell. Then came the inevitable, impulsive inhale.

The pain was instantaneous. It was as though she had swallowed a dozen pin needles that had been held over a flame. Her lungs felt as though they would inflate and burst through her chest. Saegusa pushed off the solid chunk of rubble and crawled on her stomach, gagging viciously.

Footsteps approached, growing louder and quicker. She reached out in search of the rifle. Spitting blackened saliva, she glanced over her shoulder. Through her mechanical eye, she saw hazing images of two men standing above her.

"There you are!" one of the troopers said. "Having trouble breathing, are you?" He grabbed a fistful of her hair and pulled her up. Saegusa yelled like a crazed animal, staggering up onto her toes as the trooper continued pulling back. She felt the muzzle of his plasma rifle pointed against the back of her knee.

"You know, we really just need what's in your head. I doubt Command needs your legs! What do you say, Ellis?" The trooper waited for his comrade to respond. "Ellis? You got a cork in your face?" Still nothing.

Keeping a firm grip on the doctor, the Trooper glanced back where his body stood. The Trooper he called Ellis was only a couple of feet away. His legs were bent, barely holding him upright. His back was arched, his rifle dropped from his hands. There was someone standing behind him. He had one hand over the trooper's mask, and the other pressed against his back, as though he was trying to drive his fist through his spine.

Firebird glanced at the second trooper as he drove the gauntlet blade further into the soldier's back.

"Would you understand the reference if I said 'stick around'?"

The trooper tossed Saegusa aside and pointed his plasma rifle at the wisecracking merc. With a twist of his hips, Firebird ducked behind the deceased trooper's body to use it as a human shield. It jolted violently as it absorbed two plasma blasts from its living comrade. In an effortless motion, Firebird drew his Gravestone auto-pistol. The squeeze of the trigger launched three armor-piercing bullets from the muzzle. The first struck the trooper through the collar bone, the second punched through his adam's apple, the third right through his front teeth and out the back of his head.

The trooper flailed and fell back in a vivid display, his white uniform now covered in red streaks.

Firebird holstered the sidearm and yanked his blade from the other trooper's back. The body fell limp onto the ground as he tossed it aside and approached Saegusa. She had fallen to her knees, weak from breathing the polluted air.

The exhausted doctor looked up at the mercenary. He was wearing a bio-filter facemask and a pair of mechanicalized goggles. She recognized the type. They allowed thermal vision to filter out elements in the air, allowing a clear view of human targets.

Firebird shook his head, as though judging her.

"All you had to do was sit tight. But noooo! Had to show off your girl power and try escaping yourself," he said.

"I thought...I thought..." she struggled to speak.

"Don't speak. Don't *think*," Firebird said. He sounded impatient. He didn't expect the doctor to try and make an escape. It added time he wasn't planning to spend. The remaining Rhino forces would be closing in shortly. But first, he would be forced to deal with the four remaining Troopers. "Stuart, bring her down and get the lady aboard. I'm gonna need about thirty seconds."

"Sir, I'm obligated to inform you the ground troops from the platoon are moving in. Would you like me to engage?"

Firebird grimaced with frustration. They were approaching more quickly than he anticipated. He should've considered the nano-performance enhancers the Rhino Clan injected into their troops.

"Negative. Just get the package on the boat."

"Copy that, sir."

Firebird looked back behind him. The motion detector in his goggles showed four figures rapidly approaching their location, drawn by the sound of gunfire. He unslung his rifle and prepared to charge, only to stop after hearing the doctor coughing.

"Won't get paid if she suffocates..."

He knelt down and tore his bio-filter from his face and placed it on hers. Saegusa put her hand over the top and helped to press it over her mouth. Her eyes widened and her body quickly relaxed as clean oxygen entered her body.

Now I have to hold my breath, Firebird thought. *Eh, shouldn't take too long anyway.*

He could hear the ground trembling as Stuart placed the Ash-Cloud down nearby. Holding his breath, he ran north to engage the four Rhino soldiers.

Metal spider legs clunked against the floor, carrying Stuart out of the aircraft. The fuselage door slid open and he entered the world of smoke and dust that his master created. Being a machine, it did not impair his vision. Thermal imaging directed him straight to the doctor. She was visibly in a weakened state. He stood over her.

"Hello, my name is Stuart," he said. Saegusa looked up at him, her biological eye burning red. "I am here to help you. Please remain still while I lift you up over my platform."

The ports on his body opened up, and jointed mechanical arms stretched outward. At first glance, they didn't appear able to bear much weight, as each arm was only about a centimeter wide with a claw-like hand on the end. That perception ended quickly. The arms lifted her off the ground effortlessly. Stuart raised up on the tip of his six legs, and laid Saegusa over his back as though it were a medical stretcher.

Firebird crouched low behind a piece of rubble, watching the four soldiers approach. The first two were spaced out by about five feet of each other. The third was another twelve or so feet back, and the fourth was lagging behind, probably another twenty feet.

"Hmmm...guns? Knives? Guns? Knives?" He poised as the first soldier drew near, oblivious to his presence. "Ehh, there's always compromise."

Firebird sprang from cover and drew his left arm back as though prepared to throw a haymaker. The twelve-inch blade shot from its shaft, still dripping blood from its last victim. The soldier froze and turned to his right, taken off guard by the sound of rapid footsteps.

Even with the performance enhancers, his reaction time was too slow. With a single bound, Firebird closed the distance and rammed the blade through his neck, severing arteries and tendons.

"This little piggy went to market...."

He ripped the blade free. The second soldier, five feet away, spotted him and aimed his rifle. Firebird ducked into a summersault. His back felt the hot air from the plasma blasts as they passed by. He completed the roll and sprang to his feet, bringing himself face-to-face with the soldier.

Firebird closed a fist and raked his right arm inward, striking the barrel of the soldier's plasma rifle and knocking it from his grasp. The soldier stumbled back, then raised his fists. He lunged forward, hands moving out to grab Firebird by the throat. Firebird waited for him to close the distance, then sidestepped. The soldier's hands missed, grabbing nothing but air, leaving his ribcage completely unguarded. There was no time to correct this mistake. The mercenary threw a punch, ramming the blade deep between bones. The soldier grunted as his lungs deflated. With a twist of the knife, Firebird ripped it upward, turning the puncture into a giant gash. The soldier fell to the ground, dead.

"This little piggy stayed home..."

The third soldier ran into view and spotted the mercenary. A kick to the muzzle of his gun sent the weapon flying out of his hands. Firebird drew his knee back, then thrust out a second kick, planting his heel square in the chin, breaking the soldier's jaw and some teeth. The soldier fell backward, his hands floundering for his sidearm. The inside of his facemask had turned red from the blood spilling from his guns. That red exploded outward as the glass goggles ruptured from the impalement from Firebird's twelve-inch gauntlet blade. With his knee on the enemy's chest, the mercenary pressed the blade into his brain, finishing him off.

"This little piggy had roast beef…"

Green energy pulses ripped through the air, missing him by inches. Retracting the blade back into the gauntlet, Firebird dove to the left, summersaulting again. He came up on his knees and threw his hands out to catch himself. Dust swirled on the ground near his hands, covering up the corpse of a nearby Rhino Trooper who had been caught in his minigun extravaganza.

"This little piggy had none…" he realized the trooper had been blown into at least three pieces… "or too much."

Firebird rotated and pressed the stock to his shoulder. Numerous other shots singed the air, missing him entirely, and pinpointing the final trooper's position. Firebird fired a single shot.

The explosive-tip round passed from the muzzle into the trooper's center mass in less than a millisecond. The tiny warhead on the tip discharged upon impact, blowing the trooper's spine out of his back, along with various other tissue. With the help of the thermal imaging in his goggles, Firebird watched the trooper fall backward, his body splitting in two in the process, the deathly grunt echoing in the air.

"And this little piggy went 'wee wee wee' all the way home!"

"If you're not too busy reusing dumb quotes that mean nothing, I suggest we get a move-on…sir."

God, Stuart's voice was annoying on the radio.

"I swear Stuart, you keep this up, I'm gonna make *you* squeal like a pig."

"Beggin your pardon, sir?"

Firebird thought for a moment.

"That did NOT come out the way I intended…"

Several plasma blasts tore through the air from behind him. Firebird ducked his head and ran as fast as he could. The platoon, what was left of it, had arrived. And they were pissed.

"Droid! Get the boat in the air!"

"Sir, you're not aboard yet."

"No fucking shit! Keep the fuselage door open and drop the fast rope!"

"Yes sir. Would you prefer the nylon or the polyester?"

Firebird zig-zagged, avoiding numerous plasma blasts. The troopers had his general location down, though they couldn't see him directly.

Firebird dipped into an impact crater and turned around, his rifle at his shoulder. He could see the figures approaching. The nearest ones were about twenty yards away, spaced only a few feet apart. With a flick of the lever, he switched the rifle to full-auto. A dozen rounds blasted away from the muzzle into the crowd.

Bullets punched through body armor, exploding the targets from within. Three Rhino Troopers jolted as their chests popped like water balloons.

"Droid, you're about to find out how the recycling bin tastes!"

"I'll be passing over your location in twenty…"

He could hear the turbines coming to life, one of the few occasions the Ash-Cloud could actually be heard. It would be a long twenty seconds. Firebird ducked as another series of plasma fire zoomed by. Several of them punched the ground near the crater, launching dirt and cement fragments in his face. Firebird lifted and fired another shot. The bullet struck the target between the eyes, blowing his head into tiny shards.

Firebird panned left and fired a round into another trooper who was shooting about five yards away from his headless comrade. The round landed in the middle of his gut. The white center mass of his armor suit opened up like tissue paper, revealing a huge gaping red hole, spilling intestines and stomach contents.

"They say it takes guts to be a Rhino Trooper," Firebird quipped to himself. He glanced back as the roaring of engines intensified. Through his headpiece, he could hear Stuart's countdown continuing.

"...eight...seven...six..."

He could see the ship approaching, the rope dragging from the port side. Firebird crouched on his feet, ready to sprint.

"...four...three..."

He fired another barrage at the Troopers, scattering and disorganizing them further. With their shooting at a brief pause, Firebird leapt from the crater and dashed for the ship. The ship passed in front of him, the rope dragging on the ground. With his rifle hanging by its sling, Firebird reached out with both hands, wrapping his finger around the braided polyester material. Stuart elevated the Ash Cloud, evading rifle fire from the remaining troops below.

Stuart activated the winch, bringing the rope aboard and Firebird with it. After a few moments suspended over the side, he was back on the metal flooring of the ship's cabin. The fuselage door slammed shut and the stealth systems came online. The ship quickly achieved elevation as the droid pointed the bow south. They had successfully escaped.

"Hot damn!" Firebird said, triumphantly throwing a fist into the air. He jumped to his feet, wearing a bright smile over his face. He walked across the cabin, passing Saegusa who was laid out on a couch, exhausted. The mercenary opened a small cabinet near the armory, revealing a humidor stocked full of cigars. He severed the end with his teeth and placed it in his mouth. He raised his mechanical arm, tilting his wrist to expose a small port on the underside. At the press of a button, a small flame poured out, singeing the tip of the cigar. A plume of smoke escaped Firebird's mouth as he stepped into the hallway.

Stuart was at the helm, with one arm stretching to the next computer to run a diagnostic over the ship.

"Any damage, Stuart?"

"Negative, sir," the droid responded. "Mission went smoothly, all things considered."

"Yeah, since somebody thought she'd make a break for it," Firebird said, looking back at the doc.

As he started to step back into the cabin, he did a double-take back at her. "Oh, shit!" he said in surprise.

CHAPTER 3

Firebird found himself staring at the doctor, not with lust, but with a rare sense of fascination. He hadn't seen many cyborgs other than himself. But there she was, in the flesh…and metal. In fact, she was more machine than him. Her right eye had been entirely replaced by a mechanical counterpart, offering her thermal vision in addition to normal. It resembled a regular eye. Hell, it even looked like it could blink. If nothing else, it was an upgrade. Covering the 'eye' was a metal frame that formed a ring around her head like a skeletal helmet. It was his guess that the surgery brought an infection that required additional medical attention to her skull. The hair seemed real. It was the dark hair of a Japanese woman, the last of what that country had to bring in this world. Ironically, the first nation to suffer the devastation of atomic power was the first to be hit in the war, or so people claimed.

Firebird eyeballed her, noticing additional mechanical aspects. He could see the silver joints that made up her ankles. Though both legs were covered by trousers, he could see the skeletal outline as the pants hugged down on them. As his gaze moved further up, the crude thoughts started pouring through his brain.

Wonder it that's all woman, or bot. He glanced at her rack. For a Japanese woman, she was fairly well endowed. *DEFINITELY curious about those.*

Most people didn't survive the surgical process. It wasn't the procedure itself that killed people in need of new body parts, rather it was the infections that would set in. It was a time of mutated viruses and diseases, many of which mankind had not yet conquered. It was one of many consequences of nuclear war. The radiation in the atmosphere had caused many new forms of cancers as well. As though it had a sick mind of its own, the cancer would eat away at specific parts of the body, like a hand or a foot, then metastasize to the rest of the body like an infection. Sometimes it would go 'old-fashioned' as Firebird phrased it and attack an organ. There was no chemo that would stop this cancer. Only the cut of a knife would do that, and only if it wasn't too severe for the patient. And here was a person who was worked on from head-to-toe. Either she was immune to death, or she had a serious will to live. Considering her importance to so many Territories, he figured there was more to that second possibility.

Saegusa straightened herself into an upright seated position. She glanced up at the mercenary, who stared back, specifically at her robotic eye.

"So, you *do* exist," she said. Like Firebird, she was impressed by the sight of another cyborg. The mechanical left arm fitted seamlessly to his body. It was an advanced model, almost appearing exactly like a human arm. Except for that wrist gauntlet, however. She looked up at his face. He was covered head-to-toe in dust, the only clean spot being around his eye where the goggles had been. He had a muscular figure, which came as no surprise. What skin that showed through his combat vest displayed various scars, all undoubtedly received from a history of combat. "Never thought I'd meet you."

It took a few seconds for Firebird to answer, as he was still lost in determining the rating of her hotness. It wasn't a simple task, as the mechanical components were something he hardly considered.

"*Existence?* Am I a Bigfoot or something like that?"

"No, but most people don't buy that one man could do all that. I'd be lying if I said I was a believer myself. But I just witnessed you eliminate a whole Rhino armored division. Nobody with any allegiance would have the guts to do that. Not even the Sovereignty."

"In other words, you haven't met many badasses in your life," Firebird said. He puffed on his cigar, filling the cabin with tobacco smoke. Saegusa waved her hand in front of her nose to repel the smoke from her face. Firebird removed the cigar from his mouth. "Whoops, my bad." He glanced back at the cigar. "I guess I never was the most considerate type of guy. Already, I forgot you practically suffocated yourself out there."

"Yeah, I wasn't good with being caught in a cloud of plasma fumes," Saegusa said. "I have an iron lung. It doesn't do too well if I inhale too many contaminants."

Good God! She must be at least fifty percent bot. Now he *really* was wondering if that rack was real.

"You'd have gotten out a lot sooner had you waited. I had a nice game plan set up for those bad boys surrounding you."

"Oh. I thought I would've made it easier for you by luring them to you," Saegusa said.

"Running through smoke with an iron lung. Sounds like the logic of someone who thought she could outrun the Rhino battalion all alone. Though I will give you some credit. I saw what you did with your revolver, and I caught a glimpse of you giving that one bastard a taste of his own rifle."

"Thanks," Saegusa said, her voice smug.

"Don't thank me. I just do what I'm paid for," Firebird said. He returned to the armory and replaced his Predator Rifle. After shutting and locking the door, he moved to the back of the room to a refrigerator unit. He opened it and reached in for something, though with the door in the way, Saegusa couldn't see specifically what it was. She could see the top of his head moving side-to-side slightly as he maneuvered something. He then stood straight and shut the door. He held a metal canteen in his hand, which dripped water from the cap. He extended it out to her. "Probably thirsty after running through all that smoke."

Saegusa looked at the canteen, then back at him before slowly accepting it.

"How much were you paid?" she asked.

"Enough," he said. "Why?"

"Just curious," Saegusa said.

"Two-hundred thousand gold coins," he answered. "Your extraction demanded a heavy toll." He held the canteen out to her again. He tilted his head, scrunching his face. *You gonna take it or not?*

Saegusa accepted the canteen. "Thanks."

It sounded as though there should've been a question mark at the end of it. "Sorry, we don't have any peanuts to offer on this flight," Firebird said. He marched to the mouth of the hallway leading to the cockpit. "We'll have you back on the ground in no time. In the meantime, get some fluids in you and rest up."

"Okay," Saegusa said. She watched the mercenary disappear into the cockpit. He exchanged a few words about aerial dynamics with Stuart before the room went silent. She sat in the cabin alone with her thoughts.

Espinosa couldn't have paid in that large a quantity of gold coins. The mine collapsed a month ago. The last she heard, there wasn't much in the reserve. Definitely not two-hundred thousand worth.

"Maybe LaFerrier footed the bill," she said aloud to herself. It seemed plausible. They certainly paid enough in blood.

Her throat felt as dry as a log, breaking her train of thought. She unscrewed the cap to her canteen and took a quick slug of water. She tensed, preventing herself from swallowing. That taste…a slight bitter taste…

Not all water was the cleanest, and she couldn't expect the same from something provided from a container like this. But there was something else. A faint smell emitted from the canteen. It was sweet, almost fruity. An average person wouldn't pick up on it. But Dr. Saegusa, a medical professional and bio-chemist, picked up on it instantly.

She spat the mouthful of water onto the floor. It was a sedative extracted from the roots of Bannon plants out near the west coast. Part of her training had been to learn how to grind it up to use on patients. She tossed the canteen to the floor and stood up. She put her face to the nearest window. The sun was on the west side. Wherever they were going, it was south. Espinosa was not south.

"Oh, son of a bitch," Firebird muttered. Seated in the pilot's chair, he watched Saegusa through the security monitor.

"I believe she has established we are not taking her to Espinosa," Stuart whispered.

"Congratulations, genius. You win a prize," Firebird said. He watched as Saegusa started exploring the cabin. Immediately, she started displaying interest in the armory. "Oh, no you don't," Firebird muttered, as though speaking directly to her.

"It appears she is either planning to hijack the craft, or possibly make an escape," Stuart said.

Firebird glared at him. "What would I do without you? If she was eating, would you make sure I was aware she was providing sustenance to her body?"

"If I believed that to be the case," Stuart said. "In some cases, people eat to simply boost their endorphine levels, possibly to alleviate stress, and in some other cases they starve themselves to…"

"Okay, I seriously can't tell if you're being a typical smartass, or if the computer in your head is doing that stupid dictionary thing, explaining everything on God's green Earth to me. Or both."

"You're well aware the computer is not in my head…" Stuart paused, his illustrated eyes fixed on the monitor. "It appears she does not want to be seen."

Firebird glanced back to the monitor. The side of Saegusa's head was only an inch away. She was clearly manipulating something behind the cameras. The last thing they saw was a yank before the screen went black.

"Oh, yeah, like I wasn't gonna notice that," Firebird quipped.

"Would you like me to attempt tasering her?" Stuart asked.

"Not with all those gadgets in her system," Firebird said. "Let me just do it the safari way." He stood up from his seat and hustled to the back of the room. Located near the compressor unit and junction boxes was a metal compartment, similar to the armory in the cabin. He punched in the access code and opened the door. Inside was another assortment of weapons. One Predator Rifle was racked up on top, while another rifle was racked beneath it. It was a bolt-action model, with an assortment of tranquiller darts secured to the edge of the container. He was not transporting any big game this time, so he diverted his attention to another weapon secured at the bottom of the container.

It was a pistol, though unlike any other model he owned. Like the rifle above it, it had a bolt action for inserting smaller tranquiller darts. The brown muzzle had turned grey from a history of scraps. It was not the first time Firebird had to capture a live subject, though Saegusa was proving a rather unique example. He grabbed the pistol and pulled back on the bolt to open the breach. He grabbed a tranquilizer, checked the dosage, then inserted it into the breach. After pushing the bolt forward, he entered the corridor, pistol gripped tight.

He slowed down as he approached the cabin. He listened for any sounds of espionage. It would take much effort to get into the armory without an access code. Considering how desperate the doctor was getting, he expected to hear all sorts of clamoring. But there was nothing but silence. In a way, that made him more nervous.

"Two-hundred thousand," he muttered to himself. It seemed fair that such a price wouldn't entail a simple task.

Firebird bounded into the cabin and rotated to the left, extending his pistol to shoot. To his amazement, there was nobody there. He looked to the back of the room. There was only one other corridor leading to the escape pods, and he could see the door. It was sealed with an access code that she didn't have.

There was only one other place he didn't look: up.

"Shit..." Firebird looked to the ceiling and extended his pistol. There she was. At the start of the glimpse, she had held herself flat to the ceiling by clinging to the pipes. Yelling at the top of her lungs, she freefell with closed fists bearing down on him. With the aid of gravity, she hammered down hard on the pistol, knocking it to the floor.

Firebird staggered back, alarmed, amazed, and even a bit amused. He raised his hands defensively and dodged left and right as a flurry of punches came at him. Saegusa jabbed at him with lightning speed, the several motions almost appearing as a blur. The only speed that matched hers was Firebird's defense. He swept his open hands side-to-side, parrying each strike.

A glance to the floor spotted a warning which gave away the doctor's next attack. Her leading foot inched forward: a pre-step, a mistake made when one was about to throw a hard kick.

He sidestepped to the right, rotating left to keep himself facing his attacker. In that same moment, Saegusa threw a high kick, hitting nothing but air. With her lungs still hot from the smoke, she was getting winded fast. She staggered, struggling to catch her breath.

Firebird felt the instinct to move in with an elbow to the back of her head. He lurched back, stopping himself. He couldn't risk injuring the doc, or else lose a very substantial payment.

"Don't make me hit a lady," Firebird quipped.

His words ignited a new anger in her. Saegusa turned, her face like that of a wild beast. She lunged again, this time with a bounding leap. She came down hard, throwing a haymaker into Firebird's guard. The strike brought his hands down, opening his face. His shit-eating grin disappeared as Saegusa plowed a left jab to his chin, knocking him back a step.

"Damn girl...FUCK!!!!" A kick landed to his gut, knocking the wind out of him. He suddenly felt foolish for taking it easy on her. He had seen her handle herself against the Rhino Troopers, which should've been enough to warn him that she might have had some training.

Though the blow to his gut was hard, he kept himself from folding, which would've opened himself to another attack. Enduring the pain, he leaned back and left, dodging another fist.

She threw another right-handed haymaker, putting all of her body weight behind it. Firebird sprang forward, catching her by the arm. Twisting his hips counterclockwise, he used her momentum to fling Saegusa over his shoulder. The world spun as Saegusa felt herself lifted off her feet. She flipped over his shoulder, landing hard on her back. The impact was hard, causing her to bounce a few inches before settling. Her vision was hazy and her head throbbed. Yet, she wouldn't give up. She rolled to her hands and knees, ready to launch herself at the mercenary again.

"Oh, for Chrissake," Firebird muttered. He raised his voice, "Just give it a rest..." his voice trailed off as he noticed Saegusa feeling for something on the floor. He had dropped her right next to the damn tranquiller gun. "Shit..." Saegusa grabbed it with both hands and rotated to aim it at him. As she did, he lunged forward, grabbing her wrists and redirecting the muzzle toward the ceiling.

The two cyborgs tossed and turned, struggling for dominance over the pistol. Saegusa grimaced as she tried to angle the muzzle down at the merc. Firebird kept a firm hold on her wrists, keeping the gun locked up.

"Tisk tisk. Sorry, sweetheart," he said. His condescension did what it planned to do: enrage her further. She struggled more violently, wearing herself down in the process. Firebird had to hand it to her, she was by far stronger than any woman he had met. As he locked her up, his inevitable crude side crept into play. Being so up close, he took a glance down the slit of her shirt. From what he could tell, they were actually real.

"Hot damn...UGH!"

Saegusa's knee smashed his groin. Firebird finally folded, his equipment feeling as though put through a trash compactor. He had been struck there before, but never with a metal leg. She kneed him again, this time in the gut.

Firebird's whole body juddered from the impact, his ribs now feeling as crappy as his balls.

So much for wearing her down. Firebird could see that she was about to throw another knee strike. He straightened himself out and focused his strategy on the gun. He took a long stride backward, over extending the doctor's arms and causing her to lean forward. As her arms reeled, Saegusa felt one hand slip from the pistol grip. She tried to strike, only to fall down to one knee, her right arm feeling as though it would be twisted out of her shoulder. He whipped his hands around, rotating her wrist clockwise until her arm was locked out.

"You bastard!" Saegusa yelled in pain as he bent her wrist and pried the gun from her hand. He tightened her wrist with his metal hand, over extending her arm again.

"I am many things, Sweetie," he said, positioning the gun in his hand, "but born out of wedlock, I am not. Was not…whatever the proper way of saying it is." He pointed the pistol at her ribcage and squeezed the trigger. He heard a metallic 'clink' sound, followed by another as the dart bounced off of her and hit the floor. Firebird stared dumbfounded, still keeping her wrist locked up. "The fuck?!"

Saegusa always hated that metal plate that made up the right side of her ribcage. She hated the way it looked, how it felt, especially during winter time. But now, she had a whole new appreciation for it.

She dug her feet down into the floor and sprang forward, summersaulting in mid-air like a ninja. Firebird watched, flabbergasted as she completed a complete rotation, un-twisting her arm in the process. She landed and instantly pivoted on her left foot. Her body rotated, putting all of her weight on her other leg as she thrust her heel into Firebird's chest. Blood and spit ripped from his mouth as the robot leg made contact, driving him back into the fuselage door.

The mercenary hit hard and fell to the ground. Saegusa approached, ready to kick his head as though it were a soccer ball. He could see her foot rearing back, half a second from swinging up at his face. The merc thrust his metal arm out, palm open, deflecting the kick inward. Saegusa staggered off balance toward the back of the cabin. Firebird's eye turned to the floor. Laying just a few feet away was the dart. The needle was intact, the vial still containing the sedative. The merc rolled forward onto his hands and knees and reached out. His fingers wrapped around the metal body of the dart and lifted it from the floor, pointing the needle downward like a dagger.

Saegusa's feet pounded the floor. He could see her charging from behind, fists raised for another attack. Firebird sprang up from the floor and rotated clockwise on the balls of his feet. Sweeping his metal arm across, he deflected a right-handed haymaker, brushing it clear from his face. With her arm crossed over her chest, Firebird went for her exposed neck. He struck the needle down in a stabbing motion, plunging the needle into the skin.

A piercing pain ripped through her body, causing Saegusa to yelp and recoil. She reached at her neck with both hands and tore the needle free. It was too late. The sedative had entered her body. This was verified further as the wooziness began to set in.

No…I can't be taken…

Desperation and frustration mashed together, throwing Saegusa in a frenzy. She sprinted at Firebird and leapt. Several feet in the air, she threw a kick at his head. She missed by a few feet, her heel smashing into the armory, denting the frame.

Saegusa landed and collapsed to the floor. She pushed up on the palms of her hands, desperate to continue the fight and escape. But the sedative had done its job. All of her strength had vanished in just a few moments, and after a few more, she would lose consciousness.

Firebird released a strong exhale. With the fight over, all the pain sustained from the skirmish began to amplify. His chest felt as though it was hit with a battering ram. He ran his fingers over his jaw, relieved that none of his teeth were loosened. But the worst was the strike to the groin. He leaned forward with his hand on his knees and took a deep breath.

Right next to his foot was the canteen.

"Should've started with the damn dart," he muttered to himself. Saegusa's arms quivered as she held herself up from the floor. A tear formed around her left eye and streamed down her cheek.

"You..." her voice was shaky and weak, "you're taking me south... Espinosa is not south..."

Firebird straightened his posture. "No, they are not."

"South..." she continued to mutter. "Sovereignty...they paid you to capture me..."

Firebird took another breath. "Yep." His tone was casual. Careless. Like this action would have no repercussions. Saegusa wanted to strike him again but couldn't muster the strength.

I escaped one hell just to be traded for another...might as well have been left with the Rhino Territory.

Her whole world felt as though it was falling apart. The LaFerrier troops had died for nothing. She would not be able to resist giving up information. The chip in her head, attached to the metal part of her skull, held much data storage. All they would have to do is access it and duplicate it. They had the computers to do so.

"You bastard." She looked up at the mercenary. "Do you have any clue what you've done?"

"A job, dear," Firebird said. "I did a job I was paid to do. Nothing more, nothing less."

"A job? Money? What's that worth?" Her voice was trailing off. She was now on her elbows, still desperate to keep away. Her head bobbed, her one eyelid closing despite her will. "You're giving nukes to a superpower...they will...kill...kill...Espinosa..." She was now flat against the floor. One last word escaped her breath before she slipped away. "Murderer..."

The word didn't affect Firebird. He believed the very thing he had stated. He did a job that he was assigned to do. Northing more, nothing less.

He dragged the doctor to the passenger seat and shackled her hands to a lock on the handrail. Before returning to the cockpit, he noticed the damage done to the armory door. Those metal legs could really do some damage. He was lucky his breastplate wasn't caved in. Being cautious, he placed another chain link over her ankles, fastening her legs together and linking them to a shaft under the seat.

"Sleep tight," he said.

Firebird returned to the cabin and collapsed in his pilot seat. He could hear the gears whirring in Stuart's 'neck' as he turned his head to face him.

"How was safari?" the droid asked. It was more of a remark than a question. The fight had been very audible.

"Oh, shut up, you trash bin," Firebird remarked.

"You should have known, because she is a doctor, she would not have been fooled by the spiked water."

"Oh, NOW you say something," Firebird said.

"I didn't believe I had to. You claim to be smart," Stuart said. The droid handled the controls, working various instruments to adjust for temperature and windspeed. "Shall we make contact with the client?"

"No," Firebird said. He leaned his head back as far as it could go. "I don't feel like talking to anyone right now."

"Because the doctor beat you up?"

"Hey!" Firebird came alive, his face flaring with emotion. "I…never fought a cyborg before." His angry expression transformed into a sarcastic grin. He leaned back in his seat. "Plus, I couldn't hit her. Don't think Lord Sauron wants his package to arrive damaged in any way, even though they just need her brain."

"Lord Sauron?" Stuart asked, confused. "I believe the Sovereignty leader is named Cornelius."

"Yes, I know…" Firebird said. "It's sarcasm. You use it all the time!"

"I did not understand the reference."

"*Lord of the Rings.* It's in our storage library! It's a movie! Three movies…well six if you count the hobbit ones…"

"Oh! I was of the understanding they were books…"

"Well yeah…the movies are based off books… like *Jaws*! You understand this concept…"

"I see," Stuart said. "I have more to review of Man's culture before the war. Six movies and six novels."

"Well, no, the *Hobbit* was just a single book. They just milked it into three movies and… how the fuck did we segway into this topic?!"

"You were referring to Supreme Leader Cornelius of the Sovereignty Territory."

"Yes. Him."

"He's like an evil lord named *Sauron*?"

"Yes…only he's not a big fireball eye thing…" he sensed a series of questions on the verge of escaping Stuart's speaker box about that concept. "Just watch the movies, you'll understand. Anyway, Cornelius is a douchebag. But…I suppose you have to be one if you're gonna rule the biggest bureaucracy in the continent." Firebird put his feet up on the console and thought for a moment. "Eh, who am I to talk. I'm the one providing the capabilities for him to be Supreme Douchebag of all of America."

"If this Leader is such a...douchebag...then why are we delivering a top scientist who is capable of developing immense bio-weapons?"

"Because we work for money. And they paid us to do a job. If Espinosa got in touch and made a better deal, we'd be delivering Saegusa to them instead. It's a simple thing, bot. We work, we get paid," Firebird said. "Well, *I* get the money. You're a droid. All you need is a battery."

"But is it possible that if Sovereignty reverse engineers Saegusa's data, and develop hazardous bioweapons, that they might expand?"

"Yeah. They've been wanting to do that for years."

"If they expand, and commit massacres in the process, wouldn't that affect future business opportunities?"

"Well..." Firebird shrugged his shoulders. "I'm sure they won't kill *everybody.*"

"Just those who propose a viable threat to their expansion, then," Stuart added.

"Are you going somewhere with this?"

"To be straightforward, is it ethical to deliver Dr. Saegusa to the Sovereignty when it may result in so much collateral damage?"

"*Ethics?* You're asking me about ethics? We're mercenaries. We kill for a living. We've assassinated. We've brought back prisoners. We've conducted sabotage. We've done this for years, and NOW you're asking about the ethics of it?"

"Now is different, sir," Stuart said. "In all previous missions, we've kept collateral damage to a minimum. Our actions only directly affected the client and the target, with little to zero effect on the world around them. But this is different, sir. This mission will have large repercussions."

"The repercussion I care about is the weight of my pocketbook," Firebird said.

"But what if Sovereignty kills future clients?"

"Oh, for Godsake, you're worse than a headache," Firebird said. "Let me sum it up for you. They pay, we deliver...or in this case we deliver and they pay...but you know what I mean! You wanna get ethical and save mutated five-legged cats from trees, you do it on another ship. Or a refinery. Now, get us to the drop-off point."

"En route, sir," Stuart said.

Firebird worked with some of the instruments and watched the world pass by through the side window. From up high, he could see the changing landscape as it went from a ruined city to a rural countryside. He could see various homes and settlements, some vacant, others prosperous. It was the way of the world. The strong survived. That's how he perceived it. And now, he was working for the strongest player. Stuart's words started infecting his mind like a cancer. He began to wonder how that landscape would change. Would those homes still be housing the same occupants in two years? Or would they be homes for Sovereignty troops. Would there still be farms, or missile silos?

He didn't know. He didn't care. At least, he convinced himself he didn't care.

It would not be long until they reached Sovereignty's border. Not long from his biggest payday yet.

CHAPTER 4

Minutes prior, he was walking through a valley of immense green. It was a simple job: Lead the First and Second Battalion of Cornelius' Third Army to the Central Banks, where they would await the arrival of the contractor and their prize.

Dressed in his Imperial Uniform with the lightning insignia over his right breast representing the striking force of the Sovereignty, Commander Zolnar walked through the foundation of what had previously been a farmhouse. Now, it was a pile of rubble, with little to no identity remaining. Its fragments had scattered for hundreds of feet, each one scorched by the T-32 Plasma Cannon blast that struck it. Within the rubble were bits of bodies of the rebels who foolishly took shelter.

Foolish indeed. Their plan of attack had not gone in their favor. It never did, and Zolnar would see to it that it never would.

Through the smoke were the blue flashes of pulse rifles, carried by the infantry units. Uniformed soldiers, dressed in black tactical outfits with a dark green lightning symbol streaking through their helmets, charged the side of the hill, chasing back the worthless peasants.

No, they were worse than peasants. Peasants at least knew their place. These scum were rebels. Traitors, who claimed they were part of a Rebellion. They didn't know how lucky they were to be part of the largest growing nation in the Western Continents.

Zolnar strolled through the rubble, his demeanor lacking any sense of urgency. The Army had better weapons and soldiers, compared to the measly resources of the petty Rebellion. A line of his infantry units, nicknamed 'Strikers' pushed back the few dozen rebels that remained. The Commander could see them in the distance, through a field that was green with vegetation, now greyish black from the aftermath of plasma exchange. They moved beyond a large wooden gate, where several brick structures had been erected. By the looks of it, they had converted an old farm and well into a makeshift fortress. Amateur move. It would not withstand the force of the Sovereignty's Armored Division.

Zolnar watched the exchange of rifle fire as though it were a stage play. The rebels, all spread along the gate, fired standard Five-Star Plasma Rifles down at the advancing Strikers. Five-Star. Zolnar grinned. If he could, he'd rename the weapon as Five-Shot, as many of them would overheat after five consecutive blasts. It was one of the early Plasma Rifles after all.

He could see the muzzle flashes from what appeared to be old-fashioned cartridge rifles. The Rebellion scrounged for whatever they could get, usually going through borders and black-market routes to collect them. It was hard, if not impossible to obtain a military style Plasma Rifle. Any civilian obtaining one would instantly get the death penalty.

After watching the exchange of gunfire, Zolnar yelled to the nearest Lieutenant.

"Get over here. On the double!"

The Lieutenant hustled, zagging around rubble and bodies as he crossed the farmyard. A man of thirty-five, he approached the Commander and saluted. He was a man eager to please, like all good soldiers. Zolnar enjoyed having him under his command, as he lacked the typical nervousness many would get in the presence of a high-ranking Commander. It was demeanor like that that got Zolnar promoted to his position. Perhaps, the same would happen to the Lieutenant one day. But for now, he belonged to Zolnar.

"Yes, sir," the Lieutenant said.

"We've indulged these idiots long enough. Have the Armored Division move in. Five T-32 blasts should do the trick."

"Aye-aye, sir," the Lieutenant said.

"Let the Strikers continue to hit them with rifle fire. Keep them occupied. Then order them to fall back when the tanks are ready. After they're done, have the boys move in and do a sweep. Make sure none remain."

"Aye-aye sir. Sir, I'm obligated to ask. What should we do with any survivors?"

A smile creased Zolnar's face. Like all officers, the Commander didn't wear a helmet. For him, specifically, it would be a hinderance. He wore a visor over his eyes, or rather, in place of his eyes. It was a casualty of a long history of combat, in this case, it was one of his first missions. In these days, battles would not simply be range war of gunfire. It often got hand-to-hand. He would always remember the face of the one who slashed him across the face with a knife. It was the first fight he'd ever lost…and the last.

"Make examples of them," he said. "Take 'em prisoner, and have a squad deliver them to the Radon Swamps. I'm sure the reptiles over there are hungry."

"Aye-aye, sir." The Lieutenant saluted and started to walk away to complete his duties.

"One more thing," Zolnar said, as though suddenly remembering. The Lieutenant waited. "Keep one handy for interrogation. It's no coincidence that these bugs launched an attack in this particular time and location. Somehow, they got word that Dr. Saegusa is being delivered. I want to know how."

"Aye-aye, sir," the Lieutenant said. He hustled to a radio unit that had set up near one of the trucks.

Zolnar continued walking through the obliterated farmhouse. The smoke had mostly cleared, as had the smoke trails from the surrounding structures that made up the small farm community. Bodies of several resistance fighters lay everywhere, their flesh and clothing scorched by plasma fire. Well deserved, in Zolnar's opinion.

He heard a grunt from somewhere off to his left. It was a pained sound. Whoever was making it sounded as though their lungs were full of knives. There was a wetness to the sound, making him think of blood in the back of the throat. Zolnar saw nothing but dismembered bodies, human and animal alike, and a field of blackened debris.

The sound came again, and this time, one of the large fragments moved. It was a jagged piece, containing no ordinary shape, like a puzzle piece. Somebody was under it and lacked the strength to push it off. No surprise. It was a portion of a wall, which had been comprised of pure granite. And the wells in this territory were large, some the size of the farmhouses. They contained inner mechanics to draw the water out and treat for potential radiation. In these days, even taking a sip of water was dangerous.

As Zolnar approached, he saw the remains of a Five-Star Plasma Rifle, now broken in two pieces. There was blood around the edges of the chunk of debris, some of it blackened from the heat.

Standing alongside it, he reached down and slipped his fingers under the edge, then lifted with his knees. He lifted the wall like the lid of a can and flipped it over its other end. Laying on the ground was a rebel. His brown deer-skin jacket was covered in fresh blood. His body trembled, almost embedded in the dirt. His legs were smashed, as was much of his trunk. He held his arms close to his chest. His teeth were clenched, and as Zolnar had predicted, the unfortunate rebel was spitting up blood.

The relief the rebel felt only lasted an instant before being replaced by a sense of dread. With the sight of Commander Zolnar looking over him, the rebel suddenly wished he had been fatally crushed by the wall. He prayed that the Commander didn't recognize who he was. His regular features had been marked by burns received in the blast. If not, then he would receive a quick execution.

It wasn't himself he was worried for. He knew Zolnar had a knack for inflicting psychological wounds on his enemies. He knew there was more to warfare than two sides blazing guns at each other. Zolnar understood strategy, and if he recognized him, he would have a tool to enact that strategy.

There was no sympathy behind that visor. If nothing else, there was a sick pleasure in seeing the rebel choking in his own blood. The only thought beyond personal amusement was the analysis of what to do with him. He did want prisoners for interrogation. But this one? He was broken, hardly able to speak. He was not worth the medical resources to keep alive, even if just for a few days.

But that wasn't to say he would not be useful. What the rebel didn't know was that the visor contained facial recognition from a large database. The files ran over his vision like a computer before settling on a name and profile image.

Paul Albright.

The son of Beretta Albright. Rebellion leader. Wanted for arson, sabotage, murder of the Supreme Leader's troops, espionage, and so many more.

Perhaps this one would be worth the resources.

"It seems today has no lack of gifts for me," Zolnar said to the rebel. Paul groaned. He knew he had been recognized. He couldn't be taken alive! He reached for his belt and pulled his knife. Raising it high, he lunged up at the Commander. The effort came to an end after Zolnar stomped his boot down on his wrist, pinning his arm and weapon to the ground.

"It'll take more than that little toothpick to ruin my day," Zolnar said. "You should've known. You were the one foolish enough to lead yet *another* failed assault on me."

"You keep chipping away at a boulder, eventually it'll be a pebble," Paul groaned.

"Unless the boulder keeps growing. Building. Like molten lava becoming an island. Eventually, it'll grow into a continent."

"If you think the Sovereignty can last, you're in for a huge awakening," Paul said. Blood and spit shot out of his mouth with every word. "Read history. Dictatorships never last. You steal from those around you, eventually you run out of people to steal from."

"It's more like reclaiming," Zolnar said. "We'll be bringing unity to the territories."

"By obliterating all of them!"

"If that's what it takes," Zolnar said. "But I don't expect you to understand that. You who claims he fights for freedom and hides behind history. Tell me...if you're so knowledgeable, why do free people eventually sacrifice their freedom in favor of security? I've read the archives of times past, and it always plays out the same way. It always seems to come back around. I believe, deep down, people *want* to be controlled. They never admit it. Instead, they hide their intentions behind concepts like justice and inequality, and yet their proposals always involve power."

Zolnar reached down and grabbed Paul by the collar of his jacket. The rebel yelled in immense pain as the Commander lifted him off the ground with one hand. His broken legs dangled several inches, his hands gripping the wrist, unsuccessfully attempting to pry himself loose. But the Commander was strong. Much stronger than him.

"What we are doing is simply bypassing all the nonsense. It's called order."

Paul looked past the Commander as five T-32 tanks rolled through the rubble. Twin tracks carried a sixty-foot armored platform. Rotating at their centers was a large turret carrying a fifteen-foot plasma cannon. Zolnar glanced over at the vehicles and then back up at the rebels at the top of the hill.

"Tell me: Is your mother up there?"

Paul swallowed.

"You wish!"

"I do," Zolnar growled. He looked Paul in the eye. "And you're about as good a liar as you are a fighter."

Paul gritted his teeth and lashed out with a fist to Zolnar's jaw. The Commander took the blow, the force tilting his head a bit. He smiled. For such a broken man, he packed a decent punch.

"Maybe you're more a man than I thought. But in your case, that's like saying you're a duck when I thought you were a pigeon. At the end of the day, you're just a bird that's about to be fried."

"You speak like you're some great leader," Paul said. Zolnar snickered. Did the peasant not see the army he led? Paul forced a smile. "Yeah, you're a Commander. One of... how many? At the end of the day, you're just a disposable piece of trash that works for Cornelius. If he says jump, you say "how high?" That's the problem with your belief. What you fight for will eventually turn around on you."

Zolnar's smile disappeared and his electronic stare seemed to burn through the rebel. For a moment, the Commander was deep in thought. Paul knew he hit a sensitive nerve. He understood men like Zolnar. They craved power. The worst part about men who craved power and nothing else was that they could never get enough. It was like a drug. And Cornelius was the supplier.

Zolnar glanced back up at the hill. "I'm glad your mother's up there." He marched toward the hill, raising Paul by the throat as if he were a trophy. The rebel gagged and struggled, unable to overpower his captor.

****

Hands pressed down on warm soot as Beretta Albright pushed herself off the ground. Her ears still rang from the I.N.T Plasma blast that struck the windmill behind her. Shards of brick and wood rained down over the group, opening up the side of the structure.

A piece of glass hit the ground, nearly grazing her face. She glanced down at it as she stood up. The war had visibly aged her. At forty-five, she looked as though her features were made of marble. She was rugged, worn down, fighting an enemy who was bigger, stronger, meaner, and more ruthless. Her black hair had turned pasty white, while her muscular frame had gradually grown more brittle in appearance due to the lack of good nourishment.

The rebels held the line, raising rifles over the fence and barriers as they fired back. They were men and women of different ages, their faces smothered with grime and smoke. Less than thirty remained. They fired down at the Strikers, their Plasma Rifles overheating quickly from heavy use.

They needed to continue the fight. They HAD to! On the other side of the large valley, they had another counterstrike planned. The Sovereignty forces were moving in, just as intended, though they had inflicted more damage to the rebel unit than they were prepared for. But they still had their attention, which would leave an important target open for attack. It was a target the Sovereignty wouldn't consider high value. A radio dish? They had hundreds.

But only this one had a frequency that led to the contractor. A contractor who carried a special prize on his ship. It was one that they could not afford to let Supreme Leader Cornelius to obtain.

Rebel fighters ran about, switching firing positions in a disorganized fashion. It was unclear who survived the canon assault. Beretta found her leadership abilities faltering as she looked for a specific face in the crowd. She had called out for Paul numerous times. She didn't want him here but a man of his age would never listen to his mother. He believed in this mission more than her. Hell, he was the one to set it up. Unfortunately, the young man rushed the reconnaissance. It was a costly error, one that put the mission at stake.

The Sovereignty stopped their advance about a hundred meters down. Their rifles, more powerful and durable, had increased range. And the sights were better. It was easier for a Striker to pinpoint a target through a scope which easily adjusted for range, while the older models were stuck with iron sights, which didn't adjust well.

"Armor! We have armor!" one of the rebels shouted.

Beretta stood up and approached the fence. As she expected, the T-32 tanks were rolling to the edge of the farm.

Another striker fired an I.N.T. plasma blast. The rebels scattered and dove for the ground. A ball of plasma, strobing like a disco ball, hit the fence line and erupted. Beretta's ears rang again. The I.N.T.'s were the grenade launchers of energy-based assault weapons.

She could see the uneasy panic starting to engulf the rebels. It came in the form of numerous glances directed at her. Every face that looked to her communicated the question of when they could finally pull back. It was obvious this attack had not gone well in the slightest. They didn't expect an armored division to escort the rendezvous team. And in a few moments, they would have to move. The T-32 cannons had already claimed many of their militia. If all three opened fire at once, the hilltop would resemble an erupting volcano.

"Collins!" Beretta called out.

Captain Steve Collins fired a burst of five plasma shots down the hill before looking her way. He stood up and ran from the edge of the barrier, steam pouring from the frame of his weapon.

"Beretta, we can't continue. We're no good to the Rebellion dead."

"I know. Order everyone back but keep the Striker's attention on us. And radio Daunhauer! Tell him to hurry the hell up!"

"On it!" Collins dashed several feet behind the windmill structure, where one of the rebels tried to reassemble the damaged radio equipment. It had been struck with debris from the I.N.T. strike, denting the antenna and burning the speaker wire.

The radio tech was frantically putting his equipment back together. Collins shouting at him to hurry up didn't help matters.

"I'm handling it, sir!" the scrawny forty-year old said.

"Hurry it up fast. If Daunhauer doesn't hack into the satellite dish, we're all dead!"

"Take it up with him! I just work the radio!"

"Then work it and do it fast because in two minutes we're all gonna be part of a smoldering cinder that is this hilltop." Collins hustled back to the defense line. Beretta was now running through the group, her movements uncharacteristically frantic. He had always known her to be calm in the face of overwhelming odds. He had seen it many times since she started this resistance movement against Sovereignty's bureaucracy. He knew the problem. Paul Albright was nowhere to be found and it was compromising her guidance over the rebels.

"Withdraw!" she shouted. "Withdraw to Zone Thirty!"

"Zone Thirty is a canyon!" the radio tech yelled out. "I'll never get the message out!"

"We won't lose them otherwise," Beretta said.

"We're not trying to lose them! We're trying to keep their attention on us! That's what you said!" Collins said.

"Except their attention WILL be on us. Zolnar's not one to…"

Suddenly, the endless assault of plasma fire came to a sudden end. The air went quiet, with the exception of a few return shots from some rebels eager to get a kill.

"Shit," Collins muttered. "They're getting ready to fire. Wherever we go, it can't be here. Everyone! Fall back now!"

"Wait..." Beretta watched the movement on the hill. The tanks were in place, though the plasma generators did not appear to be winding. The soldiers had divided into two groups on each side of the armored division, each in standard formation, ready to flank.

One figure walked in front of the tanks. He was a large man. No helmet. A tiny red glint reflected off his visor eye. Zolnar himself. Whatever he was doing, it was a display.

"This is something else," Beretta said.

The man was dragging something across the field. Whatever it was, he dragged it with one hand.

Beretta looked closer.

"Collins...get me the binoculars."

"General, we have to move!"

"Do as I say and keep getting everyone else back. Fall back to Zone Thirty."

"But General..."

"...And break out the mortar units," Beretta said. Collins nodded. He opened a pouch in his tactical vest under his dust jacket and handed a pair of binoculars to Beretta. She snatched them from his hand and hastily spun to look out at the field.

She saw what was in Zolnar's possession. It wasn't a *what*, but a *who*. Her heart sank to her stomach. Suddenly, all the slashes, burns, and concussions she endured on this day meant nothing. She had finally found the face she had been searching for in the crowd. And he was in the worst hands imaginable.

A loud booming voice echoed over the hill. It was deep. Commanding. As Zolnar's voice always was. He was a feared leader, and he knew it.

"General Albright!"

The whole rebel squad froze. This was nothing they had ever seen from the Sovereignty's Army. Communication? From Zolnar of all people? The only talking they ever did to rebels was interrogation, which usually ended in death or imprisonment in conditions so unbearable that prisoners longed for the former.

"General Albright! I know you're up there!"

Collins watched as Beretta approached the fence line.

"No...General!"

Beretta ignored his calls. The General stood in the open space between two barriers, watching the Commander as he held her son by the throat. She bit down, partly from physical and mental anguish, partly from confined rage. That rage so desperately wanted to escape.

It was the question she hoped she would never have to answer: Would she sacrifice family for the cause? It had been asked many times before, and she always avoided the question. And her motherly instincts had kicked in immediately. She wanted to raise a sword and lead a charge to his rescue. She even felt her hand touching the hilt.

The Strikers stood in formation, resembling black statues with their rifles held across their bodies, muzzles pointed skyward. Standing in front of the tanks, Zolnar threw Paul to the ground, his broken legs touching down first, inducing a horrific yell that made Beretta quiver.

Beretta removed an amplifier from her pocket.

"General...don't..." Collins beseeched.

"Make the call to Daunhauer," she said. The rebels pulled back, leaving the defense line vacant except for the General herself. The plan was to keep the Army's attention on them. And that was what she was doing. She just didn't expect it to come at such a cost. The question of cause and family had been answered.

The radio tech clipped down the plastic covering for the radio unit and lifted the antennae. Beads of sweat ran down his face as he turned the knob to Daunhauer's frequency. Hopefully, they weren't too far away. Radiation in the atmosphere always played havoc on long distance radio signals. Any call more than a couple of miles usually resulted in static.

"Come on," Collins said to him.

"I got it," the tech comforted him. He lifted the microphone and handed it to him, uncoiling the black cord that attached it to the box. "Here. Hope it works. It's the best I can do!"

Collins snatched the mic and held it to his lips. He knew Daunhauer would be unable to respond, or risk attracting attention to himself. His mission required stealth. All Captain Collins could do was hope that the message got through. "Mother Bird to Echo-Four-Nine-Zero. Status is Code Red. Time frame elapsing. Main unit retreating to Zone Thirty. God be with us."

Collins took a sharp inhale, during which he made a quick silent prayer that the plan on the other side was working. Otherwise, this was all for nothing, and all hopes of stopping the Sovereignty would come to an end.

"General Albright. I have something special to show you. Something worth negotiating for. That is, assuming you have a heart."

Lord knows you don't have one.

She lifted the amplifier to her lips. "This is General Beretta Albright. I am here to negotiate..." she took a breath, watching the Commander smile through the lens of her binoculars... "the terms of your surrender."

The smile disappeared into a look of shock, which then turned into amusement.

"*MY* surrender?" the Commander called out. "I know you have glasses, General. You can see I can blow you off that hill at the snap of my fingers. But I'm offering you a deal."

It was no deal, and Albright knew it. Zolnar was well aware, that even though she was the leader of the Rebellion, there were other respected officers, all of them well trained and ready to take up the mantle if she was killed. It wasn't a simple matter of killing her and winning the conflict. Otherwise, they wouldn't be communicating right now. This was the ultimate chance for Zolnar to get the intelligence he needed. And he had the best tools at his disposal: Compassion and love. Not his. Hers.

It almost worked. She opened her mouth to speak against him, but her words wouldn't flow easily. There was a war blazing in her mind. Logic vs. Emotion. How could she put her son through this, let alone watch it take place? She felt foolish enough for letting him get involved with this conflict. She wished she convinced him to migrate to Espinosa, or one of the other smaller territories that didn't suffer oppression. She felt evil for what she was about to do. That was the emotion.

But there was the reality of the contractor and the death he brought to the Sovereignty, which would therefore bring death to them and, in time, the rest of the continent. Those territories that currently weren't oppressed soon would be if Supreme Leader Cornelius obtained Dr. Saegusa's memory chip. Beretta was left with two choices. Both of them presented an outcome she would have to live with. One outcome was staring her directly in the face. Just as Zolnar had planned, it tugged at her heartstrings like nothing she ever felt in her life.

Beretta glanced down, realizing she now tightly gripped the handle to her sword.

No. She couldn't do it, no matter how much she wanted to. The most successful negotiation was not about getting to 'yes'; it was about mastering 'no'.

"There is only one deal. Have your men lay down their weapons and no harm will be done to them."

"Let me be clear," Zolnar's voice boomed, "I have your boy here. He's dying, but he can be saved." The Commander looked down at his hostage. "His body his broken. The blast has shattered his legs..." Zolnar pressed a boot down on one of Paul's knees, drawing out a massive scream.

Beretta shook, her hand lifting the hilt a few inches from the sheath. Zolnar lifted his foot and pressed down on Paul's ankle, drawing a second scream of pain.

"I can stop whenever I want," Zolnar called up to her, his voice as calm as if on a morning stroll. "You should be proud of him. Not everyone survives a T-32 cannon blast. Though, maybe it would've been better if he hadn't." He reached down and ripped open Paul's shirt. "Ohhhhh," he feigned compassion, "I see bruising and swelling around the abdomen here. Your boy's got internal bleeding. Won't survive without a hospital and proper surgeons...which you won't find except in one of my infirmaries."

"Commander Zolnar..." she said, allowing urgency to slip through her voice.

Zolnar pressed a fist down into Paul's gut, sparking new pain. The young man groaned, trying to prevent another yell from escaping. He knew that every sound he made weakened his mother's willingness to continue on. Zolnar wasn't done. He pulled a knife from his belt and pressed the blade into his right side. He sank the blade a half-inch into the skin. Finally, Paul screamed again.

"All it takes is your surrender," the Commander said, smiling wide.

"Zol—" Beretta stopped herself. This was the cost of the mission. She glanced across the valley to the hayfields beyond. From her position, she could see the trucks driven by the Strikers. Those trucks carried troops, which now stood in formation, ready to charge the hillside again.

Among those trucks was another vehicle, long and wide, carrying a large device on its platform. From this distance, it was difficult to see its fine details. In fact, it was hard to see the few people moving about. But there were people there. And not all of them were Strikers.

Hurry up, Daunhauer, you slow bastard.

****

They had moved silently and swiftly. The plan had worked. General Albright and her son had sprung the attack, hitting the lead truck with rocket propelled grenades. The battalion came to a dead stop, the Strikers unloading from the trucks and engaging the rebels.

Despite the presence of artillery, General Albright had successfully distracted Commander Zolnar and his forces and had drawn them away from the communications truck. Only a few Strikers were on guard, their eyes fixed on the distant hill where the clash had moved. The exchange of plasma fire appeared to have come to a standstill.

Daunhauer knelt low in the tall grass, watching the Strikers like a cheetah stalking wildebeest. His eyes gazed past the soldiers to the hillside. The ceasefire worried him. Had the hill been overrun? Had he moved too slowly? It wasn't easy to sneak into this position unnoticed. Strikers were very alert. One false move and they would open fire into the brush without hesitation. He had to be silent. He, and the four rebels that were with him. ,

A voice rang through his earpiece.

"Mother Bird to Echo-Four-Nine-Zero. Status is Code Red. Time frame elapsing. Main unit retreating to Zone Thirty. God be with us."

It was Captain Collins. It was a breath of fresh air to know they were still alive. The voice was loud in his ear, though out of the Strikers' range of hearing. He couldn't respond, or else he would draw fire. But he couldn't wait. Time was running out and there was no room for failure.

Daunhauer, Recon Specialist and Lieutenant of the Albright Rebellion Forces, watched the radio truck. The dish, black on the inside while bright silver on the outside, stood ten feet above the platform. There was no driver in the truck. That particular Striker stood about three feet away from the door, Plasma Rifle in hand. Daunhauer watched his actions. He kept his gaze fixed on the west, right at the valley of tall grass where the rebel team hid. Four other Strikers patrolled around the radio truck and the personnel carriers. There was roughly ten feet of space between them, and luckily for the rebels, they did not seem suspicious that they were being watched. Two of them had moved to the other side of the vehicle, while one stood near the engine. They seemed intent on the event taking place at the hillside. Commander Zolnar was up to something, and it interested everybody, including them. The only two on alert seemed to be the driver and another Striker who patrolled between the carrier trucks parked ahead.

Daunhauer looked to his right at his friend and ally, Marvin Jones. He was crouched low, his dark skin easily blending into the terrain. Even at this close range, Daunhauer had to focus intently to see the rough details in his facial skin. Jones glanced back at him.

"Yes, Lieutenant?" he whispered. His English was broken, not because of it being a second language, but due to an injury to the throat that injured his jaw and tongue.

"Think you can hit him?" The Lieutenant nudged his head toward the radio truck driver. Jones nodded. Very slowly, he pulled his weapon of choice from the ground beneath him.

Daunhauer had to resist the instinct to recoil as Jones lifted the Shuriken. The blades were insanely sharp. The weapon was the size of a Frisbee, the blades extended six inches from the handle, covering two thirds of the circular base, which the final portion served as a handle.

Jones slowly pushed himself to his knees, drawing the weapon back. He watched the guard carefully, gauging distance, airspeed, as well as keeping an eye on the other guards. They hadn't moved yet, with two on the opposite side of the truck and one near the engine.

Exhaling smoothly, Jones flung the disk in a fast flickering motion. The guard jerked, aiming his rifle toward the movement in the grass. It was his final movement before the six-inch blades plunged into his neck. He leaned against the truck and slid down, his limp hands dropping the rifle to his lap.

Daunhauer watched the Striker near the engine. Jones had done it again. The shuriken had moved swiftly and silently. The Lieutenant pulled his knife, revealing a six-inch serrated blade.

"Keep low and follow me."

He stood up and advanced for the truck. The grass and cornstalks folded beneath his feet as he reached the edge of the field. He kept a low stance, knife held downward as he cleared the thirty-foot gap to the truck. The nearest Striker stood near the engine, his back to the rebels. Daunhauer could tell by the way he tilted on his feet that the soldier was about to turn around.

Jones approached the back of the vehicle and worked his way around, followed by another rebel fighter. In addition to the Striker standing at the engine, there were two others around the passenger side.

Daunhauer glanced at him and nodded. They struck at once. The Lieutenant lunged at the unsuspecting soldier and plunged the knife into the back of his skull. Jones sprang from the back of the vehicle and slashed his shuriken like a knife, the blades ripping the Striker's throat to shreds. The third soldier turned and raised his rifle. But his reaction had come too late. Jones flung the shuriken, the blades rotating through the air until sawing through the helmet and skull.

Daunhauer held his target tightly, his arm around his throat until the twitching stopped. Pulling the knife from the soldier's head, he quickly moved up around the nearby carrier truck which was parked only a few feet ahead. He caught a glimpse of the Striker that patrolled nearby. He was moving back toward the communication truck, having heard the faint sounds of the skirmish.

The Lieutenant moved around the engine and came around to the passenger side of the vehicle, now facing the back of the suspicious patroller. With the knife raised high, he leapt onto the soldier, driving him to the ground. He slammed the hilt down, putting the blade through his jugular.

He stood up, his long Native-American black hair covered in residue from the field. Daunhauer looked back, seeing no other Strikers in the immediate vicinity.

The radio truck was theirs. Daunhauer sprinted back, seeing his fellow rebels pulling the bodies away from the vehicle.

Barber, the tech wizard, had already climbed onto the platform. He held a briefcase-sized object in his hand. He opened it up, revealing a series of wires over a console with several knobs and a keyboard. For a man nearly sixty-years old, he moved as spry as someone twenty years younger. He was a hustler, and very good with technology. He had to be. Being drafted into the Sovereign Army forty years prior, he was assigned to the various missile silos as a radio repair tech. They expected precision and punished those who did their jobs poorly. Luckily, he had an open mind and could learn quickly.

One of those skills happened to be hacking signals.

He stretched out the console's antennae and pulled out several cables. At the end of the cables were metallic clips he could insert to slots in the base of the radio disk.

"This unit here is like a big computer," he explained, speaking like a professor in a college class. "It'll have the list of frequencies that have been used in recent days. Long range signals require specific wavelengths. Kind of like a call list. Luckily, I don't suspect that the Sovereignty typically makes long distance calls to Rhino Territory."

A series of codes flashed on the console screen. It was nothing that Daunhauer could understand. He didn't care to, as long as the wizard knew what he was doing.

"Albright can't wait. We got to get this going now. We need coordinates for the contractor. Speed, direction, and current location."

"He'll be hard to hit with that camouflage," Barber said.

"That's why the gunners are gonna need those details. With the right calculations, we can intercept."

"Yeah, I know the plan," Barber said. "I just hope it works." He tapped various keys, hacking into the radio platform. Daunhauer grew impatient but had to keep silent. It was frustrating that such a device couldn't be as simple as picking up the speaker and making a radio call. But Barber was right. They needed the specific frequency to covertly get the information from the pilot, without him suspecting anything.

Jones was starting to pace nervously, keeping watch for other Strikers.

"Perhaps we should consider getting the pilot to land somewhere, instead of trying to gun him down."

"He'll smell a rat for sure," Daunhauer said. "I guarantee this guy, if he's any good, is already on edge doing business with the Sovereignty. If he gets a transmission asking for him to meet in a different location, he'll possibly suspect that he's being led into a trap because they don't want to pay the cost."

Another series of codes trickled on the computer screen.

"I think I got it!" Barber said, his voice lively. He rubbed his hands together and brushed his faint white beard while reading the codes. He then pointed to Jones. "Get me the speaker from inside the truck."

Jones opened the driver's side door and reached for the radio unit in the center console, which was connected to the disk through wires which ran out the back. He disconnected the speaker and handed it to Barber, who connected its wire to his portable unit.

"Can't you just use yours?" one of the other rebels asked.

"The wires in ours are old and rusty, one of the reasons the transmissions always sound so jumbled. Theirs are cleaner, more top-of-the-line. If we want him to think we're with the Sovereignty, we'll need to sound like them one-hundred percent." He held the mic to his face and adjusted the knob. Behind him, the disk powered on as it boosted the signal.

Here we go…

"This is Delta-Nine-Bravo-Two. Scavenger, do you read?" *Scavenger* was often the code used in the rare instances that Sovereignty used outside resources. It was the only part of the operation that required guesswork. Hopefully he guessed right.

****

Firebird awoke from a deep nap as the *incoming message* signal startled him out of his chair. He looked to the monitor, which read where the message was coming from.

"What do they want now?" His voice was groggy. His chest and groin still ached from the fight with the doctor, which left his mood sour. He contemplated ignoring the transmission.

The voice came over the transmitter: *"This is Delta-Nine-Bravo-Two. Scavenger, do you read?"*

"I would suggest responding," Stuart said. "We do not want to anger Lord Sauron."

"Cornelius," Firebird corrected him.

"I'm aware. I was using sarcasm."

"Oh, in the name of…" Each word was long and drawn out. With his feet up on the dashboard, Firebird connected to the radio signal. "This is Scavenger. We read. We have the package, don't worry."

"Do not get quippy with me, Merc. We are paying you a grand sum. We are requiring an update on your arrival."

"You haven't paid me *anything*. Yet," Firebird said.

"The Commander meeting with you needs your current location, speed, and trajectory."

Firebird scoffed and looked at Stuart. "Why the hell do they need that? Check the signal. Figure out where it's coming from."

"Yes, sir," Stuart said. His mechanical arms protruded from his body and began operating the signal tracker on the computer monitor. He punched in several keys with effortless precision. A small antenae protruded from the bow of the ship, with a blinking light strung near its tip. A grid appeared on the monitor, then a map of the region. "It's coming out of Central Valley. Source is a Sovereign Army Com Disk unit."

"Ooookay," Firebird said. His suspicion that somebody hacked the signal had subsided. And it wasn't out of character for the Sovereignty to be so uptight. Cornelius was like an impatient child, always ready to throw a temper tantrum. But that impatient child had power, and the ability to execute anyone who pissed him off. Firebird sighed. Despite how good the money was, this was certainly a one-time deal. He pressed a finger on the transmitter. "Standby."

****

"Roger. Forty-two-point-four degrees north, fifty-one-point-three degrees east. Going south at two-six-eight. Copy. E.T.A.: forty-five minutes. *You satisfied?*"

"We'll be satisfied when you bring the package. Unharmed," Barber said, mimicking the voice of an officer.

"Just have the money ready. Firebird out."

The signal muddled into static. Barber disconnected the device and quickly unhooked the components of his equipment from the disk.

"Got it!" he said triumphantly.

"Good! Collect the Strikers' weapons, and let's get the hell out of here," Daunhauer said. His voice was low, but urgent. He pulled his handheld radio from his belt. "Recon Team to Motherbird, coordinates received. Get the hell out of there now."

****

The rebels retreated down the back of the hill to a flat plain that led down to the canyon area that was Zone Thirty. The hilltop was abandoned, leaving it a smoldering collection of ravaged farmhouses and equipment. Only three people remained while the others retreated.

Beretta closed her eyes and winced as Zolnar intensified her son's torture. The air was full of his screams. Each one hit hard as though it were a physical blow to her head and chest. Several physical reactions elevated at once. Nausea. Psychotic rage. Exhaustion. Lightheadedness, yet, also a bizarre focus. It was a series of feelings she didn't know could exist together.

Zolnar was twisting Paul's broken left ankle. The young man screamed, with only one word leaving his mouth. "DON'T!" It wasn't directed at the Commander, but to his mother. He knew what he was doing, and she did too. They were using Zolnar's twisted antics against him, allowing the Recon Team to hack the radio truck.

"We got it," Collins said. The signal had come in. Daunhauer had done it! They had the coordinates for the upcoming vessel. Their job here was done. It was the strike team's responsibility now to conduct the operation. "General, we have to go!" Beretta didn't move. He wasn't sure if she heard him. "Albright! Daunhauer did it! We can't stay here. We must get back with the rest of the team!"

Beretta looked back at him. Her face was red and glistening with tears and sweat. Collins could see the agony that she was experiencing. Luckily, she was far enough away from Zolnar that he couldn't see it, though he probably knew the mental damage he was inflicting, regardless. It wasn't his first rodeo. He had inflicted this tactic successfully on other enemies. Some of which were allies of hers. And those who gave in, no matter how much she sympathized with them, had to be dealt with. Sometimes in ways that didn't make her sleep so good at night. Wars were never clean, even for the ones on the right side of history.

Beretta took one last look down the hill. "Paul!" she called out. The torture came to a pause. Zolnar looked back up at her.

"Surrender yourself," he demanded. "And his suffering will cease! You turn away, not only will you die uselessly, but you will die knowing that he will die slowly and brutally." He glanced over his left shoulder at a Striker in a brown uniform. Instead of a rifle, he held an electric rod. He stood next to a cage on wheels. Inside were two hounds. They were mutated by radiation, looking more reptilian than like dogs. Their snouts were elongated like a crocodile's, and their inch-long teeth were thin and narrow like curved construction nails. They snarled from behind the gate, eager to seize the mangled piece of meat in their master's possession.

Beretta could hear their wretched sounds. She shook, on the verge of collapsing to her hands and knees.

"General?" Collins called out. His voice helped her focus. Another voice reminded her of her priorities.

Paul called out once again. "GOOOO!"

"General..." Collins said again. He tensed as he watched Beretta step through a section of battered fence. She lifted the amplifier to her lips.

"Commander Zolnar..." she said. The Commander stood up straight, his boot planted on Paul's chest, waiting for what would hopefully be Albright's surrender. Beretta summoned all of her strength to hide any sense of pain from her voice. She spoke loud and confidently. "As I've stated before, you have one chance to surrender. Proceed with your actions, and you will face annihilation. We will give no quarter."

Zolnar leaned backward, impressed by Albright's gall. How could she possibly think she would win? Some questions he didn't care enough to seek out the answers.

He shrugged his shoulders. "Okay. Have it your way." He leaned down to look at Paul. "Some mother you have there." He stepped back and snapped his fingers toward the handler, who unlocked the cage. The two hounds ripped from the gate and raced over, baring fangs as they drew near Paul. The injured rebel closed his eyes and accepted his fate.

Teeth ravaged his flesh as the two beasts attacked him with carnivorous ferocity. Blood splashed the grass as they opened his mid-section, alternating between his now-open belly and his limbs. Tossing him around like a ragdoll, they slashed with their claws and bit, each injury felt by the helpless Paul Albright.

Beretta didn't watch. She had turned around and joined the others in their retreat. Collins waited with the radio tech near their speeder. It was a small vehicle, not much bigger than a four-wheeler. But as the name suggested, it was fast and it could hold all three of them. Collins and the tech were already seated, the Captain at the controls. She hopped into her seat and fastened the safety belt.

Collins gunned the engine, sending the vehicle zipping down the back of the hill through the plain. Behind them, the countryside lit up in a world of plasma fire as the T-32 opened fire.

"General. I'm...I'm sorry," Collins said. He didn't know what else to say. He didn't dare look back at her. What was there to say to somebody who just suffered the worst trama imaginable?

Beretta sat silently, listening to the blasting taking place behind her. Paul's screams echoed in her mind. It would be a torture that would last for the remainder of her lifetime. She stared straight ahead, her face expressionless.

They would die. No matter what happened next, they would die. All of them. The Sovereignty had made their final mistake today.

"Have Daunhauer get the guns in place. Track the location. Have a salvage team prepped."

"A salvage team?" Collins asked.

"Yes." She glanced to the radio tech. "What are you waiting for?"

"Oh! Right," the nervous tech said. He was not going to ask questions, as for the first time ever, someone scared him more than Commander Zolnar. And he was seated next to her.

CHAPTER 5

Radiation lightning flashed high above as Firebird steered the Ash-Cloud into Sovereignty airspace. Dawn was here and the sun's rays beamed through the red atmosphere down onto the vast landscape. Through the viewing screen and side windows, the mercenary watched the world passing beneath him.

The area was a rural landscape, with miles of farmland with a few towns in-between. To the west were the crocodile swamps, home to thirty-foot reptilians. The mercenary had heard the stories of these beasts and their insatiable appetites. Their hides were reported to be so thick, they could withstand an I.N.T. blast. In addition to these swamps were numerous lakes and ponds, many of them quartered off. Though he didn't know what lived in there, there was no doubt that these water sources were off limits due to their toxicity. Several roads stretched through the territory like veins connecting the communities together. Armed patrol vehicles, operated by Strikers, moved about these roads. The region was under military control, and these patrols were symptomatic of the grip the authority had on the throat of its citizens.

The towns were like those he had seen in the old western films he had watched in his video archive. Each had one main road cutting through the center of the community, with various shops and services placed within. It was the most civilized part of the region, as various outlaw groups moved within the countryside.

He could see green flickering of plasma exchange coming from one of the patrol vehicles and a small group of civilians. From what he could see, the Jeep was on a standard patrol when it came across a small group of Rebels. The Army patrol Jeeps, armed with a mounted turret, shredded the enemy with ease. The bullets came out so rapidly, they almost appeared as one laser blast.

"Probably didn't pay their cable bill," Firebird mentioned as he looked away from the massacre.

"There have been reports of increased rebel attacks on the Sovereign Army," Stuart said. "It is possible we are entering a warzone."

"Stuart, the whole continent is a warzone," Firebird said. "In every territory you'll find somebody trying to kill someone else. Why do you think we get so much business?"

"Those conflicts are insignificant to what's developing in these superpower territories, like Sovereignty and Rhino. It's different here. These are large scale military regimes. The only thing keeping them in check is the risk of conflict with each other."

"Hence the paycheck is bigger," Firebird said. "Be happy. I can buy you some upgrades. Or at least a few spare parts."

The droid didn't offer a response. Firebird audibly scoffed as he realized the bot was still hung up on the ethics of the situation. Whether it was a sense of self preservation, or just moral grandstanding, he wasn't sure. Regardless, Stuart was under his command and would do whatever was demanded of him.

"If it makes you feel better…not that bots like you can feel…but I've already decided not to do business with these super nations again," he said.

"That would be advisable," Stuart said. "Studies have shown that, throughout human history, governments, especially totalitarian ones, are by far the least trustworthy. We may be considered a loose end to what Sovereignty is planning."

Firebird thought about this. All sense of amusement was gone. What Stuart said actually made sense, and it drew a dull feeling in his gut.

"You suspect that they won't let us leave?"

"I cannot say that for certain," Stuart said. "But the more I analyze the recorded history of the Sovereignty, the more red flags I discover. You should have allowed me to run a thorough strategic analysis before we accepted the deal."

"It was a spur of the moment type of thing," Firebird said. He leaned back and thought about it. Would the Sovereignty betray them? He would no-longer be a valued player in their game once they had the data. And what would stop another nation from hiring him against them? He wouldn't accept such a deal, of course, but Sovereignty didn't know that. "What other red flags are you talking about?"

"You are familiar with The Burrier?"

"Yeah. Another mercenary. I knew him. The guy had a whole team. They did a lot of Black Ops type of stuff. I worked with them on one espionage trip before I met you."

"Their last recorded transmission was over the Pillar Banks to the north. Two months ago. They have never been seen again," Stuart said.

"The Pillar Banks…" Firebird knew where that was. It was a rocky region on the southwest Sovereignty border. Last he heard, Gordon, the Burrier founder, had been spotted fleeing the west coast territory, though what he was doing there was unknown. There weren't any military regimes out there, though several small warlords occupied the area. It was rumored that top scientists worked out there, something to do with chemical engineering. Though, Firebird wasn't aware that Gordon was doing any work for the Sovereignty.

"You think he was shot down by the Sovereignty?"

"If they are planning a massive assault on the surrounding territories, would you want any loose ends?" Stuart asked.

"Hmmm…"

Firebird was now deep in thought. The greedy side of his brain sang loudly in his mind's ears. It was two-hundred thousand gold coins, for crying out loud. It was over three times his previously best payday, and the job had gone relatively smooth up to this point. But there was a dark reality to working with certain types of people. Sovereignty had used their own highly trained operatives for special missions abroad. The only reason they chose him in this instance was to avoid Rhino Clan tracing the interference in their territory back to them. If any questions arose, they could deny involvement.

What good was the two-hundred thousand gold pieces if he was going to be too dead to spend it?

Firebird stared at the world below through the viewing screen. *Would've been nice if the damn droid had figured this out beforehand.* He sat silently, deep in thought for another minute, mentally debating whether he wanted to go through with this plan. One thing was for sure: No way was he going to come out of this without getting paid.

"How much you think Espinosa would pay?"

"Quite a significant sum, though I doubt they would match Sovereignty's bid," Stuart said.

"Well, at least we'd come out alive. Find their frequency and get 'em on the horn."

"I will begin immediately," Stuart said. "Shall we maintain present course in the meantime?"

"Yes. After all, I haven't made up my mind."

Saegusa twitched in her seat, the world within a series of flashes and lights. Ever since the conversion, dreams were sporadic and bizarre. It was like being inside a circuit, like a living bolt of electricity. She was told the microprocessor, the cybernetic portion of her brain, would not affect her dreams. Then again, she was only the fifth person to ever successfully get the implant and survive. There were many unknowns about cyborgs, and cybernetic brain implants were a new invention from Espinosa's medical field.

Her eyes opened, half her vision foggy as her organic eye adjusted. The cabin was empty, except for herself. She sat up and allowed the haziness to subside. It didn't take long for her brain to kick into gear. She instantly recalled her location and destination.

The skin on her wrists felt tight. Saegusa looked at her hands. The metal cuffs were locked together by a single chain link, which was fastened to a lock near the armrest. As she adjusted her position, she realized her legs would only move a couple of inches. She leaned forward and looked to the floor, seeing both ankles cuffed together and linked to the floor. She immediately tried lifting her legs, hoping the robotic limbs would be strong enough to break the metal binding. Her knees whined as she tugged high. Alas, they lacked the strength.

"Damn it," she muttered. She stood up as best she could and glanced out the window at the world below. She had seen much of the continent during her many travels. The fact that she didn't instantly recognize this land was an indicator that she was in Sovereign airspace.

This can't be happening.

She tugged violently against her restraints, again to no avail. She inhaled a deep breath and calmed herself. She leaned down so she could touch the tiny lever on the mechanical platform on the side of her head, which accessed the controls to her eye. Her colleagues had added a little bonus item to the eye itself. She opened the tiny door, exposing a lever inside the panel. She clicked it all the way up and aimed her eye down to the chain between the cuffs. A thin stream of hot energy flared from the eye like a blowtorch. The metal chain link turned hot red as the material gradually began to melt away.

Saegusa leaned closer, focusing the stream as much as possible. If she ever made it back to Espinosa, she would owe her colleagues an apology for including this ridiculous gadget to her cybernetic system.

****

"Okay, if my math is correct, he should be coming up on the Orion Fields in the next few minutes!"

Barber had to shout to get his voice heard over the roar of the truck's engine and the wind that surged through the broken windshield. After overtaking the radio truck, the team hurried back through the tall grass, just as the hillside lit up in a wall of cannon fire. Their objective now was to get in touch with the gunners and give them the coordinates. The first major issue was getting close enough in time.

"It'll still be hard to hit if that damn ship has camouflage," Jones said.

"It's our only chance," Daunhauer said. "Besides, those anti-air guns pack a punch. They'll turn the sky into one big ball of flame. If Barber's coordinates are right, that contractor prick doesn't stand a chance."

"Sucks for the scientist lady," Barber said, his voice sounding uncomfortable. Daunhauer kept both hands on the steering wheel as he drove the truck south. He glanced to the former Striker. The man was genuinely uncomfortable with what they were about to do. It made sense. None of this was the doctor's fault. But he wasn't going to lose any sleep over it. He believed in Beretta Albright's leadership, and agreed that this was the best course of action.

"If that scientist gets handed over to the Sovereignty, we're all as good as dead," he said. He sped the truck over a deep pitch of earth, jostling in his seat as he steered the truck out the other side. "It's all for the greater good, radio man. Now…get on the radio and give Delta Team the coordinates."

"If they're still alive," Jones said.

"If they hit the outpost the way I instructed them too, they should be fine. Barber, do it."

Barber opened up his radio console and opened up the frequency to Donnelly's, the officer in charge of Delta Team.

"Bravo Team to Delta, come in. Over."

"Delta Team here. It's about time, old man. I was starting to think it all went downhill." There was a genuine sense of relief in Donnelly's voice.

"Didn't go *quite* as planned. Rather, the cost was more than we expected. But more on that later. You only have minutes, Donnelly! The contractor's coming in hot. You need to aim your guns in the airspace over the Orion Fields. Target Zone, Charlie-four-nine-Foxtrot. Go broad range. Pepper the atmosphere if you have to. Just don't let him through!"

****

"You got it, buddy. Over and out." Donnelly slammed the mic down and ran from the Jeep to the anti-aircraft cannons, dodging the dismembered bodies of Strikers and rebels. Burning Jeeps and turret units obscured the base in smoke. It was a costly aftermath to overtaking this gun base. At least two-thirds of his squad had perished in the sneak attack. And with the hint of loss that Barber had let slip through the radio, it seemed that a large number of the rebel forces had perished on this very day. With very limited time to prepare, he was amazed the plan even got this far. But never in human history did victory come without the price of blood.

There were five anti-aircraft cannons, the barrels pointing fifteen feet high into the sky. They were arranged in a straight line, separated by twenty meters. A long, ten-foot deep trench connected the guns, each widening into a large operating chamber that surrounded each cannon's operating system. A dozen rebel fighters hustled in and out of the channels, loading artillery and finishing other necessary prep work.

The unit's corporal climbed up from the channel. He saw the short, lean figure that was Donnelly running toward him. Like the rest of the rebels, his face was unkempt, with stringy whiskers protruding nearly a centimeter from his jawline.

"Corporal, are we all set?" Donnelly called out to him.

"We are," the Corporal said.

"Target area is Charlie-four-nine-Foxtrot. Two minutes! Get the guns ready! And make sure we have eyes in the sky when it goes down. Apparently, the General wants the crash inspected. It'll give us something to do." Donnelly glanced back at a dead Striker slumped over a radio console. It was unclear whether he got the transmission out in time. If so, the squad could bet that a whole damn circus would be coming in to meet them. "Won't be staying here much longer anyway."

The Corporal gave the order. The air filled with the echoes of soldiers passing the instructions down the channel. Their voices disappeared under the mechanical whirring of gears as the anti-aircraft barrels shifted in place. The extenders protruded from the base, giving the shells longer range. In moments, all five barrels pointed to the northeast, each one moments away from unleashing hell onto the sky.

****

"Eighty-five?!" Firebird chuckled as he heckled the Espinosa official. "The fate of your nation apparently depends on this cyborg scientist lady, yet all you're willing to pay for her to be brought back is eighty-five thousand gold coins?!"

"I did suggest they would not offer the same substantial amount as Sovereignty," Stuart said.

"Yeah, what I forgot to tell you after you said that was...what's the word? Bullshit!" He turned and leaned into the microphone. "You hear that? Buuulllshit!" He looked back to the droid, who kept his mechanical limbs fixed on the flight controls. "They have money to fund all this research crap. They have the coin for this cyborg idiot."

"Just because she hit you in the balls, doesn't make her an idiot."

"Anyone who goes into Rhino Territory to pick a few plants is an idiot," Firebird said.

"Would you agree to ninety-three?" the official asked. His voice was alarmed, much like the Sovereignty official he had trolled earlier. There was a sense of pleasure Firebird usually felt in having leverage over others. However, this time was somewhat frustrating. He at least expected to get a hundred-thousand out of this. He didn't think it would be hard to get the money out, considering the situation. But to his surprise, the Espinosa official couldn't even do that.

"I'll give you her legs and eye for that," Firebird said. "I'm sure somebody could use them. Sovereignty just needs her brain."

"I don't..." the voice trailed off. Firebird tapped his fingers on the dashboard as he waited. The voice came back. *"Two-hundred thousand. Deal?"*

"Two-ten," Firebird said. Stuart whipped his head to look at him. Even through those blank 'eyes' Firebird was feeling the heat of a scornful look. "I've known women less uptight than you."

"Yes...we can do that..." the voice said. Firebird disregarded the ambiance of stress in the official's voice. He couldn't have cared less. Hell, he just came out ten-thousand ahead!

"Make preparations for the exchange. Give me a location when you're ready. In the meantime, we'll be changing course. Firebird out." The mercenary disengaged the radio and threw his metal fist in the air victoriously. "Ha! Bastards tried to play cheap. I would've accepted fifty percent if they didn't try to jerk me off. Eighty-five thousand..."

"They will probably have to get into their reserves to pay that off. Or borrow from one of their allied territories," Stuart said.

"Not my concern," Firebird said. "Free market, bolt-head. How do you think we get paid?"

"As you mentioned before, I don't receive money," Stuart said.

"Yeah, but you need oil changes," Firebird said. He leaned back, his face bright with a wide smile. He placed his feet high on the dashboard. "Prepare to alter course."

"Altering course..." Stuart's voice trailed off. His visual scanners watched the viewing screen. His emotionless, robotic voice suddenly exploded with urgency. "Emergency. Evasive maneuvers!"

The world seemed to shake as the air around them erupted into fire. The Ash-Cloud juddered violently as though caught in an earthquake, startling the mercenary. Firebird yanked his feet from the console and leaned into the controls. He watched the viewing monitor and side windows.

The sky was a swirling mix of orange and black. He caught the glimpses of projectiles streaking through the air, their journey concluding in a tremendous POP of fire and smoke. From each blast, a mid-air shockwave ripped across the surrounding sky, forming a ring of smoke, flame, and razor-sharp shrapnel. Pieces of debris clunked against the hull like metal rain. He could hear the blasts through the hull, each growing louder as the blasting intensified.

"Christ! Bot, get us out of here," Firebird said.

"Working on it," Stuart said. Firebird and Stuart got on the controls to bank the ship to starboard.

"These are anti-aircraft shells," Firebird said. "Why the hell are they shooting at us?!"

"It is possible they traced your radio call to Espinosa," Stuart said. The ship shook as another shell exploded nearby. Shrapnel peppered the hull. The viewing monitor turned black as smoke encompassed the Ash-Cloud like fog in a shipyard.

"Even if they could act that fast, how the hell do they know where to shoot?!" Firebird growled. He pressed on the controls, angling the Ash-Cloud down to take it below the point of bombardment. Another blast rocked the aircraft to port. The starboard window cracked, flames clinging to several sections of the hull. The lights went out, replaced by swirling red emergency lights.

"Shall we make a radio transmission to Sovereignty?"

"No point. Let's just get out of here..." Firebird's voice trailed off as a thought came to mind. The radio transmission...the request for coordinates... *Those bastards were looking for where to put the bullseye...*

A deafening explosion rocked overhead. Audible alarms sounded. Emergency alerts rang throughout the ship. Red letters flashed over the monitors. *Alert! Hull Breach! Alert! Hull Breach!*

The explosion threw Dr. Saegusa onto her side, tugging her wrists against the weakened restraints. Her laser ripped through the air, fizzling out a foot from her bionic eye. The restraint lock, steaming and red, snapped from the sudden pulling motion. Her hands flung free over her head.

She felt the ship pitch again. Saegusa straightened herself in her seat and switched off the laser flare. She then glanced out the window, seeing the airspace around her now a world of hot flame. Several shells burst throughout the sky as though the Sovereignty was trying to shoot down an entire squadron of fighter jets. But the air was void of other aircraft. She looked to the portside window. On both sides, the sky was empty, except for the hurtling storm of shrapnel that assaulted the hull.

She fell backward as the glass shattered. She hit the seat then fell to the floor, her feet twisting over each other. They were still bound to the lock below. Another blast shook the Ash-Cloud. Through the thundering sounds of mid-air eruptions was the groaning sound of metal. Saegusa froze, listening to the hull groaning louder and louder, as though the ship was screaming in pain. It was clear that sections of the hull were coming loose. And they were quickly succumbing to the strain of the shockwaves and flight.

A large crack ripped across the ceiling, confirming her fears. The crack widened, exposing internal wirings and components. She felt as if she was sitting inside a huge metal chicken egg. And it was splitting rapidly. A crash was inevitable. Being stuck on the floor, bound by a chain did not present a strong likelihood of survival. There was no time to waste wondering who was shooting at them or why. She had to figure a way out of this predicament.

She untwisted her legs until she was sitting up on the floor, then leaned forward as best she could to zap the chain link with her eye. She flicked the lever back on and blasted the metal, turning the link bright orange.

"Engine Two is failing," Stuart announced, amplifying his voice to be heard over the alarms. The monitor hummed as the camouflage failed, exposing the Ash-Cloud's crumbling design into view. Several breach alerts scrolled up on the main monitor.

Another explosion cracked nearby.

"Engine One now showing signs of heavy damage," Stuart continued.

"Damn it. Damn the bastard Sovereignty!" Firebird cursed.

"I did warn about how unsafe it was to do business with…"

"Not now, Bot!" Firebird snarled. He looked through the flickering viewing screen. From what he could see, they were near the edge of the bombardment. He banked the ship to port, both engines trailing smoke as the Ash-Cloud soared from the chaos above.

After several tense moments, the shockwaves subsided. However, the Ash-Cloud continued shaking violently. Firebird could hear metal clanging throughout the ship. In the background was the hefty moan from the ship. The monitor repeated its list of damage alerts, with the most significant ones flashing red in all caps.

"We're gonna need a place to set down," he said. "Are the elevators functional?"

Stuart ran a diagnostic.

"Elevators One and Two are inoperable. Three is functional. Four is damaged, but functional to a limited capacity."

"Not comforting," Firebird said.

"I simply answered your question," Stuart said.

"All you needed to say was 'we're fucked.'"

"If you insist. Firebird, we are fucked."

Firebird grimaced. *Damn freaking machine is sarcastic even when he's about to be spread all over the countryside.*

"If we're not gonna set down pleasantly, then we're gonna have to find a place to land," he said. "Let's find a patch of land that's relatively flat."

"I already have a location," Stuart said. "Dead ahead. Two-thousand meters."

Firebird checked the location on the monitor. "Where the hell is that?"

"On the edge of the farming landscape," Stuart said. "We will be risking collision in the swamps. But at this point, sir, we have no choice."

"Yeah, no kidding," Firebird said. He reached up and flicked the switches to engage the elevators, despite knowing most of them were damaged. He looked ahead and watched the landscape. With the engines failing, the Ash-Cloud was quickly losing altitude. His eyes widened as he noticed they were drawing near the tip of a large rock mound directly in their path. He pulled up on the controls with all of his might. "Come on, baby." The engines spat and sparkled. The ship leveled out. They passed over the rock.

Firebird tensed.

The tip of the rock mound, like the head of a spear, grazed the hull, generating a dull squealing sound underneath his feet. The Ash-Cloud passed over a half mile of rocky landscape before descending low on a flat plain. For a few hundred meters, the ground appeared dry, with a few trees scattered about.

But as they moved further, they could see the wet texture of the region. They were approaching the marsh.

"Oh, this won't be good," Firebird muttered. He mentally braced himself for the inevitable touchdown. He cleared his throat and barked his orders with a commanding tone. "Engage landing gear."

"Landing gear engaged," Stuart said. "Front wheel's not responding."

"Of course not," Firebird groaned. "That would mean something would actually go right in this shitheap scenario."

"Clearly the objective was to have us killed. Clearly, we are still alive. Thus, technically, something *did* go right for us."

"We? You are *technically* not even alive to begin with," Firebird said. "And a big part of dying when your plane is shot down is the CRASHING PART!"

"Sixty seconds to impact," Stuart said. Firebird reached over his shoulder and began to strap himself into the seat. As he started to clip the binds together, he noticed the blank security monitor.

"Oh, SHIT!"

During the chaos, he had forgotten about Saegusa. She was in the cabin. The way she was restrained was not ideal for a crash. She was fastened to the floor and seat by her hands and feet, which could easily be torn free if the Ash-Cloud hit hard. Firebird launched himself out of his seat. The turbulence increased, causing him to stumble as he moved toward the corridor.

"It is not ideal for you to stand at this time," Stuart said.

"I gotta strap in the doc!" Firebird said.

"I am impressed that you would put her safety above your own."

"I couldn't care less about her safety, aside from the fact that I'm gonna need that two-hundred grand to buy myself a new ship! For that to happen, she needs to survive this damn crash."

****

Zolnar stood at the top of a smoldering hill amongst the charred ruins of farmland. Bodies lay about in fragments, charred to the bone. Down the hill behind him, the hounds continued to feast on Paul Albright's corpse.

Strikers spread for hundreds of yards, executing injured rebels that lay in the grass with plasma shots to the forehead.

"How many are dead?" he asked the Lieutenant.

"Four, sir."

"Then my suspicions were confirmed," Zolnar said. "Those rebels are more cunning than I'll give them credit for. They were after something specific. Something in that radio truck…"

"I don't understand, Commander," the Lieutenant said. "We've got numerous radio trucks. We've had them as part of standard patrols. Why sacrifice an entire platoon to hack into a dish?"

Zolnar thought about it, then swiftly turned to look north as the echoes of artillery echoed through the air. The horizon was red and black, as though a volcano had erupted in the distance. Several artillery shells crackled hundreds of feet high in the sky, the only armament used by the Sovereignty that didn't rely on plasma power.

"What the hell's going on?! Who the hell told them to open fire? Lieutenant! Get in contact with Station Four!"

"Sir!" Zolnar glanced to his left. A Striker was running up the hill toward him as fast as he could. "Sir, I already attempted to communicate. That station's not responding! And there's been no other authorization by any other official for any gun station to open fire."

Zolnar watched the horizon as numerous shells burst in the air. Why were they shooting there? There were no reports of aircraft as far as he knew. Was there some invisible ship that he just wasn't aware of...

...Or one that he was aware of...moving south from the Rhino Territory, like an Ash-Cloud! He glanced back at the radio truck that had been hacked. Suddenly, it all made sense.

"That cunning bitch," he mumbled. The Lieutenant and communications specialist staggered back. It was unclear whether the Commander was angry, impressed, or both. "This whole thing was a setup! I can't believe I fell for that woman's trap." A sneer widened across his face. Then a thought came to mind, and that sneer became a sadistic smile. "It's time we use her strategy against her. Lieutenant! Get eyes in the sky! Look for the contractor."

"How will we find him?" the Lieutenant asked.

"Anything falling out of the sky will be him. You can be certain the Rebels will send a team to inspect the crash site."

****

The Ash-Cloud pitched again, tilting hard to port. Firebird stumbled and hit the wall of the small corridor. The nose dipped, and he felt himself starting to slip back into the cockpit. Like climbing a mountain, he pulled himself up into the cabin.

Stuart leveled the craft as best he could, but the turbulence was increasing. Firebird entered the cabin, immediately noticing the various breaches in the sides and ceiling. The fuselage door had caved in completely, bringing the entire wing into view. The minigun had been knocked off its mount and thrown across the room. A crack widened along the ceiling. Air surged into the cabin as though trapped in a hurricane. The ship was about to snap in half.

And there on the floor was Saegusa. She was...awake? She was sitting upright, facing away from him. Her hands were no longer bound to the link on the arm of the seat. There was no time to analyze the situation. He hurried over to her and reached down to get her into the seat, where he could get the safety harness on.

She could hear his footsteps rapidly approaching. She kept her head low, concealing the laser. The metal was red hot and steaming. Firebird was standing directly behind her now. She pulled away as hard as possible with her feet. The weakened chain snapped as though it were a toothpick.

Saegusa jumped to her feet and whipped herself around, laser sweeping across Firebird's chest. The mercenary, surprised and off balance, threw his hands up to protect his one eye.

64

Mechanical legs helped to balance her weight as the Ash-Cloud tilted forward again. She threw a hard kick into his chest, driving him back toward the open fuselage door. Firebird cursed in considerable pain. He could feel the sucking force of the wind pulling him back as though it were an invisible hand. He threw his arms out, his metal hand catching the rough edge of the breach. He shifted his weight forward as best he could, as the heels of both feet were extended over the ledge.

As he hurled himself several steps into the cabin, Saegusa had pulled herself into the passenger seat. She pulled the safety harness down on herself and secured all the locks. She took a breath and prepared for impact.

"Touchdown in five…" Stuart called from the cockpit.

"Oh…fuck," Firebird muttered. He lunged into the cabin as far as he could. The countdown ended. The Ash-Cloud touched down.

Like a train off its rails, the aircraft skidded for several hundred meters, shredding the ground beneath it as it went. The force of the landing lifted Firebird off his feet and slammed him hard into the wall behind him. He hit the ground just as hard, his mind a blur.

The overhead breach widened, and finally, the aircraft broke in two. The two halves spun as they flew in separate trajectories, ripping sediment as they went. The wings separated as well, their armaments detonating.

Firebird felt himself jolted in multiple different directions, his mind fading away the entire time. He could hear Stuart's voice, but couldn't make out what he was saying. Sparks and metal flew everywhere, battering the floor before shooting out into the world behind the open cabin. Then, it all went black.

The forward section rolled like a barrel in a raging river before skidding another few yards.

Finally, it all stopped.

CHAPTER 6

It was like watching a film strip with a blinding light shining through it. In what seemed like a blink of an eye, his whole life seemed to roll by in a flash. There were his parents, two vastly different people. His mother, the peaceful caregiver, and his father, the warfighter. Then the rise of Estis. The shining light became fire and brimstone. And for what seemed like the millionth time, he watched the Clan leader, Estis, aim his pistol at an unarmed woman, kneeling near the broken body of her husband.

The gunshot rang out, echoing for what felt like eternity. It rang again. And again. And again.

The core reactor detonated, triggering numerous secondary explosions in the debris field. Firebird woke up, seeing a flash of plasma rippling across the landscape. He sat up, though not of his own free will. He was being lifted and dragged backward. He looked down, seeing soil bunching along his legs.

His brain registered the pinch from Stuart's mechanical arms.

"It is miraculous that you are in one piece," the droid's dull voice said.

"I've been through worse," the mercenary moaned. His whole body ached. Considering the amount that the Ash-Cloud had been spread over the area, he had probably been thrown several yards. Still, what hurt the most was his chest where the doctor had kicked him…for the second time. "That bitch…"

"Are you referring to the doctor?" Stuart said. Firebird reeled his arms forward, prying himself from Stuart's grasp. He stood himself up, his head throbbing something awful.

"Who else would I be referring to?" he said. Stuart retracted the arms into his body then mimicked a shrugging motion with his spider legs.

"There have been many human females whom you have referred to as bitches," he said.

"Oh…my…God…I swear you drive me so insane…I wish somebody would put a price on your head."

"The Hoelzer Refinery, where I was previously assigned, had initially offered a price of…"

"JESUS!" Firebird said. Stuart silenced himself, then realized that Firebird wasn't yelling at him, but at the sight of the battered Ash-Cloud. The cockpit looked like a tin can, which had been through a trash compactor. The frame was crumpled inward, the inside crushed entirely. Firebird ran on wobbly legs to it. He entered the ship through the open neck where it separated from the cabin. The inside was caved in, providing little access to the tunnel. Glancing back at the droid, he noticed several scratches along his platform and neck. One of his six spider legs appeared loosely connected at the main knuckle. If anything was miraculous, it was the fact that Stuart got out in such relatively decent condition.

The mercenary looked back and scanned his eye over the landscape. The area was relatively flat, with the cockpit settling on the edge of a heavily wooded area. The trees stood over a hundred feet high, their branches and leaves displaying the many signs of mutation that the plant life had undergone. Twin leaves extended from each branch, some large and round as though containing a sac of some kind. As he had learned through the mistake of a former associate, don't inspect the leaf to find out.

Scraps of metal lined the long crease in the ground where the Ash-Cloud streaked. Smoke swirled in the air and began to spread, darkening the red sky above. At least the Ash-Cloud's defense system managed to jettison the reactor core before it detonated. Had it detonated on the ground, he wouldn't be standing here watching it.

"Those Sovereignty bastards…" Firebird groaned.

"We must plan to move back across the border," Stuart said. Firebird didn't listen. He was in a fit of rage as he gazed at the remains of his ship.

"This was not easy to come by," he snarled. "Oh…those pricks! The whole thing is destroyed. My coin bank! My video archives! Those bastards are going to pay…they're going…I'm gonna!" The mercenary was tongue-tied, consumed by anger. "They think they can shoot me down!"

"They did," Stuart said.

"I'm gonna rip their tongues from their throats!" Firebird continued his tirade. "I'm gonna gouge their eyes out! I'm gonna…" he paced, body tensed, fists clenched. "I'm gonna kill them! They're gonna die…I'm gonna…I'm…" so enraged, the mercenary could barely get his words out. "Those…those pricks! They're gonna pay! They're gonna suffer. I'm gonna kill them…I'M GONNA KILL THEM TO DEATH!!!"

Stuart glared at him. He tilted his head, as though trying to analyze that last statement.

"I wasn't aware there were any other possible outcomes to such an action…"

"Oh, shut up," Firebird said. Still seething through clenched teeth, he looked back across the debris field. The fuselage landed several hundred yards down, near another patch of trees. Behind it was the rock fields, the tan sediment looking like a mound of sand from where he stood.

"Shall we see if the doctor is still alive?" Stuart asked.

"If she isn't, she's gonna wish she was."

"Do we still plan on delivering her to Espinosa?"

"Definitely not giving her to Sovereignty," Firebird said. He inspected the edge of the section of cabin still connected to the cockpit. Amazingly, the armory was still intact, barely. The locking mechanism had shut down, allowing the mercenary to yank the door open with minimal effort. The weapons, detached from the rack, came pouring out, clattering at his feet. Firebird snatched up a Predator Rifle and loaded a fresh magazine. Strapping it over his shoulder, he grabbed extra mags for his pistol and speed-loaders for his revolver. He reached high to the top of the compartment and grabbed his seven-inch serrated knife along with its sheath. He looped it onto his belt then pulled back on the cocking mechanism to his rifle. "Let's get our asses moving."

The duo ran as fast as they could to the fuselage. Though the ground appeared flat, it was far from even. Various pieces of debris stuck out of the soil like posts. Wires and electrical equipment sparked along the grass, catching fire to some of the dry brush. The area appeared like it hadn't had any rain in some time.

The fuselage wasn't much better than the cockpit. The hull was completely ravaged with numerous breaches on the outside. It had rolled repeatedly before settling upside down over the flat edge of a huge slanted rock.

The mercenary marched near the busted end of the cabin. The passenger seats, now above them, were empty. Stuart scurried around the back of the wreckage and scanned the area for motion.

"I do not see anyone in the immediate proximity of this vessel. It is possible that the doctor was thrown from the crash and killed."

"No," Firebird said, looking up at the harness. It was intact, the clips undone by hand. "She's out there somewhere."

"The chains are broken," Stuart said. "It is not likely she was able to..."

"She got out of them," Firebird interrupted. "Turns out she can shoot a laser out of her mechanical eye thing. She's like her very own Mechagodzilla."

"To my knowledge of that franchise, she would have to be over fifty meters tall and reptilian. And she would have to be controlled by aliens..."

"No, no, no... I meant..." Firebird took a breath. "I meant she had a lot of gadgets. Hell, she's practically more machine than woman. I guess *Darth Vader* would be a better description. And don't get started on how she needs to be a *Jedi*, you literal hunk of junk."

"As you wish," Stuart said. "I suggest we leave and go northwest."

"We will. But we have something to do first," Firebird said. He started examining the ground. There were several slight indentations in the loose soil near the rock. Each one was separated by a few feet, the trail disappearing into the woods. "Not without our bounty."

"If the Sovereignty come across this area..."

"We won't be here," Firebird said. "Newsflash, droid, we're broke. Worse than that, we're stuck on foot. Now, we can hijack a land vehicle at any point, but without that doc, we don't have any coins to continue our business. The tracks lead that way. And judging by what lies beyond these trees, I doubt that the doctor knows what she's walking into. So. You coming? Or staying here?"

"I will come. Might as well," Stuart said.

"Yeah, *might as well*," Firebird muttered. The duo hustled into the mouth of the woods and followed the trail. "And just so you know...only the first *Mechagodzilla* was controlled by aliens. The other timelines had him piloted by the military..."

CHAPTER 7

Hellish streaks of sunlight peered through the canopy, lighting the path ahead of Saegusa as she ran through the woods. Her neck and shoulders were sore from falling after she unfastened the harness. She wondered who shot down the Ash-Cloud and why, though right now it didn't matter. She was in the Sovereignty Territory, and as far as she knew, somebody wanted her dead. The Sovereignty definitely didn't. They wouldn't dare risk it, even if they did plan on double crossing the mercenary. Which meant there were two entities she had to avoid.

The doctor kept her distance from the trees and various plants growing in the woods. Being a biochemist, she had seen the mutative effects on the environment and its evolution in the last hundred years or so since the war. Many plants, which were common in previous generations, had mutated into poisonous, sometimes carnivorous florae.

She ducked down under a low-hanging branch containing many inflated leaves then continued further into the woods. The ground squished under her boots. At the same time, the air grew thick and moist. She felt as if she was entering a bog. She passed by several bushes, their leaves thick and soppy. The doctor stopped and stared at a dead tree standing ahead of her. The branches were long and void of leaves, the trunk hyperextended, like the belly of somebody who had eaten too much. Water trickled from cracks in its back. Looking past it, Saegusa saw several trees, all in the same haunted condition.

"Oh, hell. What am I doing?" she said to herself. She looked back, feeling terrified and overwhelmed. She didn't want to go back, but she certainly didn't want to press forward. There had been a flooding of some kind here. And it had been here a while. One thing was for sure: This water was NOT safe to drink. Hell, she didn't even want to touch it, even with robotic feet.

Judging by the angle of the sunlight, she had been moving east. From what she could see, the water was getting deeper the further east she could go.

She looked over her shoulder and watched the trail where she came. A dreaded feeling was coming over her. Though she couldn't see anybody, she had a feeling she was being followed. She kept a hand on her pouch, which remained strapped over her shoulder. She peeked inside, making sure the samples were secure. She HAD to get these to Espinosa. Everything depended on it.

The nearest border was likely north, though she had no idea how far it was. They couldn't have gotten too far into the territory before being shot down. Feeling she had no other option, she took a deep breath and started north.

The ground seemed to dry up for a few dozen meters, leading the doctor to believe she was heading away from the bog. But before long, the ground began to squish under her feet again. Water pooled with each step, and the air thickened even worse than before. The humidity drew a sweat from her skin, adding to the sticky feeling.

There was another large pool of water. Like before, it seemed to deepen the further it went. She seemed to be on the edge of a large pond or lake, or maybe it was just a swamp. The only thing that was certain was that she couldn't go further. Her mechanical components were resilient to water. However, prolonged exposure could damage them. And from what she could tell, she'd be wading pretty deep for a while. Once again, it appeared the only way out of this bog was back the way she came.

Saegusa stopped, frustrated, and began to contemplate her options.

She barely started to think before the snapping of a branch caused her to jump. She turned and looked back. Whatever caused it, it had occurred where she had previously been standing.

The mercenary?

She couldn't see anything. She ducked down and watched. The air was thick and the grouping of trees made it difficult to see too far. If it was him, she might get another opportunity to jump him. Her confidence on the matter was high. She had kicked his ass twice. Once more didn't seem too difficult. This time, she would see to it that she finished the job. She would take his gun and blow his brains out. The famous mercenary, Firebird, would be no more. Even if she didn't make it out alive, it would at least give her a miniscule amount of satisfaction to take down the person who foiled her objective.

Another *SNAP* echoed through the bog, causing her to jolt. This one came from somewhere off to her left. Beyond the large pool of water. She raised her hand to the panel and enacted thermal imaging from her bionic eye. No figures appeared to be walking through the trees. Any human would be easy to spot.

She slowly continued along the waterline. Several broken branches marked the ground, as though something large had come through. Beneath the shattered pieces of wood were strange markings in the mud. The gashes were deep, as though an oversized cat claw had sliced the ground.

Saegusa looked back and scanned the area once again with her thermal vision. Nothing. Gazing at the swampy area around her, she grew increasingly uncomfortable. The place looked haunted, like something out of a dark fairy tale. There were no sounds. No birds. Only a slight breeze of the wind.

She moved over the brush and stopped. There was something resting near the shoreline. Whatever it was, it was bulky in shape, and covered in dead leaves and mud. Despite its size, the thing, whatever it was appeared hollow. Much of the mud seemed to 'sink' into its side.

Saegusa slowly approached, then stopped and gasped. It was the skeleton of a large animal, possibly a steer. It had been stripped to the bone and discarded, with one of its legs torn completely from its socket. Though it was dead, it carried an ominous presence. She felt a sense of danger creeping up her spine. There was the portentous feeling of being watched from something beyond those trees. She crouched down again and watched the area. Something was moving out there, and it wasn't the mercenary.

A high-pitched chirp caused Saegusa to straighten her stance. She switched her bionic vision back to normal. The murky water was rippling at her feet.

Those ripples elevated to three-foot swells, like miniature ocean waves during a storm. But it wasn't wind stirring this water. It was something underneath.

Saegusa stepped away from the water's edge as an enormous shape emerged from the surface. She saw a brown segmented body with serrated pincer-like jaws clamping over its oval-shaped head. It was an ant, mutated by exposure to radiation during the war. Drool dripped from its open jaws as its six legs, all dripping water and a saliva-like substance that secreted from its body. It hauled its twelve-foot mass toward the shore, where its three-foot long antennae detected fresh meat.

Behind it, another of its species emerged from the water, chirping from its open mouth. And behind that one, another rippled the water as it neared the surface. Seeing the water stirring further out, Saegusa knew there were more, each ascending from a nest that was somewhere beneath the deeper areas of the swamps. Not only did the mutation affect their mass, but it, along with a hundred years of evolution, changed their environmental needs.

Now the choice was clear. RUN!

Saegusa turned on her heel and took the first stride to sprint toward dry land, only to immediately stop. Inches in front of her face were the open jaws of another humongous ant. Behind it, two more marched at her, chirping from their jaws. Twigs snapped under clawed feet as they scurried at her. Behind her, the others moved in, now numbering six.

Saegusa dove to her left. The jaws snapped, missing her by an inch. The cyborg landed on her stomach and immediately clawed at the ground. She could hear the six legs of the nearest pursuer thumping the earth as it neared her.

The ant clamped down on her angle and tugged back. Saegusa's stomach hit the ground, her hands now outstretched ahead of her. Her curled fingers scratched the dirt as it pulled her backward toward the rest of its colony.

She would not die like this! Not torn apart by ravenous beasts, alone in these strange woods.

Saegusa pushed up on her hands and twisted around, seeing the two bulky eyes of the giant ant. She leaned down as far as she could and grabbed the bastard by one of his antennae. With a firm grip, she pulled herself close to the insect's face. Its horrid stench filled her nostrils. Its shell was rotting, possibly a side effect of the mutation and over exposure to water. With a flick of the lever, she blasted the flare from her eye.

The laser scorched the softer tissue of its eye-sack, boiling the fluid beneath until the individual eyes burst. The jaws opened, dropping Saegusa on her back. The ant scurried back in a frenzy, brushing its legs over its face to put out the flame.

Saegusa pushed herself to her feet and turned to run, only to once again end up in the jaws of another ant. She pushed off her left foot to reroute to the right, again, stopped by the presence of another ant. They were scurrying everywhere, at least ten of them. They chirped wildly, a hungry call for blood. Her blood.

Saegusa backed away. After only a few steps, she was at the water's edge. The ants converged on the shore. They snapped at each other, many of them fighting for the space. Driven by hunger, they all wanted the first bite.

Her heel hit the water.

"No…" she said out loud. She was cornered. An ocean of giant insects were now less than ten feet from where she stood. And somewhere behind her was the nest, where more bugs likely awaited.

A moment later, that suspicion was confirmed.

A tremendous splash sprayed her back. In the same moment, a loud screech rang her ears as another ant lunged. Saegusa's evasion got no further than a single stride. The ant sprang forward and rammed its head between her shoulders. Saegusa fell forward and hit the ground in front of the other ants. In the next moment, sensory detectors in her metal leg felt the jaws clamp down on it. The ant dragged her backward, bringing her toward the edge of the water.

"No!" she yelled desperately, as though her words would have any effect. She tried to reach back in hopes of singeing it with her laser but could not reach far enough. The water was now up to her waist. Baring teeth, she reached again for the antennae, only for her fingers to stop short.

A thunderous crack pierced the air. The ant's head erupted into shards of shell, dripping huge strands of orange goo. The headless ant slumped beneath the water, its jaws unclenching.

Saegusa sprang to her feet as several more shots rang out. She turned around, seeing splashes of orange blood spraying the woods as explosive projectiles pierced shell and detonated.

Firebird leapt over a series of coiled tree roots and blasted a three-round burst from his rifle, swaying it from right-to-left. The three rounds each struck a different segment of the next ant's body, bursting gaping holes. Blood, intestines, and brains spilled as the ant dropped to the ground.

The horde zigzagged, breaking their gathering. Three of them followed the sound and converged on the mercenary, unwittingly lining themselves up for easy headshots. Firebird shouldered the rifle, setting the lever to semi-automatic fire. He fired a single shot into the nearest one, planting an explosive round between its antennae. The top of its head ripped open, resembling the mouth of a volcano, spewing blood and silky chunks of brain tissue. As it collapsed to the ground, the mercenary aimed over its corpse and placed a round between the eyes of the two brethren that followed. Their heads ruptured, the blast carving them in two all the way down to the neck. Between the open 'flaps', chunks of brains and muscle tissue fell as freely as if they were spilled from a salad bowl.

Firebird grinned, feeling the nostalgia from an early memory of watching a certain black & white movie with his father.

"Too bad those army guys didn't have this baby," he said to himself, patting the frame of the Predator Rifle.

Another ant charged him from the left. The mercenary turned and repeatedly squeezed the trigger, blowing its head and thorax into shards. As it settled, he could hear the thumping of feet behind him. In the fray, the other ants had circled around him. He turned around, seeing the two bulging eye sacks staring him right in the face.

"Oh CHRIST!" He jumped back as the ant lunged, scissor jaws opened wide. They snapped shut, catching nothing but air. Firebird stumbled back and aimed his rifle. As he started to squeeze the trigger, his heels struck the outstretched leg of one of the other dead ants. He staggered to keep from falling, his rifle firing high into the canopy. The ant closed in for another bite.

Mechanical whirring overtook its chirps as the spider-shaped droid scampered into view. Stuart sprang like a grasshopper and landed atop of the ant's head. He raised his two forelegs, the tips extending and twirling, functioning as drill bits from his refinery days. He plunged the two drills into the top of the insect's head. Tiny flakes of shell sprayed the air like wet brown sawdust. The drills sank deep, shredding the brain.

The ant's body convulsed into a violent seizure. Its legs curled under its body and lost their strength. The creature sank onto its underside and died. Stuart ripped his legs from the two holes and leapt from the corpse. Two other ants moved outward and darted between the trees.

Saegusa crawled away from the waterline, her damaged leg unresponsive to her brain signals. She sat up and examined it, realizing a wire shaft had been knocked out of place by the pincers. She reached under her calf and shoved the mechanism back into place and fixed the screw that had come loose.

Dripping wet from the waist down, she watched as the mercenary and his droid battled the horde. There was a sense of relief after nearly getting dragged to her death and torn apart. But more than that, there was a strange captivation watching the cause-and-effect of the rifle fire and resulting explosion of insect anatomy.

Another splash erupted from the water. Another ant breached the surface like a whale, jaws aimed directly at the doctor. Saegusa dashed from the shore as the ant scampered over the waterline. It scampered after her, jaws snapping repeatedly.

Jumping over debris and weaving around the bodies of other dead insects, the doctor ran to the mercenary...the very person she was originally running from. Firebird's eye was fixed on the woods as he watched for the two ants that had darted into the trees. He could hear them rustling between branches, preparing to make another run. Those sounds were soon overtaken by the sound of splashing water, then running feet. He looked back to the shore, seeing the doctor running toward him with one of the bugs hot on her trail.

"Holy..." he rotated and aimed his rifle past her. Seeing the muzzle of the gun, billowing thin smoke from the previous gunshots, Saegusa ducked. The ant reared up, seeing the new threat behind its prey. Firebird blasted away, shredding the ant with explosive rounds to its jaw and neck. The force of the blast knocked the ant over onto its back. Its legs kicked high into the air as rivers of blood spilled between the joints.

The rustling within the woods intensified.

"Sir, we have another to your seven-point-eight o'clock," Stuart announced.

"Seven-point...what?" Firebird turned to his left, seeing the ant busting down a low hanging branch as it began to charge. He aimed the weapon and placed his eye to the scope. A single shot struck the beast in its left eye, exploding the entire left side of its face. The ant swayed back and forth, blood spilling from its half-head, then fell. Firebird shot the droid a stern look. "Dude, just say eight o'clock. Or seven o'clock. Not this seven-point-two-five crap."

"Is it not part of my job to provide accurate information to you?"

"Just round up or down," Firebird said.

Saegusa watched the trees as she approached the mercenary and droid. She could hear the snapping of twigs in the distance. There were at least two ants remaining. The bird-like chirps were now high-pitched screeches.

"Get behind me, Doc," Firebird said, guiding her with his metal arm. He watched the woods for any movement. Every few seconds, he'd catch a glimpse of the six-legged carnivore but would lose track of it as it weaved between another grouping of trees.

Saegusa listened to its movements. Her ears picked up a strange scraping sound. She envisioned a garden rake being dragged against a two-by-four. Flakes of barks rained down nearby, directing her attention upward. The last ant had climbed up into the branches, ready to drop itself down on them.

"Up high! Six o'clock!"

Firebird twisted his hips and aimed high, seeing the naked branches bending under the bug's weight. He fired a shot, exploding the branch sustaining most of the insect's bulk. A series of wood rained down, followed by the creature's segmented body. It hit the ground with its legs thrashing about. Firebird stepped closer, ready to fire the final shot.

Saegusa looked back into the woods. She could hear the sound of several footsteps growing nearer and nearer. The other ant was charging at them, jaws pouring milky saliva under its face.

The doc lunged for the mercenary and grabbed the pistol from his right thigh. With the pistol gripped in both hands, she aimed and fired at the approaching ant. Armor-piercing rounds punched through its shell, spilling orange goo like water through a dam. She fired rapidly, emptying the entire magazine into the monster's face. The ant slowed down, its face covered in dark orange. Its legs bent at the joints. After another moment, its body slumped to the ground, dead.

Saegusa took a breath and lowered the empty pistol. Adrenaline coursed her veins, making her hands shaky. A loud bang caused her to jerk. Firebird shot the flailing ant in the head.

"Whoa!" he called out. Blood poured outward, trailing smoke as if it were molten lava. He reloaded his rifle and moved out to check the area. Saegusa took several deep breaths, holding the pistol in shaky hands.

CHAPTER 8

"It is fascinating, really," Stuart explained. "To my understanding, there has been no documentation of such a species ever recorded. While there have been many mutations since the war, I do not believe any species have been so drastically changed as much as these giant ants have."

"Yeah, there's a reason we haven't heard of them," Firebird said, kicking over the bodies of one of the huge corpses. The ant rolled, causing blood to freefall from the gaps in its body. "These things are close to the border. Anyone wanting to sneak in undetected would have to go through these woods. You can bet that the Sovereignty is using these bugs as a defense system for any sneak attack."

The droid analyzed the possibility in its mechanical brain.

"You do raise a fair point."

"It worked on her," Firebird said, pointing a finger at the doctor.

Saegusa stood several meters away from the waterline, taking several deep breaths to calm her nerves. Sweat soaked her brow and streamed down her cheeks like tears. It took several minutes for her heart to stop thumping so hard. Each beat felt like a battering ram in her chest trying to break out. Though she had no organic nerves in her legs, it didn't stop her imagination from causing her to 'feel' those jaws clamping down on her. It would have been a horrible, painful death. There had been reports of other giant insects in other parts of the continent, and from what she had read, their victims were usually still alive when consumed.

Her thoughts were broken as she felt the pistol yanked from her hands.

"Yeah, that's mine," Firebird said. He holstered the weapon and stepped away while checking his compass. The needle spun, not settling on any specific point. "I don't know why I have this thing. It never works." He then glanced back at the doctor. "Hey, you have like eight-hundred gadgets installed in ya. None of them happen to be a compass, do they?"

"All you have to do is ask me," Stuart mentioned. "And it would be ideal to move away from the nest. If my analysis is correct, there are probably other nests in this water. Or, at the very least, other worker ants from this colony that could arrive any moment."

"Yeah, I get that, bot," Firebird said. "However, I don't want to go in the wrong direction and run into anyone I'm not a fan of. Particularly those jackasses who shot us down. It's bad enough I'm not coming out of this ahead financially anymore. If anything, I'm breaking even. If I'm very VERY lucky."

Saegusa stood quiet. It was clear that Firebird still intended to sell her for his bounty. She leaned against the tree, silent, seemingly unbothered. In the depths of her mind, she was screaming in agony. She could not seem to catch a break. Being captured by the Sovereignty was, in a way, worse than being eaten alive by giant ants.

The objective had not changed. She must head north and cross the border. The first step was to get away from these mercenaries.

Damn! I had his pistol. I should've saved one for him. The thought did seem cruel. After all, he did just save her life. Then again, he was the reason she was in this mess to begin with. And it wasn't like he was saving her for kindness. Like he had stated, she was nothing more than a financial transaction.

Saegusa pushed away from the tree and darted through the woods.

Firebird looked back, seeing her running between the trees.

"Oh, damn it!" He had forgotten that she didn't know he was diverting to Espinosa.

"I can still taser her," Stuart said.

"No!" Firebird yelled as he took off after her. He tossed the rifle to the droid, allowing himself to run more freely after the doctor. He could see her zig-zagging along the uneven ground several yards ahead. Her damaged leg slowed her down considerably. Not only that, but she was already fatigued. Though cybernetic components helped with cardio function, it still took energy to use those limbs. "Hey!" he called out. His voice fell on deaf ears. Why would she listen to him anyway?

Something rattled in her leg, like a nail in a tin can. The main shaft in the 'thigh' was coming loose, thus it was struggling to support her weight. With each step, Saegusa felt her knee was about to give out. It became clear very quickly she was not going to outrun the mercenary.

"Back to Plan B," she muttered to herself, recalling her thoughts about overpowering the merc in close quarters. She had done it before. But first, she would need to get the jump on him...

She noticed the edge of a steep hill off to her right, which led to a thick area of woods. The doctor pivoted and flung herself down the slope, using gravity to give her an extra ounce of speed. Angling her shoulders, she zipped through the narrow space between two trees.

"Oh, for crying out loud," Firebird muttered as he watched the doctor disappear into the woods. If he was going to transport her alive, he would have to get her out of these woods. It was clear that Saegusa wasn't familiar with the quarantine areas in Sovereignty. There were more to these areas than oversized ants.

He raced down the hill. With a bigger frame than the doctor, he had to slow considerably to slip between the line of trees at the bottom of the slope. He pried himself through, scraping bark off the trunks, then stopped to watch the area. This section of the woods was somewhat darker than the other section. It wasn't just that less sunlight was getting through. The actual terrain was physically darker. Blacker. Even he was taken aback by the sight of black tree trunks and their outstretched branches. The air was clear, yet there was a strong stench in the area. That stench worried Firebird more than anything else. It wasn't the stench of tree rot.

Firebird looked at the ground, seeing Saegusa's tracks trailing to the left in a semi-circular path. He followed the steps, but with caution, watching the space between the trees as he went. He wanted to call out to Saegusa, but knew it was best to keep as quiet as possible.

"Oh, you dumb bot-person," he mumbled under his breath.

Dumb? You're the one stupid enough to follow her in here.

This brought back bad memories. Each tree looked as though it was reaching out at him like a starving beast. And starving beasts were exactly what he was afraid of. He followed the trail, constantly looking around him. He kept a hand on his pistol and his other on the revolver, ready to draw both.

The trail now arched to the right, beyond another cluster of trees. Firebird now had his Gravestone Pistol drawn. He kept its muzzle pointed high, his arm poised to aim it at anything that came at him.

The trail came to an end, with no obvious sign of departure. The mercenary stopped and gazed down at the final tracks. They were in an open space between two large trees. Glancing to the nearest one, he could see the arm of its branch. It extended out several yards...directly overhead. He allowed a moment of amusement to show, as it was obvious where the doctor was hiding.

Before he could look above, a low rumbling sound caused him to swiftly turn around. Gun pointed, he watched the woods intently for the source of the noise. He heard it once again. The rumble was very faint, like a canine warning away another animal. It wasn't thunder, that was for sure.

Twigs cracked above.

Firebird felt both cybernetic feet land on his shoulders, driving him to the ground as Saegusa descended from her hiding place in the trees like a bird of prey. The mercenary flattened out, the doctor standing directly on his shoulder blades. Agitated, he rolled, causing her to stumble off of him.

"Listen, Doc..."

Saegusa lunged with closed fists.

Not again...

Firebird sidestepped to his left, causing Saegusa's strike to hit nothing but air. He moved again, avoiding a kick from her undamaged leg. Saegusa, exhausted from what she had endured prior, now grew frustrated from two unsuccessful attacks. She had hoped for this to be fast and easy. Now, she was getting clumsy.

And Firebird knew it. And, like he did best, he exploited. Yet, he seemed somewhat distracted. He glanced repeatedly into the trees, as though searching for something specific. Saegusa didn't care. She just needed to get free and clear.

"Listen up, Doc," he said. "I'm gonna take you to..."

His sentence stopped short as she lunged again, this time in an attempt to get the weapon from his hand. The mercenary took a single stride back, causing her grab to stop short. Saegusa came again. There was no fear in her eyes. Why would there be? She knew he wouldn't shoot her.

As she moved for another lunge, he noticed the way she shifted her weight to her right leg. As he suspected during the chase, something was mechanically wrong with the left, likely due to the ant attack. A series of thoughts rippled through his mind in an instant.

This wouldn't be considered striking a lady, would it?

Whether it did or not, he had lost all patience. Firebird thrust his right leg out, connecting the heel of his boot to her knee.

Saegusa yelled out as something detached in her thigh. Her leg gave out, the forward momentum causing her to faceplant into the ground. She called out again as she pushed her torso up. Firebird circled her like a vulture, keeping himself out of reach in case she was desperate enough to grab at him.

She rolled over and sat up to inspect her leg. The shaft had come loose again. The shaft acted like the femur, providing the most support for her weight. The ant's jaws had bent it slightly, though it was still sturdy enough. The problem was the titanium screw would not hold. It would have to be welded. Firebird's blow was the final touch.

"You jackass," she snarled at him.

"Hey, if you had just shut up and listened for a sec…"

She lunged again, falling short, the attack resulting in her faceplanting again. Firebird stood still. A smirk formed on his face. He couldn't deny it was a little funny watching the doc floundering in the dirt like a fish out of water.

The amusement ended as he noticed movement in his peripheral vision. Suddenly, he remembered where they were. He aimed his pistol into the distance. Saegusa looked back to where he aimed, catching a glimpse of the black humanoid shape as it disappeared behind some dried brush.

"What the…"

"Fun time's over," the merc said softly. "We have to go."

For once, Saegusa was in complete agreement. "Help me up." Firebird scoffed. It sounded like an order. He hated being given orders. However, there was no time to make a snide remark. He brought her arm over his shoulder and lifted her up.

"The hell was that?" she asked.

"Not something you wanna get to know," Firebird said. He guided her back the way they came, keeping his pistol pointed out. He felt her other hand reaching along his belt as they went. A big smile formed on his face.

"Don't thank me yet, doc," he said.

That hand jabbed him in the ribs, then moved back to his belt, locating the cross-holster for his revolver. His smile disappeared.

"Ah-ah, no you don't," he said. He tapped her hand with the muzzle of his Gravestone.

"I can cover our asses," she protested. "I know how to shoot."

"I'm aware. One of the reasons you're not getting one."

"Listen," Saegusa said. She glanced around in search of that thing, whatever it was. "It's not like I'm able to run off."

"Yeah, sure. Like you can't tinker with your mechanics after you blow my brains out…"

A loud snarl echoed from the dark forest. Firebird aimed the pistol. There was more movement between the trees. He squeezed off a three-round burst. Bullets ricocheted in the distance. The black humanoid creature darted off. Saegusa watched, frightened and fascinated at the same time. It was hunched over, its outer body exhibiting a scaly appearance. Its arms were elongated. In the brief moment she saw it, she noticed twelve-inch pointed fingers protruding from the wrists. It was hunched as it moved, making its height difficult to determine. But the worst part was the profile of its head. The skull seemed human. The face on the other hand, was elongated, baring needle-like teeth.

"Good, lord," she muttered.

"Yeah. We're lucky he's not used to the sound of gunshots. But that'll change if we don't get out of here. Come on."

Saegusa hobbled on her good leg while Firebird accompanied her up the hill. She looked up and gasped, seeing a spider-like shape awaiting them. At first, she thought it was another mutation, until she recognized its metal texture.

"Nice of you to help, Stuart," Firebird said.

"I did assist. I was holding your rifle, was I not?" the droid said.

"Fine. I'll give you that," the merc said. He placed Saegusa on the ground and took the rifle from Stuart. The doctor pulled up her pantleg and inspected the loose shaft above the knee. The lower end was completely separated from where it connected to the joint. The electronics appeared to be mostly okay, with the exception of one of the tendons on the backside, which had been damaged in the ant jaws. The screw had been ripped entirely from the outlet, the thread worn down. As she suspected, the shaft was slightly bent, though its end was still able to touch its connecting place.

"Shit," she muttered.

"I heard gunfire," Stuart said. "Did you encounter more mutations?"

"What the hell was that?" Saegusa asked Firebird.

"We ran into a rasilisk," Firebird said. He noticed from Saegusa's dumbfounded expression that she wasn't aware of what they were. "Basically, lizard people."

"Never heard of them," she said.

"They tend to stay within the Black Forest during the day. They mostly come out at night...mostly."

"Only one?" Stuart asked

"We're lucky it was only *one*." Firebird looked down at Saegusa. "Hell...*you're lucky* it didn't get you before I got there. That's twice now you've almost turned us into breakfast."

"You seriously blame me?!" she retorted. "You're the one who kidnapped me! You're taking me to Sovereignty, remember?! You expect me to let you just hand me over?"

"Get a grip, you human tin can," Firebird said. "We're getting out of Sovereignty."

Saegusa's hostile expression disappeared. She perked up, intrigued.

"Beg your pardon?"

"I changed my mind," the merc explained. "Turns out, Sovereignty double-crosses a lot. As you learned about a half hour ago, it turns out I was right."

"Wait..." she said. Something didn't make sense. She closed her eyes, trying to fit all the pieces together in her mind. "Why would they shoot you down if they knew I was on board?"

"I don't know!" Firebird said, his arms raised outward. "Sorry, I didn't think to stop and ask while I was trying to keep us from getting blown up."

"It just...it doesn't make sense."

"No, it doesn't," Firebird said. "Who cares at this point? You wanna get home to Espinosa, right?" Saegusa nodded. "Then I'm your only way there. So, fix your leg so we can get moving."

"I can't get this reattached. The screw's fucked. It can't support my weight. I won't be able to walk." She pointed to the shaft and where it was supposed to attach to the bearing.

"Any other way you can reattach it?" Firebird asked.

"Not without a welder," she answered.

"Can't you use that laser eye thing?" he asked.

"That'll be difficult."

"Difficult? You had no problem freeing yourself from the restraints!"

"This is a little more delicate than simply burning through a chain link," Saegusa said. "I'd have to get the shaft in a precise position. Problem is, I have to lean close to apply the laser. That close, I won't be able to see what I'm doing. I might damage it even more."

Stuart approached, his narrow forelegs protruding under her knee. They guided her foot out until the leg was fully extended. One of the ports protruded from the breastplate of his platform, sparking a small welding flame.

"If I may, I can be of service."

Saegusa glared at the droid, then back at Firebird.

"Don't look at me. I'm no mechanic," the merc said.

Saegusa sighed. "Go ahead."

Stuart got right to work, steadying the components with its other arms, then applied the torch.

Saegusa waited as the droid operated. Meanwhile, Firebird paced back and forth, watching the edge of the Black Forest. The rasilisks usually stayed in the forest, only coming out at night to scavenge for food. His mind began to ponder the distance and terrain of the trip that lay ahead. Even without knowing how far they were from the border, it was obvious they had a tedious journey ahead.

He needed a drink. A cold stiff drink. He looked back at Saegusa. Her cybernetic features stood out like a sore thumb.

"You don't happen to have a bar installed in ya as well, do you?"

She wasn't amused.

"I am almost complete," Stuart said.

"Good, because I wanna get out of here," Firebird said.

"And where are we gonna go?" Saegusa asked. The mercenary looked around, then inspected his compass.

"I don't want to travel in the open. Then again, I don't wanna travel too deep into the forest either." He pointed toward the Black Forest. "I believe that's north…" He panned his finger left. "If we go this way, we should be able to work our way around this patch of woods."

"Should we continue west, sir? We can collect another rifle for the doctor to use in case we run into trouble," Stuart said.

"By now, Sovereignty probably has a search team out to inspect the crash site," Firebird said. "Personally, I don't feel too safe going back there. Too bad we had to run off after somebody, or else we could've fixed her up with some weapons."

"Hey, man!" Saegusa said, ready to defend her actions.

"Oh, chill. I know why you ran off. Blah blah blah." He tucked the compass back into his pocket then thought for another moment. Stuart had a good point. They would be better off if Saegusa was armed. He glanced down at his revolver and sighed. It was his favorite possession. Handing it off was like giving away a piece of himself.

He took the holstered weapon and its speed-loader pouches off his belt and handed them down to Saegusa. She watched him, surprised he would trust her with a weapon. She slowly reached out and accepted the revolver. She took it out of the holster and opened the cylinder. Six .38 caliber rounds were loaded into each slot. She holstered it back and checked the pouch, finding three speed-loaders. Twenty-four bullets altogether.

Stuart retracted the torch and stepped away. Saegusa brought her knee up and examined her leg. The refinery droid had done a decent job attaching the shaft. Unfortunately, the part would have to be replaced eventually, but that was a problem for another time. She stood up and tested the weight. The leg was a little weak, but it was good enough to endure some more punishment. She strapped the holster and pouches to her belt.

"I expect that back when we're done," Firebird said.

"Fair enough," she said. "Let's get out of here."

Firebird led the way, rifle aimed low, as they walked east around the edge of the Black Forest.

CHAPTER 9

The wind rushed through Beretta Albright's hair as Captain Collins steered the speeder over rough terrain, jolting the three occupants in their seats. She held a Plasma Rifle in her lap as she kept an eye out for any Sovereignty patrol units. Target-Seekers, low altitude patrol ships similar to Rhino's Harriers, normally didn't patrol the forest area, though she wouldn't be surprised if they were ordered to infiltrate. If the Rebels were able to detect the crash site, the Strikers definitely were on it.

Collins was quiet as he drove the speeder along the edge of the forest. He wasn't sure what to say to the General. Not only had she lost her son in a gruesome way, but she had to endure his torture for the sake of the mission. What was there to say? "I'm sorry for your loss?" Though technically appropriate, it somehow felt shallow. Then again, so did saying nothing.

"Is there any word from Donnelly?" Beretta asked the tech.

"Affirmative," he answered. "They've evacuated the base. Scout Team Seven has reported Striker movement near Alevia Field."

"They're moving in toward the base," Beretta said.

"You think they've detected the crash?" Collins asked.

"I hope not," Beretta said. "Either way, we're short on time."

"Daunhauer is on site," the tech said. "The signal's a bit jumpy, but it appears that the area is clear."

"For now," Beretta said. "Get us there, Captain."

****

Daunhauer stepped out of the fuselage, holding the Plasma Rifle obtained from one of the Strikers he killed at the radio truck. Smoke still trailed high in the air, dimming the random flashes of lightning above.

Donnelly's team had arrived a few minutes prior. It was a solemn sight to see only twelve of the thirty-six team members disembark the trucks. It was a cost that, unfortunately, was unavoidable. The fact that Donnelly was able to overtake the anti-aircraft base was a feat in itself.

Donnelly was walking toward him, stroking a hand over his unkempt face. The Lieutenant was visibly exhausted. He kept glancing back to his men, who were continuing to examine the Ash-Cloud's smashed cockpit. The entire faction seemed jittery, partly due to the aftershock they endured from the heavy explosives they detonated on the anti-aircraft weapons after shooting the Ash-Cloud down.

"Lieutenant," Donnelly called out to Daunhauer. They were the same rank, though Donnelly was more recently promoted and was still used to addressing Daunhauer as the higher-ranking officer.

"Not there either, huh?" Daunhauer said. Donnelly shook his head. He stopped at the edge of the fuselage, his hands patting the blackened sides of his tactical pants. His face was stained with dirt and smoke. He had a forelorn expression on his face. He eyed the horizon, worried that Striker units would arrive any minute.

"Have you heard?"

Daunhauer knew what he was referring to. It didn't take long for word to spread about the death of Paul Albright. Some of it was patriotic, stating how he allowed Daunhauer's team to successfully complete the mission. Yet, nobody in the unit felt uplifted. Daunhauer understood the distressed feeling that Donnelly tried to mask. He had shot down an aircraft with a passenger who had done them no wrong.

The feeling that Daunhauer had to mask was anger. He had known Paul Albright and was incredibly loyal to Beretta. Whether Paul should've taken part in the mission was beside the point. The General would want blood. Whatever she wanted, he wanted for her. And now, that was the death of the Sovereignty.

The men had branched out in search of any bodies. The debris field was vast. They could be anywhere, if there was even any trace of them left. There were several signs of plasma burns from the core's eruption. Their remains could have been burnt to ashes and they would never know it.

Jones trekked several yards to the east, the tan skin of his arms and shoulders marked by burns and soil. He held his shuriken in his hand as he studied the ground. Daunhauer watched the tracker, his muscular frame almost as wide as the trees behind him. Judging by his body language, he was suspicious of something.

The Lieutenant's thoughts were interrupted by the groaning sound of a speeder engine. The vehicle whipped into view along the north end of the woods. It was a smaller vehicle, though very fast and maneuverable in rough terrain. Inside was a driver and two passengers, one a woman.

The vehicle came to a stop and all passengers disembarked.

It was impossible not to set eyes on Beretta. Everyone expected her to be worn down. To their surprise, she seemed focused and impervious. Daunhauer knew her better than most of the others. There was a reserved tension behind those eyes.

"Say nothing," he warned Donnelly.

"Would it not be proper to offer condolences?"

"Not at this time," Daunhauer said. "She probably doesn't know the word has spread. Keep your condolences for a more proper time."

The General arrived at the cockpit, her brown duster jacket swaying in the wind. She spoke with the men inspecting the cockpit, then began marching to the fuselage.

She looked dead ahead at them and called out. "No bodies?"

"Negative, General," Daunhauer said. "We have men searching the whole crash site. It appears that the ship touched down before those rocks then broke in half as it skidded. By the looks of the hull and all the shrapnel, there were several breaches before they even touched down. For all we know, they could've been suctioned out in midair before this thing even touched down."

"I have cause to doubt that," Jones said. The tracker rose from his crouched position and approached the wreckage.

"What do you mean?" Beretta asked.

Jones looked to Daunhauer. "Did you notice the armory?"

"No," Daunhauer said. "I haven't inspected it for myself yet. Donnelly?"

The younger Lieutenant nodded. "Yes, I saw it. It's broken. Like the rest of the ship."

"Did you count the weapons?" Jones asked.

"Negative," Donnelly said. "We're short on time and the forward section of the cockpit is caved in. We're trying to determine if the contractor is inside."

Jones looked to Albright. "General, come with me please."

Beretta, Daunhauer, and Donnelly followed the tracker to the cockpit. Captain Collins and Barber awaited them, standing near the other rebels who were inspecting the wreck. Jones led them to the section where it had broken from the fuselage. Four rifles were scattered on the floor, with several discarded rounds of ammunition lying about.

"This could've been broken during the crash," Donnelly said.

"Look at this locking mechanism," Jones said. "The components are bent inward. It was precise contact. The unit was already damaged, but this particular portion was done deliberately by somebody trying to get in. Couldn't have been bandits. They would've ransacked the entire supply."

"How many rifles does this unit hold?" Beretta asked. Jones opened the door, exposing the empty gun rack.

"It's a small case. It holds five rifles at max. Looks like there's storage space for ammo and sidearms. Possibly grenades." He glanced to the ground. "I only see four rifles."

"That just means the contractor's still alive," Daunhauer said. "Doesn't mean the doctor survived."

"Possibly," Beretta said. "But I want to be sure."

"Yes, General," Daunhauer said.

"Jones, I noticed you were examining the ground near the tree line. Did you discover tracks?" Barber asked.

"It's hard to tell with this hard soil," Jones said. "I'm not as good a tracker as my father was, and he died before he could teach me all of the secrets. However, once we enter the trees, we could possibly find new clues. There is one other thing you should know, though."

"That is…?" Barber said.

"You saw the chain links?"

"On the passenger seat in the cabin? Yes. They're broken. The actual chain, not the lock. If the contractor removed her from the seat, he would have unlocked it, or if he had to, he'd break the lock itself."

"It wasn't simply broken. It was melted. Extreme concentrated heat," Jones said. "Whether it was done with a torch or laser, I'm not sure. But those restraints were broken deliberately. And the safety harness was intact."

"Then she's still alive," Donnelly said. His voice had a hint of excitement. The heavy feeling that weighed on him felt like it was lifting. Perhaps he would be able to sleep peacefully tonight.

"That settles it then," Beretta said. "Get your squads together. We're moving out in five."

"We're entering the woods?" Captain Collins asked. Beretta nodded. "Ma'am! I must implore you to reconsider. These woods are hazardous. If those people went in, chances are they are already dead."

"I don't want that contractor taking the doctor to the Sovereignty," Beretta said. "We cannot risk it. If they get her, then it was all for nothing." The group stood silent. Each of them knew what she meant by "it". Every one of them knew better than to incur the wrath of a mother. And it only seemed reasonable that the only wrath worse was from a mother who had lost a child.

Collins belayed his attempts to caution, instead, he simply replied, "Yes, General."

"Orders shoot to kill?" Daunhauer asked, resting the butt of his rifle to his shoulder. Beretta looked him in the eye. She appreciated his undying loyalty and eagerness to serve. The indentation in his jaw was a constant reminder of the debt he felt he owed her. He remembered the blood spilling from his face and the mask of the Striker that had bested him. Had she not arrived when she did, machete in hand...

"Kill the contractor," she said. "Do not kill the doctor."

"Do *not* kill her?" Donnelly was relieved, yet surprised. There was no more time for questions. "Yes, General." He grabbed his hand-held radio and announced to his crew. "Assemble at the cockpit. Hide all vehicles forty yards into the tree line. Prepare to move ASAP."

The rebel soldiers gathered, the combined units numbering twenty including the officers. They gathered into the vehicles, ready to ride the forty yards into the search area. Many of them now sported the Omega Plasma Rifles looted from the dead Strikers. If anything went right today, it was the quantity of the loot. If only there were more hands to hold those rifles.

The group of officers broke as they joined their rebel soldiers into the vehicles. Beretta sat silently as Collins carefully drove the speeder into the trees. After carefully maneuvering, they found a spot where they would be out of sight. They disembarked and continued on foot, with Daunhauer and Jones in the lead. The tracker was right. The soil was softer here. They found two sets of human tracks and a third set that was different, as though a giant bug was marching beside them.

"Watch yourselves," Daunhauer said. "The mercenary and doc aren't the only ones in these parts."

CHAPTER 10

The sun now shone from directly overhead as the group ventured northwest around the Black Forest. They were a hundred feet or so from the tree line, just enough to keep out of sight from anyone on the outside while managing to keep far enough away from the territories of the mutations that lurked within.

The woods here did not appear nearly as haunted as they did further in. In this section of the woods, the trees actually displayed signs of life again. The area displayed vast amounts of green. It brought an ambiance of normality for the doctor, though the limbs carried some of the same hazardous growths similar to what she had seen before. Per her warning, they stayed as far as they could from each branch to protect themselves from any surprises the mutations might have brought.

Saegusa kept a hand on the revolver as she walked ahead of Firebird. She did so deliberately. Despite that he was now helping her, she couldn't bear to look at him. It wasn't easy to simply rid one's self of such animosity. It was like her brain had split into two sides, each taking a stance for and against the mercenary. On the one hand, if not for him, she'd be in the Rhino's hands right now. She'd also be ant food, though the other side of her mind argued that she wouldn't have been in that situation in the first place if not for the merc. The mental arguing did not do much to get her to dread his presence any less. She still wished she bested him on the plane. She almost did it too. If not for that damn needle on the floor, she could've crushed his skull or burnt through his temple with her eye-flare and flew the ship back to Espinosa.

That damn needle…

"That damn needle," she muttered.

"What?" Firebird asked.

Oh shit.

She hated when that happened. It was the one negative side-effect of her neurological implants. Occasionally, some of her thoughts escaped her mouth. It didn't happen often, luckily. And fortunately, when it did, the results were usually funny rather than embarrassing or incriminating. It usually happened when she was thinking about more outlandish things, like when she was intimate with a colleague of hers. They had been working together on the anti-radon formula. Apparently, her mind had trailed off and reminisced about a particular night. Good thing nobody else was around.

"Hey, Doc-bot? You glitching?" Firebird called out. Saegusa shot him a stern look.

"Of all people, *you're* mocking me for being a cyborg?" She jabbed a finger at his arm.

"Yeah, except I don't have wires in my BRAIN," he said. He stopped and looked her over. Saegusa noticed he was fixed on her midsection.

"Can I help you with something?" she said. Her voice was restrained. She didn't want to escalate into an argument. After all, considering their clashes leading to this point, he probably wasn't her best fan either.

"You mentioned needles," he said. She stared at him.

"What do needles have to do with you checking me out...oh..." She remembered he had shot her in the midsection, only for her steel ribcage to block it.

"I'm just surprised," Firebird said. "It's usually arms or legs. Sometimes an organ. Assuming you survive the process. But Doc, I've never seen anyone with so many parts."

"It's not an accomplishment," Saegusa said. She turned around and continued walking. That weird spider droid walked ahead of her. At least she didn't find him annoying. He was artificial. It would be like blaming a lawn mower for a problem.

"So, you mentioned needles," Firebird continued.

Saegusa scrunched her eyes shut. *Oh, you've got to be kidding.*

"Don't talk to me. You want a conversation, I suggest talking to your pet."

"Okay. Hey, Stuart."

The droid turned its head a-hundred-and-eighty degrees to look back at him. "Yes, sir?"

"Any analysis?"

"She is irritated at being captured by us," Stuart said.

"Yeah, no duh," Firebird said. "I meant what she meant about needles."

"Clearly she is angry about you tranquilizing her."

"Wouldn't have had to if you drank the water," Firebird joked. Saegusa didn't say anything. It was clear that the mercenary was bored and was getting immense pleasure from antagonizing her.

They walked for several more minutes without a word spoken. Firebird stayed back several feet as he continuously eyed her from behind.

Saegusa enjoyed the silence, though it bothered her that she had to keep a rein on her subconscious to keep from blurting anything else out. She was just grateful he didn't push the subject. She watched the droid, fascinated by its design. One of its legs appeared slightly wobbly, though it didn't impair its function too badly. Droids were mainly used in manufacturing facilities. Never were they allowed to pilot ships. A few had been invented to do so, but the project had been scrapped due to lack of resources.

The droid's head rotated again and looked past her at Firebird.

"Are you inspecting her for mating purposes?"

Saegusa's eyes went wide as she spun to look at him. His eye was locked on her rear. He froze, caught in the act, and smirked. It was a mix of amusement and awkwardness.

"Thanks Stuart. You're a real help."

"I merely asked a question."

Saegusa was on the verge of coming unhinged. "I should've figured you for a pig," she muttered.

"No, no, I'm just curious how much more of you is bot, is all," Firebird explained.

"Yeah? You're curious if my ass is mechanical?"

Firebird shrugged. "Weeell…it could be. I didn't expect your ribs to be, so perhaps…"

She gave in to the infuriation and took a swing at him. Firebird leaned to the left and stepped away, allowing the punch to harmlessly pass by. Saegusa rotated with her fists raised, only to lower them. She regained her composure then continued walking the path.

"You know? I probably don't even need your help," she said.

"Oh great," the mercenary remarked. He glanced at Stuart. "She's about to get all feminist on us. *Don't need no man! Take down the patriarchy!* We all got to see how well that concept worked at the bog."

"That is a correct analysis," Stuart said.

"Ha!" Firebird exclaimed, as though he had won a great debate.

"What? Is whatever the crab says considered gospel?" Saegusa said.

"I am not modeled after a crab…" Stuart started to explain.

"Can we just go?" Saegusa interrupted. Firebird cocked his head as he followed her.

"Hey, *I'm* the one who should be pissed. I lost my ship! My guns. My video and literature archives! That shit wasn't easy to come by."

"We do have replacement files at your place called 'home' sir," Stuart said.

"That's great…if we ever make it there," Firebird said.

"That's *your* stupidity to blame. Doing business with the Sovereignty, heh!" she scoffed.

"The doctor does have a point. We should've considered alternative options before proceeding across the border," Stuart said.

"Ha!" Saegusa mocked. "Maybe he does speak gospel. Then again, I don't know why he'd stick with you if he was so smart."

"Somebody's gotta supply him with batteries," Firebird said.

"What batteries? You don't have a ship anymore," Saegusa said.

"The doctor makes another good point," Stuart said.

"Okay, are *you* trying to get laid, or something?!" Firebird snapped. Now Saegusa was the one grinning.

"Face it, merc. You're broke, and therefore as useless as Dwayne Johnson's hairbrush."

Firebird stopped.

"Wait…you know who Dwayne Johnson was?"

"Yeah. He was famous. They nicknamed him *The Rock.*"

Firebird felt his heart flutter. Never had he met anyone who understood all the pop culture he had grown up with in all of his years. In the blink of an eye, he was looking at Saegusa differently. Perhaps he just met the woman of his dreams.

"He was a famous chef before the war," she continued. "Hence the *smell what the Rock is cooking* line. Probably liked to barbeque."

And in the blink of an eye, those feelings crashed and burned.

"Ohhhhh…I'm starting to think of giving you to the Sovereignty again…" Firebird marched on, shaking his head. Saegusa shrugged his shoulders, uncertain what she said that was wrong. Whatever it was, it shut him up. She would settle for that.

Stuart kept several feet away, abiding by the doctor's wishes to be alone. He trailed behind Firebird. He stopped, his sensors picking up a hint of vibration behind them. He scanned for several yards in search of motion of any kind. His readers picked up nothing. He was an aging machine and his components were in need of a tune-up. Not only that, but he had taken a bit of a beating in the crash. Possibly, his systems were malfunctioning slightly.

The droid continued on, following Saegusa and Firebird north.

****

Platt knelt low behind the overexposed roots of the tree and watched as the wanderers walked away. For a moment, the scout was nearly spotted as he moved for a better view, kicking up dirt as he skidded into place. The robot seemed to be suspicious, but luckily it didn't detect him.

He could hear the rustling of dead twigs as his companion crawled to join him. Platt looked back and raised a finger to his lips.

"Shhh." The sound was barely audible. The second scout, lean, bald, and wearing ragged black clothing, watched in awe as the strangers moved off. He thumbed the rings that hung from his necklace. It was his trophy display of all the women he had stolen from. He could only imagine what he could get from this female.

That is, if the Leader didn't take it all for himself first. It was the perks of being Leader of the Razor Gang.

They waited until the wanderers moved further off.

"We're clear," Platt said.

"Should we follow?" his fellow scout asked.

"No. Let's report back to Wallace."

The two scouts moved slowly at first, trying hard to be sure not to bring attention from the people they tracked. They moved southeast for a few hundred meters then moved to the edge of the woods.

The Razor Gang awaited. Two dozen men, the Razors, stood around their leader, armed with knives, blades, swinging chains, and various other melee of weapons. The gang spread out, many of them resting against fixed up speeders and motorcycles as they waited for the scouts to bring word.

The scouts stood straight as they approached Wallace. He was a large man. A giant. He stood proud, his hair braided and arms crossed, like the tribal warriors from centuries past. He wore no shirt or vest, but several thick chains over his breast. They signified the link that was the Razor Gang.

"Report," he said.

"You were right, Wallace," Platt said. "There are strangers here. Northerners by the looks of one of them. They probably belonged to that aircraft."

"How many?" Wallace asked.

"Two. A man. A woman...and a droid."

"A droid?" Wallace was surprised. Not many droids that were privately owned. "Interesting. I can reprogram it to put to good use. What other items did you see?"

"They carry weapons," the second scout said. "A Predator Rifle. Ammunition. A couple of handguns. And most interesting…the woman…she's a cyborg."

"A cyborg?" Wallace uncrossed his arms. "I've never seen a cyborg before."

"They were heading north. Toward Matten Gate. We can ride ahead and intercept."

"No," Wallace said. "It sounds like they're trying to avoid the Sovereignty. If they encounter patrols, they'll double back. Once they do, we will corner them. Follow them. I want some of you traveling with me along the tree line. The rest of you, follow the wanderers. Kill the man but preserve the droid and woman. If they resist, drive them to us."

CHAPTER 11

Saegusa took a breath and leaned against a tree. She felt immensely fatigued. The excitement from the day had caught up with her. Surviving a crash. Nearly getting eaten. Twice. Fighting with Firebird. Then there was the stress of being in Sovereignty Territory. On top of all of that, she believed she was suffering the after-effects of the tranquilizer. She was feeling drowsy, though not overwhelmingly so. At least, not yet.

Walking wasn't doing much to help. She just wanted to lay down. Moments like this made her grateful she had metal legs. Otherwise, her feet would be aching like hell by now, which would further impede her will to keep going. At least she was spared that discomfort.

But her brain felt like it was fogging up. She tried to entertain it with mentally going over the formulas for the chemical extraction she would retrieve from the samples in her pouch. That only helped for a few minutes. There was one thing that would help. She needed basic human interaction. Just to chat: to feel somewhat normal in this wacky situation.

And there was only one person to talk to.

Oh, God help me, she thought.

Firebird was moving off. He never even bothered to look back, never noticing that she stopped for a break. Even the droid seemed oblivious. At least Stuart was a machine with no real moral compass. Then again, why would she expect more from a mercenary? She disregarded the idea of chatting for a few minutes, thinking the silence would be better. She pushed off the tree and followed.

It was the longest few minutes of her life. Her eyes were getting droopy now and her feet were dragging. It was definitely the tranquilizer. She could overcome it, but she needed something to occupy her mind. She bit her lip and thought of something to say that would least likely draw an immature response, which she was in no mood for.

"So, what about your name?"

Firebird looked over his shoulder at Saegusa, surprised to even hear her speak.

"You went on a whole tirade about how you wanted to be left alone, and now suddenly you want to chat?"

"We've been walking in dead silence for an hour now. Hell, there's not even any bird singing we can listen to out here," the doctor said. Firebird turned forward and continued walking in silence. He had his rifle gripped firmly, as though hunting in the African Tundra. "So, I'm assuming your folks didn't name you Firebird. If so…it explains a lot right there."

Firebird stopped again.

"My guys in C-Company gave it to me," he said. Saegusa nodded. It seemed obvious that he had been in the military.

"C-Company. Which military?"

"Helios Territory. Over on the southern east coast," he said.

"Helios?" Saegusa said, surprised. "They're all dead."

"All but one," Firebird said. "Well…that's not completely right. When the Sovereignty invaded, many of the surviving men were given the opportunity to serve in Cornelius' armies."

Saegusa stuttered. It was twelve years ago when the word spread that Helios Territory no longer existed. The Sovereignty was always trying to expand in Cornelius' quest for dominance. The Rhino Clan would not interfere with the invasion of territories south of Sovereignty. The way Saegusa figured, the bastards didn't want a foreign military presence on their southern border in case war ever did occur against the rival superpower.

"Is that where you got the Ash-Cloud?"

"No, that came later," Firebird said.

"Oh," Saegusa said. "I just thought flying that thing and shooting everything up was how you got your nickname."

Firebird snickered. She was obviously referring to the incident at Rhino Territory when he 'rescued' her.

"Not quite," he said. He continued walking.

"Was it not the Battle of Terras Mountain?" Stuart spoke up. Firebird's grin turned into a grimace. He had almost gotten out of talking about the subject. The droid continued. "I recall reading the letter one of your comrades had written. C-Company was being bombarded with plasma artillery. The sky had turned a fiery red, and the author wrote how…"

"It's called snooping," Firebird interrupted.

"I was trying to download all available information to help increase maximum capabilities on flying the ship," Stuart said. "Your letter was among the documents."

"When we get out of here, I'm gonna find your vocal circuits and snip them," he said.

"Okay, so you escaped somehow and became a mercenary," Saegusa said.

"Wow, you must be a fortune teller," Firebird remarked.

"You've done all sorts of jobs under the radar…" she paused. "You were gonna give me to the Sovereignty…"

Firebird stopped again and blew out an exacerbated exhale.

"We're not seriously on this topic again, are we? I told you, we're going to Espinosa. If we can ever find our way out of here."

"No, it's not that," she said. "It's just…how could you do business with Sovereignty?"

"Because it was *business*," Firebird said. "At least, I thought it was. Bastards."

"How could you do that?" Saegusa said. "They destroyed your nation. They took everything and everyone you knew. Your friends in the military. Family. How could you even consider doing business with a nation who did that to you?"

"Again, it's business," Firebird said. "I look out for me, Doc. That's all. I work for the highest bidder."

"So, all that matters is money?"

"Gotta fill my belly somehow," Firebird said. "I'm no thief. I pay for what I have…except him." He gestured toward Stuart. "Why is that a bad thing?"

"It's 'how' you're getting it," she said. "The only reason you're diverting is because they betrayed you. More personal gain. It's that you refuse to consider how you could've affected others with your actions."

"What? You gonna get on a moral high horse?" Firebird asked. "Don't act like you're not gonna enjoy the fruits of your patent when you make your radiation-sickness drug."

"No. I'm looking to save lives," Saegusa said. "You're just looking out for yourself."

"Oh, really," Firebird stepped up to her until they were nose-to-nose. "Let's talk about looking out for one's self. Like you and this little formula thing." He shook her pouch, rattling the vials.

Saegusa withdrew, her face tensing with frustration. "Careful with that!" She tucked the pouch behind her hip. "How is this the same?"

"How is it the same? How is it not *worse*?" Firebird said. "How many people have died in your place escorting you across the continent to get everything you needed?"

"What?"

"Don't act like you don't know what I'm talking about," Firebird said. "Hell, when you went snooping around in Rhino Territory, how many LaFerrier troops did you get killed? How many other territories did you sneak into? How many gangs and bandits did you need 'rescue' from? All so you could cure yourself of the radiation cancers?"

"Cure myself? What are you insinuating?"

"Oh, give me a break," Firebird said. "Look at you. All those metal parts. You didn't have all of those surgeries at once, Doc. I'll admit, you've had some bad luck if you've needed that much of you cut out. Most doctors would stop after a couple surgeries, since these parts aren't easy to come by. Not only that, but your likeliness of surviving the operation decreases each time you do it. I bet the doctors told you they won't install any more cybernetic replacements. Hell, I guarantee it was your research that manipulated them into giving you more parts than they would the average joe."

"That's neither here nor there…" Saegusa's voice rose with each word.

"You can deny it all you want, Doc. But I know the truth. You preach about saving others, when really, you're trying to save yourself."

Saegusa opened her mouth to speak, ready to argue him down. Yet, no words would come out. She didn't know what to say. Her mind was a storm of thoughts and fears. Particularly, the fear of a slow painful death. The conversation had done its job. She was feeling wide awake and alert. But yet, she was still fatigued, though this time it was mentally. The pain in her gut didn't help.

If anything, she longed for the drowsiness that she was trying to rid herself of.

"Let's just keep moving," she said. She walked past him, inadvertently bumping against Stuart along the way. They had to be close to the edge of the forest by now. She quickened her pace, forcing the others to keep up with her.

Firebird leaned toward Stuart as they followed.

"I think I pissed her off," he whispered.

"It seems you are very accomplished at doing so," Stuart replied. "And not just with her."

"I'm not in this business to make friends," Firebird said. "I just want to get paid. Get a new ship, and move on…"

The group stopped as they heard a large boom directly ahead. A moment later, a light tremor swept under their feet. Firebird looked ahead as far as he could. So far, he could see nothing but trees. Another large blast echoed, this one sounding fiery.

"Artillery," Stuart stated.

"That's not good," Firebird said. Saegusa looked back at them, alarmed. She gripped the handle of the revolver, not yet pulling it out of the holster.

"Is it the Strikers?"

"More than likely," Firebird said. "Let's move a little closer and check it out." They moved north with caution. "Just don't go rushing off. Let's make sure we stay unseen."

"Yeah, no shit," Saegusa said.

They kept low as they weaved between trees northward. Firebird had his rifle shouldered, the barrel down slightly, poised to be raised and fired in an instant.

As they pressed forward, the sounds of rifle fire grew distinct. Firebird and Saegusa crouched low near a cluster of logs and other brush. Hiding behind the barriers, they looked ahead, discovering the edge of the forest. Beyond the clearing was movement. Lots of movement.

"Stay here a sec," Firebird said.

"What are you gonna do?"

"I want to get a better idea of what's going on," he whispered. "If they're looking for you, we're gonna need a new game plan."

Firebird sprawled onto his stomach and army crawled through the narrow space between the bushes. After clearing the thorns, he approached the stump of a fallen tree. It was only about fifty feet or so from the tree line. The trees between it and the clearing were spaced out, granting him a good view.

Crouched behind the stump, he watched.

Armored vehicles moved between several brick structures. Large turrets rotated on the platforms, the muzzles growing red from heavy use. Firebird recognized the models. They were T-27s, armed with heavy plasma machine guns capable of firing three-hundred shots in a minute. Soldiers dressed in black uniforms marched between the armored units, shuffling through the civilians living in the small town.

He couldn't see the entire community, but from what he could figure, there were only about thirty or so families living in this area. The Strikers were jostling them around in the streets, knocking several of them to the ground while others ransacked the properties.

Smoke swirled in the distance. Firebird tilted to the right, his eye catching the edge of the crumbling structure. It was hard to see, but judging from the foundation, it was a larger structure than the houses. Probably a church. The Strikers likely did that out of spite.

Dead leaves rustled on the ground behind him. The blade protruded from his gauntlet. Firebird turned around, his fist drawn to his shoulder. Saegusa gasped, seeing the tip of the blade level with her throat. Firebird held back, caught a breath, and lowered his arm.

"For a doctor, you're not too bright," he muttered. He grabbed her by the shoulder and forced her to the ground. "I told you to keep back."

"What are they doing?" she asked. Firebird looked back and watched. The soldiers were going through each building and interrogating the civilians.

"I think they're searching for somebody," he said.

"Us?"

"Possibly," he said. "Though, I say it's odd that they weren't right there at the crash minutes after we went down."

"Hard to predict a landing," she said. "They probably expected us to be disintegrated in midair."

"Maybe," Firebird said. "One thing's for sure: we're not getting out this way. Too many troops."

"We can wait and see if they move off," Saegusa said.

"You want to chance that? If they don't find what they want, they might expand their search into the woods. And we don't want to move too far inward."

"Is there more Black Forest?"

"The Black Forest extends mostly to the north, so yeah," he answered.

"And more of those things," Saegusa clarified.

"Did it take a doctorate to figure that out?"

Several rifle shots drew their eyes back to the conflict taking place ahead. Several red plasma bullets singed the air as several armed civilians retreated from the back door of one of the larger houses.

A squad of Strikers flanked them, returning fire with Omega Plasma Rifles. The T-27 moved in and opened fire on the house. A stream of plasma bullets pummeled the front of the structure, ripping the bricks to powder, exposing the interior and helpless people inside. Their screams were short-lived as plasma tore them apart.

Saegusa covered her mouth as the four armed civilians engaged the Strikers. One of them was immediately hit in the face by a green plasma blast, searing away his features and leaving a blackened skull. As the other three attempted a retreat, a second one took a round in the back, just below his neck. He hit the ground hard, his weapon bouncing off the cement.

The remaining two fired off a few more shots before the inevitable burst of steam spat from the frame. Discarding their overheated weapons, they ran toward the trees.

The T-27 rotated its turret and lined the muzzle up with the targets. Green golf-ball sized plasma bullets ripped from the gun. The two rebels arched backwards as the first of the bullets struck them in the back. The bullets that followed finished them off, tearing both men to scorched pieces of meat.

Firebird shoved Saegusa down as several residual shots entered the woods, striking trees and exploding into a small puff of energy flame. The mercenary waited a few moments then peeked back out.

The Strikers continued marauding, with several of them examining the bodies. The T-27 turned its barrel away as the vehicle moved further along the street until it was out of view.

"We've seen enough," Firebird said.

"Can't we do anything?" Saegusa said.

"Like what? Take them all on with that revolver?"

Saegusa took a deep breath. "How can these people live like this?"

"It's simple," Firebird said. "They don't have a choice. You think the Sovereignty would let any of them leave? Who do you think works in the factories? Who do you think farms and provides rations? The government here does what any of them do best: Take. Only Sovereignty isn't afraid to put a gun to your face to do it." He stood up and started to move back. Saegusa was frozen in place, her eyes locked on the event taking place. "You coming?"

"Yeah," she said. They kept low and moved back. As they retreated, the putrid smell of burnt flesh entered the trees.

CHAPTER 12

Stuart waited as the humans moved on to inspect the military conflict taking place outside of the forest. He kept his mechanical eyes focused on the west. There was more movement taking place again. He sent out a scan, only for the results to come back fuzzy. There were too many obstacles in the area to get an accurate reading. But his mechanical brain knew something was wrong, and it wasn't just the Sovereignty.

He could hear his master approaching with the doctor.

"Come on, droid," Firebird said. "We're gonna have to double back."

"We might not want to do that, sir," Stuart said.

"I think we do," Firebird said. "Can't go that way, unless both of us want to end up as spare parts." He waved his mechanical arm.

"What's the problem?" Saegusa asked Stuart.

"My readings are not coming back accurately, but I think we are not alone in these woods."

"Oh no," Saegusa muttered. She looked at Firebird. "More of those reptilian humanoids?"

"Rasilisks? No. They only stray from the Black Forest at night," he said. He kept his rifle at his shoulder. He glanced down at the weapon, then listened to the distant sounds of Plasma Rifles discharging. "Let's hope there's nothing. If we have to shoot our way out of trouble, you can bet we'll draw the attention of the Strikers back there."

"What do we do?" Saegusa asked.

"We can't wait here." He took the first step, leading them back where they came. Stuart and Saegusa followed.

The mercenary watched carefully. That sixth sense started to rise inside him: That feeling of being watched. He knew Stuart was right. Somebody was in these woods.

Saegusa pulled her revolver and gripped it with both hands. She held it with both hands, close to her chest, muzzle pointed to the sky. She watched the trees. It was hard to see anything.

They stopped.

Something disturbed the brush in the distance. An eager scavenger, or possibly a marauder on the verge of launching an assault.

Firebird thought of giving them warning, whoever it was that was out there. But he had dealt with looters and gangs plenty of times in the past. If they were watching, they knew he was armed, and didn't care. This worried Firebird more.

"You see anything, Stuart?"

"My readings are being interfered with," Stuart replied. "I think my systems are damaged."

"Hang on," Saegusa said. She raised her hand to the frame on her temple, engaging the thermal vision in her bionic eye. The world turned blue all around her, with the exception of Firebird's body heat signature.

She looked ahead and panned left.

A glimmer of orange peeked from behind a tree several yards out. Straight ahead, she saw a couple of human shapes moving between trees. She glanced to the right. There was a tree, just out of Firebird's reach. Its trunk was thick, but not enough to conceal the outer traces of a heat signature behind it.

"Merc. Three o'clock," she announced. Firebird saw she was looking at the large tree on his right. Only one reason that would indicate a threat. He moved in a fast semicircle around the trunk. He came around to the other side and thrust the butt of his rifle outward.

The Razor gang member had been confident in his stealth. When he heard the wanderers approach, he vowed to be the one to take down the male. His confidence turned to shock as he saw the one-eyed mercenary flank his position. He sprang to his feet, intent on tackling him to the ground, only to instead charge straight into the butt of the Predator Rifle. A moment later, the thug was on his back, warm blood moistening his dried face.

They were so close. Platt believed he had set the perfect trap. Had the wanderers moved another hundred feet or so, they would've been in the middle of an encirclement of bandits. Had the plan worked, he would've had the Leader's favor.

His enthusiasm was gone in the blink of an eye when the female miraculously detected one of his foot soldiers. Platt watched in utter shock as the male swiftly moved around the tree and smashed Oakie's face.

"Bitch can see us," he muttered. In the blink of an eye, it seemed his ambitions were about to tank. Wallace had never had a cyborg before. Or a droid. Platt knew that if either one got away on his watch, he would be crucified.

The wanderers were already aware of their presence. There was only one thing left to do. Platt sprang from his hiding position, raising his machete high over his head as though summoning great powers from the sky.

"Gut him, boys!"

Firebird rejoined the others as several thugs rose from their hiding place. There were six of them, all dressed in various tattered clothing. Some were shirtless, while others wore frayed leather vests. They were all lean, each accustomed to fighting in close quarters. It didn't take much imagination for Firebird to know this wasn't the first time they robbed somebody.

They all wielded a handheld weapon of some sort. Two of them sported knives. One held a large pipe like a baseball bat. A couple of others swung chains as though they were nun chucks.

Then there was the one standing straight ahead. He yelled at the others, his open mouth baring blackened teeth. In his hand was a machete. The blade was two feet long. Though slightly rusted, it was sharp enough to do the job.

"Gut him, boys! Get the girl and the bot!"

Platt led the charge, pointing his machete straight ahead like a Cavalry sword.

"Ah-ah!" Firebird aimed his rifle, lining up Platt's forehead with his scope. The Razor Gang came to a stop, some of them visibly nervous by the sight of the weapon. They all remained still, their formation like a half-moon around the wanderers.

Platt watched the muzzle of the rifle. He was only about twenty feet away from the mercenary, close enough for him to look him in the eye. Platt had seen enough wanderers in his time. He knew which ones weren't afraid to kill and which ones didn't have what it took. This particular one was a prime example of the former. It was a scenario where Platt considered himself lucky, as circumstances favored him.

"You won't shoot me…"

"You really want to count on that?" Firebird said.

"I do," Platt remarked. "We've been watching you. You don't want to be found by the Strikers. You shoot me. I die…but you bring the Army down on you." His mouth widened into an ugly smile.

He took a step forward, testing his own theory with his life. Firebird's trigger finger twitched as he resisted squeezing. His fear had been realized. They were between a rock and a hard place.

He returned the smile, which caught Platt slightly off guard.

"You know, you're right. Can't shoot you," Firebird said. "Stuart, do that thing you've been constantly offering."

The droid reared on its back legs, opening a wide port on its underbelly. An electric rod protruded from the port, and in that same moment, two taser prods ejected, striking the gang leader in the chest.

Platt convulsed and fell to the ground, spit and sweat shooting off his body like from a sprinkler.

The five other Razors shuddered with surprise as they watched the head of their group go down. With only a second to prepare, Firebird twisted a lock on his rifle frame, jamming the trigger and preventing the weapon from being used against him.

All at once, they charged ferociously. Chains and blades flickered in the morning sunlight as they closed in on all sides.

"Hope you're still pissed off, Doc," he muttered, dropping the rifle and tucking away the key. Firebird lunged for the nearest Razor. The thug swung his chain for his head. It was a predictable move, which Firebird easily evaded by ducking. As the chain passed overhead, he pounced with his cybernetic arm pulled back.

His closed fist plowed the Razor's face, crushing his nose against his skull. Blood spewed from his mouth. The Razor had been struck many a time before, but never with the increased strength of a robotic arm. With his vision reduced to a foggy haze, he fell backward, landing in the brush.

Firebird could hear running feet rapidly approaching him from behind. He glanced over his shoulder, seeing two Razors coming at him, each sporting knives.

He rotated clockwise, his right knee raised. Pivoting on his other foot, he thrust his leg upward, his heel striking the charging thug in the jaw. Teeth rained from a bloody mouth as the gang member staggered backward. His companion maneuvered around him, knife held downward in his right hand.

Hesitation struck as the Razor witnessed a twelve-inch blade protrude from the mercenary's gauntlet. Firebird pulled his tactical knife from its sheath, holding it in reverse grip as he waited for the now-nervous thug to attack.

"Your move, creep."

Stuart ripped the taser prods from Platt's body as two other thugs approached the doctor. Saegusa held her revolver out and cocked the hammer. The larger thug wielded the pipe, which could easily shatter a person's skull. He smiled as he approached.

"You can't shoot me," he said. "You know what would happen."

"I'd improve your facial features," Saegusa said.

The second thug whirled his chain in a circle, gradually approaching her from the left. Stuart poised like a jumping spider, giving both of them pause. The larger thug stopped, wary of what the droid was capable of.

A moment or two passed before the thug regained his confidence. He figured the droid would just taser him like it did Platt. But it didn't. It probably had to recharge. It was probably defenseless now.

"Stupid bug droid. You're coming with me..."

Stuart leapt, tackling the thug to the ground. His forelegs transformed into drills. The Razor screamed as he watched the spiraling tips ram into his belly.

As the droid attacked, the other thug moved in for the doc.

Saegusa placed one foot ahead of the other and rotated clockwise on the balls of her feet. As she completed the turn, she raised her right leg high, swinging her foot toward his head with lightning speed. The metal heel connected with his jaw, breaking the bone and launching teeth far into the woods.

The Razor spun twice, blood freefalling from his loose mouth before he stumbled to his knees. Still holding the knife, he looked up at the doc. In this moment, he turned into a ravaging beast. He no longer contemplated the consequences of what Wallace would do: he wasn't capable of thinking that far ahead. His ego was now in the way. This *girl* dared to break his jaw. He would gut her like a pig. Slowly and painfully. But not before allowing himself the carnal pleasure of...

Saegusa moved in and kicked her foot high, bringing it up close to her face. An instant later, she brought her heel down in an ax-like motion. The metal heel struck the top of his head, fracturing the skull and silencing his thoughts.

The knife-wielding Razor moved in with a slash at Firebird's head. The merc stepped back, allowing him to miss. The thug slashed several times, each strike falling short by an inch or less. Frustrated, the thug changed his grip to a forward grip. Yelling, he moved in for the kill, thrusting his knife out.

Firebird stepped slightly to his left and swept his right arm upward, his forearm catching the thug at the wrist and deflecting his attack skyward. He punched his metal fist into the exposed ribcage, driving the blade all the way through the stomach. He yanked the blade free, slicing a lung in the process.

By the time the thug felt his chest deflate, the merc sliced his other knife across his throat. The blade cut two-inches deep, just below the jawline. His face pale and blank, the Razor fell to the ground.

His companion stood to his feet, his jaw bloodied from the kick, just in time to witness his comrade be bested by the wanderer.

Snarling like a wild beast, the Razor slowly approached, pointing the tip of his knife at the merc.

Firebird awaited the attack, lining his shoulders at a forty-five-degree angle. He could hear the rustling of twigs behind him. The chain wielding Razor stood up, his face flattened. Dirt had peppered his face, mixing with the still wet blood that spilled from his nose and mouth. He whirled the chain repeatedly like a Ferris Wheel.

Finally, he moved in, swinging the chain down from overhead. Firebird turned and raised his gauntlet, allowing the chain to wrap over his metal arm. The merc yanked his arm back, ripping the chain from the thug's grip. The gang member staggered, dumbfounded, his hand bloodied from the metal slicing through his palm as it pulled away. Firebird thrust a kick, smashing him in the chest.

As the thug stumbled backward, Firebird rotated left. He swung his metal arm, unreeling the chain and lashing it like a whip. The tip of the metal struck the charging thug in the eye, blackening his vision. He swung wildly, hoping to land a lucky shot. A kick to his ribs folded him over. Before he could recover, another kick connected with his kneecap. The kick followed through with tremendous force, bending the joint backward. The thug yelled out, his leg bent back into a V-shape.

His face bloodied, chest aching, and disarmed, the broken-nosed Razor stood up again after being floored twice by the mercenary. Firebird glanced his way and took another fighting stance. The thug reached behind his belt and pulled a rusty knife.

"I'm gonna take that other eye," he said, spitting with each word. He took a step forward. "I'm gonna carve it out, and then I'm…"

Firebird gripped his tactical knife by the blade and flung it. The knife rotated like a wheel before its blade plunged deep into the Razor's throat, shutting him up. Gagging, the Razor dropped to his knees, gripping the weapon.

Firebird leaned forward.

"Oh, sorry, did I interrupt?"

Platt twitched as he rolled onto his hands and knees. His fingers trembled as they clutched the handle to his machete. He looked straight ahead, witnessing the robot overtake Grizzly the Brute. Never did he expect the Brute to go down so easily. Not too far away from that skirmish, the woman had bested Mingle the Savage. She moved with grace. He had never seen a cyborg before, much less one that could fight.

He gritted his teeth in anger. The attack couldn't have gone any worse. Wallace had trusted him. He could not report failure! He couldn't! If by some miracle they didn't crucify him, he would be forever ridiculed by the Razor Gang. Never would he find himself promoted within the ranks. Hell, with so many of his group deceased under his watch, he might even be banished.

There was only one solution. And it was a simple one: come back with the girl. The Leader never specified she had to be COMPLETELY unharmed. Just alive enough to perform the needs he so desired.

Platt stood up and rushed the droid, machete raised high.

Detecting the advancing threat, Stuart pried his forelegs from the dead brute's body and scurried back. The blade came down, catching one of his legs at the knuckle. Sparks flared from a busted circuit, causing the droid to stumble. Before he could recover, Platt drew down again and struck another leg.

With two of his legs disabled, Stuart toppled. His remaining legs flailed at the attacker, keeping Platt from striking again.

"HEY!" Saegusa yelled. She sprinted toward him and pointed her revolver. A loud *cling* echoed. Platt had swung his machete, striking the gun and knocking it from her hand. He drew the weapon back and closed in before she could react. He hammered the machete downward, hitting her forehead with the bottom of the handle.

As the thug died with the knife embedded in his neck, Firebird turned his attention to his companions, just in time to witness Saegusa falling to the ground. The group leader stood over her, simultaneously victorious and enraged. Behind him, Stuart floundered on the ground, damaged.

"Do I have to do everything myself?"

The leader looked his way. By the looks of it, he was further enraged by the sight of the gang members the merc had bested.

Good. I hope he's pissed.

Intent on enraging the leader further, Firebird shrugged nonchalantly with both palms held up.

"At least I saved bullets."

The leader growled and sliced his machete angrily. He stepped over Saegusa and began to charge. Firebird leaned forward slightly, ready to sprint. He went to take his first step, only for his foot to remain seemingly locked to the ground.

The broken-legged thug clutched at his leg. He yelled and cursed as he attempted to pull the merc to the ground. Firebird pulled away, unable to free his ankle.

"Shoo!" he muttered. The leader was only a few meters off. Balancing on his captured foot, Firebird raised his other leg and stomped down hard on the thug's head. The injured attacker's grip released as he sprawled out on his back, unconscious.

Platt closed the distance and swung the machete for the mercenary's neck. Firebird ducked and rolled, passing underneath the weapon. He sprang to his feet and turned. Platt had already redirected and progressed the attack.

Firebird angled his gauntlet blade up and parried the first strike. Platt immediately swung back, missing the merc's head as he leaned back and sidestepped. A kick struck his ribcage, followed by a punch to his head.

Platt fell to his knees. Firebird moved in, ready to make the kill with his gauntlet. The Razor Gang warrior summersaulted. He completed the roll and came up on his feet. Immediately, he charged at Firebird again. He brought the blade down like an ax. Again, it was parried outward as Firebird waved his metal arm in a circular motion, clanging the blades together. The mercenary shifted his weight forward and raised his elbow, striking Platt in the nose. Platt yelled and stumbled a few steps backward, then lunged again with a wild swing of the machete.

Firebird stepped inward and closed the gap, catching Platt by the arm. Rotating his hips, he used the thug's momentum against him and flung him over his shoulder, plowing him headfirst into the ground.

Though disoriented, Platt quickly rolled away to avoid a follow-up attack.

Oakie's head ached from where the wanderer had struck him with the rifle. In the minutes that followed, he was in the realm between consciousness and unconsciousness. The world seemed bright and in constant motion. The sounds of combat were faint at first but grew louder and more meticulous as his mind gradually came back to him.

Oakie sat up, only to discover that the group had been massacred by the wanderers. Several yards away, the Savage lay motionless on the ground, his head smashed. Even the Brute had been killed, his torso impaled by something sharp. He could see hints of the others beyond the trees, all of them limp in the grass.

The only one who stood was Platt, and by the looks of it, he would not last long. He was bloodied and visibly fatigued. Each of his assaults were easily parried by the male wanderer. Oakie watched as the stranger threw Pratt effortlessly over his shoulder. Though Platt successfully evaded a strike from the strange gauntlet blade, it was clear the scout leader was minutes from meeting his end.

Oakie stood up and raced west, where Wallace waited. Winding between trees, the thug passed through over a hundred yards of wooded area before he saw the gang patiently waiting by their speeders.

Rather, they were *impatiently* waiting, as was expressed in Wallace's eyes. His chains rattled over his large chest as he stepped away from his bike. His eyes narrowed as he watched his subordinate stumbling from the trees, his head bruised and bloodied.

"What is happening?" Wallace's voice boomed with anger, causing a few nervous jitters among the crowd.

"These people...they're not like anyone else we've come across..." Oakie said. "The man...he is a cyborg too. And he can fight. They have bested all of us."

"Nobody bests the Razors!" Wallace announced. The gang cheered, raising various weapons high in the air. "Looks like I'll have to take it upon myself! Are they still there?"

"Yes!" Oakie said. "Platt is engaging the man in combat...though he won't last long."

"Disembark!" Wallace announced to the gang. "Gather your weapons! Let's finish this ourselves!"

The gang cheered as they armed themselves with various handheld weapons. One eager thug approached Wallace, sporting a Five-Star Plasma Rifle in his hand.

"Shall we bring these?"

Wallace briefly pondered the idea.

"Bring them, but do not use unless necessary." He glanced to the north. "If there's anything we have in common with these strangers, it's that we don't want to alert Sovereignty."

Five of the thugs happily armed themselves with Plasma Rifles, while a dozen others stormed the woods with their hand-held weapons. It was dishonorable to turn down a good fight, and from the sounds of it, this stranger was the best fighter they had come across in years.

****

With a sharp pivot to the right, Firebird kicked his left leg upward in a near-horizontal swing, connecting the top of his boot to Platt's temple. Sweat and blood spouted as the thug staggered back. He still clutched the machete, though his hand was shaky. He teetered on his feet, keeping the blade pointed directly at the wanderer.

The frustration was overwhelming. He could not seem to land a blow on this bastard cyborg. Not only that, but the wanderer did not advance. He waited, his eye unblinking, watching him. Why did he not advance?

Platt steadied himself and sucked a deep breath in through his nose. He waved the blade back and forth while waving Firebird over with the other hand.

"Come on. That all you got?"

Firebird lowered his fists. He stood in a non-threatening manner and pointed a finger at Platt.

"This is your one chance," he said. "Beat it. Live. And find a dentist."

Platt snarled. He would not dare retreat! That in itself was a death sentence. Wallace would have his head. And if Platt departed on his own, the Leader would undoubtedly hunt him down to the ends of the Earth.

"You fool! You prick!" he growled. He sliced the air with the machete then advanced.

Firebird grinned with delight as the Razor approached, clumsy with rage.

Thought that'd piss him off. Offers of mercy were usually taken as insults by road gang members. Angry people often fought sloppily. This fellow proved that point.

He raised his gauntlet high and connected the blade with that of the machete. He parried, throwing Platt's balance off to the left. The thug swung back. With an inward thrust of his gauntlet, Firebird deflected again. Platt drew back, growling madly. He raised the machete high and brought it down vertically.

Firebird moved in with precise timing, catching his arm as it came down. With a firm grasp on Platt's wrist, the mercenary yanked back, overextending the arm. Firebird slammed his metal forearm into Platt's locked elbow, snapping the limb. Bone punched through skin as the arm folded backward, the limp hand releasing the machete.

The weapon only fell a few inches before its handle landed in Firebird's hand. He swung high and brought it down like an axe, cleaving Platt's forehead directly between the eyes. The Razor took a shaky step back, the machete still embedded in his skull. It took a moment for his brain to shut down entirely. And when it did, the thug collapsed, the look of failure implanted on his blood-caked face.

"Took you long enough," Stuart said.

Firebird collected his rifle and revolver off the ground and hurried to his companions. The droid was attempting to push himself off the ground with his four functioning legs. His forelegs were damaged, the exoskeleton cracked at the knuckle. Beneath the steel, the tendons had become loose. It was fixable but Firebird needed tools that he did not have handy at the moment.

Saegusa rolled to her side, her head bruised. Firebird stepped away from the droid and helped her up.

"You suck," he said.

"Wha—wait…WHAT?!" Saegusa came alive with confusion and irritation.

"You attack me like a freaking *terminator*, yet you let that punk get the best of you," he joked.

"Yeah, well…you're more annoying. Besides, why aren't you yelling at him?" She pointed at the droid.

"Eh, he's not as fun to piss off. Can't really piss him off at all really."

"How you've managed to live this long, I'll never know," Saegusa said. She balanced herself and checked her forehead for blood.

"Just a little bump," Firebird added. "You'll live, though I recommend stop getting hit in the head. Everyone's after all that data stored in that noggin."

"No kidding," she said. She looked at the dead gang members. "Who the hell are they? Do they know who I am?"

"No, they're just some bike gang looking to rob. Simple as that," Firebird said.

"Sir, I suggest we leave immediately," Stuart said. "My readings are still fuzzy, but I believe I am detecting motion from the east."

"Great. Just great," the mercenary grumbled. Saegusa enacted her thermal vision and looked into the woods.

"Oh God…there's several of them! They're closing in fast." She switched the vision back to normal. Her normal eye widened as the gang came into view. They were only a hundred or so feet away. Firebird could see them too. There were too many to engage hand-to-hand. And shooting them would attract an even worse presence. There was only one other option.

"Let's go! Doc, can you run?"

"Hell yes!" Saegusa was the first to take off. Firebird ran behind her, only to stop and notice Stuart struggling. He started back to help him.

"Negative, sir! Keep moving! I can run. Protect the doctor!" The droid spaced out his four functioning legs, adequately balancing himself to run. Several of the gang had entered the small spacing of trees. Armed with various blunt and bladed weapons, they maneuvered around the corpses of their brethren in pursuit. To Firebird's shock, some of them carried Plasma Rifles.

Firebird sprinted as fast as he could. Saegusa was thirty feet ahead. She weaved between the obstacles with precision, despite being dazed from the blow to her head. Stuart kept pace despite his handicap.

The ground drummed from the running feet behind them. Chains rattled and waving weapons cracked against trees as the wild gang closed in on their victims. Firebird knew they weren't gonna lose them. All he could hope was to keep going south. With a little more distance, they would be out of hearing range of the Striker unit, and he could then engage the gang in a firefight. Picking them off one-by-one would not be a difficult endeavor. These punks were fierce. But they were also clumsy and disorganized. On top of that, he doubted they were great marksmen.

Firebird leapt over a small mound and landed, his feet propelling him faster down the small hill. He checked the ground in front of him to make sure there was nothing to trip him up. Looking back up, he realized he was about to plow into Saegusa. She was standing still, looking dead ahead.

"What are you doing? We need to…" Firebird stopped, realizing what she was staring at.

A group of at least twenty armed individuals stood in their path. They were armed to the teeth with various models of Plasma Rifles, including the Omega models used by the Sovereignty. Though they didn't look like Sovereignty, they definitely didn't look friendly. They looked like they had been through hell, with their clothes battered and faces marked with burns and smoke.

A middle-aged woman stood at the front of the group.

"That's her!" she yelled, pointing to Saegusa.

"And that's the contractor!" a Native-American individual shouted.

Before Firebird could react, the drumming from behind him grew increasingly loud. The gang closed in, shouting various obscenities. Suddenly, their advance came to a stop as they locked eyes with the new group of strangers.

"The Razors!" somebody shouted.

Beretta Albright had run into these cut-throats in the past. They were thieves and murderers, who had raided small bands of rebels in the past. They had no allegiance to anyone, including the Sovereignty. If there was any loyalty, it was to the leader of their group, Wallace. Beretta knew the kind of man Wallace was. He was a sick individual. He gave off the demeanor of a disciplined leader. But beneath that rugged exterior was an immature boy, who carried little more discipline than the thugs that followed him.

He emerged at the crest of the small hill behind the doctor. At once, they stared into each other, mirroring each other's hate. He was after the cyborg for himself.

She would not have it. Her son had sacrificed himself for this plan. She would not let it be ruined by a bunch of bandits who had no use for the doctor other than to fulfill their sick desires.

"Open fire," she yelled, raising her rifle and discharging it into the group of bandits.

Several guns discharged at once as the rebels dispersed. Each shot echoed through the trees, traveling far and wide.

CHAPTER 13

Zolnar seethed through clenched teeth. His suspicions that the contractor had been shot down were now confirmed. He stood at the compound at the artillery unit, staring at the dead bodies of Strikers and Rebels. The fort itself had been absolutely obliterated by explosive charges, rendering the artillery guns useless.

A part of him admired what General Beretta Albright had managed to pull off. One couldn't organize a concentrated effort like this without guts. Guts, and a little help. Somehow, they had received word that the contractor was bringing the doctor to Sovereignty.

The radioman had informed the Commander that Supreme Leader Cornelius was requesting an update on the situation. It was the one person that Zolnar actually feared. With a snap of his fingers, Cornelius could reduce Zolnar to a measly peasant, and have him spend the rest of his days rotting away in a dungeon for this colossal failure. The Commander delayed the call, ordering the radioman to relay that the Commander was occupied with handling the situation.

He would have to get back to Cornelius at some point. Each time he put off the call, he risked the Supreme Leader's wrath. In desperation, he ordered his battalion far and wide across the region in search of any downed aircraft. An hour ago, he had been riding in a T-32 tank with five-hundred strikers around him. Only one report had come in so far, but it amounted to nothing. After ordering all of his men to search, he was left with fifty. He waited anxiously with a portable radio on his belt.

Few reports had come in, with only one being of any interest. A patrol on the northern border had discovered some rebels hiding out in the small town bordering the Restricted Forest, but so far, it appeared unrelated. Other than that, the radio was silent.

Finally, Zolnar considered updating Cornelius of the situation. He would need a longer range than what the portable could offer. As he walked to the radio disk, static crackled through his portable. Through the static came words.

"Europe-Three-Echo-Four, calling Motherbird."

"This is Motherbird. Report!" Zolnar responded.

"Something's going down in the Restricted Forest!" the Lieutenant reported. *"I don't know who it is, but several of our troops are reporting rifle fire. There's something going on in there!"*

Zolnar's blood rushed through his veins. He felt like a wolf that had smelled a herd of sheep.

"Excellent," he said. "Remain at your location in case they try to flee north. Send a couple of your T-27s along the east edge of the forest to help us pinpoint the location. We're on our way."

His voice boomed over the platoon of Strikers.

"LET'S GO! LET'S MOVE IT OUT!" The Commander snapped his fingers at the nearest radioman. "Call for some Target-Seekers. I want some air-support!"

"Yes sir," the radioman said.

"Sir!" a Sergeant called to Zolnar. "What about the tanks?" Zolnar glanced to the large armored vehicles. Great weapons they were. Excellent for open warfare. But as powerful as they were, they were slow, with a maximum speed of thirty-miles per hour.

"If we wait for them, we'll lose time," Zolnar said. "Have them guard this station. They won't be of much use in the forest anyway. Now, get moving!"

In seconds, the Strikers were mobilized. Engines roared as carrier trucks ripped onto the paved road. They raced northeast, trailing dust behind their rear tires.

****

Firebird grabbed Saegusa by the waist, picking her up off the ground as he raced behind cover. Stuart was right behind him, galloping like a horse. Behind them, Rebels and Razors scattered. Like two swarms of bees, the two groups massed together in a vicious clash. Laser rifles, spewing red and green colored energy, blasted away. The air grew hot and thick, and the smell of burnt flesh soon permeated the forest.

"Get down," he said, tucking the doctor behind a cluster of trees. He shoved the revolver into her hands. "Anyone comes at you, you blow their brains…"

Saegusa shoved him aside and extended the gun. She fired, putting a round through the skull of a charging thug. His face exploded into a heap of blood and bone. He hit the ground, rolling head over heels before settling in the dirt.

Firebird glanced at him, then back at Saegusa.

"Like I said…" He shouldered his rifle and ducked behind the next tree as several plasma shots streaked by. Several Rebels advanced on their location, rifles raised at eye level. Firebird pulled back on the cocking mechanism of his rifle and watched from the edge of the tree, ready to return fire.

As he prepared to move, a series of red plasma struck one of the rebels from behind. The unlucky soldier was dead instantly. His two comrades turned and flanked the Razor who had shot him.

The warring groups branched out, some locked in close combat with the Razors. Albright led the charge. She shot from the hip, burning cavities into the chests of two thugs that stood in her way. She looked around. In the chaos, she lost sight of Saegusa and the contractor.

Several feet ahead of her, Wallace joined the fray. He held a plasma pistol in his hand. It was a military-class weapon, undoubtedly looted from a dead Sovereignty officer. It was an accurate weapon with a built-in ventilation system to keep from overheating.

She aimed her rifle to shoot, though not in time. The gang leader fired his weapon behind the skulls of two unsuspecting rebels, who were already under fire from a couple of armed thugs. Albright squeezed the trigger. Wallace had already ducked down, unwittingly evading her shots. He saw the plasma bullets streaking by and sprinted for cover. Beretta followed him with the barrel of her rifle, each shot zipping inches behind the running target. A moment later, he disappeared behind a thick cluster of trees.

"Damn it!" she shouted.

A flash of red zipped in front of her. A thug had taken a shot at her and missed. She saw another flash, this time green and going in the opposite direction. A spray of plasma bullets hit two armed thugs, cutting their pathetic lives short. Daunhauer darted toward the General.

"Where are they?" she asked.

"They're here somewhere," he said. Smoke twirled from the muzzle of his rifle as he let it cool.

They ducked down as more plasma shots singed the air. It was Wallace again. Like a mole in the ground, he peeked out from cover and fired at them. Daunhauer fired back, his shots going wide. Wallace ducked behind cover again. Daunhauer stood up to flank him, only to see another thug approaching in his peripheral vision. The Razor rushed him. In his hand was a crowbar, covered in the blood of a deceased rebel soldier.

Daunhauer turned to fire, but a swing of the crowbar knocked the gun from his hand. The Razor reared back to swing again. Daunhauer lunged, locking the thug's arms across his chest before slamming a fist into his mouth. He struck repeatedly before the thug pulled away.

The Razor swung again, the jagged tip of the crowbar grazing Daunhauer's chest, ripping his shirt. The Lieutenant pulled a knife and charged again, locking in combat with the Razor.

Albright aimed her rifle as they tussled, hoping to pick the thug off. Their movements were too frantic, the Lieutenant too close to the target. She could not get a clean shot.

There was more movement from beyond the fight. Another thug, sporting a knife in each hand, rushed Daunhauer as he struggled against the other Razor. The General crouched to one knee and placed her eye along the barrel. She squeezed the trigger and watched the flash of green turn a fiery orange as it hit the thug in the throat. He dropped and rolled, his knives bouncing aimlessly from his dead hands.

Daunhauer raised a knee, striking his opponent under the ribs, and followed with a left cross to the jaw. The thug retracted, his muscles tensing from pain. He attempted another two-handed swing, which was effortlessly blocked at the wrists by Daunhauer. The Lieutenant thrust his knife under the Razor's outstretched arms, plunging the blade deep into his belly. The Razor yelled out, which quickly settled into a groan as he died. Daunhauer yanked the knife free and allowed his fresh corpse to fall freely.

He sheathed his knife and collected his rifle, only to duck again as Wallace began shooting again.

Firebird watched the clash. Before long, the battle grew out of control. Rebels and Razors were everywhere, shooting projectiles from behind cover. The chaos was perfect.

"Good. Let them kill each other," he muttered to Saegusa.

"I suggest we go this way," Stuart said. He was moving west toward the outer edge of the forest.

"I'm with him," Saegusa said.

"We're gonna have to go now," Firebird said. He stood up to provide cover. Stuart took the lead and guided Saegusa to the forest's edge. Firebird waited another minute, assuring himself that the two groups were too busy fighting to notice them, then followed the doctor.

Jones squeezed the trigger of his Omega Plasma Rifle, burning several holes into the charging Razor. The careless thug had rushed him with a fire axe and was foolish enough to think he could clear the distance.

Jones released the trigger after the dead thug collapsed to the ground. He looked ahead. Behind the frantic movements of clashing rebels and thugs, he saw Daunhauer dispatching a thug in close combat. Shortly after, he and the General dove for cover as an assailant, whom he couldn't see, fired at them from behind cover.

He eyed the patch of trees carefully in hopes of spotting the shooter and picking him off from his location. He could see some movement where the plasma shots originated from but couldn't get an exact placement.

His concentration came to an end as he felt the presence of someone approaching from behind. Jones turned around to shoot. The thug was only a few feet away. He was armed with a chain which had been lined with razor wire. He swung the chain like a whip, wrapping it around the barrel of the rifle, and yanked back, prying it from the rebel's hands. The chain unfolded, launching the rifle through the air to a destination obscured by the trees.

Jones jumped back, narrowly avoiding another swing of the chain. The thug laughed as he approached, believing himself to have the upper hand. Jones reached along his belt and pulled his shuriken. That smiled disappeared as those large spikes protruded from the disc. Before he could react, Jones flicked his wrist as though tossing a Frisbee.

The blades cut across the thug's neck, slicing arteries and tendons. The thug fell on his back and twitched, his last thoughts being anger of his defeat as his vision faded to black.

Jones hurried past his defeated enemy and secured his shuriken from the tree it had embedded in after its strike. Movement up ahead caught his attention. Believing it to be another Razor, he ducked down and drew his shuriken back for another throw.

There were three individuals moving across the section of woods, nearly sixty feet ahead. They weren't moving toward him but in a diagonal route. The first was a droid with spider-like legs. Behind him was the cyborg. The doctor! She was using the skirmish as a distraction to escape.

Jones remembered the orders had changed. General Albright ordered she be taken alive. He could not use his shuriken to stop her. Doing so would incur the wrath of the General, and she was already pissed off to say the least. He would have to chase her down on foot.

Trailing behind her was the contractor. He was slightly taller than average-size. An eyepatch covered his left eye, the skin around it marked with burns and scrapes. But what really caught his eye was the metal arm. This man was a cyborg too. And he was the only thing in the way between Jones and the objective.

Jones brought the shuriken high to his shoulder and launched it.

Ducking under low branches lined with poisonous leaves, Firebird started catching up to the doctor and droid. Weaving around a thick tree, he nearly ran into a thick thorn bush. He twisted himself to the left, narrowly avoiding being embedded in the thick barbs. As he turned, he noticed a figure poised several dozen yards away. It was a large individual with a muscular frame and a height which easily had six inches on him at least.

The man whipped his hand outward. The sharp silver object glinted in the sun as it spiraled at his face. A shuriken!

Firebird threw his left arm up over his face.

The shuriken hit hard, the blades clanging against the gauntlet. Firebird reeled backward, losing his rifle. He hit the ground near the root of a tree. Sparks flared from the gauntlet where the shuriken had bounced off. Its blades had breached the steel.

Saegusa looked back, seeing the mercenary on the ground.

"Merc!" she yelled.

"I have a name," he muttered through gritted teeth. He leaned up, seeing the large figure charging his way. For a large man, he sprinted with the speed of someone half his size. He had already cleared about half the distance.

Firebird sprung to his feet and waved Saegusa away.

"Stuart, get her out of here!"

The man was ten feet out. Firebird drew his Gravestone pistol and fired from the hip.

Jones saw the man's organic hand move for the holster. He recognized the wide stand. He'd seen it before. The contractor was going to attempt a fast draw. As the gun left the holster, Jones dropped into a summersault. Shots fired, sending bullets zipping over him harmlessly.

He came up on his feet, now face-to-face with the contractor. He threw both hands out and clutched his wrist. With a sharp twisting motion, he bent the wrist back, dropping the gun.

Saegusa watched the two men as they locked in combat. She extended the revolver to shoot the attacker, however couldn't get a clear shot. They wrestled on foot, twisting each way with no predictability.

"Dr. Saegusa, he has ordered us to leave," Stuart said.

"I know, but..."

"Firebird has fought bigger men than that...and, as he phrased it, 'gotten his ass kicked'..." Stuart said. "Ah, he'll be fine. But we must go. He'll catch up."

Movement from the battle caused the doctor to look right. Two men, armed with Omega Plasma Rifles quickly approached.

"There she is!" one of them shouted.

Saegusa gasped and squeezed the trigger. The .38 caliber round struck the one who spoke in his center mass. His eager expression turned into one of surprise. Jaw agape, he looked down to his chest, seeing his blood freefalling from the hole in his breastplate. His face paled before collapsing.

Saegusa fired another shot, missing the second man. With no time, she turned and ran with Stuart for the forest edge.

Lieutenant Donnelly ducked as a second shot fired. The woman retreated, leaving him crouched behind a critically wounded Captain Collins. Donnelly pulled some gauze from his pocket and pressed it to the wound.

The Captain was motionless. His eyes stared blankly at the sky. Donnelly realized he had gone limp. The Captain was dead. Donnelly tensed. He had been so relieved that he hadn't killed the doctor. Now, it wasn't relief he felt, but regret. He should've lit up the entire countryside with those artillery guns.

The Lieutenant shot to his feet, seeing Jones fighting with the contractor.

"Bring him to me, Jones! Let me at him!"

The big man glanced in his direction and shook his head no, then tilted it to where the doctor had run off.

"Get her! I got this!" he yelled. Donnelly nodded then shouldered his rifle as he darted after the objective.

Firebird's nerves lit up as his wrist twisted back. The jolt had launched the pistol from his hand. Adrenaline coursed through his veins as he heard his opponent shout to his comrade to chase Saegusa. The man called Jones had him locked up pretty tight, now with one hand on his wrist, the other wrapping around his neck like a python.

The mercenary banged his gauntlet against his leg to trigger the blade. But it wouldn't extend, likely due to the damage. He was down to his fists and feet.

"Just my luck," he muttered to himself. Closing his metal hand into a fist, he threw several hard punches into the attacker's ribcage.

Jones grunted in pain, caught off guard from the excessive force of the blows. Another hard blow struck under his bottom rib. Firebird lifted a foot and stomped down on Jones' knee. The grip on his wrist loosened. Firebird seized the opportunity and pulled his arm free, immediately smashing his elbow into Jones' eye, severing his hold on his neck and driving him back.

Firebird followed up the strike with a hard kick to the chest, driving Jones to the ground.

The rebel quickly stood up and threw his arms over his face, blocking a punch to his head. Firebird jabbed low beneath his guard, hitting dead center in the chest and blowing the wind out of the Rebel. Jones folded, his guard lowered, resulting in Firebird kicking high. His foot came high, connecting the toe of his boot to Jones' eye socket.

Jones felt his vision flash. The kick snapped his head back, sparking a sharp pain in his skull. He stumbled back, barely managing to keep upright. He held his fists up to guard against his opponent. His vision was cloudy now. The contractor was moving in, though he couldn't properly gauge the distance.

Jones threw several jabs, successfully backing Firebird off. Open hands deflected each strike as he moved in. Though not landing any blows, it gave Jones the few seconds he needed for his eye to clear up.

He moved in, deflecting a punch from the mercenary, before grasping a hand on his throat. Firebird gagged as the fingers closed around his airway. With one arm, Jones lifted him up off his feet. He extended his arm upward, dangling the mercenary two feet off the ground before choke-slamming him hard on his back. Firebird hit the ground and bounced. A heartbeat later, the rebel stomped down on his ribcage. Jones stomped again, then kicked the mercenary in the side.

The kick struck his upper ribs. The force of the blow rolled Firebird onto his stomach, where he quickly pushed up onto his hands and knees. Before he could stand, Jones threw another kick, bringing the tip of his boot into his stomach. Firebird gagged, the blow launching him inches from the earth. He came down on his back again. His ribs caved in again as Jones brought his knee down on him.

Pinned by his weight, Firebird threw his hands up to defend against a series of punches to his face.

Jones pounded his fists with all his might, intent on pancaking the mercenary's face to the soil. He struck with a right, then a left, then another right. Suddenly, he felt an intense tightening around his wrist. It was caught in the grasp of Firebird's metal arm. The fingers squeezed tighter, the mechanical force far exceeding that of a human's. The muscles crunched down into the bone, sparking intense pain.

Jones did something he rarely did. He yelled out.

Firebird thrust his other hand up, smashing his palm into Jones' nose, disorientating him.

Grasping his arm with both hands, he raised both legs, wrapping his right over Jones' left shoulder, and his left leg under the extended arm. His feet locked together behind the shoulder blades. Firebird leaned back on his shoulders, lifting his rear and extending his locked feet outward, thus, squeezing his knees inward. The right pressed down hard into his jugular, while the left knee pressed Jones' extended shoulder under his jawline.

Jones gulped as he felt his airway cut off. His feet clawed the ground behind him as he tried to scurry out of the hold, which only resulted in a tighter squeeze.

****

Daunhauer sprinted wide, placing a plasma shot between the eyes of another Razor as he flanked Wallace's position. As planned, he drew the gang leader's fire, while Albright worked her way around the right.

Wallace cursed, his calm demeanor quickly fading as he failed to land a shot on the Rebel Recon Specialist.

He glanced back to where he originally had them pinned, realizing Albright was nowhere to be seen. He continued shooting, each shot going further wide of the target. Daunhauer dove behind another tree for cover.

Wallace pelted the tree with several more laser blasts before giving up. He turned around in search of the General. It didn't take long to find her.

She stood ten feet away, her eyes lined over the sights of her Omega Plasma Rifle. Though a proud man, Wallace was able to accept when he had been bested. He would not be able to fire off a shot fast enough. He dropped the pistol and raised his hands high.

Behind him, Daunhauer emerged from cover and saw the gang leader kneeling before Albright. He started forward, ready to place binds on the prisoner's hands.

Albright didn't waste time with words or consideration of mercy. She squeezed the trigger and watched the ball of plasma punch through his eye. Smoke billowed from his flaming skull as Wallace slumped to the ground.

Daunhauer jumped back, shocked by the unexpected execution. He looked up to Albright, his face displaying his surprise. There was no sense of remorse in Beretta's expression. Her face was cursed with a dark rage. She returned his gaze, her eyes cold as ice.

Daunhauer nodded his head. If this was to be the new way, he would still follow her. His loyalty was undivided. He owed her his life, and fighting a war required cold decisions. Wallace would just have been another mouth to feed. Besides that, he had killed some of their people. Why waste time with their trial process?

The Lieutenant examined the battleground. The clash had come to a close. The rebels had overpowered the Razors, and only suffered five or six casualties. The remaining rebels had the remaining Razors kneeling in a row. There were three of them, all kneeling with their hands raised. Daunhauer glanced back at Albright, who nodded with approval. Daunhauer raised his rifle and placed the nearest one in his sights. The thug looked, his face alarmed and surprised. That expression disappeared, as did most of his face, as a plasma blast burned it away. Daunhauer let off a barrage of shots, killing the other two, much to the surprise of his comrades.

There was no time to discuss, as the Lieutenant immediately started running through the trees toward one final skirmish that was taking place. He could see Jones locked in combat with the contractor. He was locked tight in a triangle choke, his face now purple from lack of oxygen.

"Get him!" Daunhauer yelled.

Firebird grimaced as he maintained the triangle choke. Jones' attempts to break the choke slowly weakened as oxygen failed to reach his brain. Finally, the man was nearly unconscious, his body slumping over the mercenary.

It was that moment when Firebird realized that the shooting had stopped. Glancing right, he saw the squad of armed men converging on his location. A Native American man led the charge and pointed his rifle down at his face.

Firebird separated his feet, releasing the choke. He brought his legs back and pressed his boots under Jones' ribs, then launched him like a catapult toward the Lieutenant.

Daunhauer stumbled as Jones plowed into him, causing his aim to jerk sideways. Firebird sprang to his feet and charged the Lieutenant. Daunhauer pushed the dazed Jones out of the way, then repositioned his rifle.

A kick from the mercenary knocked the gun clean from his hands. Firebird followed-up with a left hook to the jaw, knocking Daunhauer to the ground.

Another rebel stepped forward and aimed a rifle at his face. Firebird threw himself at the rebel and grabbed the gun by the barrel, shifting it toward the sky. A few shots ripped into the air before he slammed the barrel into the Rebel's face. Still holding on, he pulled the gun back and bludgeoned him again, bloodying the rebel's face.

Another appeared to the right. Still holding onto the rifleman, Firebird threw a kick, striking the companion in the chest. The rebel reeled backward, shooting plasma into the branches above.

Returning his attention to the man in front of him, Firebird hammered a fist on his gun hand, severing its grip from the gun. Now in possession of the weapon, he swung it like a club and struck the rebel in the head, driving him to the ground.

The other Rebels scattered as the mercenary fired from the hip, spraying plasma bullets wildly into the crowd. With the group distracted, he turned to run, only to see Lieutenant Daunhauer blocking his path. He held a knife in his hand, the blade angled toward the merc. Aiming for his midsection, Donnelly thrust the knife. Firebird swept the gun barrel across his body, deflecting the blade.

"Seems like everyone's out to piss me off today," he said. Placing one foot ahead of the other, he spun counterclockwise, shifting his weight and cocking his left foot. Using the momentum of the spin, he plowed a kick into Daunhauer's chest, driving him to the ground for a second time.

Firebird started his retreat. Unfortunately, the delay caused by Daunhauer had allowed the others to rearrange their formation. Several rifle shots zipped past him. Each one grew nearer. Firebird zigzagged, but the terrain ahead made it difficult to run smoothly.

He yelled out as a fiery hot blast struck his leg, dropping him. He rolled twice, bumping over roots and busted branches, losing the gun in the process. Groaning in pain, he brought his hand down to his leg. The plasma had ripped a hole through his hamstring, singeing the surrounding tissue. He contorted in pain, listening to the numerous footsteps approaching him.

The woman leader stepped up along with several other rebels. One of them, vengeful for being shot at, slammed his rifle down on the mercenary. Another followed with a kick to the side, while Daunhauer, bruised and bleeding, stomped a foot down on the injured leg. Firebird yelled out and writhed.

Albright cooled her weapon, ready to execute the useless prisoner who had nearly given the Sovereignty so much power. As it did, they heard several gunshots from the outskirts of the forest.

She snapped her fingers at Daunhauer. "Go. Get the doctor. I've got this prick," she said.

****

Running as fast as he could, Donnelly squeezed the trigger at the target. A barrage of plasma energy sprayed into the forest.

Saegusa was only a few meters from the tree. A thick gathering of trees blocked her way, the space between them filled by enormous thorn bushes. She ducked as several shots whizzed past her.

A hot blast of energy grazed her left shoulder, sending her into a spin. Saegusa cried out as the flesh along her upper arm burned. She crouched low and pointed the revolver. She only managed to catch glimpses of the shooter. He was advancing quickly, firing behind trees and bushes.

She followed his movements with the muzzle of her gun and fired back. Four shots blasted away before the cylinder emptied. It took several more empty clicks of the trigger before her frantic mind realized she needed to reload. She removed the cylinder and slid the ejector rod, removing the empty cartridges before slamming in a fresh speed-loader. Clicking the cylinder back in place, she realized Stuart was nowhere to be seen.

The droid circled wide, trying to work his way around. He armed his tasers, which had adequately recharged. After trekking between some thick terrain, he spotted the gunman about twenty yards ahead. He reared up, opening his ports to stun him.

Before he could fire, a volley of plasma fire whipped by him. Two of them passed by his underside, grazing his exoskeleton and damaging the taser rods. The droid scuttled back, avoiding another group of plasma blasts. Unable to repel them, he moved, keeping low and silent until he was out of sight.

The Rebels swarmed the edge of the forest, surrounding Saegusa. She trembled nervously, overwhelmed by the numerous armed men that approached. She swept the gun barrel from left to right, then back again.

"Don't...I'll shoot," she said.

The group laughed except for Donnelly.

"She's serious," he announced. The laughter gradually faded.

The team leader stepped forward. She pointed the gun at him and cocked the lever.

Daunhauer stopped and shook his head. "Tisk tisk tisk." He extended his arm. "There's no getting out of this, ma'am."

"Wanna place a bet on that?" Saegusa said.

"You can fire all six rounds if you want, and you'll still be outnumbered." He reached out slowly, touching his fingers to the revolver. She shook, unsure if she wanted to squeeze the trigger. Feeling defeated, she allowed it to slip from her hands.

Daunhauer uncocked the lever and examined the weapon. As he did, another rebel grabbed at her pouch.

"What's in this, lady?"

Saegusa rammed an elbow into his nose, driving him backward. She stepped away, tucking the pouch behind her.

"These are my samples. You're not getting these," she said.

"Let it be," Daunhauer ordered his men. He continued checking out the revolver. "Haven't seen one of these in a while. You've taken good care of this thing, considering how old it is."

"It's not mine. It's Firebird's." She stopped and looked around, realizing he wasn't anywhere to be seen. "Where's Firebird?"

"Firebird?"

"The merc?"

"Oh, him…the General's taking care of him. Don't worry. You'll be coming with us."

"Fat chance," Saegusa said. She stepped back, only to collide with a rebel standing directly behind her. Without warning, he bearhugged her. His arms clasped around her waist, he lifted her off the ground.

"Speak for yourself, Miss Saegusa," Daunhauer said. "The General has use for you. Consider this your lucky day."

"No!" Saegusa yelled. She screamed in agonized frustration. She should have shot the bastard. She tried to strike the rebel carrying her, but the man was strong, and had angled her up on his shoulder, making it nearly impossible to reach back.

Daunhauer noticed Donnelly. The young Lieutenant was looking uncharacteristically incensed, watching Saegusa get carried off.

"You okay there?" Daunhauer said. Donnelly took a deep breath and glanced at his rifle.

"Look at what she's done to us," he said.

Daunhauer nodded and watched Saegusa get carried off. "She's a tough cookie, I'll give her that."

"No…the General," Donnelly said. "She should've gotten in touch with General Drake back at the ship. We should've connected with reinforcements." Daunhauer stared at him a second time. The rebel, having calmed down a bit, no longer looked angered. Instead, he looked ashamed. So much so, that he was on the brink of tears. "Captain Collins took one in the chest from that revolver you're holding there. He's dead. And I just…lost it. I was gonna blow her head off, had you guys not gotten here in time."

"Once we get what we need, you can blow her head off," Daunhauer said. Donnelly looked at him in disgust.

"Is this what we do now?"

"We do what it takes to win," Daunhauer said. "General Albright understands this."

"She just lost her son," Donnelly said. "I don't think she's in a position to make decisions."

"What are you saying?" Daunhauer said. He stood nose-to-nose with Donnelly. Donnelly watched the Recon Specialist's eyes flare. He looked at the young Lieutenant as though he was a traitor.

Donnelly grew nervous. He took a brief moment to keep his thoughts collected and not backtrack on his point.

"I'm saying she's compromised by grief," Donnelly said. "I don't like this talk of *using* the doctor. I think the General is going too far with her actions."

"Let me explain something to you," Daunhauer said. "We're fighting a war, which means to win, we have to do some things that might not seem very, let's just say *moral*. General Albright understands this. She knows that to win, we have to…"

He stopped as a loud mechanical hum filled his ears. The air was filled with the sound of turning wheels and clattering engines. Among those mechanical vibrations were the thuds of boots on the ground. Then all at once, the edge of the forest flashed as plasma blasts filled the space between the trees.

CHAPTER 14

Daunhauer and Donnelly ducked and retreated deep into the forest. Sovereign Strikers, at least forty of them, stormed the tree line. Behind them, a T-27 turret fired into the woods. Plasma blasts filled the forest, cutting through anything in their path. Trees splintered and toppled, catching aflame as they hit the ground.

"Go! Get out of here!" Daunhauer yelled. The rebels scattered. With at least four of their team killed in the skirmish with the Razors, they were overwhelmingly outnumbered. He fired back into the invading force before ducking behind the base of a tree. Everywhere he looked, he saw hot energy soaring by. Smoke twirled from various impacts. Trees and other plants burst into flaming bits of sawdust. In moments, the sounds of gunfire were joined by the distressed screams of soldiers caught in the wake.

The rebel holding Saegusa stumbled as he tried fleeing from the Sovereignty, still holding her over his shoulder. Saegusa yelped as a hot streak of energy zipped by her head. Adrenaline ran fast through her bloodstream. The rebel stumbled again, angling to the side as he steadied himself.

Saegusa seized the opportunity and twisted her body, loosening his grip. With her hip on his shoulder, she rotated toward him and brought her knee up into his face. The rebel fell to his knees, dropping the doctor. Holding on tight to her pouch, Saegusa ran as fast as she could into the woods.

"Shit...SHIT!" Daunhauer growled as he watched her escape. He couldn't fail the General like this. He ran from cover in pursuit, crossing the paths of rifle fire as he ran into the forest.

General Albright had her rifle pressed against Firebird's forehead. Her rebels had continued stomping on him to keep him from escaping. The one who took the most pleasure in doing so was Jones. The color had returned to his face, though his neck was thoroughly bruised. The mercenary yelled as he stepped down hard on his injured leg, grinding his boot into the burn. He stepped back, waiting to watch his General rupture the enemy's skull.

It was then they heard the gunshots. Plasma passed by, causing the rebels to duck and scatter.

"What the hell?" Abright grumbled. She looked up to see the invasion of Strikers.

Firebird kicked up with his good leg, striking the General in the knee. Albright twisted and fell, landing on her hands and knees. She turned to point the rifle back at the mercenary, only for his metal arm to grasp it at the muzzle and redirect her shots upward.

"Hate to hit a lady...but..."

Firebird plowed a right hook into her jaw, knocking Albright backward. With her rifle in hand, Firebird turned to the right as Jones moved toward him and rammed the stock into his groin. The large rebel grunted and folded over. Firebird kicked high, catching him in the nose. As the rebel fell backward, Firebird stood up to his feet and started to flee.

The nerves in his left leg flared with each step. Firebird grimaced and kept going, limping heavily as he raced into the woods.

Chaos engulfed the forest. The air boiled and steam swelled into the canopy. The Strikers pressed inward, driving the rebels back.

Zolnar followed the frontlines into the trees, watching with glee as his men cut through the thin rebel forces. A few return shots claimed the lives of some of his Strikers, but it was nothing that caused great concern. He was moments away from completing his objective; thus, being looked at with great favor from the Supreme Leader.

"Disperse!" he yelled.

The Strikers broke formation and swarmed the forest. Serrated bayonets glistened from their rifle barrels. Some of the rebels retreated. Those who stayed behind were quickly overpowered.

The forest edge became a disarray of gunshots and soldiers clashing hand-to-hand. Strikers converged like bees, easily overpowering rebel soldiers and thrusting bayonets into them.

Hot energy singed his arm as Donnelly sprinted. Looking back, he watched two of his brave comrades attempt to make a stand, only to be driven backward by numerous Strikers. They plunged down with their blades, only to pull out and plunge again. As the life left their victims, they continued into the trees.

Rebels from Albright's group took firing positions, catching several Strikers off guard. The General herself looked mad with rage. She held a pistol in hand and joined the fray, quickly putting an energy blast between the eyes of a Striker.

Jones threw his shuriken into the throat of another. As the target collapsed in a bloody display, the thirty-plus remaining troops took cover, uncertain as to how many rebels were engaging. Several of them started circling from the sides. Albright could see the black figures weaving between the trees. It was a buffalo horn formation. Zolnar was a scholar in military history, and he was undoubtedly taking a page out of the playbook of the Zulu tribes in Africa.

She looked around. In addition to herself, there were maybe eight rebels left in her squad. If they stayed here, that number would soon be reduced to zero. Watching the movements again, there were only a few soldiers to the north.

If we move now, we can break through, she thought.

"I got this," Jones said. He knew what she was planning. The recon expert sported two Plasma Rifles that he had found and began laying suppressive fire from a thick cluster of trees. The space between them was covered in bushes, allowing him to shoot while remaining unseen. From the perspective of the main group of Strikers, it looked like multiple shooters.

"Damn it," she muttered. She stood up and yelled to the squad, "To your nine! Go! Go! Go!"

Jones laid down cover fire, killing at least two Strikers as the rebels fled. Albright led the charge with Donnelly. They blasted the few Strikers in their path, killing them. Jones watched through the bushes and aimed his rifle at some Strikers who attempted to pursue. His rifle shots were perfectly timed, hitting each target in the head. Helmets ripped open, releasing a large misty display. It was enough to keep other followers crouched low. He continued shooting, keeping the Sovereignty back long enough for Albright to escape.

****

Saegusa didn't dare to look back as she ran. The terrain dipped into a small hill, which caused her to gain momentum. As she moved deeper into the woods, she could still hear the cracks of rifles discharging. Though numerous, she noticed there weren't nearly as many stray shots passing by. She was making distance.

She watched the ground to avoid any tripping hazards as she hustled down the hill. Finally, she looked up. A world of black awaited her. Black, rotted trees, extended over an equally black mushy ground. The Black Forest.

Saegusa stumbled to a halt. She balanced herself and began to catch her breath. She barely had a moment to think before the sound of running footsteps caused her to turn around.

Daunhauer leapt like a leopard and tackled her to the ground. Saegusa felt the pouch fling from her arm as she fell. Daunhauer pinned her, his face almost red from the heavy activity.

"You're not getting away," he warned. "Either you come with us, or I'll twist that pretty neck of yours around and take that chip out of your head myself. Either way, you're not going with the Sovereignty. Make your ch—AGH!"

Saegusa brought his warning to a close with a knee to the groin. With one arm free, she raised her elbow to his chin, knocking him upward and allowing her enough space to bring her feet under his stomach and propel him backward. With him off of her, she got up and ran to her pouch.

The pouch had opened as it fell, spilling her vials of Radialem all over the place. She couldn't leave them. Her entire journey teetered on these samples getting to the lab. Peeking into the open bag, only two remained, meaning six others were lost. Three of them were close by. She scooped them up and placed them in the bag and scoured the area for the others.

Daunhauer crawled to his feet, enraged. He had been struck too many times today, first from the contractor, now the doc. His groin was throbbing. Being in hundreds of fights, that area was no stranger to being hit, but not with the increased velocity of a cybernetic leg.

The gunfire behind him was a reminder that they had limited time. He removed the revolver from his belt with the intent to pistol-whip her. He stood up and raised the weapon back.

Hearing his movements, Saegusa jumped away, dodging his strike.

"I'm done playing games," Daunhauer said. "You have any idea what we've been through! If you did, you'd hand yourself over."

"What *you've* been through," Saegusa said. "You think you're the only one who's had a rough life. You think I've had it easy? Why do you think I've acquired all this machinery?!"

"All I care about is what you've acquired inside that head of yours," Daunhauer said. "Now, I'll give you one more chance. Easy way...or hard way..."

Saegusa took another step back, feeling her hair brushing against a low hanging branch. In her peripheral vision, she saw the leaves extending from it. Near the end, dangling inches from her head, was a mutated leaf, filled with corrosive acid.

Daunhauer raised the revolver again and began to move in. Saegusa reached high and grabbed the leaf by its stem, snapping it loose. She could feel the soft skin of the leaf rippling as the acid swayed inside. She tossed it like a softball. It struck Daunhauer's face and exploded, spraying acid about.

The Recon Specialist clutched his face and yelled as the acid started eating into his skin. Smoke billowed from between his fingers. Dropping the revolver, he dashed off into the woods out of Saegusa's view, trailing smoke as he went. He pressed his hands to his face, only to retract them as the acid started to burn his palm. He blindly fumbled at his belt for his canteen.

He continued running blind, overcome with unbearable pain. His foot hit a piece of debris, causing him to trip and fall. Rolling on his back, the rebel groaned. His hands felt along his belt, feeling his holster, ammo packs, then finally his canteen. He yanked it free and opened it, then felt the cool wave of water washing over his face.

Saegusa combed the ground, finding two more vials. She placed them back into the pouch. One to go.

"Where the hell is it?" she muttered. She moved back and forth, overturning branches and dried leaves in search of it. She froze, hearing more approaching footsteps. She tensed, not with fear, but with rage. She was tired of being chased. She reached up and grabbed another Radialem leaf, then spun back and threw it with all of her might.

"Whoa! Holy shit!" Firebird exclaimed, leaning right to dodge the leaf.

"Oh!" Saegusa put a hand over her face. "Sorry."

"Yeah, right," he said. Saegusa noticed him limping as he approached. His pantleg was soaked in blood and charred.

"Oh, God, you're hurt," she said.

"Don't have time to worry about that," he said. He looked back and forth. "Where's Stuart?"

"I don't know. He took a hit where the second group cornered me. I don't know if he's still functioning."

"Damn it." He watched her search the forest floor. "What are you doing?"

"I dropped my samples!" she said. "I found most of them but one's still missing."

"It's right there," Firebird said, pointing at the ground past her. Saegusa turned around. With the situation being so frantic, she hadn't even thought of looking into the edge of the Black Forest. She crossed the border and collected the vial. As she returned, Firebird picked up the revolver and handed it back to her. "I told you to take special care of this."

"Sorry...I, uh..."

"Gotta go. Can't stay here." Firebird took her by the hand and pulled her back up the hill.

****

Jones squeezed off another barrage of plasma before one of his rifles finally overheated. Billowing smoke from its frame, the weapon would be useless for several minutes. With the Sovereignty closing in, a few minutes was a lifetime. Thus, the weapon was useless.

Down to one rifle, he sprayed several more shots, while keeping an eye to the north. Albright's team was out of sight. He could only hope they made enough distance to evade the Strikers. He fired again, hitting another Striker between the eyes, then sprinted away.

Zolnar could see the rebel retreating. He groaned, realizing that the bastard was alone and had diverted his squad's attention. General Albright and her band of filth was nowhere to be seen.

"Kill that son of a bitch," he ordered. He ran along with his Strikers and swarmed after Jones. He pulled a radio from his belt. "Target-Seekers, keep watch over the forest perimeter. Our target might attempt to make a break for it. If you spot her, DO NOT FIRE. I want her alive. It is imperative she be captured."

Jones aimed the rifle back over his shoulder and sprayed several shots aimlessly as he ran. He came to the summit of a hill and retreated down. Hopping over branches and various other hazards, he quickly made it halfway down.

"Oh, shit," a voice called out.

Jones stopped and looked directly ahead. At the bottom of the hill stood the contractor, and beside him was the doctor. Jones turned the muzzle of his rifle, ready to shoot. But as he prepared to aim, he noticed that the contractor wasn't watching him but staring past him, at the onslaught of enemies gathering at the top of the hill.

Zolnar joined his men at the crest of the hill, intent on being the one to shoot the lone Rebel. He looked down, seeing the human filth standing halfway down the hill. Standing several feet past him was the objective, standing near the mercenary known as Firebird.

"By the Gods, the Rebels didn't get her," he said to himself.

Jones felt a cold sweat on his brow as he realized that the Sovereignty was within seconds of capturing Saegusa. It was critical enough that they failed to capture her themselves. If the Sovereignty got her, the war effort would be obsolete.

He turned around and opened fire, hitting at least two Strikers before Zolnar and his squad opened up. His body danced in place as a series of energy shots punched through him.

As the energy blasts tore Jones to pieces, Firebird and Saegusa turned back and retreated, avoiding several strays of hot green. Up above, Zolnar directed his men after them. The Strikers charged down the hill, bayonets pointed forward.

"I want the girl ALIVE!" Zolnar announced, his voice echoing through the trees. Those echoes reached Saegusa's ears as she followed the mercenary through the forest.

Firebird groaned constantly. The pain in his leg was unrelenting. His flesh still felt as though it were sizzling. He wasn't sure how deep the plasma cut into him, but there was no doubt it had damaged much of the muscle tissue.

Saegusa ran alongside him, keeping an eye on him as they went. His body dipped with each step on that leg. It didn't take a medical degree to know he was on the verge of collapsing. She leaned in as she noticed his weight shift on the next step, catching him over her right shoulder as he started to fall.

"You can't keep running," she said. Firebird glanced back to the sound of approaching footsteps.

"Don't have much choice," he said. He stood himself up again and limped as fast as he could.

"They're everywhere," Saegusa said. "There's nowhere for us to go."

Firebird looked ahead at the valley of black.

"There's one place."

Saegusa looked at the Black Forest. Realizing where he was indicating, she shook her head. Her mind flashed to the image of that...whatever it was...that stalked them earlier.

"Oh, no...you're not thinking we..."

"Come on!" he interrupted her. Taking her by the wrist, he pulled her over the edge of the rotting section of forest. The repugnant smell hit them instantaneously. The ground felt wet and loose with each step. The doctor applied her thermal vision to look out for any lifeforms.

"Hey!"

Firebird yanked her off to the side. She pulled her wrist back.

"What the hell?"

Firebird pointed at what appeared to be a long, twirling tree trunk. It stood fifteen feet high without branches. Vines clung to the bark, appearing like veins. Looking closely, she noticed a slight pulsation taking place in those vines. There was no need to ask the merc what this was. She knew what she needed to know: It was no ordinary tree.

They could hear the Strikers closing in behind them.

"Keep going," Firebird said.

The Strikers converged on the edge of the Black Forest. All at once, they looked back at Zolnar. Though he couldn't see their faces through their masks, he could picture the rare display of cowardice in their eyes. Nobody dared to venture into the Black Forest. Nobody.

"What are you waiting for?" the Commander yelled.

"Sir," the Striker Lieutenant approached him. "The mutations...the rasilisks!"

"You damn coward," Zolnar growled. He pulled his pistol and squeezed the trigger, shooting the Lieutenant through the eye. The Strikers surrounding the ill-fated Lieutenant jumped back as the gunshot rang out. They watched as his lifeless body dropped to the ground. Zolnar watched his soldiers with distain, sweeping the crowd with his pistol. His warning was clear: Either pursue the cyborgs into the Black Forest or share the Lieutenant's fate.

He halted his muzzle on one Striker, who stood next to the Lieutenant's corpse. This Striker was the only one who didn't jolt from the unexpected gunshot. The only one who didn't outwardly display cowardice.

"Congratulations. You've just been promoted," Zolnar said to him.

It was both a promotion and a warning. The newly promoted Lieutenant could read between the lines. Either lead these troops into the forest or face the same punishment as his predecessor.

"Yes Commander," the Striker Lieutenant called out. "Everybody on me." He shouldered his rifle and marched into the Black Forest, followed by twenty-five of his comrades.

The air was wet and thick. Though the sun shined bright through the rest of the forest, it seemed nonexistent here, despite the fact that the trees were void of leaves. A heavy mist formed up at the canopy, creating a fog that lasted twenty-four hours a day. Each tree looked like the classic image from a haunted house story: bare of leaves, limbs outstretched, black.

Firebird and Saegusa were nowhere to be seen. The area was quiet and still. Using hand signals, the new Lieutenant directed several of his troops outward, branching the unit out to conduct a proper sweep pattern. After a few moments, there was ten feet of space between each soldier. Mud splashed as they hustled, with some keeping back to patrol alongside Commander Zolnar. Without saying a word, they pressed forward.

The air seemed to thicken as they went. They began to sweat under their masks. The humidity was very high, making their suits feel sticky. Nobody dared to say a word about this. Nor did they dare to speak at all. Between the rumored horrors of the Black Forest and the wrath of their Commander, they were between a rock and a hard place.

The Lieutenant carefully watched along his rifle sights. His finger rested on the trigger guard, ready to spring into place when necessary. The forest seemed void of life. His mind began to play tricks on him. Every shadow seemed to taunt him. Every shape and twist of the tree limbs appeared like a large beast ready to lash at them. And the smell...even the masks couldn't filter it out. It was the smell of rot and death. Death was the word that kept echoing in his mind. No doubt, many things had died here.

He glanced down to the base of a nearby tree. The ground was hollow near the exposed roots...like a caved-in entrance to a tunnel. There was a near-perfect circle of mud that looked more gravely and discolored than the ground around it, as though it had been dug out and shoveled back in. The Lieutenant didn't trust it. He walked wide of the strange soil and signaled for the nearby Strikers to do the same.

The nearest Striker moved right to avoid that tree. Like the Lieutenant, he had seen the suspicious hollow area. He kept his eyes on it as he moved past, before directing his gaze forward. Another tree was directly in his path. At least, he couldn't think of any other name for it. There were no branches on this tree. Rather, it resembled a log standing up on end. He stood about five feet from it, staring at the pulsating vines that wrapped around its trunk.

He felt the hairs on his neck rise. There was a wet, slithery sound at his feet. Then there was the tightening around his leg. The Striker yelled out, drawing the attention of his comrades.

The Lieutenant and several others gathered around him.

It moved like a snake in its attack. Yet, there was no head. The texture, though flexible, appeared wooden.

"Get him out," the Lieutenant ordered. Several men pulled on the soldier while he and a few others aimed their rifles at the ground and fired. Mud splattered and steam trailed high in the air.

Like tentacles from an underground Kraken, several more roots raised high. They lashed at the intruders, driving them away from the trapped soldier. One soldier remained and continued pulling him free, only to be lashed across the face from these bizarre tentacles. He fell backward, his mask cracked.

The trapped Striker screamed as more tentacles wrapped round his legs and waist. Slowly and torturously, they pulled him to the base of the tree. Something under him lifted through the wet soil. It was a large mass, dark green in color, shaped like a coffin.

Zolnar watched as a slit opened up in the middle of this pod. The Striker yelled as the tentacles pulled him inside. The pod sealed tight and sank back into the earth.

Gunshots rang out and the darkness flickered with green flashes of plasma energy. Some of the soldiers converged on this so-called tree and blasted away at the trunk. Bark and wet inner tissue exploded. The pulsating quickened, as though the thing was in pain. The tentacles lashed out again, this time like actual whips, striking the soldiers and driving them backward.

Meanwhile, the Striker's screams echoed from under the ground.

"Get away from that thing!" Zolnar ordered. "Get ahold of yourselves! Lieutenant! Get them in line!"

Not wanting to test the Commander's patience, the Lieutenant quickly got into action.

"Back away!" he yelled to the Strikers. "Leave it be. You can't help him. He's a dead man." The soldiers backed away, with those knocked to the ground scuttling backward on their hands and feet. The Lieutenant resumed the march, walking clear of the carnivorous trunk. Trying to inspire confidence from his Commander, he tried setting the example by leading the search. "Get up! Find the doctor. And for Godsake, don't stop to admire the scenery. Remember, we're not the only ones in these---" His words ended with a dumbfounded *Umpf* as he blindly walked into something. He looked forward and froze from sheer fright.

It stood over six feet. It had a basic shape like a man. But beyond having two arms and legs, there was nothing human about it. Its hide was black and scaly, with thorns protruding from the elbows, shoulders, back, and neck. Twelve-inch claws protruded from its hands like daggers.

But the worst feature was its face. Compared to the black of the rest of its body, its eyes were huge. They bulged from each side of its angular head. They were white, and bloodshot. The pupils didn't even seem to look at him. They just stared directly outward, motionless. Beneath those eyes was a closed mouth, baring enormous fangs. The mouth reminded him of photos he had seen in archives, of deep sea fish that lived in the bottom of the Pacific Ocean.

Both hands lunged out, penetrating both sides of his ribcage with its jagged claws. His scream was short-lived as his lungs deflated. The rasilisk opened its mouth and sank its jaws down between the Lieutenant's neck and shoulder. It pulled back, trailing strands of flesh.

The Strikers fanned out, with several of them discharging their weapons at the creature. The rasilisk turned and darted between the trees, carrying its prize with it.

Various rumblings passed under the ground. Zolnar watched the soil and the trees, pointing his pistol everywhere he looked. He could hear wet clawing sounds, though the fog made it difficult to see very far.

Something growled near one of the trees.

"Eight o'clock," he announced. He turned and fired a few shots. A few of the soldiers joined him and fired off a few rounds. The Commander held up a fist, signaling for them to cease fire. Taking each step cautiously, he moved in toward the sound.

Smoke swirled, mixing in with a gradually thickening fog around the tree where the sound originated. He waved his hands to blow away some of the smoke. The fog continued to thicken, as though new moisture was rising from the ground.

Zolnar stopped. Maybe it was.

He noticed a spot where he had noticed the hollow ground. Small mounds of soil were bunched up, as though pushed out, exposing the entrance of a small tunnel. From within, hot moisture lifted like steam from a cooling tower. The ground around it was marked with clawed footprints.

Zolnar looked back to his team, though he couldn't see them. The whole Black Forest was quickly being consumed with this fog. The Commander tensed. No way could this one vent fill up the entire forest this quickly.

In the blink of an eye, the air filled with the screams from numerous Strikers, along with the ravenous snarling from carnivorous beasts. Green flashes streaked through the clouds, generating several small explosions wherever the energy blasts struck. The Commander ducked as a few blindly fired shots streaked his way. They struck a tree somewhere behind and burst into arrays of sparks.

Zolnar got up and rushed in the direction of gunfire.

"Everybody re-group!" He yelled. "Move back to the tree line! Get to the—" He spun back as a rasilisk raced behind him, arms lashing at the nearest Striker. The soldier yelled briefly, his calls stunted as the claws punched through his abdomen. The beast raced into the fog, carrying the soldier away. Zolnar pointed his pistol and fired in the creature's direction, doubting he hit it.

Another soldier yelled. Behind him, a rasilisk reared up, its bloodshot eyes staring unblinkingly to the sides. Its claws sank into the Striker's neck. With a sudden twist, Zolnar heard the snapping of bones. The creature lifted its hands, pulling the soldier's head from his neck.

"Christ," Zolnar muttered. He fired his pistol. The first shot hit the rasilisk in its torso, sparking an ear-piercing screech as it darted into the fog. Zolnar shot several rounds after it, then scooped up the rifle from one of the dead soldiers.

Behind him was chaos. Strikers scattered wildly throughout the woods. Black humanoid figures darted in and out of view, their snarls vibrating all around. Claws ripped through Kevlar and flesh, inducing bloodcurdling screams.

Zolnar raced back, finding ravaged corpses of his men scattered about. The ground was red with their blood and innards. Uncoiled intestines laid outstretched from shredded stomachs. Zolnar continued, following the sound of gunshots. As they rang out, a rasilisk screamed. There was the splashing sound of blood spraying the ground, followed by the thud of a body.

The Commander stepped over bodies, making his way toward the sound. The gunshots were growing more distant, with fewer and fewer screams.

The hot smell of burnt plasma entered his nose. At his boots was another body, torn apart by the creatures. Zolnar signaled to the Striker accompanying him to hold still. They waited and listened. Feet were pounding the ground like drums. Each step was heavy, carrying something larger than a man. He aimed at his two o'clock and fired.

The flashes brought the frame of the rasilisk into view. The shots hit dead center, stopping its advance. Dark red blood ripped from its torso as chunks of flesh exploded off its body. The creature fell backward, flailing its arms and legs like an insect. Zolnar stepped closer to it and fired another blast through its eye.

More running footsteps approached, this time behind him. Zolnar spun on his heel and aimed. The figure appeared. It was a Striker, running as fast as he could with no weapon in hand.

Another figure appeared behind him. The Striker arched backward in pain as a claw punched through his back. The tip ripped through his chest like a spear, spraying blood out. Zolnar squeezed the trigger, hitting both the Striker and the rasilisk, spilling blood from both of them.

The rasilisk darted off with its prize. Somewhere off in the distance, another Striker yelled out. Those screams quickly ended, replaced by the sounds of tearing and clawing.

"HOLY--!" his fellow Striker yelled. A few shots left the muzzle of his rifle before another rasilisk sprang from the fog. Its claws embedded in his chest and neck and ripped outward, tearing him in two. The beast cried out as Zolnar sprayed its back with plasma fire. The plasma energy carved it open, exposing inner layers of tissue and blood. The creature turned around, still intent on killing the human injuring it. Zolnar aimed high and fired again, burning energy through its skull.

With his team dead or dying, Zolnar focused on himself. He would not be able to detect the mercenary and doctor through this forest. Not in this fog, with these creatures running about. It was impossible. He tensed with anger. They had led him into this trap, and he let it happen. He shot another round into the dead rasilisk's face, spilling charred brain matter into the dirt. Gathering his bearings, he turned to face the direction where they came.

****

With the chaos echoing behind them, Firebird and Saegusa crept back to the edge of the Black Forest. The Strikers' hesitation at the edge allowed them time to move southward, where they had crouched low in the bushes and waited for them to pass. With the dim lighting and the various other hazards, the Strikers passed by.

During the confusion in the clash with the creatures, they moved back to the edge, keeping a low profile to remain undetected. The border was instantly brighter. There was an instant feeling of relief as Saegusa stepped out of the Black Forest. Firebird limped over a small hill and guided her onward.

"What now?" she asked.

"We're not out of this yet," he said. "That wasn't all of their men. They've got armor up at the edge of the forest."

"How can we escape that?" she asked.

"That's where you'll come in handy," he said. "They won't shoot you. They're after you. We're gonna use that to our advantage." He tensed with each step on his left foot. He clutched the wound with one hand, feeling as though pressure would keep it from hurting.

"I don't know about this," Saegusa said. "You're hurt. You need to stop."

"Not exactly a good idea," he said. "Pain doesn't change the situation. You can rest assured there'll be more troops coming. If we don't move now, this leg will be the least of my worries."

Saegusa sighed nervously.

"What will you need me to do?"

"You're gonna run out of the trees and get their attention. All eyes will be on you. You're like a gold medal to anyone that catches you. Believe me, they won't be looking anywhere else. And while they're focused on you, I'll do the rest."

"What will you do?"

"Take the tank," he said. "We just need to…look out!" He pushed Saegusa down as a streak of energy flashed past them. He fired his rifle, eliminating the stray Striker. As the body fell, another Striker ran out from the Black Forest, just in time to see his comrade get shot down. Tracing the energy blasts back to Firebird and Saegusa, the Striker aimed his rifle and opened fire. Firebird ducked and rolled to the side, aggravating his leg in the process.

The shooting ceased, allowing Firebird to spring up to his knees to shoot. His aim was obscured with too many leaves and branches from the nearby trees. He shot anyway, tearing up the forest in front of him.

Return shots streaked his way, forcing him to duck again. His leg throbbed, making his movements stiff and rigid. Even the adrenaline couldn't dull the pain. With plasma passing overhead, he rolled back and found another area of cover. However, his movements rustled the branches that dangled overhead, alerting the Striker, who adjusted his aim accordingly.

Firebird kept low, unable to move without getting shot. Scowling with frustration, he felt along his vest for a grenade. As he prepared to yank the pin free, the firing stopped. He could hear the Striker grunting as though in a struggle. Firebird stood up and peeked through a small clearing.

The Striker was arched, his hands clutching at his throat. Behind him, Stuart stood on his hind legs, with one of his disabled forelegs wrapped around the soldier's throat. Pulling tight on it with his other two functioning legs, Stuart choked the soldier until his airway fully closed off. The world went to black and the soldier slumped.

Stuart released the unconscious Striker and hurried to Firebird and Saegusa. The mercenary placed the grenade back on his vest and stood up.

"Where the hell did you disappear to?"

"Apolog-gi-gies...sir," Stuart's voice system was wonky. "I've taken damage."

"I can see that," Firebird said. "Me too. Seems like we've invited a whole freaking circus to this forest."

"Stuart, can you keep going?"

"Ye-ee-sssss, Doctor. I will continue to assisss-sst you," Stuart said. He looked back at Firebird. "See-ee, sir? She's n-niiiice-ce to me."

"You just haven't had enough time to get on her nerves," Firebird said.

"I don't know. It only took you about thirty seconds," Saegusa replied.

"That's called charm," Firebird quipped.

Together, the group moved to the edge of the forest, passing through the battleground where the Sovereignty clashed with the Rebels. Bodies littered the ground with weapons by their sides.

"Ah ha!" Firebird said.

"What?" Saegusa asked. The mercenary kneeled by one of the dead Strikers and picked up a large weapon. It was shaped like a rifle, though its muzzle and frame were much wider. It was an I.N.T Plasma Caster.

"This might come in handy," he said. He held it by the handle on the top of its frame. They continued through the battleground. The air was grey with stilted smoke that lingered between the trees. It thinned as they approached the edge of the forest which led to the open plain.

The group of three crouched low to remain unseen. They watched as the two T-27 tanks patrolled back and forth on their tracks, patrolling the tree line. Between them were roughly ten ground troops. Up above, three Target-Seekers circled the sky. The spiraling elevators on their wings created a heavy downdraft that kicked up clouds of dust.

Firebird watched the nearest tank. It had stopped, its front facing the woods. Its turret rotated back and forth. The operator was likely bored. The mercenary studied the platform carefully, spotting the hatch. If it wasn't locked from the inside, he would have to use an explosive to blow it open. Eyeing the ground, he saw two soldiers directly between him and the tank. It would be a fifteen-meter run. Piece of cake, if there weren't hostiles in the way. Worse than that, there was air support. He'd have to be quick.

"Yeah...you're gonna have to distract them," he whispered to Saegusa.

The doctor glared at him. "You're really trying to amp up that *annoying* factor, aren't you?"

"I might be annoying, but I speak the truth," he said. "We're not getting anywhere with these patrols in the way. And I'm not gonna get them *out* of the way without taking one of those tanks. And I'm not gonna be able to take one of the tanks with all these assholes on the lookout. Plus, there are these birds in the air." He pointed up to the Target-Seekers.

"Damn it," Saegusa muttered. She put her face to the ground and sighed. The thought of willingly putting herself within reach of the Sovereignty was excruciating. If this plan didn't work, there'd be no escape, and her worst nightmare would be realized.

"His logic is sound," Stuart said. "They w-will not fire on you, no matter the circumstances. If you dis-distract them, we can overtake the tank and eliminate their forces and vacate before reinforce-force-ments arrive."

Saegusa looked up at the Sovereignty and allowed the courage to build within her.

"Okay...okay you're right."

"Oh, I see how it is," Firebird remarked. "You'll agree when *Spock* here explains it." Saegusa looked at him, puzzled.

"His name's Stuart," she said.

"Yeah, I..." Firebird facepalmed his forehead. "Nevermind."

CHAPTER 15

"Oh Lord," Saegusa muttered as she crept further south along the tree line. She moved silently, gaining over six hundred feet of distance from where the mercenary hid. As Firebird advised, she would have to make some distance in order to draw the unit's attention. She was now past the second tank, which was now patrolling north toward the other one. Walking beside it were two of the ten soldiers. They were much closer to the trees than the vehicles. She could hear them conversing among each other, clearly in a state of confusion. There had been no contact from Commander Zolnar.

Saegusa kept a low posture as she crept by, watching the soldiers the entire time. With her attention off her path, she never noticed the branch in her way until one of its arms snapped under her feet.

She froze. *Shit!*

The doctor ducked down beside some bushes and watched as the two soldiers gazed into the woods. After looking inward for several seconds, they stepped through the tree line. Her heart thumped hard as if about to erupt from her chest. Though they couldn't see her, they were unwittingly closing in on her location.

She waited in hopes that they would stop and turn back. Holding her breath, she watched. Twenty feet from where she crouched, they closed in. In her mind, she debated her options. Her thoughts scrambled into a series of curses directed at Firebird for putting her in this predicament.

Finally, the soldiers stopped. Saegusa remained still as a brick and watched through the bush. Her blood rushed as she thought they might finally turn back. Mouthing the words "go away" she waited. Her words made her realize that she wasn't mentally ready to make the run. She focused on her breathing and reminded herself it needed to be done.

The Strikers looked deep into the forest. One of them tried radioing Zolnar's team through the radio but did not get any response. They looked to each other and exchanged words. For a moment, it appeared they were about to turn back.

Then, taking a double take, one of them looked toward the bushes. Looking through the leaves, Saegusa found herself staring right at the Striker's mask, and him right back at her.

****

Groaning in pain, he wandered blindly, bumping into trees with each step. His hands and face were hot from the acid. Though the water from his canteen had stopped it from eating away at him, the pain continued to worsen, driving Daunhauer nearly to insanity.

Finding Jones' body, completely ravaged by plasma fire, worsened the effect. His friend and fellow Recon Specialist had fought alongside him for years. They had vowed to die side-by-side in glorious battle. But this didn't resemble a man fallen in battle. He was executed. Blasted away by over a dozen soldiers.

He could hear the screams of Sovereign soldiers in the Black Forest behind him as he stumbled. With his hands pressed to his face, he continued in silence. There was residual sound of gunfire echoing through the woods, though nothing compared to the all-out conflict that preceded it. He wasn't sure of the whereabouts of Beretta Albright and the others. He wasn't even sure how many of them were alive.

Each thought was broken by waves of pain in his face. Daunhauer kept moving, unsure what direction he was going. The vision in his left eye was blurry, while his right seemed unfazed. He looked at his palms. The flesh was red, the outer layers of skin burnt away. Near the ridge of his hands, between the thumbs and index fingers, the tissue damage was even worse. He could see the muscle tissue exposed, already gaining infection. He didn't even want to know how his face looked.

He kept going, feeling increasingly worn with each step. The sun grew brighter as he went. The smoke gradually cleared. Looking ahead, he realized he was approaching the edge of the forest. His ears picked up the sound of T-27s moving about. He felt along his belt for some grenades. In his fractured state of mind, he considered a suicide attack. He could run up to one of the tanks and detonate all of his grenades. It wouldn't be enough to destroy one, but it could at least damage the tracks or the rotational gears for the turret.

He was close enough to where he could see with his good eye. The silver metal of the tank shined in the sun several meters from the forest. There it was, his target. It was moving across, the men around it unsuspecting of his presence.

As he prepared to make his run, Daunhauer noticed something else. Movement. Somebody was in the woods nearby. He heard the snapping of a twig, then the sudden jerkiness of the figure as it ducked down. Daunhauer watched for a moment and studied the person.

In a heartbeat, his interest in the tanks disappeared. It was her: The DOCTOR! The one who scarred his face. The reason they had been through so much on this day. Whether or not it was her fault was irrelevant, not in this momentary psychotic state of mind. He would not let her get away, even if he had to break those mechanical legs off of her.

With his knife drawn, he silently approached. She was watching through the bush, completely unaware of his presence. As he neared, it dawned on him that she was watching something. At first, he assumed she was watching the patrols. Then, he saw the movement ahead. By the time he had seen the two Strikers, they had already spotted him.

They pointed rifles and fired.

****

Saegusa tensed as plasma fire streaked overhead.

"Logic is sound, my ass!" she groaned. She yanked the revolver and moved around the bush for a firing position. The Strikers hesitated. For a moment, they seemed to be looking past her. When they finally looked in her direction, their body language indicated that they didn't expect to see her there. She didn't put the thought together in her head until she squeezed the trigger, emptying all six rounds into the two of them.

The time to run was now.

Saegusa launched herself into a mad dash, scooping up one of the rifles in the process. What better way to gain their attention than to shoot up the garrison? She burst from the tree line, spraying plasma fire toward the now-alerted patrol.

As expected, the plan worked. She could hear the soldiers alerting to each other that the priority was on the move. The Target-Seekers passed overhead and started a circular formation. Their turrets pointed down at her, but she knew it was nothing more than an intimidation tactic.

Behind her, the tanks rotated their turrets toward her as the gunners watched the chase.

****

Firebird watched the soldiers give chase. Saegusa was a fast runner despite the damage to her leg. Plasma blasts flashed all over the place from the muzzle of her rifle, causing some of the soldiers to scatter as they pursued.

"Son of a bitch," he muttered, watching the tank directly ahead of him. Two soldiers remained. They stood still, watching the Target-Seekers as they followed the doctor. One stood just outside the trees, while the second was right beside the tank. If not for his leg injury and the damage to his gauntlet, he would be able to take them out quietly. But as luck would have it, he would have to go out guns blazing. Luckily, it was only two.

He sprang from cover and pointed the rifle. The first soldier looked toward him just in time to see the flash of his weapon. A spray of plasma fire burned through his mask and consumed his face. With his leg in agonizing pain, Firebird charged at the second Striker. The Striker had squeezed off a couple of shots that went wide before his chest was torn open by the plasma fire.

The tank started rotating its turret. Hot flame glowed at the twin barrels, blowing smoke as though from a dragon. Firebird ran to the nearest track and jumped onto the platform. He pulled himself all the way up and stood. The barrels were now directly over his head. He moved to the center of the platform, opened the hatch, and without even looking to see if anyone was below, he fired into the control room.

His shots burned into a Striker who stood at the base of the small ladder. As the soldier fell dead onto the floor, Firebird slid down the sidebars. Two other tank operators moved toward him, drawing pistols. Firebird struck the nearest one in the face with the butt of his rifle, throwing him into a spin. He grabbed the dazed Striker around the neck and pulled him close as the second one fired his pistol. The blasts struck the human shield.

With one hand, Firebird held the rifle like a pistol over the dying Striker's shoulder and shot the enemy in the face, burning the mask and any identity underneath it.

He could hear Stuart's footsteps clunking the hull. The droid pulled himself down through the hatch.

"It appears they left the hatch unlocked," he stated.

"Congratulations, you're a genius. Now, get on the wheel," Firebird said. The droid took the driver's seat and opened the ports to allow his internal arms to unfold. They took the throttle and began rotating the platform. Firebird took the gunner's seat and lowered the targeting mechanism. It came down from above like a telescope. Looking through it with his one eye, he watched the soldiers closing in on Saegusa. They were probably a thousand meters away, well within range of the guns.

But first, there was the other tank.

He lowered the guns, placing the second tank in the crosshairs. Aiming at the center platform where the neck of the gun attached, he opened fire. Hundreds of plasma blasts crossed the short distance in an instant. The tank turned red as it absorbed the heat. The thick metal slowly caved inward. The turret started to rotate back, only to stop part-way as the gears exploded.

"How do you like that?" Firebird said, watching the tank fall apart. Flakes of metal fell from the side. The hull was not as thick as the T-32s and had not been subjected to the Sovereignty's own heavy weapons until now. The port side fell apart, exposing the internal components and the Strikers inside.

Firebird squeezed the trigger again, turning the interior into a flaming heap.

He elevated the turret and locked on to one of the Target-Seekers. A thousand rounds of plasma struck the cockpit, fracturing the hull. The aircraft descended into a spin and smashed down. Its power cell ruptured and burst into a fiery blast.

****

A rush of wind and smoke hit Saegusa, driving her left. Her ears rang from the huge blast. She looked back, seeing another barrage of plasma colliding with another one of the Target-Seekers. They struck head-on with the cockpit, ripping through into the fuselage. It fell into the tailspin and exploded upon hitting the ground, throwing shrapnel all around.

Another shockwave swept through the plain, engulfing Saegusa with smoke and dust. She staggered back, struggling to keep her balance. As she did, she switched to her thermal vision, seeing the body signatures from the Strikers through the dust cloud.

Taking advantage of the confusion, she pointed her plasma rifle and fired. She watched the nearest orange shape twist in agony and drop to the ground. She fired again, hitting the next one. And the next.

Another shockwave rippled under her feet. This one was smaller than the last two. A wall of orange expanded in her thermal vision about a thousand meters away. Looking above, she realized the third Target-Seeker was still hovering. It moved side-to-side, avoiding plasma fire.

"Oh, no..." she muttered, realizing the heat signature was from the tank exploding.

****

"Son of a dick!" Firebird yelled. The last Target-Seeker waved side-to-side, evading his shots. Its forward cannons charged and fired, hitting the tank's starboard side. Firebird and Stuart rocked in their seats as the tank tilted to port and fell back.

"In biology, sir, it would make sense that every son was originally conceived…" Stuart said.

"Shut up, bot! It's a figure of speech!" Firebird snapped. He put his eye back to the targeting viewer and tilted the joystick. The turret was still functional, though the joints grinded audibly. He spotted the Target-Seeker charging up another blast.

It moved to starboard, successfully evading his next volley of shots. Firebird scowled and adjusted his aim.

"Okay, you freaking clay pigeon, I see how it is," he said. He fired another stream of plasma and immediately rotated the turret to starboard. The Target-Seeker maneuvered again as he expected, right into his next line of fire. He fired again, this time hitting it dead center in the cockpit. The cannons detonated as it crashed down, expanding into a huge fiery ball of plasma.

Sparks sprayed the control room. Stuart checked the mechanics and conducted a diagnostic.

"We need a new plan of escape, sir," he said. "This tank's not going anywhere."

"Just our luck," Firebird muttered.

"Not luck," Stuart said. "You were just too slow at shooting down all three Target-Seekers. And your aim was poor with the third one. Otherwise, we could've continued on in this T-27 and retreated to the border."

Firebird stared at the droid.

"I swear, if there wasn't a gaping hole in my leg, I'd—" Several more sparks flashed from the starboard instruments, interrupting his threat. Firebird stumbled away from the flares. "Let's get the hell out of here."

"Do we know the whereabouts to Ms. Saegusa?" Stuart asked. Firebird pressed his eye to the targeting visor again. He lowered the turret and saw the doctor several hundred yards out. She was moving between two of the wreckages and was firing her pistol at another Striker. Six or seven of them were scattered across the field and were running for the trees.

Firebird adjusted the turret. The mechanisms were slow to respond due to the damage. He could hear the rotator grinding above him. He panned left and lowered the barrels. The first of the soldiers entered the tree line. Unable to target them, he focused on the stragglers trailing behind.

Before he pulled the trigger, he noticed two more off to the side. These tenacious Strikers continued to chase after Saegusa. They fired off several shots, clearly aiming low to get her legs.

"Loyal to the cause, I see," Firebird muttered. He rotated the barrels ten degrees starboard and targeted the Strikers. He discharged the firing mechanism and watched the two figures evaporate into a red cloud of dust. He panned back to the other soldiers, seeing the stragglers entering the forest.

"Shall we pursue them?" Stuart asked.

"Not necessary," Firebird said. "They've learned their lesson." He moved up the ladder out of the tank. The toxic fumes hit him as he exited the hatch. The tank was burning on the outside, its power cell leaking. He waved his hands to brush the smoke out from around him as he stepped off the platform. The air cleared a bit as he stepped further away from it.

From another plume of smoke, he saw Saegusa approaching. She kept her weapon gripped with both hands. Her movements were sluggish. She was ready to lie down for some real rest.

The group gathered between the sparkling wreckages of Target-Seekers.

"I need a beer," Saegusa said, breathing heavily.

"I had some on the Ash-Cloud. Damn Sovereign pricks, that's another thing they cost me," Firebird griped. He kicked a small piece of wreckage and watched it roll. The disk-shaped piece of metal rolled on its edges and settled near the engine of a carrier truck. "Hmm…I think we've found our ride."

The three of them approached the truck. It had taken a bit of damage from the explosives. The frame was chipped, the windshield cracked along the top, and there were several indentations along the compartment. However, it appeared to be functional. Firebird climbed into the driver's seat and started the engine. It came to life as though it were brand new.

Saegusa moved around to the passenger side.

"Ah-ah, you sit in the back," Firebird said to her.

"What?"

"We're cutting across hostile territory. Right now, nobody's looking for a stolen carrier truck. But if anyone sympathetic to the Sovereignty sees you through the window, we're toast. So…back in the compartment."

"I shall accompany you," Stuart said.

"She's not your type," Firebird quipped.

"I'm am not seeking to court the doctor. I need the space to conduct repairs…"

"Yes, yes! I figured," Firebird said. Stuart followed Saegusa to the rear of the truck. "The damn droid can make sarcasm but can't receive it." He leaned back in his seat and waited for them to climb in. "Sounds like most people I know."

CHAPTER 16

Daunhauer could hear the footsteps of several Strikers entering the forest. He held his knife close while he remained in the shadows. He had nearly chased Saegusa out into the field, only to be held back by the overwhelming pain. Right when he thought he had lost the doctor to the Sovereignty, all hell had broken loose yet again. Their own tank fired on them, destroying their aircraft and secondary armored unit. He hid back into the woods and awaited the soldiers that approached.

He watched with one good eye, while gripping his knife with his blistering hand. He counted five soldiers. The first two were several feet ahead of the others. Daunhauer crouched low and let them pass. In their frantic retreat, they never noticed him behind the bushes.

Two more passed by, with the fifth a few feet behind them. His nerves throbbed in his face. His mind was a hurricane of vengeful thoughts. He wanted anyone associated with the death of Jones to be punished. The fact that these soldiers were Sovereign made it even more pleasant to kill them up close.

The final Striker began to pass by. Daunhauer lunged from his hiding spot, tearing through the bush. Leaves and twigs exploded as he caught the unsuspecting Striker by the neck and stabbed him in the chest.

Throwing the soldier to the ground, he quickly turned and attacked the next two Strikers. His movements had been so quick, they were only just starting to turn around by the time he closed the distance. He slashed one across the throat and kicked him in the chest, driving him back into a tree. The other raised his rifle, only to have it slammed against his face. Daunhauer raised his knife and stabbed down deep into the Striker's neck.

He yanked it free and dove behind another tree, avoiding the gunfire from the first two Strikers. As their comrade succumbed to his injuries, they started to circle the tree where Daunhauer crept. They continued firing as they worked their way into position in hopes of keeping him pinned down.

The one on the left finally moved in, while the other provided cover. The Striker slowly worked around the tree then sprang, firing several rounds where the rebel had dived. A cloud of dirt and leaves swirled from the impact craters. The rebel was nowhere to be seen.

His partner waited, equally dumbfounded at the realization that the enemy was nowhere to be seen. He started to look around. Every swaying branch alarmed him. He felt the presence of the enemy all around. He turned around, seeing nothing. He looked left and right. Still nothing.

Then out of nowhere, Daunhauer sprang and drove the blade deep into the Striker's chest. He was a Recon Specialist with expert knowledge of the land. Sneaking around these bozos was an easy task for him, even with his injuries. He wrestled the dying soldier to the ground and finished him off by stabbing him through the eye. He rolled away as the final remaining soldier shot at him.

Ducking around another tree, he gripped his knife by the blade. Several shots hit the tree behind his back, warming the bark. He took a deep breath to concentrate through the pain, then leapt from cover. A few more shots missed him. He landed in a crouched position and threw the knife.

The Strikers yelled out and spun, firing wildly into the forest. Daunhauer watched as he steadied himself. The knife handle stuck out of his left shoulder. A severe injury, but not fatal. Holding the rifle in one hand, the Striker pointed the muzzle at him again.

Daunhauer reached down to grab the rifle from the dead soldier nearby. His fingers barely touched the weapon as numerous rifle shots discharged. He shuddered, thinking he had moved too slowly. Then he saw the Striker dancing in the midst of numerous energy flashes that engulfed his body. He hit the ground with smoke billowing from his corpse.

Daunhauer glanced to his right. Beretta and seven other rebels approached through the woods. There was Donnelly, who walked like a man three times his age. He looked ill. Demoralized. Hell, Barber looked more energized, and he actually was twice his age. Though Barber had seen better days as well. As had the rest of the unit. Especially Beretta Albright.

The General lent a hand and helped Daunhauer up to his feet. She was shocked at the horrible scarring on his face. So much of the skin had been burnt off, giving Daunhauer an almost demonic appearance. Much of it was condensed on the left, creating a gaping wound in his cheek that exposed some teeth. The acid had even burnt away his eyelid and mildly scarred the eye itself. He would need treatment or risk serious infection.

"To say you look like hell would be an understatement," she said.

"I'm fine," he muttered. His voice was broken. Spit shot through his cheek as he spoke.

"Jones?" she asked. Daunhauer shook his head. Beretta turned and angrily kicked a pile of gravel. "And the doctor?"

"I don't know. She's…" Daunhauer paused, realizing all the Strikers were neutralized in the immediate area. "She ran out this way!" He led them out through the edge of the forest. Beretta gazed at the burning spectacle of armored vehicles.

"*He* did this?" she asked.

"He must think he was double-crossed by Zolnar," Daunhauer said.

"Fine by me," Beretta said. They heard the roar of a truck engine. The rebels moved outward to where they could see around the tanks. Beretta pointed. "There! The carrier trucks were intact. Saegusa opened the back of one and climbed in along with a refinery droid."

Though they couldn't see him, it was obvious that the contractor was at the wheel. The truck pulled forward and began speeding off.

"They're going north," Barber said. "He's trying to make it across the border."

"That's perfect," Donnelly said. "Let him go. The Sovereignty won't be looking for one of their own trucks. He'll get the doctor out of here. Cornelius won't be able to make the bio-weapon. Everything will be fine."

"Fine?" Daunhauer grabbed the young Lieutenant by the collar of his shirt and pulled him close. "She killed Collins! You said it yourself!" Donnelly pried Daunhauer's scaly hands away, causing the Recon Specialist to wince in pain.

"Yes, she did! It sucks. I knew the Captain. He was a good man. But honestly, if we look at this objectively, how we've handled the situation, could we really blame her? After all, we were shooting at her. Hell, Jones went after the mercenary and almost took his head off with the shuriken. I've seen it," he said.

A blow to his stomach doubled him over. Beretta stood over him and placed a boot over his back.

"We're not letting this go unanswered," she said. "There's more to this than keeping her away from the Sovereignty now." Donnelly looked up at her, disgusted.

"General, I offer my sincerest condolences for the loss of Paul," he said. "I really do. I can't even begin to imagine, nor do I want to. But we can't abandon our principles for the sake of revenge."

"You call it revenge, I call it motivation," Beretta said. "I'm tired of this war. I'm ready to end it." She looked back to the rest of her rebels. "If anyone disagrees, you have the opportunity to walk away. There'll be no repercussions."

Almost every one of them shook their heads. There were no reservations in the group from following Beretta's lead, except from Donnelly. The Lieutenant stood up and sucked in a dust-filled breath. He was outvoted unanimously. An anger swelled inside of him. These rebels were blindly following General Albright without question. That, or they genuinely wanted the same thing as her. One probably had something to do with the other. Either way, there would be no keeping them from Beretta's next task.

"It's decided then," the General said. "We're going after them!"

"How?" Barber asked. "I don't see any vehicles except for that truck, and it looks even more beat up than the one they took."

Beretta looked down the tree line. "The bikers' vehicles! We'll take those! Daunhauer, you and I will take the truck."

The rebels hailed and dispersed. Beretta and Daunhauer moved to the truck, the latter taking a position inside the compartment. As he had hoped, there were a few weapons stored away, including I.N.T. launchers and some grenades.

"You are driving," he said.

"Just don't blow up the doctor just yet," she replied. "I want her alive."

"Fine," Daunhauer said. "Do you have any use for the mercenary?"

"No. Dispose of him. Don't need him," she said.

"Good," Daunhauer said.

Beretta started the truck and followed the mercenary's trail.

****

Firebird twisted in pain as he drove the truck onto the nearest road. No matter how he positioned himself, his wound pressed against the seat, aggravating it. Tensing, he tried to reposition himself again by shifting hard to his right. Doing so, he accidentally turned the wheel, jerking the truck to the right. The tires came off the smooth dirt paving and rocked over bumpy landscape.

"Oh, shit." He quickly swung the truck back, correcting course. The compartment rocked back-and-forth until the truck steadied. The interior window slid open over his right shoulder. Glancing back, he could see Saegusa in his peripheral vision.

"You *trying* to get us killed?"

"How many times have I saved your ass? Yet you still complain," he said. "Besides, I'm an excellent driver."

The truck shook again. Saegusa scoffed, seeing that he had veered off the road a second time. Once again, Firebird corrected course. He fidgeted in his seat and watched the road.

"How long until we're over the border?"

"I don't know," Firebird muttered. "Why? You have a date?"

"Just eager to get out of here."

"Aren't we both?" he said. "Just relax. Take a nap. Chat with Stuart."

Saegusa slipped back into the compartment and took a seat. There were no armrests between the seats, which allowed her to lay across them as though it was a sofa. She gladly did so.

Laying face-up, she tried to rest. Despite how tired she felt, she had undergone too much tension that sleep seemed impossible. Her heart was still racing, causing all of her aches and pains to throb even worse. She tried to ignore it, instead focusing on her samples. They were intact, the vials clattering together inside her pouch. She took a deep breath, grimacing from a tightness in her stomach. It continued for several long seconds before subsiding. The abuse she had been subjected to had aggravated it. She held a hand over her stomach and closed her eyes.

Across the aisle, Stuart positioned himself on the seats and started tending to one of his damaged legs. His internal gadgets extended from the compartments in his body and began assessing the damage, starting with his right foreleg. The arms found the severed tendon, and with careful, precise calculation, Stuart fused it with his torch. He extended the leg and flexed it. Though limited in flexibility, the leg was functionable again. Stuart repeated the process with his other leg.

As he did so, he looked over to the doctor. His sensors picked up signs of distress in her. It wasn't emotional distress but indications of physical pain and discomfort, along with some anxiety. He fused the damaged interior segment of his leg and stood up from the seat. With all six legs functioning, he was able to walk normally again. He crossed the aisle and stood next to Saegusa. A laser scan protruded from his cone-shaped head and ran over Saegusa's body.

She shook and opened her eye, surprised to see him.

"What are you doing?!"

"I am merely checking for injuries. I have noticed you are favoring your stomach."

"It's nothing. I'm fine," she said.

"It is imperative you remain uninjured." He resumed the scan. Saegusa pulled away, her facial expression showing irritation.

"I said I'm fine," she said defensively. She sat up and moved away. Stuart ended the scan and watched her.

"Firebird," he called.

"Now what?"

"It is imperative that we get the doctor to her lab as quickly as possible."

"Yeah, no shit! What do you think I'm doing? Haven't we just been over this? Or are you glitching?"

"Negative. My damage has been isolated to my exoskeleton and some interior joint and vocal m-mechanics. My computer is running just fine."

"Oh, for the love of…" Firebird groaned. "Just tell the doc to relax. Like I told her. If all goes well, we'll be in Espinosa by tomorrow…or the day after…I don't really know. Hell, I need a map."

Stuart turned his attention back to the doctor.

"Will that be enough time?" he asked.

Saegusa nodded. "It's progressing fast, but not THAT fast." Stuart noticed she was speaking at a whisper, and Saegusa knew he took notice of it. "Don't tell the merc."

"Why?"

"First of all, he won't care. Second of all…I simply don't want anyone to know."

"Because of what he said before?"

Saegusa sighed as she recalled Firebird's words before all hell had broken loose with the Razor Gang.

"I bet the doctors told you they won't install any more cybernetic replacements. Hell, I guarantee it was your research that manipulated them into giving you more parts than they would the average joe." But I know the truth. You preach about saving others, when really, you're trying to save yourself."

"When you were assembled, did they install some kind of human psychology data chip in you or something?"

"Negative," Stuart said. "There were a lot of books in the Ash-Cloud, and occasionally a lot of time between assignments. I'm always trying to take in more data. There was an old book about basic psychology, and…"

The truck shook and rocked violently, throwing Saegusa to the floor.

"What the hell…"

The truck veered sharply to the right. In that same moment, they heard another explosion echo off to the right nearby.

"Son of a bitch," Firebird muttered. He straightened out the truck. Three motorcycles zipped in front of him. Initially, he thought it was the gang, until he noticed the patches on their shoulders. It was that other group that was after them.

He looked into his rear-view mirror, seeing the other carrier truck directly behind them. It was pulling off to the side. Sticking out of the top hatch, he saw a man pointing an I.N.T. launcher. Moving alongside it were three other motorcycles. Every rider carried a weapon of some sort and had its muzzle pointed at the driver's seat.

He veered sharply to the right, narrowly avoiding another shot from the I.N.T.

"Alright…" Firebird snarled. He slammed the brakes, allowing the other vehicles to start speeding past him. Saegusa's face appeared in the interior window.

"What's going on?"

"We've got some assholes who think they're *The Road Warrior*."

"Who?"

"Ugh, just grab a gun and start shooting."

Saegusa saw the rifle rack just below the window. Three Omega Plasma Rifles remained, along with the I.N.T. launcher that Firebird had salvaged. She picked it up and faced Stuart.

"How's the recoil on this thing?"

Stuart mimicked a shrug. "Only one way to find out." The truck rocked again, nearly throwing Saegusa into the wall. She steadied herself and reached for the ceiling, pulling down the retractable ladder.

"I suppose there is," she said. She climbed the ladder and popped open the hatch.

The General cursed under her breath as she started speeding past the fleeing truck. She hit the brakes and turned sharply to the right to cut them off but was too late. The mercenary had generated enough space, causing her to sweep across. He had already moved left across the field.

From atop the truck, Daunhauer launched another blast. The blinding ball of energy streaked across the air toward the engine but struck ground as the mercenary veered further to the right.

"Careful, not too close," Beretta said. The vibration of the vehicle generated a shakiness in her voice. "We want that cyborg ALIVE!"

"Yes!" Daunhauer said. He waited for his I.N.T. to recharge. He bared teeth as his gaping eye endured the onslaught of the wind and dust. He wouldn't close it to protect it. Red veins surrounded the pupils as infections slowly started to set in. He ducked back down into the compartment and discarded the I.N.T. and opted for an Omega.

He was halfway up the ladder when a huge impact struck the truck, shaking him to the floor.

"How you like that?" Firebird muttered. He steered away, then cut sharply to the left again, ramming the pursuing truck. It jerked further to the left, the driver forced to go with the momentum or risk toppling over.

Firebird started to line up for another hit. Bright plasma flashes streaked near the windshield. Sparks popped along the hood of the engine. Faster and more agile, the motorcycle team circled the truck like vultures, concentrating their fire on the driver's seat.

Keeping his head low, Firebird swayed side-to-side to sideswipe them. Dust billowed from under their tires creating a thick trail behind them.

He kept his eye just above the console, carefully studying the movements while keeping the truck on the road. The bikes circled, firing at the engine each time they passed over the front.

Firebird began to veer to the right, as though ready to sideswipe. The foolish rebel passing along the front took the bait. Instead of passing from left to right, he hooked back to avoid the sideswipe, ending up parallel with the truck. Firebird cut back hard, hitting the side of the bike with the engine.

The bike shot to the left, jolted by the impact. It traveled for several feet, jittering over uneven ground. Then finally, its front wheel hit a gorge in the earth, jamming it. Driven by momentum, the bike flipped over end, launching its rider for several feet before he faceplanted.

"I believe I can fly," Firebird hummed as he floored the gas pedal. More shots struck the hood, ripping the metal plating free and exposing the inner mechanics. Other shots focused on the tires. These guys were doing everything they could to bring this truck to a stop…including killing him. He ducked again. Several shots shattered the windshield, spilling glass into the seat. A couple of rounds zipped inward and exploded into the back wall behind his head.

He kept trying to peek over the dashboard, only to be blindsided by plasma fire. The engine spat and sputtered as it endured further abuse.

A metallic echo shook the top of the truck as the hatch popped open. A moment later, several flashes flickered over the top of the truck. Several explosions ripped along the road, driving the bikers off the pavement.

With her waist pressed against the edge of the hatch, Saegusa panned left with the I.N.T. and placed another shot a few feet in the path of the biker. The bike closed the distance as the plasma connected and exploded, tossing the bike and its driver sky high.

"Holy shit," she said. She tried to fire another shot, only for nothing to happen. A warning light appeared along the trigger frame. The weapon started its cooling process, billowing hot steam. "Figures."

Brushing the glass away, Firebird looked up and studied the terrain around him. The engine was beginning to smoke. He couldn't outrun these guys on the road. There was only one thing he could think to do. He gazed out toward the field of rocks to the west.

"Screw it." Firebird veered back into the field, pointing away from the bikers. The rebels followed, jittering hard against the uneven ground.

Struggling to keep standing, Saegusa peeked into the window. She opened the slide and was surprised to be hit by wind coming through the windshield. She looked ahead and saw that Firebird was driving directly toward the rock mountain.

"What are you doing?"

"Just taking the scenic route," Firebird quipped.

The truck was now moving over solid rock. The tires hit the edge of the mountain, jolting the vehicle hard as it went up the incline. The path up the mountain was a maze of boulders, many as tall as a man and as wide as the truck he was driving.

Behind them, the bikers pursued, weaving wildly around the boulders. The rebels were quick to realize they could not travel in a tight group. They spread out like flies, slowing their speed to keep from toppling out of control.

"Oh no you don't," Beretta snarled. She drove her truck after Firebird. The engine shook as the tires hit the rock, nearly causing her to faceplant into the steering wheel. Behind her, Daunhauer emerged from the hatch with his Omega Plasma Rifle in hand. The mercenary had gotten several yards ahead, and there were too many obstacles in the way.

"I can't get a shot from here," he called to Beretta. The General grabbed her handheld radio and raised it to her mouth.

"Bikers, I need you to slow him down," she ordered.

The bikers began to converge. The truck bounced hard like a sailboat tossed in a storm. Firebird steered back and forth, narrowly avoiding the solid masses of rock that protruded from the mountain like mushrooms. Plasma flashes glinted in his left mirror. A moment later, the mirror snapped off, leaving a steaming stub.

"Stuart, I need you to be my lookout!" Firebird called.

"You have two coming in from the right. One on the left, and two trailing behind," Stuart said.

"Hey Doc, if you're looking for some target practice, now's the time!"

"I'm starting to think I'm earning a cut of whatever you're getting paid," she replied.

"Yeah...don't kid yourself," Firebird said. "Now stick your pretty face out there and shoot people!"

Saegusa gripped the ladder. She braced as the truck raced over a small ledge. It went airborne for several feet before touching down, zigzagging slightly back and forth before steadying it.

Behind them, several motorcycles hit the same incline and flew over the edge. One landed in a crazy spin, throwing the rider face-first into a boulder.

Saegusa emerged from the hatch and braced again. Firebird conducted a sharp turn to avoid collision with a tight group of boulders. Leaning forward, the doctor faced the rear of the truck. The motorcycles spread again, while the leader in the carrier truck pursued directly behind them.

She could see the woman in the driver's seat. Saegusa shouldered her rifle as best she could and sprayed several rounds into the windshield.

The General ducked her head as plasma fire shattered the windshield. With her eyes off the path, she didn't realize she tilted the wheel slightly in the process, causing the truck to sideswipe a boulder. The truck reverberated, shaking the Omega rifle from Daunhauer's hand.

"Damn it," the Lieutenant cursed. He ducked below as another volley of shots sprayed his way. He freefell to the floor, landing on his back.

"You alright?" Beretta yelled to him.

"I'm fine," he said. He stood up and examined the armory. He grabbed a pistol from the rack. "Get me close. We're gonna have to do this the hard way."

"Hasn't been easy so far," Beretta said. She cleared the glass out from her lap and stepped on the accelerator.

Rocking hard against the sides, Saegusa sprayed plasma energy at the bikes. The constant zigzagging made it nearly impossible to aim. However, the shooting was enough to distract the bikers and prevent them from shooting back.

"Sir, there's another formation ahead," Stuart announced.

"I see it," Firebird replied. He veered left, closing in on one of the motorcycles. The biker pointed a pistol at the window.

"Doctor, rotate yourself one-hundred-eighty degrees," Stuart said. Saegusa turned around and saw the bike getting up close and personal. She pointed her rifle and fired down at him. The blasts caught him in the leg and in the tires, causing the bike and its driver to flip repeatedly before crashing down hard.

The three remaining bikes slowed down to trail the truck. The nearest one steadied the bike and pointed a pistol. He shot for the rear tires. A stream of plasma from Saegusa forced him to evade.

"Sir, there is an unfortunate update in our situation," Stuart said.

"Can't you just state the problem?" Firebird grunted.

"Sir, we have a ridge up ahead," Stuart said.

"Oh, great," Firebird said. He started to turn but was boxed in by a barricade of rocks. There was nowhere to go but straight. And stopping was no option. "Just lovely. The only way this could get any worse is if I was driving a damn bus!"

"If you were driving a bus instead of a truck, the scenario would be no different…"

"It's a reference, bot!...and it would be different! They had a damn bomb keeping them from slowing down." Firebird groaned, watching the opening appear a couple of hundred meters ahead. The stress aggravated his leg injury even worse. He could hear the vibrations of pistol blasts hitting the back of the truck. He thought on his pop-culture reference. "Well, I've heard that jump wouldn't work in real life. I guess it's time to find out!" He floored the pedal, putting the truck to its maximum speed.

Gravel crunched under the tires as the vehicle approached the ledge.

"Doctor, you may want to take a seat," Stuart said to Saegusa.

"And put on a seatbelt," Firebird called.

The doctor slid down the ladder and strapped herself into a seat. She took a nervous breath and braced for the inevitable jump.

"What the hell is he doing?" Daunhauer said.

"He's making the jump!" Beretta said. They slowed down and watched from afar as the mercenary made his suicidal approach to the ledge.

The gap was thirty feet, leading into a dark abyss that seemed to stretch down to the center of the Earth. As Firebird had hoped, there was a slight upward incline at the edge of the rift.

"Hang tight!" he alerted. In the compartment, Saegusa ducked her head down while Stuart held himself firm to his seat.

The truck passed over the edge. For the longest moment of their lives, the truck was airborne. They were engulfed by a sensation of weightlessness, followed by the helpless feeling of falling. The fall only lasted a moment. The truck hit solid ground, bouncing hard several times while teetering back and forth.

"Ha!" Firebird cheered himself. "Proved that old trivia wrong!"

"Actually, the distance in question was fifty feet," Stuart said. "The rift we passed over was barely more than half that distance…"

"Oh, shut up," Firebird quipped.

"Get after him! Get after him now!" Beretta ordered. The bikers accelerated toward the ledge. She could see Donnelly and Barber at the front. She felt a slight cringe as they jumped the edge, followed by the last remaining biker.

Donnelly landed and descended into an uncontrollable spiral that knocked him over. Barber landed right after. The tires exploded from the sudden pressure, forcing his bike to fall over as well.

The third biker fell short, smashing hard into the edge of the cliff. The front of the bike smashed into several pieces, pummeling its rider against the granite before they both freefell into the deep.

Donnelly stumbled to the edge, too late to grab his comrade. Looking back across the cliff, he saw the truck making its jump. He and Barber ran in opposite directions out of the way.

The truck came down hard, its rear tires striking the corner of the ledge. One of them popped in an enormous balloon, throwing the truck into a fish tail. It hit several smaller rocks before Beretta gained control of it. Not waiting for the rebels, she pressed on to catch up with the mercenary.

Daunhauer reemerged through the hatch. The I.N.T. launcher was fully charged. With both vehicles moving in a straight line, he was finally able to get a decent aim. Directly behind them, he couldn't hit the truck without destroying the compartment. And with the rocks all around them, it would be difficult to swing wide and line up a proper shot.

With the barrel resting on the truck, he aimed carefully left of the truck and fired off several shots.

Each blast erupted inches near the mercenary's left tires. Flame expanded and clung to the side of the vehicle. The tires popped, causing the truck to shift to the left, striking several rock formations along the way.

Daunhauer discarded the I.N.T. and drew his pistol.

"Now's our chance. Get me close!"

Flame swirled over the frame of the truck and into the driver's seat, scorching Firebird's metal arm. He waved his hand, extinguishing the flame with help from the wind. The truck shook like dice in a cup. Sparks flew from the wheels as he steered away from a wall of rocks. He continued steering right to avoid other obstacles.

"This…has been…a very…VERY long day," Firebird griped to himself, his voice shaking from the constant battering of the truck.

"We have a truck coming up on our left," Stuart warned.

"Saegusa, shoot the prick!" the mercenary yelled. The doctor was already halfway up the ladder, holding the I.N.T. launcher. She flung the hatch openand started to emerge.

The truck slammed hard against theirs, driving it to the right with tremendous force. The launcher fell from Saegusa's hands and smashed against the rocks.

"Shit!" she yelled, brushing the hair out of her face. She looked back. The trucks were still pressed together. Leaping from the top was the scar-faced man who nearly captured her in the forest. He landed on top of their truck and reached for her.

Saegusa slipped down the ladder and pulled the hatch shut. She could feel the rebel pulling against it. She twisted the latch, sealing the door in place.

"Damn it," Daunhauer cursed. He rested on his hands and knees. The wind stung his injured face. Unable to open the hatch and pull the doctor out, he looked to Beretta and motioned for her to move away. The General did as instructed and stayed back, allowing for Daunhauer to crawl to the front of the truck.

Holding onto the top of the frame, he jumped down along the driver's side and shoved his pistol into Firebird's face.

"Hot damn!" the mercenary yelled. He raised his metal hand and clutched Daunhauer's wrist, thrusting his aim outward as a shot rang out. Daunhauer grunted as he struggled against the bionic appendage.

The truck swayed from side-to-side as Firebird struggled to maintain control. He glanced through the window at his attacker, seeing his scorched face and exposed eye.

"Eh, it's an improvement," he quipped in a raspy voice. The remark successfully enraged the rebel, causing him to struggle harder to point the muzzle in his face. He squeezed off several shots, frying the passenger window and frame. Daunhauer snarled and rasped, desperate to put the gun in Firebird's face.

The truck bounced hard against the ground. Firebird looked ahead and saw a huge rock twenty feet ahead. With one hand on the wheel, he steered to the left. The truck scraped against it, blowing another tire. Sparks sprayed from both sides of the truck as it raced down a small hill.

The truck hit a small rock, jogging it upward. Firebird attempted to correct course, only to graze another. Finally, he let go of the wheel and made a fist. He yanked Daunhauer's arm further in, over extending his shoulder and bringing his head inside the window.

Firebird struck him hard in the nose, blowing blood out of every hole in his face. The attacker still held on. Firebird punched him again, cracking one of his bottom teeth. A third strike split his lip against that chipped tooth.

"Alright Two-Face," Firebird muttered. "Time to go!" He plowed another punch into him, connecting his knuckle to his exposed eye.

Daunhauer yelled in pain and fell backward, rolling several times before settling.

Firebird faced forward… just in time to see the upcoming boulder. The engine smashed against it, spattering pieces everywhere. The compartment reared up and twisted, throwing Saegusa against the wall and knocking her out.

The truck spiraled on its engine like a tornado before finally smashing down on its side.

Firebird crawled through the open windshield. His world appeared to be spinning around him. Everything was a hot blur of rock, gravel, and flickering sky.

He crawled on his belly, bleeding from his face and neck. His eyepatch barely held to his head. Unable to go any further, he rolled onto his back.

The enemy truck pulled up. The female driver stepped out and checked on the man who had tried to shoot him. She took his pistol and slowly started to walk toward him.

Her words sounded warped as she spoke.

"You've caused me more trouble than you're worth," she said. She pointed the gun at him. "I'll give you credit for helping me with the Strikers. But there's more that needs to be done."

He could see her finger tightening around the trigger, slowly drawing it back.

Her hand jerked upward, discharging a shot in the sky as the General suddenly convulsed into a wild spasm. She yelled and grunted incoherently before collapsing to the ground.

Firebird leaned up on his elbow, seeing the wires protruding from the woman's back. His eye followed them all the way to the truck, where Stuart stood on wobbly legs. There were several indentations in his exoskeleton from being tossed in the wreck. The ports along his 'chest' area were open. He retracted the tasers and closed the ports before stumbling off the truck.

"F-iiire—are you…okay?" The droid's voice was hardly recognizable as he approached his master. Firebird's vision was constantly fading in and out. In one instance, Stuart was on the truck. A moment later, he was on the ground. Then he was standing over him, projecting his laser scan. "Yo—u are…lucky…no broken…b-boooones…" The droid backed up and settled onto the ground. "My computer is-is j-jumbled. I…must…reboot." He rested his body against the ground and curled his legs to the side. In the following instant, all motion ceased. The droid had shut itself down.

He wasn't sure how many moments, or minutes, had passed. Firebird could see the gun laying a couple of yards from his feet. The woman was gradually regaining her senses. He knew he needed to get the pistol and check on Saegusa. But he couldn't move. The world was still spinning. It took everything to stay conscious.

He faded out. Then back.

The General was standing now. She held the pistol in her hand. She was sweaty and covered in dirt. Her three surviving companions were nearby, including the one with the acid burns. Firebird waited for the inevitable. However, she kept staring off into the distance.

Laying back, Firebird tilted his head to the left where they stared. More people approached, all wearing similar outfits. They were led by a bald man of at least fifty. He was unshaven, his eyes sympathetic but also intense.

"General Drake," Beretta said. She didn't sound happy to see him.

"General Albright," the man replied. He looked down at the mercenary and the wreckage. He signaled to his men and pointed at him. "Pick him up. Bring the droid and the doc."

"General..." Beretta protested.

"That's enough," Drake said.

Several rebels gathered around Firebird and lifted him onto a stretcher. Others approached the truck and pulled the doctor out. His vision faded in and out, and suddenly he was placed inside a vehicle. He could hear some chatter taking place between the Generals. His wonky mind couldn't make out the words, but the tones were undeniably tense.

He heard doors slamming and men boarding the truck.

"Let's go," somebody said. There was motion.

Then finally, it all went black.

CHAPTER 17

For the first time in forever, he was in a world of bliss. He was ten years old, in a house made of lumber. He could smell the ocean and see the sealife leaping joyfully in the distance.

He was in the living room with his folks. He was tucked under his father's arm, watching one of many films from the world prior. Their library was full of archives. They were more than movies and books. They were memories of family. They pointed and laughed at the special effects of some earlier pictures and jumped at the surprising appearance of a shark rising out of the water behind an angular faced actor dangling a cigarette out of his mouth.

He was in the Dojo that his father had built before he was born. He crossed the jacket of his white uniform and stepped on the cold deck floor. His father was a large muscular man. A black belt was tied around his waist. They bowed to each other, then proceeded into their first fighting form. *Kata.*

Low block, left hand. Step forward, right hand punch. Turn around. Low block, right hand. Step forward, left hand punch.

It was his real left hand. It felt so…normal.

Then, in the blink of an eye, the flesh was gone, replaced by metal.

Firebird stepped out of the infirmary, the flesh of his shoulder red from where the fusion took place. He didn't expect a metal appendage to hurt so much. It wasn't a mild pain. It was excruciating. Enough to drive him mad. Or maybe, it was having to identify the bodies of two people he loved most. The tanks had rolled over the hills. They didn't bother identifying targets. They just blasted everything in sight.

Suddenly, he was in the pilot seat of a Model-10 Hawkeye. The world below was ablaze from artillery fire. His men were below. Explosions from anti-aircraft weapons had burst all around him, turning the sky a fiery red. But he descended under the flames, the ship taking damage, but holding together. There they were, his fellow soldiers.

That was when he first heard the name…

"Firebird."

****

"Come on, wake up." The voice sounded a mile away at first. Yet, it sounded so familiar. "Firebird. Wake up." It was closer now.

"HEY!"

An electric current swept through his body, lighting up his nerves.

"YOW!" Firebird sprang from the bed with the fury of a madman. He raised two fists, ready to take everyone around. Several people turned to face him. Doctors and nurses, along with other patients in beds.

"Firebird." It was Saegusa's voice. Firebird looked at her. She was standing by his bed. She was okay. Bruised, but okay. She held both hands up, trying to signal that everything was okay.

The mercenary suddenly felt cold. He realized he was wearing nothing but a pair of shorts.

"What the hell?" he said. He lowered his hands and looked around. The smell of dirt filled his nose. Lights dangled from above, with visible wires running in-between them. The floor was made of wood. It creaked with each step. The medical equipment was old. Outdated. He glanced at the doctors. Their coats were dirty and worn, and their eyes were glossy.

A bandage was wrapped tightly around his leg. It throbbed endlessly, though not nearly as bad as it did before. It seemed that the doctors had administered some kind of painkiller. He looked back at Saegusa. Stuart stood next to her, retracting the barb of a taser into his body. Saegusa was wearing fresh clothes. She looked relatively clean compared to everyone else.

"Where the hell are we?" he said

"I don't know," she said. "I was knocked out the whole time."

"When I reactivated, we were already in this location," Stuart said. "But from my analysis, I believe we are below ground level."

"Below ground level? Like a basement?"

"Not exactly," Stuart said. "If you observe, you will see corridors and tunnels leading to other areas…"

"What I want to observe right now are my clothes," Firebird said. He turned around and marched for the nearest doctor. "You! Where's my stuff?" The doctor stumbled back nervously. "Oh, relax! I'm not working for *Skynet*. I just want my stuff." The doctor stared blankly. Firebird groaned. Another reference gone over someone's head.

Several armed rebels entered the infirmary and pointed Five-Star rifles at him. He remained still as they surrounded him. One closed in, raising a pair of cuffs.

"You know, if you were smart, you would've had those on me to begin with," Firebird said.

"I didn't see a need," another voice boomed. The door opened. The bald General stepped into the infirmary. "Gentlemen, lower your guns." The rebels glanced at him, surprised, then did as commanded. They backed out of the way as General Drake extended his hand to Firebird. The mercenary looked at him suspiciously, then at his hand. He reluctantly accepted the handshake. "I understand if you're a little confused," the General continued.

"Confused, cold, and starving," Firebird said.

"Allow me to remedy that," Drake said. He gestured to one of the rebels, who quickly moved off to get Firebird's boots and some fresh clothes.

"Where the hell are we?" Saegusa asked.

Firebird stared at the General. It suddenly made sense. "It's the Rebellion headquarters."

"Rebellion?" Saegusa said. "I wouldn't have expected the Rebellion to attempt to kill us." The General nodded, seemingly in agreement with her.

"Come with me and I'll explain," Drake said. "But first..." he turned around as the rebel returned with Firebird's clothes, "let's cover you up."

****

Though he hadn't been undressed long, it felt refreshing to be wearing clothes again. Perhaps it was the vulnerable feeling of being trapped in an unfamiliar place, fortified by several people who had previously tried to kill him.

Firebird, Saegusa, and Stuart followed the General through a narrow hallway. Dust and flakes of dirt trickled down from the ceiling as they went. They passed a few armed rebels along the way. So far, he hadn't seen the female who had chased him across the field.

They entered a round room. At the edges were several computers, and in its center was a conference table. There was some food placed in its center along with plates and some eating utensils.

Firebird wasted no time sitting down and helping himself to what was there. Saegusa sat next to him. She was slow to get some food, as the pain in her stomach screwed with her appetite. However, she was aware she hadn't consumed anything all day. She had to keep up her strength. She grabbed a plate and started loading it with food.

The beef was dry, possibly a couple of days old at best. There were a few vegetables and potatoes, none of which were particularly tasty. But she didn't complain. This was probably top-notch compared to what the rebels were eating on a daily basis.

General Drake sat at the end of the table. Another man stepped into the room. Firebird and Saegusa recognized his face as one of the rebels they had encountered in the chase.

"This is Lieutenant Donnelly," General Drake said. "You can thank him for contacting me in time."

Saegusa held her breath. This man was standing next to the rebel she had shot with Firebird's revolver. He had chased her through the forest, enraged. The fact that he kept them from getting killed came as a bit of a shock.

"What's going on, exactly?" she asked. "Why are we here?"

"I'll be frank," General Drake said. He tapped his fingers against the table as he tried to figure out what he wanted to say. "Uh, there were some major mistakes made by General Albright."

"The white-haired chick?" Firebird said.

"Yes," Drake said. "She and I started this whole operation almost twenty years ago. It's been almost nothing but war since. And death. We're outnumbered and outgunned. Our forces have been deteriorating rapidly." He breathed a heavy sigh. "Today was a particularly bad day. We've lost many. The worst part was that we shouldn't have."

Firebird swallowed a large piece of meat, knowing that the General was referring to the rebels killed in the skirmish with him and the Sovereignty.

"Don't worry," Drake said, seeing the nervousness in his eye. "What happened between our people and you is extremely unfortunate. But I can't begrudge you for what happened, especially with how Albright handled it, despite her judgement being impaired."

"Booze?" Firebird joked.

"No, her son was recently killed. Brutally." Firebird's smile disappeared.

"That's a shame. But what did that have to do with me? Or her?"

"We knew you were coming," Drake said. "We got word through an unspecified source that a private contractor was delivering a bio-engineer specialist to the Sovereignty. There was a plan to intercept, well, at least I was under the impression of it being *A* plan. Turns out Albright had her own idea how to handle the situation. Long story short, it didn't work out very well."

"The irony is that she didn't have to do it," Firebird said, spitting crumbs all over the table. "The Sovereignty shot us down. I've seen artillery like that before and it was definitely Sovereign anti-aircraft guns."

Donnelly felt a slight sweat running down his temples. He watched the General, praying that he wouldn't disclose the truth. He could sense a similar nervousness going through Drake's mind. He bit his lip, deciding it be best not to disclose that information.

"Spotters saw your plane coming down," he said. "Albright tracked you through the forest."

Firebird noticed a slight pause in his voice. His unblinking eye dug into the General's forehead as he crunched a carrot.

"I suspect they somehow traced my signal to Espinosa," he said, waiting to see what the General would say. "Then again, they called prior to that asking my exact coordinates...why would *they* do that?"

Drake acted as if he didn't know what Firebird was talking about.

"Listen," Donnelly said. "Like he said, mistakes were made. By *both* sides."

"I would not emphasize that," Firebird warned him.

"Listen," Donnelly spoke defensively, "You were the one taking her to Zolnar. Don't act righteous. You were intending to make money at the expense of us, the surrounding territories, hell the whole friggin' continent!"

"Right," Firebird said. "That explains why we were moving north...to the border."

"You were moving south first. You crossed the border."

"Until we were shot down..." Firebird watched the Lieutenant's face flush. The mercenary knew the truth.

"Like I said, mistakes were made," Donnelly said.

"I don't chalk being repeatedly chased and shot at as a *mistake*," Firebird said. "And I definitely don't appreciate being shot down with artillery. My Ash-Cloud was not easy to come by!" He pushed his plate away and stood up. Three rebels burst into the room.

General Drake raised a hand, ordering them to stand down.

"All this time, I knew it defied logic, what the Sovereignty did...or what I thought they did. I'll give you credit, though. It had to be a bitch taking over those gun units."

"More than you know," Donnelly said.

Firebird raised his metal arm.

"I know better than you ever will," he said.

"Listen," Drake said. "The mission now is to get you out of here. You already told us you were planning on diverting to Espinosa. I'm dedicating myself to helping you with that. The fact is, she's in Sovereignty Territory. We can't let Zolnar find her. The fact is, Saegusa is one-of-a-kind. Her research cannot be duplicated."

"No shit," Firebird said. "You were willing to blow us up to keep her out of their hands."

"I…" the General took another breath. "I did not approve that operation. Believe me, I will deal with Albright. But it doesn't change the situation, Firebird. They're still looking for her. We've gotta get her out of here."

"It's better we get her back to Espinosa as soon as possible," Stuart added.

"Why?" Firebird asked.

"Never mind that," Saegusa said.

"No, I mean WHY do they need her, specifically," Firebird said. "This always bugged my brain. You're telling me nobody else can figure out how to make a bio-weapon? Just this little cyborg here? The Sovereignty has their own scientists, I'm sure they can figure it out."

"It's a little more complicated than that," Saegusa said. "It's…it's the chip in my head."

"What do you mean?"

"My father…he…" she sighed. "Never mind. I'll tell you if we ever get out of here." She cleared her throat. "The question is not why, but *how*. How do we get out of here?"

"I'm working on that as we speak," Drake said. "We don't have many people left. But if there's one thing I can promise, is that I'll uphold the principles that this Rebellion is supposed to stand for. I'm not murdering innocent lives. Not even one, no matter the situation. Be ready doctor. I'm working on a plan, and your escort here will get you home. For now, there isn't much you can do. I suggest you get some rest."

General Drake stood from his seat. "Donnelly will show you to your quarters when you're finished."

He stood up and exited into another corridor. Firebird took his seat and bit into a chewy piece of beef.

"Ugh, I had some good chow on that plane too," he said.

"Quit whining," Saegusa said.

"I'll stop whining when I get my gold," he said. Saegusa stopped chewing and glanced at him.

"Wait…gold? What's Espinosa paying you?"

Firebird could sense a rising tension. He forgot she was patriotic to her Territory.

"Um, not much," he said.

"Two-hundred-and-ten-thousand gold pieces," Stuart said. Saegusa spat her food at him and stood up.

"Thanks, Stuart," Firebird said.

"You jackass," she said, sneering. "That's more than our entire reserve."

"Hey, they agreed to it," Firebird said. "Right, Stuart?"

"Well, initially they offered seventy, then eighty…" Firebird cupped a hand over his speaker.

"All you had to say was YES!"

"Are you finished?" Donnelly interrupted. Both of them looked up at him. Saegusa glared at Firebird, feeling the urge to punch him. Why not? It would only be their *fourth* fight.

Donnelly approached the table. "Let's not do this now. Listen, it's been a long ass day for all of us. I'm tired as shit. Let me show you to your quarters and you can do this in there."

Firebird and Saegusa shared a moment of tense eye contact.

"Fine," Firebird said.

"Good with me," Saegusa said.

They stood up together and followed Donnelly out of the room into another narrow corridor.

CHAPTER 18

General Albright took a long draw of her cigarette as she waited for General Drake to appear through the door. She hated the enclosed spaces of interrogation chambers. She hated these tunnels in general. It was one more of countless motivations to win this war and actually live a life on the outside.

Then again, what life was there to live? The last thing that meant anything to her was gone. She had lost much in her lifetime. But she always held on, thinking she'd eventually hold some grandchildren on her knee. Only now was it sinking in fully that that would never happen. She didn't cry. She couldn't. Not even for the death of her son would she display weakness. Even when nobody was around.

The door opened. General Drake stepped inside and silently stared at her. His eyes carried contempt, with a hint of compassion. He closed the door and sat at the opposite end of the table.

"We're in the endgame now," he said. He reached for a bottle of liquor on the table's center and poured himself a small glass. "I did a headcount when you got back."

"I know. You do it every day," Albright said.

"The thing I notice most is how it takes less time every time I do it," he said. He took a sip of the liquor, swallowed, then downed the whole glass before pushing it away. "Beretta...I'll say this first. I've been where you are. You know I've lost a son. I know what it's like to feel like your whole world has ended. I wish I had more to give than my deepest condolences..."

"I'll be okay," Beretta said. There was a slight enthusiasm in her voice. "His death won't be in vain. He died for something greater: he died for this Rebellion. And because of him, we will have victory."

"How do you propose that?" Drake said.

"I have a plan," Beretta said.

"You seem to have a lot of plans," Drake said. His tone was confrontational now. "And it seems I'm not up to date on any of them. Like your stunt with ambushing Zolnar's battalion."

"I did what had to be done," she said.

"I *had* a plan in place," Drake said. "We had land mines set up. See...*I* knew they had armor. I had a battle plan in place that would've slowed the enemy down and created enough confusion to allow us to divert the Ash-Cloud. But you had to lead a high-risk operation and shoot them down."

Beretta blew a large cloud of smoke and leaned forward. "Your plan wouldn't have worked. All you would've achieved were the deaths of many rebels."

Drake scoffed. "The deaths of many...how many did you get killed?" Beretta didn't answer. "Oh, I forgot, I already did the head count."

"At least I got the doctor."

"But that wasn't your original intent," Drake corrected her.

"It doesn't matter," Beretta said.

"Oh, it does," Drake replied. "We don't murder innocents. No matter the stakes. We're trying to rid this land of ruthless dictators. Not replace it with another one."

"I'm not an authoritarian," Beretta defensively said. "I just have my priorities in order. I'm willing to do whatever it takes to win."

"The 'end justifiesthe means' mentality; NOT consulting with me, or any of the other officers; seizing command of half our remaining forces…all that paves the road to an authoritarian," Drake said.

Beretta stood up suddenly, knocking her chair on its back.

"I'm not gonna sit here and be lectured on the rules of warfare. Not after the price I paid…"

"You didn't pay the only price," Drake said. "Look at what you've done! Grief does not justify taking a squad of twenty rebels into a suicide mission and getting them killed. All you had to do was let the contractor go. He'd be out of the territory by now. All you've accomplished was getting more people killed or injured. Captain Collins is dead. Daunhauer is severely injured. How Barber's still kicking, I'll never know."

"You're insane," Beretta said.

"No. You are," Drake said. He stood up from his seat. "I'm relieving you of your command."

Beretta cocked her head. "You don't have that kind of authority."

"Oh, I do," he corrected her. "Under Article Thirteen, Section Five. Read it yourself." Beretta didn't say anything. "Oh, right…you've already memorized it. Probably with intent to eventually use it against me."

Beretta flipped the table, shattering glass and spraying alcohol all over the floor. Drake didn't flinch. He saw it coming. Her anger was like a fuse to a stick of dynamite.

She turned around and briefly paced to the end of the room before turning back to face him again.

"How do you expect to win?"

"At this point, I don't," Drake said. "The Sovereignty has too many recruits. Too much firepower. Too much sheer will to win. For every soldier we kill, they get two more. Right now, my intent is to get Ms. Saegusa out of this territory. After that, I'm possibly looking at evacuation."

"Evacuation?" Albright smirked. "You're a coward."

"The Sovereignty is not expanding any further without risking war with the Rhinos," he said. "And frankly, we no longer have the manpower to combat them. It's just the way it is. We're down to a hundred-and-fourteen rebel soldiers. Possibly a couple dozen support staff and doctors. We've lost most of our heavy artillery. The fact is…we've lost."

"You lost. I'm not done yet," Beretta said, pointing a finger at herself.

"Yeah? That why you wanted to capture the doctor?" Drake said. Beretta exhaled, knowing he wouldn't like her answer.

"We can use her," she said. "We have the lab equipment. All we need is what she has in her head."

"And that, Beretta, is why I relieved you of your command," Drake said. "You know the truth of that gas. It can't be controlled. It'll kill everything around it. If we deployed it near a populated town, we could kill every innocent person living there." He shook his head, disappointed. "We've founded this Rebellion together, Beretta. You had principles then. You gave me hope for the future. But now..." he shook his head again and sighed, "I question if humanity is always doomed for tyranny."

He turned around and left the room, closing the door behind him. Beretta stood alone, seething with anger. She wasn't done.

So, the coward was throwing in the towel? After all the blood that had been shed, he would quit just like that? To save a few lives?

She thought of Paul on that hill, with Zolnar's dirty boot pressing on his broken bones. He didn't just die, he suffered brutally. WILLINGLY. So, they could win. Beretta wondered what he would say if he were here. But he wasn't. And that was what mattered most. He wasn't here, and Drake was willing for it to be for nothing.

Beretta leaned back against the far wall and allowed her temper to cool. Afterwards, she left the room, crunching broken glass under her boots.

****

Firebird followed the Lieutenant through a set of dirty corridors. Several light bulbs needed replacing. Some of the lights had even fallen, after breaking off of the ceiling along with the tile. Some of the walls hadn't even been covered, exposing brownish-black dirt.

"I'm starting to know how it feels to be an ant," Firebird said. "A regular one, that is."

"It's how we've remained undetected this long," Donnelly said. "We used to have headquarters on the surface but we knew we'd eventually be found."

"Yeah, but damn! How the hell did you carve all this out without being seen? You'd think the Sovereignty would notice dump trucks going in and out of here."

"It took a VERY long time," Donnelly said. "Basically, we did it little by little. We took the soil and gravel and gradually spread it out over the land. Dumped some over the ridge where our chase concluded earlier today."

"I see. You went *Shawshank Redemption* style on this place," Firebird said. Donnelly stopped and looked back at him.

"Pardon?"

"It's a mov—never mind," Firebird said. They took another left into an area that was much better insulated and furnished. The floor and walls were much more solid and cleaner. As they followed Donnelly through this corridor, Saegusa couldn't help but notice several unoccupied rooms. Inside each one was a bunk and personal belongings, with no owner nearby.

"This'll be your quarters here," Donnelly said. Firebird stepped inside. The room was wide, containing a single bunk and a desk. Saegusa followed him in, saw the room, and looked at Donnelly with surprise.

"Wait... where's my room?"

"This is for both of you," Donnelly said. "General wants to keep you all in one place to keep a better track on you."

Saegusa looked back at the room, then at the one-eyed man she'd be sharing it with.

"Oh, come on! You have all these other vacant rooms!" Saegusa argued.

"Sorry. We're going through them," Donnelly said. He stepped aside to make room for Stuart. "We'll come for you when we're ready to evacuate." He shut the door, leaving them in a dimly lit room.

"Great. Just great," Saegusa griped.

"Oh, get off your high horse," Firebird said.

"My high horse?" Saeguas kicked the leg of the desk, cracking the wood.

"Yeah, your high horse," Firebird argued. "What? You think I was gonna deliver you to Espinosa for free?"

"That'd be nice," she said. "And no, I didn't think that. But I didn't think you'd suck us dry of our finances. They'll have to collect from almost every citizen to get the funds."

"That's how it is. We made a deal. For Chrissake, quit being such a Girl Scout."

"Technically," Stuart chimed in, "the term is Boy Scout. Before the war, they incorporated girls into the Boy Scouts and intersected..."

"Girl Scouts, Boy Scouts, girls-in-boy scouts...that generation was so confused and retarded, it's no wonder they blew themselves up!" Firebird ranted.

"I'm starting to wish you'd get blown up," Saegusa said.

"I'm hurt," Firebird quipped. He flopped onto the bed and stretched his legs. Saegusa's face tensed. Something whirred in her mechanical eye, and the glassy 'pupil' lit up.

"Are you serious right now?"

Firebird looked down at himself. "Well, I'm not making jokes."

"You are NOT taking the bed," she said. Firebird slapped his arm to the side, bouncing it off the mattress.

"There's room," he said.

"UGH!" Saegusa groaned and turned around.

"What'd I do?" Firebird said. Saegusa sat at the desk chair.

"You were born," she remarked. Firebird sighed and stared up into the ceiling, then finally stood up.

"Well, your majesty! I present to you a bed!" He waved his hands at the bed as though performing a magic trick.

"It appears she is angry," Stuart said.

"Oh, WOW! Gee whiz! I suppose it took careful observation and analysis of her during the past TWELVE HOURS for you to come to that conclusion," Firebird said.

"Wait, are you implying someone has spent that long with you and felt any other kind of emotion?" Saegusa remarked.

"Hell, yes there has!"

"Sir, I do not recall previous passengers expressing positive feedback," Stuart said. He paused and went through his memory banks. "Key words from previous contacts include: Jackass: Moron: One-eyed prick. Phrases include, 'Go suck a dick': 'I hope you die': 'Please burn in the deepest darkest circle of hell': 'You're gay'."

Firebird bit his lip.

"There's no proof those were directed at me...except for the hell guy. Can't really blame him. I did cause him minor inconvenience. I might've, uh," he cleared his throat, "shot his hand off. But other than that! People love me!"

"You're a jackass," Saegusa said.

"Isn't that the hundredth time you called me a name?" Firebird said. "Look, I'm giving you the bed. Take a snooze. Sleep it off."

"Just..." Saegusa leaned forward. He noticed a pained scowl on her face. "Just shut up, please."

Firebird stared at her in confused silence.

"You alright? You hit?"

"No... I just need to lie down," she said. Her voice was weak. She stood up, still hunched over as though she was sick. This made Firebird especially nervous. He took her hand and helped her up, then guided her to the bed. Saegusa laid down and rolled on her side, favoring her stomach area.

"Need me to get a doctor?" he asked.

"No...no, nothing they can do," she said.

"Nothing they can do? You know what it is?" he asked. She nodded.

"I'll be fine. It comes and goes, especially after I eat," she said. Firebird didn't understand at first. This was such a stark contrast of how he had seen her before. She was always feisty and energetic, even when injured or knocked down. But here, she looked entirely hopeless.

He found himself looking at her numerous cybernetic components. Suddenly, it made sense.

"How far along is it?" he asked. Saegusa lay silently for a few moments.

"I'm not sure," she said. "It's advanced if it's hurting this much."

"Is the cancer in your stomach?"

"Yeah," she said. "I haven't wasted time with doctors. They'd just tell me what I already know. And they won't do any more surgeries on me. I'm not gonna use up what little time I have when I need it to do my work."

"You sound confident that your little formula will work," he said.

"It has to," she said.

"I'll give you credit," Firebird said. "It takes a lot of persistence to travel all over the place. Then again, some people will do whatever it takes to survive."

"It's not just me," she said, lifting her head. "It's everyone! I've seen so many bodies shrivel from all kinds of cancers." She laid her head back down. The pain was gradually beginning to subside. She breathed slowly, feeling her abdomen gradually loosening. But as the pain loosened, another tightness constricted her chest. It was the clutch of fear. Her temples throbbed from a stress-induced headache. The thought of death and the uncertainty of what came afterward drove her mind into a frenzy. "At least...that's what I tell myself."

"It seems a little too simple," Firebird said. He picked up her bag and looked at the vials inside. They were just simple leaves. Rare, but simple. "If these were the key, wouldn't somebody else had discovered this by now?"

"It's not just the leaves," she said. "We have to mix them with various compounds from other plants I've found around the continent. I'd explain the scientific details, but I'm sure they'd go right over your head. Basically, it'll produce a serum that'll attack cancer cells. At least, that's what I hope it'll do."

"Yeah, the medical mumbo jumbo might not stick, but it still seems too simple," he said. "I'm shocked somebody else hasn't figured it out by now."

"It's more complicated than that," she said. "It's been years of searching, experimenting, and discovery. Not just by me."

"Let me guess. Mommy was a scientist?"

"Dad," she said. "He was a bio-engineer, trained by…" her voice trailed off.

"Not Espinosa," Firebird said. "Who?"

"He was born…here. In Sovereignty," she said.

"Huh?"

"They had him travel in secret research operations to develop their superweapon. Most chemical agents that exist today would have a serious affect on the environment. Sovereignty wants to expand. Contaminating the land that they want to conquer would be counter-productive. They wanted a concentrated gas that could wipe out an enemy population and eventually bio-degrade. So, he started the research project. Until he defected. When my mom got sick, he swore to find a cure to the cancers caused by our atmosphere. He kept coming close but couldn't do it in time. Then he got sick. They replaced his heart, and he was able to keep going. Then he got sick again. And again. And again…"

"Damn," Firebird said. He stepped away from the bed. "Your family has had some shitty luck. But unless you have all of Daddy's notes on you, I don't understand how they expect you to remember all of his research."

Saegusa rolled onto her back and lifted her head, tilting the bionic casing on the left side toward him. Firebird could see the lining around the port where the memory chip was inserted.

"That isn't just yours, is it? It was your dad's."

"He was the prototype," she said. "Nobody had ever tried a partial brain replacement and lived. Until him…and me."

"Son of a bitch," Firebird said impressed. "You have access to all of his memories." He thought about it. A smug grin creased his face. "Damn, I hope for your sake it's not literally ALL his memories. You might have a few salty images of your own conception."

Saegusa allowed a smile to slip through. Only *he* would think of something like that to say.

"I chalk it up as part of the cost to saving the world," she said.

"Yeah," he said. Firebird moved to the desk table and laid himself across it. He stared up at the ceiling, considering dozing to a peaceful bliss.

A mild crackling sound entered his ear. It grew gradually more intense. Suddenly the desk tipped to one of its corners and toppled, spilling the mercenary onto the floor.

"What the—" he pushed the desk off of him and examined it. The leg that Saegusa cracked with her foot had buckled under his weight.

Seems nothing can go right today.

CHAPTER 19

Commander Zolnar marched through the middle of NorthTowne's main street, observing his Strikers as they ransacked every building in sight. Lights from the military vehicles shined far in the night air. Armored tanks patrolled ahead of him, surrounded by panicking civilians.

"I will say it again. Anybody with knowledge to the traitor's whereabouts, come forward. We will do this all day and all night until we find them!" the Commander announced to the terrified lot.

Strikers wrestled some unruly men out of a farmhouse. A steadfast teenaged boy charged the soldiers that threw his father to the ground, only to be struck in the face with the butt of a rifle. His mother's reactionary screams filled the air until another soldier knocked her down from behind.

Hours earlier, Commander Zolnar emerged from the forest, only to find the rest of his platoon devastated. Not a single Striker survived. It wasn't long before the rest of his battalion arrived at his location. Once again, the Supreme Leader was demanding an update on the situation.

Only one person could threaten the Commander's life and actually spark fear in his soul. And knowing Cornelius, he didn't bluff. Ever. Even worse for Zolnar, it wouldn't be a quick death for this failure. There would be no escape. No matter how loyal his Strikers were to him, they were more loyal to Cornelius, and would turn on him in the blink of an eye once the order was given.

There was only one thing Zolnar could do to cool the Supreme Leader's temper: lie.

"We are tracing the doctor's trail and are closing in on her position as we speak," he told the Supreme Leader. It had done little to quell his anger.

"This is unacceptable! The fact that you were outwitted by a bunch of peasants living in caves disturbs me, Commander," Cornelius replied. *"You better have Dr. Saegusa delivered to the Spahn Laboratory in twenty-four hours. If not, we can assume that she had either been killed or extradited by the Rebellion."*

"Supreme Leader, their interference came at great cost to them," Zolnar explained. "We have crushed many of their forces today with ease. Once we locate them and extract the doctor, we will eliminate their leaders and finish off their Rebellion once and for all."

"You speak as though I'm supposed to be impressed," Cornelius answered. *"You think I care for the Rebellion?! There is a reason they haven't launched an attack in months, and it wasn't solely strategic! Their forces have been degrading, due to our efforts and cloning technology. The fact that you've been in charge of handling them and have failed so far to find their base of operations, is an insult to the Sovereignty! Tell me Commander, do you mean to insult me?"*

"Hell no, Supreme Leader!" The words had a bitter taste to them. It was another indication of Zolnar's hidden distain for being obedient to someone else. Such a desire for power came with ego. Begging for his life, even though indirectly and in the form of a lie, scarred that ego with scorching burns.

"Twenty-four hours, Commander," Cornelius warned. *"If Dr. Saegusa is not delivered to our labs by this time tomorrow, I will put someone more competent in charge of your batallion."*

The feed came to a swift end. Zolnar understood the meaning of Cornelius' words. His lie had probably spared his life. Currently, he had no idea of the whereabouts of Saegusa and the Rebellion. Drastic time called for drastic measures.

"We will go through every house. Every barn! Every well! We will nail you to stakes and light flames under your toes until someone tells me what I want to know!" he yelled into the night sky.

****

The scouts lay on their stomachs as they watched the attack on NorthTowne. Several buildings were aflame and the echoes of a hundred terrified screams reached the hills.

"This is the second town they've hit," one of them said.

"That we know of," the other replied.

"They're going to hit Water Root next. Zolnar's desperate. Judging by the way they're going through the buildings, they're going to find Headquarters. No doubt."

"Looks like Drake's plan of evacuation was right on the money," the second scout said. With no time to waste, they quickly stood up and mounted their horses. Galloping their steeds to exhaustion, the scouts raced across the vast fields and farmlands until finally coming to the edge of Water Root. In the dead of night, the town was quiet. Few people walked the streets except for a few night watchmen keeping an eye out for coyotes and field rats, ugly three-foot vermin that often came out of their holes at night.

The properties were spaced out with several acres of farmland in-between. Water Root was mostly home to various vegetable farms. Of course, the Sovereignty was sure to be around in autumn when it was time to harvest. It was just one more tax that the lowly peasants had to pay to their Supreme Leader.

The scouts looked back. There were lights on the distant horizon. Target-Seekers patrolled the skies. Zolnar had his Striker battalion on high-alert. Only ego had kept him from alerting the entire Sovereign Army.

They cantered their horses through down the street, passing several properties until they came to a long, narrow dirt road that cut between a vast field of cornstalks. They followed the path for a few hundred yards until it concluded at a large barn. They entered through the open doors and dismounted. They placed their horses in their stalls and secured the door. Afterwards, they quickly moved to the end of the long aisle of stalls, glimpsing at various trucks, motorcycles, and other vehicles hidden within the barn.

They came to the last stall entered, pulling back a large tarp covered in straw and sawdust. Under that tarp was a large hatch. They tapped three times on it and waited. The wheel turned and the hatch opened.

The rebel soldier under it had a pistol in hand as he peered out. Behind him, another rebel on watch pointed a Plasma Rifle. After identifying the scouts, they opened the hatch fully and allowed for the scouts to enter.

****

Daunhauer tossed in his bed, tugging on the IV cords that were taped to his left arm. The pain meds did little to mask the continued burning sensation in his face. He could still taste the strands of his own charred flesh from his cheek. Worst of all, sleep was impossible. He had slept in horrible conditions before. He slept cold. In hot weather. Outside. In mud. In almost every circumstance, he was able to find rest. But they all had one thing in common: he could close his eyes.

In years of warfare, he and many others had made the joke of having to sleep with one eye open. He never thought it would be a reality for him. No matter what he did, he couldn't fall asleep. The doctors had given him an eye-mask to cover it up. All that did was aggravate the problem even worse. His eye was already dry to begin with. Sensitive to touch, he registered every time the fabric pressed against it.

He heard the door creak. He rolled onto his back and tossed the mask aside. He leaned up to look at the door. It was General Albright.

"General," he said.

"Don't stand up," she said. "I'm sorry to wake you. I just wanted to check and see how you were doing."

"I was already awake," he answered. His words were jumbled. Some of the muscle tissue had been eaten away by the acid. Even simple things like speaking would require a bit of therapy. "I suppose General Drake has pulled the plug?"

"He'll make the announcement in the morning," Beretta answered. "Nobody wants to volunteer anymore. We can't get any more recruits." She took a seat on his bed. "He's okay with everything being all for nothing."

Daunhauer rested in silence as his mind digested her words. He knew what she meant by 'everything'. He hated to see her in such misery. Resentment billowed in his soul. He wished he had the rank to confront General Drake and convince him to follow through on Beretta's plan. But the bastard couldn't see the bigger picture.

"I used to respect him," he said.

"I still do," Beretta replied. "I will face the truth in this matter: we wouldn't have gotten this far without him. I was no soldier back then. I was somebody who'd had enough."

"You're a soldier to me," he replied. "I'd be dead if not for you. And I think the same goes for this whole rebellion. Drake would never have started this alone. You have been as essential as him. Now, I think even more so. He's a good man. But I think he's lacking an edge that's needed right now."

"He's stripped me of my rank," Beretta said. Daunhauer sat up.

"Huh?"

"Apparently, we were too reckless," Beretta sighed. She stared aimlessly at the wall. Daunhauer wondered if she was pondering whether Drake was right.

"No. We were trying to win. We *DID* win! And we both paid a heavy price!"

Beretta gazed back at him.

"Yes, we did. We did win." She thought about those words and the events that had taken place. She thought of Paul's sacrifice. He purposely allowed himself to be tortured so that Zolnar could taunt her into capture. Except the only one who got conned was Zolnar himself. Daunhauer and Barber would have never completed their task had they not shown such bravery. It was another reason why Daunhauer knew she was the right leader for the job.

The sound of running feet drew their attention to the door. Two rebel scouts ran through the infirmary toward the conference area. Communication personnel sent a message through to Drake's quarters, alerting him to report.

"Get dressed," Beretta told Daunhauer. "I'm gonna see what's going on."

"I'm not sure he'll approve of you being there," Daunhauer said.

"Whatever's going on, something tells me he'll need my help," she said. She marched into the hallway and followed the scouts.

****

"Ow!" Firebird yelped. He kept himself hunched forward to block the flashes from Stuart's welder from waking Saegusa.

"You need to hold still," Stuart said. He straightened Firebird's artificial arm and continued working on the gauntlet. "Your blade got jammed tight in there. The metal on that shuriken would've decapitated if not for your arm."

"Probably why I blocked it," Firebird whispered. He glanced back, making sure Saegusa was still asleep. The poor doctor was out cold, understandably. Firebird had napped for a bit, but couldn't sleep for too long. He hated being in this tunnel, guarded by these rebels, who less than a day earlier, had tried to kill him.

Stuart opened the gauntlet and tended to the damaged areas. He straightened some of the metal around the knife's port as best as he could and reworked some of the inner components that blocked the blade from popping through. After several minutes of operation, he sealed the gauntlet and stepped back.

"Try it now."

Firebird tightened his fist and tapped his wrist against his knee. The twelve-inch blade shot out with a loud piercing sound. The blade glinted in the dim corner light, good as new.

"Perfect," he whispered.

"You guys done playing with your toys?" Saegusa muttered.

"Oops," Firebird said. He looked back again. "My bad. Thought you were asleep."

"I *was*. But how could anyone sleep while listening to you two flirting back and forth?"

"There is no purpose in flirting for a droid," Stuart mentioned.

"Unless that's your fetish," Firebird joked.

"Lovely," Saegusa groaned. She rolled back on her side. "Now, keep it down please."

"Yes, your majesty," Firebird quipped. He retracted his blade and took a seat on the desk chair. He leaned back and shut his eye in an attempt to doze off again. A knock on the door caused both of them to jump.

The door opened and Donnelly peered through. "Sorry to wake you. Dr. Saegusa? General Drake has requested your attention in the conference room."

Saegusa sat up. "Okay, give me a minute." Donnelly shut the door. Firebird switched on the overhead light. She winced as her eyes adjusted, then stretched. "I wonder if he's found a way to get us out of here." Firebird didn't answer. Saegusa glanced at him. The concern was plain on his face. The mercenary watched the door, thinking on Donnelly's tone and body language. The man was in a hurry, hence he didn't wait for them to answer when he knocked.

"I'm not sure," he said. He moved to the door and opened it for Saegusa, then followed her and Donnelly to the assembly room.

****

The assembly room was twice as large as the conference area. Several rows of seats were lined up like church pews. Many of them were empty now, another reminder that the Rebellion's time had ended as far as Drake was concerned. Several soldiers gathered on the south end, filling the first few rows of seats. They grew visibly nervous with the news brought from the scouts.

"You sure they're gonna come here?" a voice called out from the second row.

The scouts stood at the front of the room with General Drake and a few other officers. There was Major Krasnewski, Captain Bryan, and Sergeant Major Flinn. There were no Colonels or Lieutenant Colonels alive anymore. What was once a large and prosperous Rebellion had dwindled to this measly group.

"Commander Zolnar is being very thorough in his search," one of the scouts said. "They've hit Parch Tree, Lincoln Well, and NorthTowne. We're next."

"Frankly, I'm shocked that there aren't any Target-Seekers flying over town already," the second scout added. "But we saw them out over the fields. I guarantee they'll be here shortly."

A rebel stood in the front row. "They might not find this base. Hell, they've rolled through town before. They've never detected us."

"As I said, they're being extremely thorough. They're literally going through every home, every shop, every farm. They're tearing some structures up from their roots. I suspect Cornelius is putting so much pressure on Zolnar that his ears are about to pop."

"More like implode," Drake added. "There we have it, everyone. We can't stay here. We're gonna have to abandon this base."

"This entrance is still very well hidden," Major Krasnewski said. "It's possible it may go unnoticed."

"Our vehicles won't," Drake said. "Once they find those, they'll scour the area for anything leading to us. They'll eventually find the hatch. That is, if they don't discover one of the other entrances first."

"We need to get Dr. Saegusa out of here," Captain Bryan said.

"I understand we do not want her to fall in enemy hands," Krasnewski said. "However, I must ask: is saving her life really worth risking ours? Why don't we destroy the chip?"

"Because it'll kill her," Drake answered. His tone was as blunt as his words.

"General, you know I don't bring this up lightly," Krasnewski said. "But we're risking the lives of everyone here. For *one* person...whom if the Sovereignty obtained would lead to them developing their bio-weapon..."

"If she was voluntarily trying to help the Sovereignty, I would agree to your sentiment," Drake said. "But she's here largely because of our own doing. As you all know, we had a plan in place for her extraction, but that got sabotaged. Even the contractor almost had her out of here, yet *we* screwed it up. If not for certain actions from our own people, she would be across the border right now. We have to fix the problem. I am not going to execute an innocent person out of convenience."

"Would this lead to our own evacuation?"

All eyes went to the main entrance. Beretta Albright stepped through the doors and approached the main table. Drake stood silent, questioning whether he would have her forcefully thrown out or listen to what she had to say.

"Yes..." he answered. "But not right away. The border is heavily patrolled and fenced. We will not be able to simply stroll through."

"Then what's the plan?" another voice called from the main entrance. Firebird stepped ahead of Saegusa as he entered the assembly room. As he approached the table, he gave Albright a heated stare. Her expression was blank, her eyes glassy. To his slight surprise, she didn't return any harsh response.

"That's up to General Drake," she said. She looked to the General and stood like a good soldier waiting for orders. Drake was taken off guard. This was the Beretta Albright he had known before: tough, yet humble. Perhaps she had done some reflecting in the past few hours.

"*General* Albright," he said. "I know this day has taken a toll on you..."

"From how it sounds, this will be our last fight, General Drake," she said. "I'm ready to make it count."

"I wish it didn't have to be a fight. But it will be. That's unavoidable," Drake said. "The one good thing about our numbers is that we're small enough that we should move through the night mostly undetected if we're careful."

"Sounds like you're planning a strike," Firebird added. "Where?"

"The only way to get the doctor out of here successfully is by air," Drake explained. "There's a missile silo complex about thirty miles from here." He pulled up a large map and pointed to their town, which was on the north side. He moved his finger southeast toward an elevated region.

"A silo complex?!" Captain Bryan exclaimed.

"Silo Complex Six," Drake added.

Firebird let out a laugh. "You gonna have her sit on a rocket and ride it all the way to Espinosa?"

Drake laughed. "No. I don't think we need to pull a scene from *Dr. Strangelove*. Besides, that was a bomb, not a missile." Firebird's eye widened.

Someone actually understood one of his references.

"However, there's usually some Prime Eagle aircraft stored at these missile silos," Drake explained. "The plan is to cross the wheat fields and cross the River Pyre and go out and around until we're south of the silo."

"General!" Krasnewski spoke up. "These silos are HEAVILY defended! This is suicide."

"Not if we do this right," Drake said. "And I don't think Silo Complex Six is as heavily fortified as we think, at least not at the moment. Commander Zolnar is extracting all available forces from his jurisdiction to raid the towns. That requires significant manpower, which means he's probably pulled several personnel from the silos. They don't expect us to hit such a place."

"Even so, we'll be cut to bits just trying to storm the gate," Bryan said. "Sir, I'm agreeing with your objective, but I don't believe we can do this successfully. Those gates are armed with twin-plasma turrets. Between the rocks and the gate, we'd be wide open."

"Not if we launch the attack from inside," Drake said. He looked back to the group of rebels, focusing on a couple of mechanics seated several rows back. "How'd those repairs go?"

"It doesn't look pretty, but it'll work," one of them said.

"You're going to use the carrier truck?" Major Krasnewski asked.

"That's right," Drake said. "We'll store as many rebels in the compartment as possible, then go right through the front gate as though we're old friends. Once we're in...and past the turrets...we'll overwhelm the silo complex. We'll get Saegusa on a ship and get her out of here."

"Okay, I'm *almost* on board," Captain Bryan said. "But I think it's not like we can just go up and knock. They're going to require a code or a key swipe to enter."

"I have an answer to that," Beretta spoke up. She pointed a finger to Barber, who happily stood up. He wore a satisfied grin on his face.

"I can drive a truck. And I still have a uniform or two handy," he said.

"Yeah...but the code to check in at the gate...?"

Barber scoffed. "I helped *design* those things, as well as the algorithm. Trust me, I can get us in. The only trouble is, if these guys are searching as heavily as our scouts claim, then traveling thirty miles in a truck won't be easy. Target-Seekers will think something's off if they spot a truck, especially a Sovereign carrier truck, moving away from the populated areas."

"I know..." Drake said. "That's why we'll need a decoy; something to draw them away as we depart."

"You'll have to come up with something fast," Firebird said. "At this rate, you'll probably have Strikers crawling all over this area like ants in the next half hour. And that's if we're lucky."

"General Drake, you still have those anti-tank mines?" Beretta asked.

"Yes," Drake answered. "You suggesting we hit an armored division?"

"Sort of," Beretta said. "Rather, I'm considering we wire a Jeep with explosives and crash it into a guard tower on the border gate. Needless to say, the Strikers on post will call for reinforcements. That's where those mines will come in handy. Since they'll be responding to an attack on the border gate, they'll respond in droves. When they arrive, they'll find a nasty surprise in store for them. With trucks and tanks getting blown up by mines, they'll think we're launching an assault on the border, which'll give us the opportunity to make our trip."

"That'll be risky but it might work," Drake said. "Unfortunately, that mission has a high probability of being a one-way street. Whoever sets that mission needs to volunteer."

The room was silent for several moments.

"Sir, I'll do it," Lieutenant Donnelly said.

"You sure, Lieutenant?" Drake asked.

"Yes." He glanced over at Saegusa and Firebird. "I owe it to them."

"You don't owe us anything," Saegusa said.

"A few coins wouldn't hurt," Firebird mumbled.

"Let's stop wasting time," Donnelly said. He was already walking for the exit. "Get the Jeep loaded up. Set the explosives to charge. If anyone wants to come with me, now's the time."

After a few moments, one of the rebels stood from the front seat and followed him out. Soon after, another one followed. After a brief pause, one more stood up and hustled after them.

"Anyone else?" Drake asked. Nobody moved. "Okay, then. I want fifty men on board the carrier truck. Everyone else follow us on horseback or motorcycle. The clock's ticking, so move now."

CHAPTER 20

The base was alive with a frenzy of rebels running through the corridors. They gathered in the armory and stocked themselves with as much gear as possible before hustling to the surface exit.

Firebird went to the armory, finding the room alive with rebels. He quickly grabbed an Omega Rifle before they were all taken. No way he was going to be stuck with a Five-Star. He stocked his vest with grenades and a replacement power cell and grabbed a pistol and holster. He scanned the armory for anything else of use, eventually finding a box of plastic explosives.

Why not?

He grabbed a few blocks of the explosives and a wireless detonator, then hustled out into the hall, where he climbed the exit ladder into the barn.

Hidden within the barn, the rebels flooded the carrier truck while the mechanics conducted as many last-minute repairs as they could. They double-checked the tires and welded patches over holes in the exhaust line.

Firebird took the first seat in the carrier, holding an Omega Plasma Rifle in his hand. He looked over, seeing Saegusa taking the seat next to him. She too held a Plasma Rifle and was decked head-to-toe in body armor.

"What are you doing?" Firebird said. "You need to hang back. You trying to get shot?"

"I'm not gonna just sit back and watch you and everyone else take all of the risk," she said. Stuart scampered into the truck and folded his legs into the seat beside the doctor.

"It wasn't a request, Doc," Firebird said.

"I'm not your employee," Saegusa retorted.

"Oh, for godsake...Stuart! Tase her and get her out of here."

"I cannot do that. The doctor poses no threat," Stuart responded.

"I didn't say she posed a threat. I want her out of here," Firebird said.

"Relax," Saegusa said. "I'll stay alive and you'll get your money. Everyone knows that's what you're concerned about."

Firebird bit his lip. Before he could argue, several more Rebels flooded the carrier. He sat back down and stared at the empty seat across the aisle. A rebel took the seat and stared back at him. Firebird groaned audibly as he recognized Beretta Albright's white hair and piercing gaze.

"Greeeaat."

Drake took the seat next to her. The rebels packed themselves in tight, sitting shoulder-to-shoulder. Various types of Plasma Rifles pointed to the ceiling, resting between the knees of each seated rebel. Several others flooded the center aisle, filling the truck to its maximum capacity.

Another face peered in through the open door. Donnelly and his four men gave a final salute to General Drake, who stood and returned the salute.

"Godspeed to you, gentlemen," he said.

"Back at you. Get her out of here," Donnelly said. He started to walk away, only to stop and look back. "Hey, merc?" Firebird stood up to see him over the many heads that sat in the way. Donnelly gave a quick nod. "Sorry about blowing you up."

Firebird shrugged his shoulders. "Eh, happens all the time."

Donnelly smiled and put a hand on the door to shut it.

"Wait for our signal, Generals," he said.

"Affirmative," Drake responded. Donnelly shut the door and hustled to the other end of the corridor. His three men sat ready among one hundred pounds of heavy explosives. Two of them sat at the back, one of them at the turret mount. Donnelly took the driver's seat and steered the vehicle out the open doors. As they drove through town, he looked back. He could see the Target-Seekers in the horizon, guiding their spotlights along the ground below. They were moving in on the town. The ground forces would be quick to follow.

"God, please let this work," he said.

****

After exiting the north end of town, Donnelly sped the Jeep off the road, traveling through four miles of fields. The ground was irregular and full of dips, creating a bumpy ride for the small crew.

"Damn it," Donnelly muttered as they hit another bump. He refused to slow. Time was running out. The Jeep shook as its tires hit another small ridge in the earth. "Sorry, guys."

"Don't worry about it, sir," the passenger responded. His name was Jacob. He was actually a few years older than Donnelly but harbored no qualms about taking orders from him.

"How far to the perimeter?" Donnelly asked. Jacob looked to the map.

"Another three miles," he answered. He looked over at the speedometer, seeing the needle tilting into the red. "At this speed, we'll be there in a few minutes."

"Have the men get the explosives ready," Donnelly said. Jacob looked over at the men in the back. The gunner lowered himself off the mount and knelt by his comrade. They unpacked the mines and dynamite and passed several blocks to Jacob. He placed several blocks on the floormat and took the triggering device. It was a remote charge that would detonate the rest of the explosives. Donnelly fought the steering wheel to keep the Jeep on course. He worried that the ground would smooth out near the border. Once they propped the accelerator, there would be nobody at the wheel to steer it. At that point, the Jeep would be nothing more than a missile.

"I hope we can hit that guard tower," he said. "If we don't, those snipers will pick us off before we place the mines."

"We'll get it done, Lieutenant," Jacob said.

"Jake, you might wanna hold this," one of the rebels said. Jacob twisted to accept the pack of mines. He took the heavy bag, hearing the metal shells clunking together inside it. As he started to face forward, he noticed something in the sky. Lights—wing lights.

Suddenly, a huge spotlight beamed down on the Jeep.

"Target-Seeker!" Jacob shouted. Donnelly immediatey cut the wheel to the right. The vehicle darted out of the golden circle that encompassed it, just as a stream of plasma pulses rained down. Chunks of earth exploded along the Jeep's previous path, burning a fiery green. The air grew hot as Donnelly steered the vehicle further away. The Target-Seeker adjusted course in pursuit. Donnelly cut the wheel again, narrowly dodging another series of blasts.

One of the back passengers climbed onto the mount and clutched the butterfly grip. He depressed the trigger, firing a stream of plasma bullets up at the aircraft. The Target-Seeker elevated and zigzagged, continuing to spill artillery down on them. Donnelly gritted his teeth, seeing several pulses hit the ground just a few yards ahead of them. Flooring the accelerator, he sped the Jeep through the explosion. Hot air consumed them and singed their flesh, only to be immediately replaced by cool night air as they came out the other side.

The gunner blasted away at the aircraft, landing a few small rounds along its underbelly. They could see the red glow from the plasma burning into its thick shell. Unfortunately, it was not enough. The gunner would have to concentrate a long steady stream to cut through the exoskeleton. With the Target-Seeker zigzagging left and right and Donnelly's evasive maneuvers, that was impossible. His only hope was to hit the cockpit.

Or the guns.

He watched the green plasma cannons charge up. Donnelly swerved to the left, then back to the right, dodging a shot with each maneuver. The Jeep tilted from the force of the nearby explosions, jolting Donnelly and his passengers. The gunner sprayed back at the aircraft. He waved the barrel side-to-side, spraying plasma up in a wide fountain instead of focusing a steady stream.

Red sparks boomed from the cannons as the Target-Seeker passed through. The gunner perked his head and watched as the cannons sparkled. It actually worked.

"I got the guns!" he announced triumphantly. "Try shooting us now, motherfucker! Ha! Ha! AGGGHH!"

Twin machine guns fired from under the cockpit, raining bullet-sized plasma blasts down onto the rebels. They trailed the Jeep for a brief moment, kicking up dirt and gravel with each mini-explosion, then bombarded the turret. The gunner jolted violently, blood spouting from his chest before slumping over the side rail.

"Shit!" Donnelly cut the wheel, taking them out of the stream. He glanced over his shoulder. The gunner was dead, his body dangling over the side in a mangled state. The other passenger was okay, though shocked.

With the gunner out of commission, the Target-Seeker descended for easier aim.

"Drive straight," Jacob said.

"What are you doing?" Donnelly asked. Jacob didn't answer. He unbuckled himself and stood up. Donnelly looked over at him, thinking the fool was going to try shooting with a Plasma Rifle. "You idiot, don't..." he saw the flickering flame of a short fuse leading to a pack of dynamite. Jacob timed the distance and trajectory, then launched the explosives as though it were a football, just as the machine guns opened up again.

Jacob yelled out and fell in his seat, nearly toppling onto Donnelly. The dynamite bounced off the nose of the aircraft and detonated, ravaging the front of the aircraft. A large flash consumed the night air. The Target-Seeker smashed down, launching shards of metal through the sky.

Donnelly continued speeding north. The lights of the guard tower came into view. Roughly a dozen soldiers were on the ground, alerted to the vibrations from the crash. In addition to that, Donnelly was more than certain that the pilot let out a radio warning.

He stopped the Jeep along a dark hill then turned his attention on Jacob. He had caught a plasma bullet in his left shoulder. It had burned through, leaving a gaping hole in his upper chest. Blood trickled from his mouth as he grimaced in pain.

"Hang on. We'll get you out," he said.

"No," he moaned. He glanced back at the third rebel. "Get those mines out. Now!" The rebel took the bag and detached the turret. Donnelly moved around to help him lower it to the ground. As he did, he removed the plank from the back to prop the accelerator.

He stopped as Jacob scooched over into the driver's seat.

"Jacob, don't even think about it. Get out. That's an order," he said.

"Sorry, Lieutenant," Jacob said. His breathing was raspy. The way his head was tilting, he was quickly losing energy. He glanced at the terrain between them and the tower. "You were right. No way will this thing land where we want if we let if go on its own. I'm disobeying your order." He tossed the portable radio to the Lieutenant. "Give Drake the go-ahead."

"Jake, don't—"

Jacob gunned the accelerator, launching the Jeep down toward the tower. Shaking with each bump, he lit a fuse on one of the dynamite sticks. It was a long fuse, giving him more than enough time to reach the target. He floored the pedal, seeing the soldiers branching out. With his free hand, he lifted his rifle and smashed the windshield with the muzzle. As he entered the perimeter zone, he sprayed plasma fire wildly. Soldiers ran about, firing back at the speeding Jeep. They shouted and ducked for cover. To his amazement, he actually managed to catch a few in his spray.

He swerved left, pummeling another Striker with his engine. He was only a hundred yards from the target. Ninety.

Jacob jolted in his seat, feeling a hot punch pierce his stomach. Lurching backward, he saw the sniper high in the guard tower. There was another flash, and with it, another hot punch, this time in his chest. The rifle dropped from his hand. His vision started to blur. With the last of his strength, he put all of his weight on the accelerator and pointed the Jeep to the base of the guard tower.

Forty-yards. Thirty. Another flash streaked, striking just under his neck. His hand slipped from the wheel and the rebel slumped in his seat. The Jeep smashed into the tower, caving the engine inwards. The Strikers converged with rifles pointed. Ranking officers blared emergency transmissions on the radio. Several soldiers peered into the Jeep, seeing the flickering of sparks. Those sparks reached the end of the fuse.

The dynamite burst, exploding the hundreds of pounds of explosives. The blast shook the Earth, its flame engulfing the guard tower and surrounding Strikers. The support beams bent and caved under its weight, and the guardhouse smashed down.

A handful of Strikers staggered away from the blast, one of them continuing to alert the others on the radio.

"I say again. Echo Post is under assault. We've been hit with artillery and..." his voice was cut off, along with his head, as a hot streak of energy cut through his neck.

Donnelly charged down the hill with his fellow rebel. With a few well-placed shots, they killed the remaining Strikers. The Lieutenant caught his breath and gazed at the flame, then shared a glance with his comrade.

"Get the mines. We only have a few minutes," he said.

"Yes sir," the rebel said. As he hustled to collect the mines, Donnelly switched on the portable radio.

"Job is done. General Drake, you're good to go. Saegusa, if you're hearing this, I hope that cancer cure works."

****

"God bless you, Rebels," Drake responded. "Alright, men. Let's move out!"

Barber adjusted his Striker mask and cleared the fog from the visor. It had been many years since he donned one of these. He thought it would bring a slight feeling of nostalgia from his youth. Instead, he only felt shame. Those were bloodthirsty days when he was eager to hold a rifle and feel a sense of power. Only as the years went by did he finally mature.

"To hell with the Sovereignty," he muttered out loud. He hit the accelerator and sped the truck out of the gate, onto the main road, and out through the fields toward the target.

****

Donnelly dug with the small hand shovel and rake, digging an eighteen-inch wide crater into the ground. It didn't need to be deep, but just enough for him to conceal the mine. After brushing the dirt into a small pile, he placed the mine into the hole and primed the triggering mechanism. A small green light lit on the bottom, blinked several times, then faded. The mine was activated.

He could hear the sounds of heavy machinery approaching in the distance. The sky was full of spotlights from several Target-Seekers. Zolnar had taken the bait. The plan was successful. Donnelly released a sigh of relief. Despite the threat that loomed in his immediate future, he felt more relieved than ever. The guilt he felt from shooting the Ash-Cloud had lifted. He had righted his wrong.

He scooped the dirt pile and poured it over the mine, being careful not to throw too much dirt on at once. Any significant detection in weight would set the explosive off. With it fully covered, he glanced back, unable to see the traces of the other mines. That was just the way he wanted it. With the last one buried, he was ready to vacate.

The sound of machine-gun fire turned his attention to the east, where his fellow rebel had laid the last charge. Several vehicles rolled into the perimeter zone, each with a mounted machine gun on the back. There was nothing Donnelly could do but watch in horror as the guns literally cut his comrade to pieces.

Donnelly ran as fast as he could toward the flaming tower. Several blasts streaked by, missing him by inches. With a bounding leap, he dove behind the machine gun, which he already had propped and ready on its turret legs. Laying on his stomach, he opened fire, hitting the nearest truck. Its windshield shattered and the truck spun wildly until it overturned. The other truck veered to the side to avoid collision. Its front tires hit a slight 'bump' in the ground. That bump erupted into a fiery blast which launched the truck several meters into the air.

Donnelly aimed up and fired at an approaching Target-Seeker. Return fire rained down all around him, getting closer and closer. He tucked his chin down, enduring the heat, and continued shooting. He looked to the distance, seeing several armored units coming over the hills. A carrier truck moved in. He could see the backdoors opening up.

Before it could deploy, the truck hit a mine, sending it and its crew through the air in a fiery display. Moments later, a T-32 tank hit another mine. The blast wasn't as spectacular as the lighter vehicles, but it was effective all the same. The front of the tank lifted up under a ball of flame which had breached into the operating unit, frying all inside.

Donnelly continued shooting, cursing and taunting the Sovereignty. Finally, a blast struck, shattering the machine gun and launching him through the air. He was still alive when he hit the ground. He tried to move but couldn't. It wasn't until he looked up that he realized his legs and left arm were gone. His chest and belly were unrecognizable under the smoke that billowed from the flesh. He laid back and stared at the sky one last time. In his peripheral vision, he could see the flashes from the remaining mines detonating. He took a final breath, closed his eyes, and smiled.

He had righted his wrong.

CHAPTER 21

Firebird scooched as far as he could to the left to free up any tiny bit of space he could. The rebels were packed into the truck like sheep. Saegusa had watched their faces during the long journey. To her surprise, there was hardly a bead of sweat in the entire group. Most squads she had seen, brave as they were, usually had at least a couple of troops that were on the edge of breakdown near the edge of deployment. But they always did their duty.

I guess that's what makes them brave, she thought. But this group hardly displayed any anxiety. Hell, the officers in the assembly room were more nervous than this. It went to show that these rebels were battle hardened and ready to take on the challenge. Or perhaps it was just a hatred of the Sovereignty.

General Drake stood up and moved as best he could, despite the lack of space around him. He unfolded a large piece of paper and pressed it to the front wall for everyone to see.

The diagram showed the silo complex in great detail. The barrier walls were hexagonal shaped, with circles marking the position of turret mounts. The only opening was a gate on the south side, which contained a guard post both on the inside and outside.

Forty meters in was a radio tower on the left side and a vehicle storage area directly across on the right. In the center of the fort was the main control complex, which was a rather small building. Lines in the diagram displayed underground tunnels that led to the individual silos. There were eight of them, spaced about a hundred feet apart, from the top right down to the center. Up on the north end were the barracks and flight deck, the ladder being the largest building in the complex.

"Alright, let's go over the plan one more time," he announced. "As you know, the walls are twelve feet high, made of steel, and armed with dual-barrel turrets every fifteen-feet. We won't be able to scale them without being chopped to bits. That's where Barber comes into play. We'll be going in through the front gates, assuming Barber's as good as he says he is…"

"I'm so good, *I* could be a General," Barber quipped.

"Yeah, I'm sure," Drake said. "Anyways, once we're in, Barber will try to lure as many troops to us as possible, under the guise that they'll be loading into the truck. That's where the surprise attack begins. We'll take as many of them out as quickly as possible then storm the individual facilities. First thing's first: I need somebody to disable the guard tower IMMEDIATELY. If that fails, then this was all for nothing."

"You can bet the control center will be heavily defended," Firebird said. "They're gonna think we're after the missiles. Once they realize what's going on, they're gonna focus their defense on that."

"That's fine," Drake said. "Because we're after the landing pad. I want a team to secure the walls and prevent them from sniping us as we converge on the inner forces. The turrets can't turn inward to face the facility's interior, so we'll be safe from them. Once they're taken, I want that team to open the gates and let the rest of our people in. Meanwhile, I want the rest of our units to secure the barracks, trucking station, and flight deck. Then we'll have the center station surrounded. We'll close in and clear out the rest of the Strikers. Use explosives when necessary, EXCEPT at the flight deck. I don't want to risk any ships being damaged. If that happens, then this was all for nothing."

"What do you want me to do, General?" Firebird said.

"Do whatever you want. Just don't get yourself killed," Drake said.

"Sir, I have to ask, do we have a contingency plan if we can't get through the gate?" one rebel asked.

"Basically, we'd be screwed," another one said. "At that close distance, those guns will tear us to pieces."

"That's where Ms. Saegusa will come into play," Beretta spoke up. "If they discover us and find out she's in the truck, they won't risk firing on the compartment with those turrets."

"She's got a point," Drake said. "Sorry, doctor. I hope it doesn't come to that."

"Hey, if it keeps us from being blown up…" Saegusa remarked.

"If and when we do get in, keep out of sight…but DON'T stay in this truck," Drake said. "I wouldn't put it past the Strikers to shoot at it or blow it up with grenades. So, get out and find cover."

"Yes, sir," Saegusa said. "Thank you for this."

"No need for that," he said.

****

Barber followed a twisting road that led to a rocky landscape to the west. He had gone south as planned, and according to the map, he was on the path leading up to Silo Six. He drove onto an elevated landscape which was nearly as barren as the rocky region he had chased Firebird the previous day.

The sky was still dark. There was probably only an hour until sunrise. The moon was the smallest crescent before becoming a dark new moon. Through the flickering atmosphere, he had just enough light to see where he was going. Now, being so close to the silo, he finally switched on the headlights.

After several more minutes and bends in the road, he could see the wall. The silver steel glowed in the far reaches of his high beams. Little shapes rotated high on the walls. He knew immediately that it was the turrets rotating to face him. They had been spotted.

"Alright, everybody," he called back. "Not a peep from any of you. Including you, Generals."

A grin displayed on Drake's face. He knew Barber always relished the rare opportunity to give 'orders' to someone of a higher rank. He closed the window panel and held his gun close to his chest. It was time to be a soldier now.

Barber relaxed in his seat, recalling his memories as a Striker in the Sovereign Army. It was his way of getting into 'character'. The guard post came into view. The Striker on duty was already standing outside with his rifle in hand. Now Barber could clearly see the turrets up high on the wall. Four sets of dual-barrels pointed down at him. A couple of them pointed away as soon as their operators recognized it as a Sovereign vehicle.

This plan *had* to work. There'd be no plowing through the gate to get in. Hell, it was made of condensed steel that was only about two-inches less thick than the walls. It would require a few blasts from a T-32 cannon to breach it.

He stopped at the red line and flashed on his interior lights. Through his mask visor, he saw the guard approach his window. Barber stuck his head out as casually as if he were a delivery trucker.

"I hope I didn't wake you from a nap," he quipped.

"Shouldn't you be out participating in the search operation?" The guard clearly didn't have a sense of humor.

"Yeah, I am as a matter of fact," Barber expressed sternness in his voice. "You're gonna have to let me in and alert any available crew members for boarding."

"Boarding?! We've already relinquished half our crew to assist in the operation," the guard said.

"Weren't you guys notified of the attack on Echo Tower?" Barber said.

"Affirmative, but we've received no orders to lend additional troops."

"Well," Barber shrugged his shoulders, "that's what I'm here for. I would notify your commanding officer if I were you. And let me in." Barber extended his makeshift security card. The guard took it and gazed at it, then back at Barber. After a moment of apprehension, he slid the card into the security panel. It flashed green and the guard handed it back. He opened the gate and picked up his radio.

"Staff Sergeant Curfice, please report to Trucking Station B."

"On my way."

Barber drove through the gates. His eyes immediately went to the huge radio tower up ahead to the left. It was over a hundred feet tall. At its base was an enormous box unit, similar to the one he had hacked on the radio truck in yesterday's attack. Luckily, he wouldn't have to hack this one.

He passed the interior guard shack and steered the truck to the path along the right and parked in the designated space. He waited for several minutes, all the while observing the number of troops patrolling the wall.

He slid the window panel open a crack and whispered, "Ten guys total on the wall. Most on south end. Two on northeast." He slid the panel shut. Considering that was minimal staffing, he predicted that none of the wall security would be taken off to 'board' the truck.

Finally, he saw an officer approaching. The Staff Sergeant didn't bother to wear a mask. The Staff Sergeant had the scars to prove his worth, but something about his body language made Barber think he was somewhat laid back. Considering how clean and untouched the outer walls appeared, this fort had never faced assault since it was constructed. In military terms, this was a place of leisure. It was complete routine that had never been tested. That was exactly what General Drake had hoped for.

The Staff Sergeant stepped up to his window.

"Driver? What's this about taking away more of my men?"

"Zolnar's ordered more men to assist in the operation," Barber said.

"He's already taken over half my Strikers," the Staff Sergeant said.

"Yeah, but as you're aware, there was an attack on the perimeter. Early reports are saying there were a lot of casualties. Zolnar needs more men to continue the sweep into Water Root."

"We don't have any more to hand off," the Striker said. "We're already stretched thin."

"You have interior guard posts and internal operators?" Barber asked.

"Yes, but they're gonna be on post in the next hour or so. And we'll need them."

"You'll have to do without them, Staff Sergeant," Barber said. "The missiles will still be there when they get back."

"Listen, Driver, I've received no orders from Commander Zolnar. I don't have the men to spare."

"Okay. Feel free to contact Zolnar and tell him that. Until then, I can't leave without a fresh truckload," Barber said. There were a few moments of pause. The psychological warfare was working. The Staff Sergeant knew that Zolnar was under tremendous pressure and had a temper like a raging bull. The rebel attack on the tower had undoubtedly made it worse. He could only imagine what radioing Zolnar on this morning would be like, much less actually withholding troops.

"Shit," he muttered in frustration. He glanced back up at Barber. "Hang tight. Let me see what I can do."

"Thanks, Staff Sarge," Barber said. He watched the officer walk away. Two other Strikers gathered near him. After receiving orders, they took off running for the barracks.

With nobody around, Barber looked back into the compartment.

"In case you couldn't hear, it's game time," he whispered.

"Got it," Beretta said.

The rebels arranged slowly, careful to not make noise and visible rocking of the truck. Like revolutionary soldiers from centuries past, they positioned themselves in rows, all facing the doors. The front group pointed their rifles, ready to open fire as soon as those doors opened up.

"Okay, we're gonna find out if this plan was good or bad," Firebird said.

"It'll work," Drake whispered.

"It better. I feel like I'm on a landing craft headed for Omaha Beach, and you know how well that went for the first wave," Firebird whispered.

Several tense minutes passed. Firebird uncovered the corner of the window and peeked outside. Soldiers were hustling up to the truck. They marched along to the back and prepared to board. Firebird looked closer, growing nervous. The line stretched out to the side, not directly out in front.

"We've got a problem," he whispered. "They're not assembling where we want."

General Drake squeezed past several of his rebels and looked. Firebird saw the very faint twitches in his emotionless expression that displayed distress. This part of the plan had backfired. If they spilled out of the truck, they'd be in point blank range of these troops with no cover.

Firebird gently tapped on the window panel. "Barber, how clumsy are you?"

"Beg your pardon, merc?"

Firebird slipped a couple of grenades through the window. He looked down at them, realizing they were creator grenades. Once detonated, they would spread flame that would burn anything at fifteen feet. Barber realized what the mercenary was getting at.

He pulled the pins and tucked the grenades behind his back as he stepped out of the truck. The Staff Sergeant was there waiting, growing more impatient by the minute. Behind him were at least thirty troops. If Barber's predictions were correct, there would be at least fifty others within the complex in addition to those on the walls.

"Get the door open," the Staff Sergeant barked.

"Already on it…" Barber took a couple of steps, then took an exaggerated stumble. "Whoops!"

The two grenades rolled out into the group. Recognizing what they were, the Strikers retreated behind the truck. The grenades detonated, unleashing a circle of flame. Unlucky Stickers ran ablaze, the fire clinging to their uniforms as though they were soaked in gasoline.

"What the hell?!" The Staff Sergeant yelled, watching several of his men running ablaze.

"NOW!" Drake ordered. The back doors opened up and the rebels opened fire. Streams of plasma cut through the unsuspecting Strikers, cutting several of them down to size.

The rebels spilled from the truck, exchanging gunfire with the remaining soldiers in the squad. The Staff Sergeant pulled his pistol and fired. His eyes were wide with surprise when he turned his aim on Barber, only to see the so-called driver with a pistol already fixed on him.

"Should've called the Commander," he said. A single shot ended the Staff Sergeant's command in a hot blaze. Barber ran behind the engine, avoiding incoming fire from the dozen Strikers who survived the initial onslaught.

Drake and Beretta followed the squad out of the truck. Fifty Rebels flooded the south side of the complex. With Drake at the lead, they swarmed the Strikers. Firebird hopped out of the truck and watched as the two groups exchanged gunfire as the larger one closed in on the smaller group. He glanced up to the wall, seeing the gunners dismounting and firing down at the Rebels. He counted two on the section of wall directly ahead. He aimed his rifle and fired. Each blast hit its mark, spinning the gunners on their heels before dropping them. Firebird aimed further left, seeing a gunman aiming at him. He tucked and rolled to his right. In that same moment, several plasma shots struck the cement where he had stood.

He came up into a kneeling stance, aimed, and fired. The Striker arched his back, billowing smoke from his chest. He twisted in agony before falling off the edge of the wall.

"Sorry, Humpty Dumpty," Firebird said. He glanced back as Saegusa stepping out of the vehicle. She froze, unsure of where to go. Firebird grabbed her by the shoulder and pulled her behind the truck as a few stray shots streaked their way.

"Holy shit," she muttered. She peeked back around the truck, watching Drake's men overwhelm the Strikers.

The General discharged his rifle, dropping the last of the first wave of Strikers.

"Take the radio! Converge on the radio tower!" The men charged into the interior of the complex, while Barber and a few other rebels climbed ladders up onto the wall.

Firebird looked up again, seeing some of the remaining gunners converging on the wall section where the rebels climbed. A few shots already flared from their rifles, hitting one of the rebels and dropping him to the ground.

"Oh, hell," Firebird muttered. He moved out into the open and fired up at the five Strikers, hitting one of them and causing the others to retreat back. The distraction was enough for Barber and his men to complete the climb. They raced along the perimeter and engaged the Strikers.

Firebird continued laying down cover fire, successfully shooting another one off the wall. As he continued spraying blasts, the Rebels moved in and overwhelmed the three remaining soldiers.

An explosion caused him to turn around. Several grenades burst around the base of the radio tower, pulverizing the electronic unit.

"Good Lord," Saegusa said. More gunfire streaked from the north as Strikers moved in from the Barracks and Center Station. The two groups collided, with the rebels running along the left wall. As Drake had predicted, several Strikers had retreated to the Center Station to guard it.

She heard the creak of a door opening. Looking to her right, she saw a Striker dashing out of the vehicle garage. Gasping in surprise, she spun and squeezed the trigger. Plasma bullets sprayed wildly as she swung the rifle. One of them hit the soldier, who dropped to his knees and faceplanted.

"Ooookay!" Firebird yelled. Saegusa saw him ducking several feet to the right, having recoiled. A slight bit of smoke raised from his shoulder.

"Oh!" she said, realizing she had grazed him. "Sorry…I…"

"I'm good. You shoot like a damn girl, though," he said. He ran for the open door and waited off to the side. As he expected, a couple more Strikers were exiting, probably awoken from a deep slumber.

He greeted the first one at the door by striking him in the belly with his rifle, then grabbing him by the neck and spinning him back. Locking him tight with an arm around his neck, he moved in front of the entrance. Several shots spilled out, striking his human shield. Firebird extended his rifle over the now-dead Striker's shoulder and returned fire, dropping the target.

"What do we have here?" he said. He knelt down and picked up the Striker's weapons. "Plasma Uzis! I haven't seen any of these in forever." He discarded the rifle and picked up the Uzis, sporting one in each hand. As he stood up, he spotted movement up ahead. A small group of Strikers were moving in from the silo areas, weaving between the guard posts.

Firebird charged, winding back and forth to evade shots. Sparks splattered amongst clouds of smoke as plasma pummeled his surroundings. The mercenary angled his path to the right, weaving around their cover positions. After several yards, he angled around the nearest guard post. The Striker turned to shoot, only to get a dozen rounds to the chest.

Firebird pivoted to the right and fired both Uzis into the next Striker, watching him dance from the multiple hits before collapsing. In one smooth, dance-like move, the mercenary took a long stride forward and aimed left. The two other targets shot at him and missed before the dual-wielded Uzis plastered them with hot energy.

Firebird looked back and forth, confirming this zone had been secured. Up on the wall, Barber's team had secured the south barrier and was moving toward the gate to open it. Spotlights had come on throughout the complex, illuminating the various figures darting across. Drake and Beretta led their forces around to the barracks, where most of the remaining forces were, with many of them moving back to the Central Station.

Firebird looked further out, studying the movements of the Strikers. Some of them seemed to be running further back to another station beyond the Central Station. It was the flight deck. He looked back to the rebels, who were locked in a shootout with the Strikers. At this rate, they would not reach the ships in time.

No way are they stealing my ride, he thought. As he started to move, he felt the presence of someone approaching behind him. He turned, ready to shoot, then lowered his weapons. He should've known it was Saegusa.

"You need to quit doing that," he said.

"They're going for the aircrafts," she said. Firebird could read between the lines. She wanted to help stop them. He didn't want to risk her getting killed. However, every moment they wasted arguing increased the likelihood they'd lose their ride out of there.

The doctor could sense the conflict twirling within him.

"Hey, the safest place is right behind you," she said.

"Ohhh, FINE! Come on," he said. They ran north, hugging the interior of the wall as they worked their way around the silos to the flight deck.

"All units converge," Drake commanded. The rebels branched out from behind various guard post structures they used as cover and swarmed the barracks. Strikers fired from the windows of the two-story structure. The rebels fired away, cutting through the enemy troops on the ground.

They spread for cover again as a heavy machine gun blasted from the front entrance. The stream of energy bullets caught two rebels in the front of the pack and literally cut them to pieces. Drake's team fell back, with several of them taking refuge behind the radio tower, while others took cover behind the various Jeeps and guard posts.

Drake ducked down behind the engine and planned a course of action. His thoughts were interrupted as an energy blast zipped down and cut into a nearby rebel. He looked up over his left shoulder. Numerous plasma fire rained down from the top of the wall. The two gunners up top had a prime sniping position and were picking off rebels with each shot.

Beretta saw the problem and moved for the nearest ladder, letting her rifle hang over her shoulder by its strap. She tensed and ducked her head as a flash of energy passed by, singeing a few of her white hairs. She drew her pistol and fired back. She didn't hit anything, but it was enough to force the shooters to duck for cover. She resumed her climb, with a few rebels following her.

The shooters emerged from cover and resumed firing. The rebel directly behind Beretta was hit and flaked off the ladder like a dry leaf in autumn. Beretta took three bars at a time and scrawled to the edge. Finally, on the wall, she rolled forward, nearly getting hit by a few more rifle shots. She fired back, driving the shooters into cover again.

Her rebel comrades climbed up onto the wall and joined her as she flanked the shooters. Beretta got the first shot, frying one of the Striker's face with a single blast. The other attempted to make a glorious last stand by picking up his partner's rifle and duel-wielding, only to get pummeled with over a dozen rifle blasts.

The rebels spread out over the section of wall and began laying cover fire for Drake's team.

The Strikers were caught off guard by the sudden rain of plasma. From the wall, the rebels were able to fire through the windows. Beretta laid on her stomach and grabbed one of the sniper rifles. She placed the thermal crosshairs into the doorway and fired. Orange droplets splattered in her view as the blast cut through the gunner. She panned the rifle and fired again, blowing off the head of another enemy troop.

Each kill felt increasingly satisfying. More so than ever. She fired again, feeling the rush of watching the enemy in brief writhing pain before dying. She wanted to do this to the entire Sovereignty. For Paul...

After picking off a few more soldiers, she moved her scope out. She saw movement in the thermal display. Several soldiers were at the flight deck. However, they were already engaged with a firefight coming in the opposite direction.

Two figures moved from the east wall, their cybernetic components not displaying thermal signatures in her scope. Firebird and the doctor.

Firebird sprinted, firing both machine-pistols. He had reached the flight deck. There were two ships remaining. They were Prime Eagles, scout-class aircraft. They were smaller than the Target Seekers, with only a third of the armaments.

He moved around the bow of the nearest one. He had seen an enemy combatant hiding around there. He could hear the soldier's back brushing against the hull. He was getting ready to make his move. Firebird reached his metal arm around the nose and fired his Uzi blindly. A moment later, he heard the thud of a body hitting the deck. He checked his corners and moved along, glancing back to make sure Saegusa followed close.

Up ahead, three other Strikers emerged. The Uzis were already aimed, allowing the mercenary to fire first. The two streams of hot energy bullets struck all three, causing them to arch, spin, and fall. The merc turned to his left as another one emerged. Energy bullets struck the target in the gut then the head, exploding the mask.

Not wasting time, Firebird hustled around the tail of the second Prime Eagle, shooting another Striker who tried sniping from the right. He reached the ship, then glanced back to the sound of rifle fire. Saegusa had her gun shouldered and aimed at their six-o'clock, dropping another enemy who had tried to circle behind. After confirming the kill, she looked back, then jumped with surprise.

"Pay attention!" she yelled.

Firebird saw the movement in his peripheral vision. The shadow betrayed the presence of a Striker approaching from around the ship with a rifle in hand. Firebird rotated his body clockwise and threw his arm out, knocking the barrel of the gun away from his head. Completing the twisting motion, he extended his left arm and pointed the Uzi in the bastard's face.

"Swallow this."

The shot tore the helmet apart like glass and burned into his skull. With the target down, the mercenary completed his sweep of the flight deck. He approached the bow of the Prime Eagle then extended both Uzis as another Striker stepped out to fire. He squeezed the trigger, sending a three-round burst into the enemy. Firebird held up the guns. Steam swirled from their barrels and frames. They had both overheated.

"Well, shit..." he glanced back up, seeing another Striker peering around the ship, aiming a rifle. "SHIT!" He ducked and rolled as rifle fire zipped past him. He leapt to his feet and extended his gauntlet blade. Before he could charge, the Striker suddenly convulsed into a violent spasm. The seizure lasted for a few seconds, causing him to lose his grip on the rifle. Finally, the shaking stopped, and the gunman fell on his face with two barbs protruding from his back. The barbs retracted.

"I was starting to wonder where you were this whole time," Firebird shouted as Stuart strolled around the Prime Eagle. The droid closed its ports as the tasers reeled back into his body. The Striker groaned and lifted his head, only to be kicked and knocked unconscious by Stuart.

"My apologies. I almost took a hit." Stuart ducked down, revealing a black scar resulting from being grazed by a shot.

"Eh, better late than never," Firebird said. He moved around the bow of the ship. He observed the interior of the complex, seeing the Rebels invading the barracks. The windows glinted with the red and green flashes of plasma fire.

As the rebels secured the building, General Drake led a charge into the Center Station.

Flames flared as the defenders launched rocket-propelled-grenades. The General ordered his men to disperse. Explosions kicked up concrete and dirt, miraculously missing any rebels.

However, machine-gun fire forced them back behind cover.

Saegusa watched the rebels get pinned by machine-gun fire. There were at least two guns, one of which was aimed up in an attempt to take out Beretta's snipers.

Meanwhile, Firebird leaned against the bow of a Prime Eagle with his arms crossed. He yawned as though bored, then turned around to examine the ship.

"Wha—WHAT are you doing?!" she said.

"Getting our ride ready. That's why we came here in the first place," he said. His voice was nonchalant, with the casualness of somebody leaving a nine-to-five job for the day.

Saegusa watched the assault, then back at Firebird. "You need to help them."

"We did," he said.

"Their machine guns have them pinned," Saegusa pleaded.

Firebird shrugged. "Drake should've considered that in his attack plan. Besides, their reinforcements should be arriving any second." He opened the cockpit and checked the instruments. With the flick of a few switches, the ship was primed and ready to go. He gestured to Saegusa to come aboard.

The doctor looked back. Barber's team had the door open but only partially. Something had gone wrong, either mechanically or systematically. Either way, the remaining units would not be able to assist in time.

"Merc! You help them...or I will." She squared her rifle across her chest and pivoted to leave. Firebird groaned.

"You owe them nothing," he said.

"It's not about what you owe," she said. After a long stare, she started to go for the station.

"Okay, fine," Firebird said. She stopped, seeing him stepping out of the cockpit and scoop up the unconscious soldier's rifle. "Just stay here for once. Stuart, keep an eye on her."

"Technically, I don't have eyes..."

"Oh my...GOOOOOOODDD" Firebird shook his head in frustration and charged the back of the station. Despite the intensity of the situation, Saegusa couldn't help but chuckle at his reaction.

"You piss him off on purpose, don't you?" she said to Stuart.

"He gives quite fascinating reactions," the droid said. "It's a shame I can't laugh."

By the time they noticed he was coming, Firebird had closed the distance on the building. He ducked under the window as they shot at him, removing themselves from the machine guns. Tucked against the foot of the building, Firebird pulled a grenade from his belt and tossed it through the overhead window.

Soldiers panicked briefly before the loud *BANG* pulverized the interior. Firebird stood up and moved around the corner where the nearest entrance was. One Striker stumbled out, his uniform battered. Holding a pistol in his hand, he turned in a weak attempt to aim it at the mercenary. A quick spray from his rifle neutralized that threat. Firebird shuffled around his smoking body and progressed into the station. Controls sputtered and monitor screens were cracked. Looking out the opposite window, he saw Drake's team closing in. In that moment, he considered leaving them to finish the job. Then again, that would result in another lecture from Saegusa.

"Must do everything myself," he muttered. He moved to the stairwell door, grasped the handle, then paused. Still gripping the handle, he moved to the side, staying clear of the entry. He whipped the door open. As he predicted, a volley of gunfire sprayed out from the stairway.

After letting waste several shots, he stuck his rifle out around the edge of the frame and blasted away. Blazing energy hit all three Strikers, sending them rolling down the short flight of steps.

Firebird moved into the stairwell and proceeded into the tunnel below. It led to a door, which led to a junction that combined four separate tunnels. Two Strikers waited in that junction, only to be taken down in a fiery blaze by the intruder. After shooting them, he aimed to the entryway marked *Silo 1-2*, and fired as another soldier emerged. As the target collapsed, he looked over his shoulder, hearing running feet descending down the steps.

General Drake arrived at the door with several rebels. He gazed at the aftermath of Firebird's work and nodded, impressed.

"I'm glad you're on our side," he said.

"Each of these tunnels should lead to two missile silos," Firebird said. "There's nowhere for any of these bastards to go."

"Good. Then let's finish the job," Drake said. The group broke into teams of four, with Firebird leading a team into the tunnel marked *Silo 3-4*. They were immediately greeted with gunfire from Strikers defending the position. As Drake had predicted, they believed the rebels were after the missiles.

Firebird took out the one on the right, while several of his rebel followers eliminated the other. They proceeded further in. Echoes of gunfire boomed through the tunnels as the other teams engaged security forces. The tunnel led to a large circular atrium with a guardrail surrounding a large missile. They had entered *Silo 3*.

Out from the opposite side of the atrium came another Striker. The rebels reacted with a series of blasts, singeing the side of the missile's shell casing.

"Whoa!" Firebird held up a hand. "Dumbasses! Watch your shooting unless you want to blow us all up. You shoot this thing, it'll detonate and trigger the other missiles, and everyone gets fried."

"My bad," one of the rebels answered. They followed his lead and proceeded into the next corridor. So far, the tunnel was empty. They could see the next silo about a hundred feet ahead of them.

A Striker stepped into the entryway. Firebird aimed his gun to shoot, then stopped, realizing that the soldier wasn't holding a rifle, but a long shaft connected to a hose.

"Get back," he yelled, diving back into the hall. Several rebels ignored him, however, and charged the silo. The Striker squeezed the trigger, shooting a stream of flame. Fire swirled in the tunnel, causing the rebels to twist and turn in scorching agony. The group backtracked, with some of them aiming their rifles to fire. Firebird thrust a hand out, knocking a couple of muzzles toward the ceiling and sabotaging their aim. "You hit that fuel tank while he's in there with the missile, what do you think will happen?!"

Realizing his point, the rebels backtracked, while their blazing comrades slowly succumbed to their burns. They retreated back into *Silo 3* and took cover behind the walls. Smoke filled the tunnel and swirled out into the silo.

"Can't say this one doesn't have balls," the merc muttered.

"How do we get in there?" one rebel asked, choking on the smoke. Firebird peeked back in around the entrance, then yanked back out as the Striker blasted another stream of flame around the corridor.

"I can shoot it out of his hand," one rebel said.

"Yeah, right. Weren't you the one who almost shot the missile?" Firebird quipped.

"Doesn't your metal arm have anything we can use? What can that gauntlet do?" one of the rebels asked. Firebird protruded the blade, causing them to jump back. He glanced down at the blade and sighed.

I hate losing these things...

"Ugh," he groaned. He stood up and placed his other hand under the gauntlet, sliding a small panel back, exposing a small red button. He peeked once more around the corner. The smoke had cleared enough for him to see the target. With his arm extended, he stepped out into the doorway, pointed the blade, and pressed the button. With a loud springing sound, the blade launched like a spear and soared through the tunnel. The Striker dropped the shaft and clutched his face where the blade pierced his skull.

The rebels peered in just in time to see the soldier drop to the floor.

"Two minutes spearing," he said, speaking like a broadcaster in a hockey game.

They invaded and secured the silo. After a few moments, the echoes of gunfire ceased.

The group returned to the juncture and waited. A few moments later, the other teams arrived from their corridors. General Drake stepped into the juncture and tapped a few of the men on the shoulders.

"Well done, everybody. Area is secured."

CHAPTER 22

The doors opened with a loud whine and the remaining rebel forces flooded the Silo Complex. Jeeps and motorcycles parked throughout, deploying rebels who proceeded to secure the area. They immediately got to work moving bodies and taking control of the wall turrets.

Firebird stepped out of Central Station, which was still smoking from the damage it had sustained during the battle. He was immediately greeted by Saegusa. She wore a smile on her face, displaying true happiness. He didn't expect to see that. In fact, he didn't think such a look could exist on her.

"Thank you," she said. Firebird stood silent for a moment, taken by surprise by her reaction.

"This job was supposed to be easy," he quipped. "Yet, here I am, fighting revolutions."

"God forbid you do something out of the goodness of your heart," Saegusa said, her tone sarcastic.

Barber closed the gates as the last of the motorcycles and Jeeps arrived into the complex. With the area secured, he climbed down a ladder and joined the rest of the rebels where they gathered near the flight deck.

He passed a Jeep as he walked, immediately recognizing the rebel stepping out of the passenger seat.

"You sure you don't need any painkillers, Lieutenant?" he asked.

"I'm fine," Daunhauer answered, his voice raspy. A bandage covered the left side of his face, including his eye. It was oozing with disinfectants the doctors had placed on his charred skin, which likely stung like crazy.

General Drake stepped out of the complex building and greeted Beretta, who approached from the wall. She was glancing at the numerous Striker bodies, feeling satisfaction with each one.

She greeted Daunhauer with a nod, which he returned.

"Did they get a signal out?" Major Krasnewski asked.

"No," General Drake said. "We hit the tower in time. All of Zolnar's forces are too far away for two-way radios."

"Well, you proved me wrong, General," the Major said, looking around at the aftermath. "Not that I have the rank to argue, but I wasn't convinced this could be done."

"We had help," Drake said, nodding his head at Firebird. The mercenary didn't offer a response. He was already prepping the ship to take off.

"Glad I could be of service," he muttered. He climbed into the cockpit and fumbled with the navigation. "Are you kidding me? Those dumbasses haven't recharged the power cell." He climbed down and marched to the station

Drake then turned around and gestured a hand at Beretta. "General Albright, you did great."

"Thank you, General Drake," she replied. She looked around, her face displaying a sense of satisfaction. "We have access to all kinds of supplies here. We can really cause the Sovereignty a real headache with the missiles alone."

"I wish it was an option," Drake said.

"It can be," Beretta said. Drake tensed for a moment, fearing another debate about to take place. The respect for her that had returned was now starting to dwindle from a wave of frustration.

"But we just don't have the numbers to continue this war."

"Our people didn't fight to lose," she continued. "Everyone here is more than willing to continue the fight instead of running away like cowards."

"We *will* come back," Drake said. "Just because we're vacating, doesn't mean we're done. But as for now, I'd rather keep them alive until we can develop a new fighting force."

"It won't happen," Albright said. "Nobody outside of the border has any stake in this fight."

Drake shook his head. He could sense the desire for vengeance in her tone again.

"The most important thing is that we can get the doctor out of here and figure out a means of escape. We have time. The Sovereignty doesn't yet know this facility has been overtaken." One of the rebels approached and handed him Saegusa's pouch full of samples. He took it and passed it over to Saegusa, then shook her hand. "Doctor, I hope you have a safe journey."

"Thank you, General," she said.

"I believe your knowledge and research will be of great value," he said. Behind him, Beretta nodded again at Daunhauer, who nodded back, as though giving approval.

"Yeah, I must agree," Beretta said. She drew her pistol and fired a shot into Drake's back. The General lurched with a loud yell, then fell to the ground. Shouts of surprise and shock ripped through the crowd of rebels. One lifted his firearm to point at Beretta, only to be disarmed and knocked to the ground by Daunhauer.

"What the hell?" Firebird looked over his shoulder and gripped his sidearm. Stuart retreated into the fuselage and prepared to engage in defensive combat.

Beretta fired a shot into the air, gaining everyone's attention. Rebels pointed rifles at each other, as personnel loyal to each General took a stance on who to defend. In the middle was Saegusa, who immediately kneeled down to tend to Drake's injuries. He was still alive, though in a mild state of shock. It was obvious his mind hadn't quite realized what exactly had happened. He groaned in considerable pain as he leaned on his side.

"We did NOT go through all of this to turn tail and run!" Beretta announced to the rebels. "You all have a choice: Join me and witness the destruction of the Sovereignty. Or you can join him," she pointed down at Drake.

"General, what are you doing?" Saegusa said.

"I'm finishing this fight. And *you* are going to help me."

"You can stick it up your ass," Saegusa retorted. She rose to her feet and drew the Model 10 Revolver. Before she could point it to shoot, a hand struck from out of the crowd, knocking it from her hand. The gun flew through a broken window of the Center Station and bounced out of sight as it went down the flight of stairs.

Daunhauer grabbed her wrist, twisted it, and shoved Saegusa to her knees. She felt his fingers grab her from behind the neck, serving as a warning not to resist further.

"You can refuse all you want, but you're not going anywhere. I got what I need." Beretta gestured to the metallic side of her head.

"Go," Drake rasped. "Go with Firebird..." Saegusa took a deep breath. Desperation set in. She realized being captured by Albright was just as bad as being captured by the Sovereignty. She threw a hand back, knocking Daunhauer's grip away. She stood to her feet and started to run. She felt a set of hands grab her by the shoulders. She threw an elbow back, striking the attacker in the throat. Another rebel stepped in her path. She threw a hard kick with her cybernetic legs, crunching a couple of his ribs and driving him to the ground.

A blow to her stomach doubled her over, triggering the immense pain from her cancer. She fell to her hands and knees, gasping for breath.

"Not cool!" Firebird shouted. He started running at the crowd, only to stop after a few steps. Judging by the number of rifles pointing at him, it was abundantly clear most of the rebels were siding with Beretta. Knowing he would not reach the Prime Eagle in time, he turned and retreated, firing a few shots back at the group.

Several energy rounds zipped by as he ran. He tucked his head down as one passed a few inches overhead. He could hear the drumming of running feet behind him. After several yards, the cement ground turned to metal. He was running over the silo doors.

He stopped briefly and looked around, quickly locating the maintenance hatch. He turned the lever and opened it, then lowered himself down the ladder. He closed the hatch and latched it, then used his metal arm to smash the lever inward, jamming the latch in place.

The rebels' boots echoed over the metal ceiling. The lever creaked as they tried to open it.

"It's jammed," one of them said.

"Down the stairwell. He's got nowhere to go," said another. He could hear their feet drumming to the Central Station

Firebird grimaced, immensely frustrated. "Are things just *supposed* to go wrong?!" He slid down the ladder bars. He descended at a speed just shy of freefalling until he finally landed in the silo.

He moved around the large missile into the mouth of the hallway, snatching up a Plasma Rifle from a dead Striker along the way. Hearing the numerous feet running his way, he knew he would not be able to defend his position for long.

"Fuck it," he said. He pulled one of the plastic explosives from his vest and stuck it to the missile. The rebels drew closer. They were now in the next silo over. He armed the explosive and grabbed the detonator. They were now flooding the adjacent tunnel into his silo.

Firebird held the detonator high over his head and pressed down on the side-lever. All he would have to do is release his grip and the charge would detonate.

The rebels swarmed the silo and pointed their rifles at him. Daunhauer pushed his way to the front of the group. He had torn his bandage off, revealing his scarred face and bulging eye. He immediately realized the device in Firebird's hand, which prompted him to look at the missile. The charge was right on the tip, ready to blow.

"Shit," he whispered.

"You shoot me, I drop this…" Firebird mimicked an explosion then sang "Bye-bye, Ms.-Beretta-Albright…"

Daunhauer drew in a long breath through his nose, then held a hand up to his rebels.

"Don't shoot," he warned them. Another echo from running feet traveled down the tunnel. The rebels moved to the side, making way for Beretta. She entered the silo and saw Firebird with the detonator.

"You know what, it's fine," she said to Firebird. "You're eager to get out of here, right?"

"What gave me away?" Firebird retorted.

"You know what? I'm good with that. You and your droid are free to go," she said. Firebird stood silent.

"Not sure I trust you," he said.

"No, seriously," Beretta said. "I'm ambitious, but not stupid. I'm not gonna pretend you don't have us in a bind. And frankly, you're not worth the headache. If letting you go gets you out of my hair permanently, then let it be."

"Yeah? How do I know you won't shoot me down once I get out of here?"

"Like I said, I'm not stupid. Shooting you with the turrets while you're within range would only detonate the charge. And we blew up the anti-aircraft guns. You're free to go. Thank you for your assistance in taking over this complex. You have a ship to go wherever you please." She spoke like a businesswoman doing trade negotiations.

"I'm taking the doctor with me," Firebird said.

"That can't happen," she answered. "I need her."

"So do I," Firebird said. "She's cost me a pretty penny. I'll be lucky to break even after I collect my payment."

Beretta shook her head. "Sorry. If she goes, this was all for nothing." Firebird trembled, pretending to drop the device. All of the rebels shuddered except for Beretta and Daunhauer.

"Frankly, if she goes, I might as well let you blow us up," she said. Firebird studied her with his eye. She wasn't bluffing. He had to determine his stakes in the game.

"I'm not keen on leaving empty handed," he said.

"I might be able to help remedy that," Beretta said. "Come outside with us. No tricks, I swear." She motioned for her rebels to back out of the entrance. Firebird hesitated, then slowly followed, keeping the device raised high to keep anyone from grabbing for it.

The rebels kept their distance, none of them daring to look the mercenary in the eye as they moved up the steps up into the station. Beretta and Daunhauer were the first to step out of the station. The other rebels had already gathered around the building, waiting for them.

"Move out. Spread out," the General announced to them. They did as instructed and made way. She turned to face Daunhauer. "Did you pack the funds?"

"I did," he answered.

"Good. Go get them," she said. Daunhauer quickly raced back toward the Jeeps. As he did, Firebird emerged from the door. There were still a few rebels standing close.

"Back off! *Way* off!" he warned.

"Do it," Beretta sternly said. The tenacious rebels stepped back with their comrades. Firebird watched the group with caution. His gaze turned to Saegusa, whose hands had been shackled behind her. She was on her knees, hunched forward. Her illness was wreaking havoc on her insides.

Daunhauer brought the Jeep forward and parked it a few feet away. He stepped out, holding a thick bag. He opened it and first presented its contents to Beretta, then turned to show Firebird. The bag was full of sparkling gold coins.

"This is our financial reserve," she explained. "Some people, like those who supplied explosives and vehicles, didn't work for free."

"How much?" Firebird said.

"Sixty-thousand," she said. Firebird scoffed.

"I'm getting over three times that amount from Espinosa," he said.

"Then you'll have to blow us up," Beretta said. "Listen, you're getting a new ship out of the deal. You've got some money to help make up for some of what you lost. Best of all, you're getting the hell out of Sovereignty. You can take it for what it is, or just blow us all up."

Firebird eyed the bag of gold and pondered the options. It was clear she was serious in her intent. He was tired of this place and the unpredictable scenario he continued to play a part in.

He glanced over at Saegusa, who looked back at him, alarmed.

"Don't. Please, don't," she whispered.

Firebird groaned. "Ugh...put the gold in the fuselage," he said in an exasperated tone.

"FIREBIRD NO!" Saegusa screamed. He ignored her pleas and followed the rebels to the Prime Eagle. Saegusa sprang to her knees and twisted away from the rebel holding on to her. "You son of a bitch!"

"You had your chance to get out of here, remember?" he said.

"You can't just leave me here!" she said. "They'll kill everyone! You think they'll just stop with the Sovereignty?" Firebird continued walking away. Saying anything else would only drag along a senseless conversation. "Firebird! Please!" she was pleading now. He didn't look back.

The rebels loaded the bag into the fuselage and shut the door. Firebird climbed into the cockpit and sealed the door, keeping the device visible through the window.

Stuart climbed into the co-pilot seat.

"Are we not bringing the doctor?"

Firebird shook his head. "Just get this thing in the air." Stuart recognized the tone. The engine had already been started. He activated the elevators. The engines hummed and the ship vibrated as the mechanisms did their job.

Beretta watched the ship elevate over the complex. Barber approached from her left.

"How can we be sure he won't blow us up the minute he gets out of here?"

"Those detonators have a very short range," Beretta answered. "If he detonated, the blast would blow all eight missiles. He'd never escape the blast. By the time he clears the blast radius, he'll also be out of range of the signal."

"You okay with just letting him go?" Barber asked.

"He's a thorn in my side, but he's a thorn who only cares about money. I can live with that," she said. She turned back and walked away.

General Drake was still alive on the ground. Standing nearby were a group of nervous rebels who had been disarmed. Daunhauer stood by her side, ready to obey any command to handle any potential detractors.

Drake scowled at her. The hole in his back burnt deep, severing the use of his legs.

"You're a damn traitor," he said.

"No, *you* are," she responded. "Not only that, you're a coward. How could you think of turning back after fighting this long? You know what, don't answer. I don't even care anymore. We've got the doctor now and we have the ability to make the superweapon, and the technology thanks to the gifts that this complex has to offer."

"You develop that bio-weapon, you won't be able to control it," Drake groaned. He noticed the other rebels standing behind her. It was evident that all of them, except for the few disarmed ones standing near him, had sworn allegiance to her. "Are you all okay with this? If you use that weapon, the collateral damage will be exponential! It'll spread into the towns and kill thousands! These are the people we were trying to save!"

"Can't save everybody," Beretta said. She drew her pistol and fired a shot between his eyes. The unarmed rebels stumbled back, looking at the recently deceased General, then gazed back up at Beretta.

One of them stepped forward, his face red with anger.

"You BITCH!"

Daunhauer lunged forward and plowed a fist into his stomach, then threw an elbow to the head. The rebel fell to the ground, settling on his back. Before he could move, he felt his airway close off. Daunhauer pressed his boot hard on the defiant rebel's throat, watching him slowly gag. He struggled, gripping his foot with both hands before going pale. Blank eyes stared skyward as the life left his body.

Daunhauer stepped away then looked at the remaining rebels.

"Anyone else?"

They stared back, dumbfounded. The huge veins in that overexposed eye looked as though they were about to pop. Finally, all at once, they threw fists in the air.

"For General Albright!" they shouted in unison.

"Excellent," Beretta said. She put her pistol away and looked over at the doctor. Saegusa was still watching the Prime Eagle, still holding on to that faint glimmer of hope that he might bring the ship back down.

Those hopes disappeared entirely as the thrusters sparked, pushing the ship far into the distance. The ship gradually moved to starboard, adjusting its trajectory north.

She pounded her fist into the ground, feeling a single tear spilling from her eye.

CHAPTER 23

Firebird watched the world pass by beneath his ship. The digital map displayed their position, displaying a long red line that represented the barrier. They were almost at the border.

The plan had worked. About twenty miles from the Silo Complex, they had passed by a dozen or so Target-Seekers and numerous ground troops below. So far, it seemed they all thought he was part of the search party.

"Two-thousand meters," Stuart said.

"Keep it going," Firebird said. "Slow it down just a bit. Let's not draw attention."

"Reducing speed by forty knots," Stuart said.

"Come on, baby," Firebird muttered. He could see the barrier in the distance. Off to the east was an enormous collection of tanks and trucks, with several Strikers spread out along the border. It was the site where Lieutenant Donnelly had launched his attack on the tower. He could see the remains in the distance.

"Damn, those guys really did a number on that," he said. Stuart didn't respond.

Firebird took the controls and steered the ship west. If he crossed the border while in range of the tanks, they would likely try shooting at him. The Prime Eagle rotated to port and continued on, quickly moving out of visual.

"Nine-hundred meters," Stuart said.

"Okay, let's go for it," Firebird said. He rotated the nose to starboard and applied additional power to the thrusters. He held his breath and waited for the barrier to pass by underneath.

"Clear," Stuart said.

"Whoa!" Firebird exclaimed. He leaned back in his seat, finally feeling relaxed. It had been a very long day until now. "Okay, first thing's first, I need to go home and cook us up some steaks."

"I'm a droid," Stuart said. "I cannot consume food."

"I know. It was a joke. Why do I keep trying with you?" Firebird said.

"Some would say because you're stupid," Stuart answered.

"Well, SHIT!" Firebird said. "Didn't take long for your wit to come back, did it?" Stuart didn't give a response. Firebird felt a sense of awkwardness, as though he was with a pissed off girlfriend who didn't want to speak with him. "Okay then." He got up and went back into the fuselage.

"Where are you going?" Stuart asked.

"Checking on that gold," he answered.

"You don't want to consider a plan to extract Saegusa?"

"Why would I do that?" Firebird said. He stepped into the cabin and placed the bag into a chair. He took another glance at the gold coins then sealed it and did a brief exploration of the interior. There was a small gun rack with three

Omega Plasma Rifles and a small food storage container. "Oh, finally!" He opened it up, finding a few bins of foil sealed ready-to-eat foods. Not particularly a gourmet meal but it would certainly beat that dry stuff the rebels fed him.

"Sir, Saegusa still has cancer," Stuart said. He placed the ship on autopilot and scampered into the cabin. "She will certainly die if we do not help."

Firebird ripped the foil open, inadvertently spraying a few droplets of sauce.

"Damn!" he muttered. "Not much I can do about that, bot. In case you didn't realize, I literally had to go 'jihad' on those rebels just to get us out of there."

"I understand the matter we had at hand but what can we do now?" Stuart asked.

"Ulgh!" Firebird swallowed hard on the pasta that was in that foil tray. "Steak! Steak now! Full throttle to home. Code Red!" He tossed the food into an incinerator bin and slammed the lid shut. The edges glowed as the trash was cremated.

"I meant about the doctor?" Stuart continued.

"Yeeees, I know you're talking about the doctor," Firebird said. "What do you expect me to do? They've got control of the Silo Complex, thus they have the turrets. We'd never get close to it without being shot to pieces. And eventually, they'll go mobile once the Sovereignty's figured out their game plan, after which we'd have no idea where to look."

"We can get help and organize an attack," Stuart said.

"Yeah? Is there money involved? I don't work for free."

"You're not. You'll still get paid from Espinosa," Stuart said.

"I should add that I'd like to live to spend the money. It's not worth the effort, droid. We'd be killed before we even got close."

"Are you confirming that you will not consider rescuing Saegusa?" Stuart said.

"Yes, I confirm," Firebird said, mimicking a mechanical voice. "Does that compute?"

"Affirmative," Stuart said. He turned around and proceeded into the cockpit. Firebird shook his head. That droid was worse than a nagging girlfriend. He tried to take his mind from it as he dared to open another one of the stored foods. He opened it with caution, trying hard not to spray its contents like the last one. And like the last one, it had no label, leaving him to guess what it was.

Hopefully these Strikers weren't allergic to anything because they have no idea what they're getting.

He slowly tore it open, revealing another pasta mix. This one was more like linguini with a few vegetables. He reluctantly took a bite and to his surprise, it was tolerable.

"At least something's gone right," he said. The bow of the ship dipped, causing him to stumble back into the wall. Linguini and sauce sprayed his face. "Bot! What are you doing?!"

The ship leveled out and descended to the ground. It hit rather fast, causing more of the sauce to splash Firebird's eye. Furious, the mercenary tossed the tray to the floor and looked for something to wipe his face. As he cleared his eye, he peeked into the cockpit in time to see Stuart open the door and step out.

"Hey!" He opened the fuselage door and followed him out. "What are you doing?"

"It's okay, sir," Stuart said. "The ship is in good condition. I have navigation displayed for you. You should have no problem getting back to your place called 'home'."

"Wait, what? You're LEAVING?" Those words left a weird, bitter taste in Firebird's mouth. It almost sounded like a breakup. "Where are you going?"

"I'm returning to Sovereignty," Stuart said.

"To *Sovereignty*?! We just busted our asses trying to get out of there," Firebird called after him.

"I'm going to help Dr. Saegusa."

"Good luck with that," Firebird said.

"It is okay, sir. I do not judge you for staying behind. You are programmed to calculate decisions based on financial risk versus gain. Understandably, you don't see this action as worth the risk."

"What the hell are you talking about?"

"There is a ninety-three percent chance I will fail. So, with that probability in consideration, I wish you farewell," Stuart said. He turned and started marching to the perimeter far in the distance.

"Ninety-three percent chance of being fried...and you're going anyway?! WHAT?!" Firebird shook his head and followed Stuart. "Come on, dude. You probably just have a few wires touching together that probably shouldn't be."

"My wiring is fine," Stuart said.

"Then come on back. Let's go home. If you're jealous of the steak, I'll make you... I don't know...battery-soup or something."

"No, you don't understand. I was designed to benefit the lives of people. Before I was a refinery droid, I was a medical droid. And the refinery you stole me from was to build medical transport units and respirators. I'm sorry, sir, but my programming will not allow me to leave Saegusa behind."

"Great, you're a bot with a conscience," Firebird said.

"You will find another one," Stuart said.

Firebird started to speak but didn't know what to say. He watched the droid walk off. He was serious about going back.

"Fine. Maybe I will," he said under his breath. Droids weren't easy to come by. Especially not ones with even a hint of personality. Stuart had a lot of life experience.

"Just because she's sick, doesn't mean you owe her anything," he called out.

"It's not about what you owe," Stuart said.

"Oh, come on! You just said that because you heard her say that!"

"It's something you used to understand," Stuart said.

"I understand it just fine. I just don't believe in it," Firebird retorted.

"We were down to eleven men..." Stuart said.

"Pardon me?"

"...Enemy forces formed blockades around the mountain side. Escape was impossible. We had radioed for reinforcements, but our Air Force was decimated. The sky was ablaze, as though Heaven was besieged by Hell."

"Oh, give me a break," the mercenary groaned. The damn droid was reciting the letter written by one of his fellow soldiers in C-Company.

"We had dug out a foxhole and huddled together. The Sovereignty's leviathan army was advancing. Preparing for our deaths, we said our final prayers. I was always a believer, yet, I never experienced a direct answer to my prayers. Not until that day on the mountain. The sky opened up with thunderous bangs. Enemy ships rained down, their plasma cores blazing in the sky. Then, we saw our savior descending, the wings of his ship blazing red. Like a Firebird."

The droid gave him one last look. Firebird said nothing. His mind was warped with the memories of friends long gone. Those words were written in a much different time, of which he had nearly forgotten.

"Live well," Stuart said. He started back toward the border.

Son of a bitch. The droid was persistent. He was always looking out for her well-being. Firebird wondered if he detected the cancer all along. Finally, he got back into the cockpit. He took the pilot seat and reinitiated all of the flight systems. He grabbed the controls and prepared to lift. Immediately, his eye went to the empty co-pilot seat. Not only was the seat empty, but the whole ship felt empty. They had traveled together for years and pulled off daring missions. And now he was alone. And that empty feeling weighed heavily within him.

So what if he only worked for personal gain? He was no Rebellion fighter. He had been an honorable soldier before. He had been a rescue pilot and paratrooper, saving hundreds of men, only to see them killed the next day. He wasn't like Donnelly. Or Drake. Even if he saved Saegusa, she was more than likely going to succumb to her illness. After all, she still had to create the new serum, assuming Beretta hadn't destroyed all of her samples.

Yet, for some reason, he couldn't bring himself to lift off. He looked out the window again. Stuart was almost a silver dot in the distance now.

"A droid with a conscience. What next?" he said to himself. He gnawed on his lip, then took a deep breath. "Oh, screw it." He pushed the door open and ran out after Stuart. "FINE!"

CHAPTER 24

Saegusa tugged on her restraints, rocking the steel chair she was cuffed to. Daunhauer waited in the corner. The room was below ground, in some godforsaken tunnel between the barracks and the Center Station. She noticed all sorts of lab equipment in the room, as if the Sovereignty had conducted chemistry experiments in this silo.

She knew that the Sovereignty kept their science facilities secret, but she didn't think it would be in a silo. But it made sense the more she thought about it. These facilities were already heavily defended. Not only that, but she realized that the Sovereignty had intended to use the missiles to disperse the chemical agent.

And now, Beretta planned to do this. She tugged again on her restraints, digging the cuffs into her wrists.

"Stop wasting your energy," Daunhauer said. She stopped and sneered at him.

"How's the face?" Saegusa said. "I hear that after you get hit with leaf acid, it always feels like it's eating your flesh away." Daunhauer didn't show a response. However, Saegusa could hear the sharp breathing through his nose. The Lieutenant was in immense pain. She wondered if it was driving him mad. He'd HAVE to be mad to be so willing to follow Beretta.

A door opened directly across the room. Beretta stepped in, followed by three of her rebels. They carried in large glass tubes, along with small circular glass vials. Two more rebels followed them in, carrying computer consoles and hooking them up to the lab monitors.

"Sorry this had to happen this way," Beretta said.

"Don't patronize me. You're not sorry about anything. You wanted this the whole time."

"Fine," Beretta said. "I'll admit it. I didn't expect you to survive the crash when we shot down your boyfriend's ship, but I assumed that pretty memory chip would. Hell, it has a metal plate and your skull protecting it."

"First of all, HELL NO, not my boyfriend," Saegusa said. "Second of all, you think you're actually gonna develop the superweapon? Even if you analyze the data from my chip, you don't have all of the materials you need to develop the weapon."

"Oh really?" Beretta said. "Why don't you dig a little further into your memory banks. Better yet, your *daddy's* memory banks."

"I try to stay out of there," Saegusa said.

"Then you know about the crash in the West Mountains. A mercenary had crossed the border, delivering a very special sample of *acidium folium.* Acid Leaf from the Pacific Northwest. I think you've delved into those memory banks a time or two. If so, you'd know that the leaves from the mutated northwest acid flower generates a teaspoon-sized orb of acid, hence the name. Of course, we can't just harvest the flowers, because even with a whole field, we'd only have enough of the bio-weapon to defeat a small patrol unit. That's why we needed your samples here." Beretta held up the pouch. Saegusa lurched in an attempt to free herself. Beretta shook her head. "Stop fighting."

"If you apparently have all the ingredients, then why do you need me?"

"Just because you have milk, eggs, and batter, doesn't mean you know how to make pancakes unless you learn the amount of each, how to cook it up, how to serve it…you get the idea."

"Let me guess? You double crossed the mercenary too?"

"No, the Sovereignty did that for us. They correctly assumed he was delivering supplies, though they caught him on his way out, lucky for us. Of course, they had to keep that quiet because the idiot knew Firebird, and they knew they needed him to get you eventually."

Saegusa saw the men loading the samples into the room.

"This worked out for you, didn't it? No wonder you were so eager to help Drake take over this Silo."

"I've lost a lot in this war. The biggest price was paid only twenty-four hours ago. If we leave, it means my son died for nothing."

"Yeah? What kind of a mother leads a revolution and lets her son fight?"

Beretta grabbed her by the jaw.

"He was a grown man doing what he believed in," she growled. "Unless I'm mistaken, you've never cared for a child and watched him grow into someone better than you."

"Girl, I could throw a rock and hit somebody better than you," Saegusa said. Beretta backed away, tempted to throw a punch. She stopped, knowing she would have the last laugh anyway. She stepped aside as one of the rebels stepped out. After a few moments, he came back in carrying a bag of tools. Saegusa felt a chill sizzle her spine.

"What's that?"

"These domes tend to be a little complicated. After all, they're part of your skull," Beretta said, tapping Saegusa's head above her mechanical eye. "We'd prefer it if you just dig into those memories and tell us what we need to know. Otherwise, it might get a little messy. It's your choice."

Saegusa sucked in a deep breath as the rebels hooked up all of the computers. Some of them put on lab coats and gloves. Only now did Saegusa look them in the eye. They were the doctors from the infirmary.

She trembled visibly in her seat. She was faced between two tough choices, neither of which were good. Talk and live a little longer, only to be killed slowly and painfully by the cancer or sit helplessly as the doctors tried to dig into her head.

She sat for a bit and thought about it. There was a third option…

"Well?" Beretta said. She held her arms up and sighed. "We don't have much time. Let's go, docs."

"Wait…" Saegusa said. The doctors stopped and all eyes went back to her.

"Yes?" Beretta said.

"You idiots are going to screw it up and blame it on me," she said. "Let me up. I'll do it."

The group stared at her, then glanced at the General, anticipating her decision.

"*You'll* do it?" Beretta said.

"Might as well be on the winning team, right?" Saegusa said. Beretta glanced back at the doctors. They were good at the craft of healing but had no experience in developing medicines or serums, or anything of that nature. Though she wouldn't admit it out loud, Beretta knew that the odds of them butchering the formula, even with Saegusa's supervision, were high.

"Alright...fine," Beretta said. "Daunhauer, cut her loose. But know one thing, Doctor. You make one wrong move. You butcher this thing, you put one pinch of salt in there that doesn't belong, we'll break you apart limb by limb. You got it?"

"Been there, done that," Saegusa retorted. Beretta nodded at the Lieutenant, who proceeded to unlock her restraints. Saegusa stood up and rubbed her wrists. Beretta stood to the side and presented the tools.

"Well? What are you waiting for?"

CHAPTER 25

Firebird watched the ground below as they passed over the border back into Sovereignty. Immediately, he could see the army of Strikers spread out over the countryside. Target-Seekers flew in the air, covering low over the town of Water Root.

"Didn't we just leave this party?"

Stuart kept the ship at a standard cruising speed. Just as they did when they were leaving, they tried not to draw any attention to themselves.

"Saegusa will be pleased that you came back," he said.

"Yeah, if we don't get her brains blown out first," Firebird said.

"We could try an E.M.P. attack on the silo," Stuart said.

"And where would we get the E.M.P.?"

"I believe some of the storage trucks might have E.M.P. shells that we could steal and possibly…"

"Let me stop you right there," Firebird said. "I'd like to LIVE at the end of this shenanigan."

They continued passing over Water Root. Stuart watched the activity below, noticing the familiar sight of a large barn being torn apart by Striker vehicles.

"It appears they have discovered the rebel's place of headquarters," Stuart said.

"Too bad we didn't get out of here when we had the chance," Firebird said. "The Sovereignty would've found these rebels and taken care of Beretta Albright for us…" his voice trailed off as the thought came to him. "What are the odds Zolnar is down there?"

"Assuming they found the base, I would estimate an eighty percent chance he is either on site currently, or within radio range." Firebird fumbled over the dashboard for the radio transmitter. "You're trying to contact him?"

"The best jobs are when we can get someone else to do our dirty work for us." He adjusted the frequency and spoke into the microphone. "Prime Eagle, uh…" he realized he didn't have the ship's number and code. "Oh, the hell with it. Commander Zolnar? Are you listening? You better be!"

****

The signal began to broadcast from all of the radio units across the battalion as Zolnar raced from the barn to the nearest radio truck.

"Commander! Are you sure you want to speak with this guy?" one of his Lieutenants asked.

"Shut up. It's the mercenary. I'm curious what he has to say. He might have the girl," Zolnar said. He arrived at the truck, shoving through hordes of Strikers. "Get out of my way, damn it."

The broadcast was still ongoing as he picked up the microphone.

"Come on Zolnar. I know you can find your way with those funny glasses you call eyes."

"Little prick," Zolnar responded. "You must have a serious death wish if you are trying to push me now."

"Death wish? I'm not the one repeatedly embarrassing myself in front of my dictator! Supreme Leader Cornelius has got to be pretty fed up with you right now."

"What do you want, mercenary?"

"It's more like what you want," Firebird said. *"Clearly, you're such a great General that you're keeping tabs on all of your jurisdictions."*

"I've been busy. Where's the doctor?"

"Oh, aren't you gonna freak when you find that out."

Zolnar could hear laughter over the transmitter. All of the stress of the night had reduced his patience to a hair-trigger temper.

"What are you talking about? Clearly, she's not across the border, or you wouldn't bother with this conversation."

"Use your head, Commander. Where do they normally store Prime Eagles?"

Zolnar froze. There was only one answer to that.

"Prime Eagles are support ships for the Missile Silo Complexes, but…" he removed the transmitter from his lips, "they couldn't have." He pointed at one of the other officers. "Someone try and raise Complex Six. Right now!"

"If you're trying to radio the Complex, you're wasting your time. Your girlfriend Beretta is running it now."

"So, what are you doing?" Zolnar said. "You working for her now? What are you doing, telling me this?"

"Hell, NO! She's tried to kill me so many times, I think I'm down to my seventh or eighth life. All I'd like is a little bit of payback. And you might want to act fast before she gets a little touchy-feely with those missiles. Oh, and she has the doctor there as well."

"This better not be a trick, Merc," Zolnar said. "You double-cross me, and I'll…"

"Oh, we both know you'll be crying at Cornelius' feet, begging him not to cut your balls off and stuff them down your throat," Firebird interrupted. *"Besides, I've been shot at so many times today, I'm thinking of changing my name to Stallone."*

"Who? What?"

"Oh, for godsake. Nevermind. Over and out."

Zolnar tried to keep his composure as he stared at the silent radio. He noticed a hundred soldiers watching him, waiting to see what he would do. Rumors had already spread through the battalion regarding his fate. Many of them believed Saegusa was gone, especially after finding the empty base. What these rumors really implied was that they had lost confidence in their Commander, though they still feared him enough to keep it to themselves. Time after time, he had been outwitted by the mercenary and the rebels. He, a military expert, had been outdone by a band of filth!

And now, he was at a crossroad. He suspected a trap. Yet, something in him believed the mercenary was telling the truth. If the Silo Complex had been overtaken, Cornelius would make sure his death was slow and painful. It would be medieval, lasting for days. On the contrary, if it was a lie and he fell for it, the consequences would be just as dire.

"Sir?"

Zolnar snapped into reality. He looked around for whomever spoke up, finding the radio tech.

"What?"

"We've tried reaching Silo Complex Six, and…there's no response, sir."

It was the answer Zolnar dreaded. For once in his life, he was visibly perplexed. There was no time for a middle-ground-decision, such as sending scouts. If the facility truly was overrun, the response would have to be immediate and strong.

"Sir?" another Striker asked. "What's the plan?"

Several moments of silence passed. He had to make a decision.

"Lock and load," he said. "Prepare for full assault on Silo Complex Six. I want all air units to go in first. Do not bombard the interior with explosives. You'll risk setting off the payload inside. These silos are the Sovereignty's major line of defense against our enemies on the outside."

"How will we get in?" another Striker asked.

"I want men in the Target-Seekers. You're gonna drop inside and open the gates. If you're unsuccessful, then we'll just have to hit it with artillery until we bust it open. All units converge on Complex Six. Immediately."

CHAPTER 26

"Open the capsule," Saegusa ordered. One of the doctors placed the replacement warhead near the mixing equipment and unscrewed the cone-shaped cap.

"Is it ready yet?" Beretta asked.

"Of course not," Saegusa responded, holding up her pouch with all vials still inside. The chemical mixer hummed as it processed the *acidium folium* samples. The doctors stood by, awaiting instructions. "Okay, apply dispersal agent." A man in a lab coat approached the large machine and extended a large clear tube from the side. It was like an IV line but thicker. At the end was a screwcap which attached to the end of the vial. The machine gradually sucked the container dry. "Okay, we're going to have to remove this formula from the machine."

"Wait, you haven't added the herbs and flower components," Beretta said.

"I know. They are loaded into the capsule separately," Saegusa said. "They can't go in mixed together. Not with the technology we have available. Any contact between the chemicals will cause them to disperse prematurely. Therefore, we have to load them separately."

Beretta didn't say anything. She knew nothing of chemistry, other than that it could produce deadly results. Right now, she had no choice but to take Saegusa's word for it.

The machine dispersed the formula into a large, oval-shaped container. The machine hissed as it pressurized the container and automatically sealed the opening. Saegusa removed it and examined the opening to make sure it was secure.

"Okay, run the machine again and extract any residue, then run a rinse with water. After that we'll prep the flower sample."

"Yes," the doctors said. Saegusa screwed a standard receiving vial into the extractor and inserted a cap into the injector port for the machine to seal it with. The machine whirred again, this time sounding more smoothly, as there were hardly any contents inside being mixed. The machine expelled nearly ten milliliters of mixture into the vial and sealed it. Saegusa removed it and nodded to her assistants, giving them the go-ahead to commence the rinse.

As the machine went to work with the rinse, she eyed the small vial, watching the light-brown substance swirling about in the glass tube. There was nothing but death in this tube. Only combined with her flower samples from the Rhino border could it be made tolerable. It was the balance of life and death which was about to be separated into two vials. The flower would help break down the acid leaf upon dispersal. The gas cloud would spread long enough for the acid component to kill any living thing coming in contact with it, while the cells from the Radialem would eventually neutralize the chemical compound, keeping the attack area from becoming uninhabitable.

"Doctor, we are ready," one of the medical doctors said.

"Okay," Saegusa said. She placed the pressurized sample down and grabbed one of her samples from the pouch. She gave it a long somber look. This was not what she intended its use for. Her moment came to an end after she recognized Beretta Albright's impatient stare.

Saegusa removed the dark grey leaf from the vial and laid it in a small processing machine. She spun the blades as though processing it were a food blender, grinding the leaf into tiny pinhead-sized pieces. She added solution to the mix and spun the machine again, liquifying the herb.

"Prepare the dispersal agent. We'll need double the amount for this mixture," she instructed. She loaded the cannister filled with solution and herb and into the machine. The processer began its process. The doctors mixed in the dispersal as instructed. After a few minutes, it spilled the solution into the receiving container and sealed it. Saegusa removed it and placed it on the capsule with the other. "When the warhead detonates, it'll disperse both solutions at once. The flower solution will immediately start neutralizing the acid-leaf, but the effect will take time, allowing for the chemical to do its work."

"Perfect," Beretta said. She peered into the open capsule and admired the creation as though it were a new child. "Absolutely perfect." Saegusa initiated the machine, extracting any residue into a small glass tube.

"We should test it immediately," Daunhauer said.

"No. Not yet," Beretta said. "Let's fill the rest of the warheads first. I want as many missiles as as possible ready before we launch our assault."

"You should've picked a newer machine," Saegusa said.

"What do you mean?" Beretta said. Her sinister smile disappeared and a scowl took its place.

"This machine is already on the verge of overheating. Something tells me you've robbed an old abandoned Sovereignty lab, or probably had some equipment delivered to you for cheap, since you couldn't squeeze too much from the Rebellion's funds and hide it from Drake."

Beretta's lack of response was enough for Saegusa to know one of those guesses were correct.

"Can you make it work?"

"Yes but we're going to have to allow a cool-down period between each mixing," Saegusa said.

"Fine," Beretta said.

Saegusa scooped up the flower-leaf samples. Only five remained now. She watched as Beretta picked up the capsule and screwed the cap on tight. The General's smile returned as she carried the capsule like a newborn infant. "Soon, we will test these elements on the Sovereignty. We will take refuge underground until the gas wears off. And when we emerge, we will find ourselves in charge of a brand-new world."

"You're really not concerned about the people in the towns, are you?" Saegusa said. Beretta didn't even blink.

"There might be a little collateral damage," she said. "Nothing that can be controlled. They're just going to have to accept what's happened."

Saegusa scoffed. "You know, listening to you, you'd think Beretta Albright was the only person EVER to lose someone she loved in war." Those eyes turned back toward her. "It's tragic, yes. You were fighting a good cause and lost. But it's not justification for mass genocide. The end does not justify the means."

"Doctor?" Beretta's voice was low and intense. "I thought you were on the winning team?" She took a step closer. "Judging by those words, I'm starting to wonder if this formula will even work."

"Oh, it'll work," Saegusa said.

"How can I believe that?" Beretta said.

"Because I always test my inventions," Saegusa said. She raised the two vials of excess solutions high over her head then threw them to the floor. The glass shattered, spilling a thick brown mist into the room. The rebels erupted into a panic. Guards and staff collided as they ran for separate exits, knocking each other over.

Saegusa lunged forward, thrusting an elbow into Beretta's face, driving her to the floor. The General hit the ground with her eyes closed and felt the capsule yanked from her hands. A pair of arms wrapped under her shoulders and pulled her away.

"Come on, General!" Daunhauer yelled as he pulled her away from the cloud. It was small but rapidly expanding. Guards and doctors caught in its wake grabbed at their throats, gasping for breath. Their skin reddened as the acid ate at their flesh. Beretta turned and ran out with Daunhauer, listening to the horrid sounds of the rebels coughing up blood.

"That bitch! Where'd she go?!" she snarled. "She's going to die so slowly...I might unscrew her head myself!"

Saegusa ran as fast as she could down the corridor then turned at the first bend. She had no clue where she was going and couldn't recall the exact specifications from Drake's sketch of the complex. The corridor led to a set of doors. She tugged on the handle, only to find that they were locked.

The echoes of running feet drummed behind her.

"Can't believe I'm admitting this, but I should've gone with Firebird when I had the chance," she grumbled. She squatted and fired her eye flare into the lock, melting it. She looked back, seeing Daunhauer coming around the corner with a pistol in hand. "Shit." She stood up and kicked the door, plowing it open. She ran into a dimly lit juncture with three separate directions to go. With no time to decide, she took the one on the right.

It was the brightest of the choices. She ran past a series of rooms with control boards and panels. There were several radar stations and an armory locked behind a thick steel door.

Beyond that armory was a dead end.

"Great. Just great," she said. The door lock was three times as thick as the last one. After seeing Daunhauer and Beretta turn the corner, she knew she would not be able to break through it in time. She opened the capsule and withdrew the two glass containers stored within it and held them up.

The rebel leaders stopped. Daunhauer kept the pistol pointed at her head. His hand twitched, either from pain or simply an eagerness to kill.

"Go ahead. Shoot me," she said.

"Yeah?" Beretta said. "You gonna smash that and kill yourself? Firebird had the guts to do it, but not you. I should've known you were stalling before. You, who is so afraid to die, would even build a weapon of mass destruction that would kill thousands before she would let herself die. You lecture me on principles, while you continue to put yourself ahead of others."

Saegusa glanced up, seeing the vents in the ceiling.

"You're almost right, except for the principle part. I won't be killing thousands."

"Oh really?" Beretta laughed.

"Just a hundred or so murderous Rebels who lost their way. I guess I won't be able to save myself and millions of others who suffer from the effects of our radioactive atmosphere. But I'll settle for keeping you from killing several thousand innocents. Besides," she pressed a hand to her stomach, "I'm dead anyway."

The Rebels stood silent, testing Saegusa's resolve. Beretta looked serious for a moment, even mildly afraid. Then that smile returned.

"Nice try," she said. "But those aren't fragile glass vials like those little test tubes you smashed back there. That's reinforced glass that *needs* the impact of a freaking ROCKET to breach it." She pointed to the floor. "Go ahead. Try and smash them. Kill us all."

"Don't need to," Saegusa said. She tossed the container carrying green solution at them. It hit Daunhauer in the nose, knocking him backward. The pistol fell from his hand and spiraled back into the hallway.

With her free hand, Saegusa reached for the lever to ignite her eye flare.

The General dashed across the short distance and grabbed her wrist. She plowed a fist into Saegusa's midsection and grabbed for the container. The two twisted and spun, with Saegusa fighting against the newly triggered pain in her stomach. She arched her back then snapped her forward, headbutting Beretta and driving her back.

The General regained her balance. Blood spilled from her nose and onto her jacket. She ducked and leaped, grabbing Saegusa by the waist and tackling her to the floor. The container fell from her grip and rolled several feet past her.

Beretta drove a fist into the doctor's face then grabbed at her throat with both hands. Saegusa gulped and clutched at the General's wrists. She pushed and twisted, unable to pry her grip away. Her airway closed and her gag reflex started to kick in.

"Sorry Doc...but not too sorry," Beretta said. Her chuckle degraded into a stutter as she felt the doctor drive a knee into her rear, driving her forward. She steadied herself, her face less than an inch away from Saegusa's. In that moment she noticed one of her fingers flicking a lever inside the open panel.

"Don't be."

Saegusa ignited the flare. Beretta yelled as the flame cut into her face. She reeled backward and sprawled onto the floor.

The doctor pushed herself up and grabbed the bioweapon. She flinched as a plasma blast zipped by her head. She glanced back, seeing Daunhauer pointing his pistol. She moved to the other side, narrowly avoiding a second shot, only for a third to hit her in the shoulder. She yelled out and fell in a spiraling motion, ending up once again on her back.

Daunhauer approached and stood over her. Blood leaked onto the cement floor under her. She was truly helpless now. He pointed the pistol at her face and prepared to squeeze the trigger.

"Not the head," Beretta said. Daunhauer hesitated. The General sat up. Smoke twisted up from the dark red circular mark which surrounded her left eye and ran down her cheek. "The chip! Shoot her in the chest....OR..." she motioned at his face, noting the injuries she had inflicted on him, "feel free to make it slow. Shoot her hands and feet first. Then the real punishment begins."

Daunhauer smiled and pulled a knife while keeping the pistol down at Saegusa.

****

"Do you have any music requests, sir," Stuart asked Firebird. Firebird thought about it as he watched the Silo Complex come into view.

"Oh, I don't know. I don't think this thing has any music in its inventory."

"No, but I have a few files downloaded into my computer," Stuart asked.

"What? Really?"

"Yes...you installed it, remember?"

"Oh, yeah. Sorry, it was a long walk through the Torrek Desert. I needed something to listen to. To answer your question...uh..." He watched the perimeter wall. Several Rebels were moving into position. The gate had been sealed tight. All weapons were being mobilized.

He glanced at the rear monitor. There were several silver spots in the distance. Target-Seekers, dozens of them, were soaring at top speed to engage the threat.

The Cavalry was on the way.

"Scorpions."

"I do not detect any arachnids in the cockpit..." Stuart said.

"No...the band," Firebird corrected.

"Oh! Searching files."

"While you do that, take us on a perimeter sweep and prime the missile. Hopefully those douchebags didn't move the cargo truck."

He activated the targeting computer and gripped the joystick. The computer displayed the aim for the weapon. He watched through the screen as defense turrets started to spin on their platforms.

"Music on, sir," Stuart said. Rock music pounded from his speakers. Firebird bobbed his head to the music then squeezed the trigger, blazing the wall.

The blasts cut into the wall and tattered the gunner's seat of the nearest turret, ravaging the man seated inside. In his agony, the rebel hit the controls, accidentally rotating the turret to starboard, striking another rebel with the barrel.

Activity boosted within the Complex as soldiers rushed to the fort's defenses. Rebels climbed the walls and manned the turrets, while others carried rocket launchers up to assist the gunners.

The Prime Eagle evaded, dodging several turret blasts. The gunners' aim followed the aircraft, their blasts missing it by several feet only to disappear into the atmosphere.

"Hold up! Five o'clock!" one of the rebels shouted. A wave of anxiety swept through the defenses as several Target-Seekers filled the sky. All guns took their aim off of the Prime Eagle and focused on the greater threat coming from the northwest.

Following orders from their leader, the pack of Target-Seekers branched out. They swarmed the fort like locusts. An exchange of plasma fire filled the air as turrets on all sides of the facility engaged with the frantically moving aircrafts.

On the south wall, Barber scrambled to the portable radio. Hot flames burst as plasma fire from wing turrets struck the floor behind him. Fifty feet ahead of him was a radio tech, who scrambled to notify the units below ground.

"Have you notified Albright?"

"I haven't been able to reach them!" the tech said. "I'll boost the frequency and try—" A barrage of plasma fire rained down and punched through his body, shattering his equipment. Barber dove behind the wall, feeling the hot radius of the bullets streaking above him like shooting stars.

The Target-Seeker passed into the center of the Complex and began firing down at the rebels below. It picked off at least two ground troops before truck mounted turrets drove it away. As it passed over the west wall, an RPG spiraled up and struck the tail. The thrusters broke apart into flaming flakes of metal, throwing the Target-Seeker into a tailspin. The pilot steadied the aircraft with the elevators, only to be finished off by the wall turrets.

Barber stood up and studied the battlefield. With so much activity in the air, it was impossible to get a good estimate of how many ships were attacking. He dashed for the nearest turret. The gunner was dead, the back of the seat blown out and billowing smoke. He pulled the body out and took over. He angled the gun up and fired. The seat shook as though he were riding a galloping horse. Target-Seekers moved to-and-fro, evading the defenses while trying to fire back.

He chose a target and kept it in his iron-sights. He traced its movements, aimed accordingly, then opened fire. A volley of plasma streaked into the enemy's path, causing it to fly right into his shots. The cockpit imploded, bursting smoke and flame through the breaches. As it spiraled and smashed down, Barber rotated his gun to focus on another target. His shots trailed the chosen Target-Seeker. He followed it with his aim, missing its tail by inches. It moved off toward the north, exiting the battlefield.

"What the--?" Barber dismounted the gun and ran north along the perimeter, dodging explosions the entire way. He raised a set of binoculars to his eyes and looked northeast. "Ohhhhh SHIT!" The landscape was filled with Sovereign tanks and trucks, carring thousands of armed Strikers to lay siege. The Target-Seeker moved off toward it and was starting to land.

****

"Commander? Are you sure you want to do this?" one of the Lieutenants said. Zolnar put the pilot helmet over his head and strapped it tight.

"You're damn right," he said. The Target-Seeker touched down after being recalled back to the battalion. The boarding ramp opened and the pilot stepped out. "I'll be commandeering your ship, Pilot." The pilot knew better than to ask questions and simply stood aside.

"Sir, it's a chaotic mess…" the officer said.

"I don't care. It's personal now. I'm going to kill that bitch like I did her son. And I'm tired of that mercenary. He's MINE."

"Sir! We need you to command—"

Zolnar drew his pistol and shot the officer in the face. The surrounding Strikers stumbled back in surprise, watching the officer fall to the ground with a smoking black hole between his eyes. All at once, they looked at Zolnar, none of them daring to speak. He turned his pistol to the side, pointing it at the nearest Striker.

"You! Corporal Grimes, isn't it?"

"Yes sir," the Striker answered.

"Congrats. You're now a Lieutenant," Zolnar said. Grimes simply nodded, though he wasn't pleased about the ordeal. It seemed more like a death sentence than an honor.

"Thank you, sir," he said, hesitantly.

"I want tanks surrounding the complex. Have T-32s assault the main gate. They'll be in range of the turrets, so have T-27s and ground troops converge on the side walls to keep them occupied."

"Sir, our men will be out in the open. We will lose many Strikers," the newly promoted Grimes said. He instantly regretted expressing that concern. The Commander shot him a glare. Even with that expressionless visor, he still looked like a crazed maniac. Grimes had to correct or pay the price. "Of course, it's a sacrifice we're happy to make."

"Good," Zolnar said. He boarded the Target-Seeker and lifted off. Lieutenant Grimes got on the radio truck and relayed the Commander's orders to the battalion. The armored vehicles moved at top speed. In minutes, they surrounded the north and east sides, with several units moving around the south.

Up above, Zolnar steered his ship close into the action. Target-Seekers whizzed in and out like moths dancing around a flame. He watched them all, searching for the Prime Eagle that he knew didn't belong in the group.

"Where are you?" he whispered as he searched. He flew high and around, watching as Target-Seekers attempted to land a boarding party into the complex. Several rocket-propelled-grenades soared up to meet them, striking both ships under the cockpit and sending them spiraling into a frenzy. They smashed down outside the gates, killing all units on board.

His eyes went back to the center of the complex.

There he was. The Prime Eagle attempted a landing, only to take off again, narrowly avoiding an RPG, which was now heading directly for Zolnar.

"Shit!" The Commander banked to port. The RPG zipped by, missing the starboard wing by a couple of feet. He steadied the ship and pursued Firebird. He prepped the machine turrets and placed the mercenary in his targeting computer. He fired, his shots going wide and exploding on the ground several feet past. The Prime Eagle banked to starboard and evaded.

"Damn you, Mercenary," Zolnar growled. "All ships, don't let the Prime Eagle get away."

****

"Hope that ugly bastard knows I can hear him," Firebird said. He engaged additional power to thrusters and flew across the Complex. He twisted the joystick, forcing the ship into a twisting motion. Plasma fire from both Rebels and Sovereign pilots sprayed toward him as though he was suddenly the prize target.

"It appears both sides want you dead," Stuart said.

"Them and the rest of the world," Firebird quipped. He watched the rear-view monitors, seeing the pursuing Target-Seeker positioning for another shot. He had seen the aircraft leave the battlefield. Not even five minutes later, it was back, attacking him. It didn't take a genius to know that Commander Zolnar was in the pilot seat.

He angled the ship upward and elevated, dodging another barrage of plasma. He swerved to port and spiraled back down, only to bank to starboard to evade turret fire.

"Son of a bitch," he said, unable to make a landing run into the complex. He maneuvered it into a tight circle, unable to get the Commander off his tail. He listened to the music booming from the droid's speakers, then gave the rear-monitor another glance. Zolnar's ship was closing in, its machine turrets red hot. He killed power to the thrusters. The ship freefell like a comet, causing Zolnar to pass over them.

Firebird reengaged the thrusters and sped the ship to full power, now behind Zolnar's aircraft.

Here I am! The song boomed.

Firebird fired the machine gun. Zolnar elevated and dipped in an attempt to evade. Two bullets struck the topside of its hull, causing fire and smoke to spit.

Rock you like a hurricane...

Firebird moved in to finish the Commander off. As he did, another Target-Seeker whipped into view from their eleven-o'clock. Stuart responded first, dipping the ship and turning back toward the complex. They soared high, performing a tight vertical loop. They completed the loop and descended down nose-first, putting the pursuing ship right in their line of fire.

Firebird fired the machine gun, hitting the enemy's cockpit and ripping it apart. The Target-Seeker flipped in midair and smashed down right in the center of the complex, exploding several yards from the Center Station.

****

A thunderous boom shook the Earth. Daunhauer looked up just in time to see the ceiling cave down on top of him, driving him to the floor. Saegusa rolled to her left as another huge block of concrete smashed down where she had lain. A huge windgust filled the corridor, driving General Albright backward and filling the tunnel with thick dust.

Saegusa stood up and collected the bioweapon. She felt Daunhauer's pistol bounce against her boot. He was still on the ground, buried in rubble. She picked up the gun and studied the ceiling. There was a massive gap leading to the world above. The vent dangled from one of its ends, serving as a ladder for anyone wanting to climb out of the breach.

Through the hole, she could see ships flying about. Lasers fired in every direction. Soldiers ran and climbed the walls, their officers frantically yelling orders to each unit.

She didn't know what was going on. At this point, it didn't matter. She tucked the pistol in her waistline and climbed.

****

Barber raced back to the south wall and boarded the nearest turret. T-32s and T-27s rolled up the hill and were starting to bombard the wall with plasma fire. Huge balls of energy struck the gate, shaking the entire wall.

Rebels raced to the wall with RPGs and I.N.T. launchers from the armory. They fired the weapons at the armored vehicles. The weapons hardly even scratched the T-32s and were slow to penetrate the armor of the smaller T-27s. Rapid fire struck the walkway, causing the defenders to duck. Barber waved his hand to clear the smoke from around his face. Another blast hit the gate. It was already glowing orange and bending inward.

His eyes went back to the battlefield. The landscape was blanketed by an army of troops charging the wall.

"They're crazy. They are absolutely insane!"

He aimed his turret and fired into the crowd. Exploding shots of plasma tossed waves of Strikers into the air, ripping many of them to pieces. By now, the complex was being bombarded on all sides.

He and the other defenders focused their fire on the swarm of Strikers closing in on the walls. RPGs exploded into tight groups, sending bodies flailing for several yards. Turret blasts sawed through the attack lines like butter. Yet, they kept coming.

Another explosion rocked the wall somewhere on the north end. Target-Seekers pounded the defenses with their cannons. A series of blasts hit one of the turret mounts, sending metal fragments spitting into the complex. He aimed high and successfully hit the enemy aircraft responsible, causing it to spiral out into the field where it struck down in the middle of a swarm of Strikers.

He continued the punishment, hitting the incoming hordes with another few bursts of plasma fire. Then he saw the Prime Eagle circling above, evading pursuit from another Target-Seeker. It was the contractor.

The bastard, no doubt he betrayed them.

Barber pointed the muzzles upward and fired a volley of shots at the smaller aircraft, meanwhile, never noticing the incoming barrage of plasma energy raining down from the T-32s. All he saw was a huge blue flash.

His vision went to white, then to permanent black as his body was blown apart instantly, along with a half dozen of his fellow rebels.

****

Beretta coughed so hard she thought her lungs would burst. She stood on wobbly knees and walked blindly through the corridor. Her ears rang and the dust stung the fresh burn on her face.

The dust began to clear near the breach. Below it, she saw a pile of rubble shifting. She hurried to it and pushed the largest block away. Daunhauer stood up and turned around to face her. As horrible as he looked before, he was worse now. Blood was spilling from the hole in his cheek. The teeth behind the wound were chipped, looking like those from a crocodile. Blood trickled around his exposed eye, which was so swollen and so red it looked demonic.

He leaned toward her, allowing her to give his right arm a tug. He yelled as his shoulder popped back into place, then yelled again as he leaned down and shifted his dislocated knee back into place.

He looked at the breach. It was obvious that the doctor had escaped out into the open.

"I'll get her," he said, snarling. Beretta watched the chaos taking place in the skies. Target-Seekers fired down into the complex, focusing their fire away from the silos. RPGs and machine-gun fire sprayed back up, forcing the ships to weave in and out of view. And in the middle of it all, the Prime Eagle zipped into view, firing at some unknown target.

"It's him," she said. She watched the Prime Eagle weave in and out of view. Blood leaked from the burns into her eye. She whipped it away with her sleeve, sparking new pain as she brushed against the burns. She clenched her fists and punched the wall in a murderous rage. "This is it. If this is how it goes, then so be it. First, HE dies. Then Zolnar! Daunhauer, GET THAT CONTAINER!"

She had barely finished speaking when Daunhauer leapt onto the vent and pulled himself up through the breach.

Beretta turned and retreated down the hallway. She entered the juncture and took a right into the next tunnel. After about a hundred feet, she was in the control room beneath the Complex. Several computers were already on standby. She sat in the center seat and punched in a few codes, bringing the screen to life.

The targeting system came on the main screen. She flicked a switch, launching a targeting drone from a small port near the silos. The twelve-inch wide drone easily flew through the chaos, safely emerging undamaged a quarter mile above the complex. It flew in a circle, monitoring the events taking place below. She operated the camera by remote and searched the sky for the Prime Eagle.

She located Firebird, who was currently flying several yards outside of the wall. She locked on to his ship and linked the feed to Missile One. Emergency codes flashed on the screen, alerting her of the Complex's proximity to the blast. She overrode the alert system and pressed *launch*.

"See if you can get away from this one, you cybernetic freak."

****

Saegusa stumbled across the open complex, ducking low to avoid being seen by the Target-Seekers below. Several explosions ripped from the walls and the gate. Rebels caught in the wake of bombs were launched from the walls, trailing clouds of smoke like volcanic debris.

She looked around in search of a way out.

"HEY!" somebody shouted. She looked ahead, seeing a small group of rebels charging toward her.

"She escaped!"

Saegusa pointed her pistol, "Great, just great. Like this hasn't been hard enough so far!"

She squeezed off a few shots, hitting the rebel in the lead and causing the others to scatter. Another one continued his charge, only to be hit in the face by a plasma bullet.

She heard movement behind her. She glanced back, seeing Daunhauer emerging from the corridor. He looked and moved like a member of the undead. Judging by his actions, the pain had put him into a near-psychotic state. Yet, he was still loyal to the General.

Everyone, including Daunhauer stopped. The ground vibrated under their feet. Saegusa's heart pounded in her chest. She grew nervous, feeling as though something beneath the earth had awoken. She wasn't entirely wrong.

The Silo doors opened with an ear-piercing alarm.

Saegusa gasped as the nose of the missile emerged from the open doors. The ground was now shaking violently. Smoke rolled in huge clouds as the thrusters pushed the rocket high into the air.

It traveled high then arched down to pursue its target.

****

"Holy mother of ass! That's a big missile!" Firebird said. He could see the projectile shooting high into the sky, cutting through the swarm of ships before curving its path.

"Sir? We are being pinged," Stuart said.

"Pinged? Wait… they're shooting that at US?!" Firebird said, his eye wide. He looked back to the missile, seeing it turning toward them. "YEP!" He pressed on the throttle, pushing the thrusters to the max.

Immediately he had to bank to dodge incoming fire from Zolnar.

"Son of a bitch! He's relentless!" Firebird said.

"My analysis indicates he is angry at you and wants you to die," Stuart said. Firebird shook his head in silence.

"Let him keep chasing us. If the guy wants to go into the danger zone, let him!"

Alarms rang out as the missile closed in. Firebird pointed the ship skyward. The missile followed, gradually closing in. Traveling beside it was the Target-Seeker.

At this point, Zolnar realized the rocket was locked on to the Prime Eagle.

"That crazy bitch!" he yelled. He had assumed she was launching an attack on the armored units, which despite being devastating, would've kept him out of the blast radius. But she was actually trying to get the mercenary, and once that missile hit, it would turn the sky red with flame.

He reduced speed and steered away.

It was the exact opportunity Firebird was waiting on.

"Kill the engines now. Put port elevator to full power!" Firebird ordered. Stuart killed the thrusters, stopping the ascent. The port elevator spun into action, flipping the Prime Eagle repeatedly as it fell away. The missile flew by and continued several hundred feet into the air before turning to track its target.

Stuart re-engaged the thrusters and aimed the ship downward, placing Zolnar in the sights. Firebird squeezed the trigger, sending a dozen blue streaks into Zolnar's ship.

"What the..." Zolnar's ship juddered with each hit. Warning signs popped up on all the monitors.

System failure. Brace for impact.

"Merc! You son of a bitch!" he yelled. He steered the ship out as best he could, crashing several yards outside the wall. It skidded along the ground as though on ice, kicking up dirt and ground units before settling down.

Sparks spit from the monitors as he straightened himself in his seat. He looked out, seeing the missile descending on Firebird. The remaining Target-Seekers continued to engage with the Rebels, with some of them converging on the Prime Eagle.

He grabbed the radio transmitter and shouted, "All air units withdraw! Withdraw now! With—" he looked at the console as several more sparks ripped from it. The unit was busted. His signal would never get out.

Firebird and Stuart steered the Prime Eagle in a variety of directions, constantly moving up and down. The rocket followed their every move and was closing in. In addition, plasma fire from both Target-Seekers and defense turrets blasted in every direction.

"Sixty degrees starboard," Firebird ordered, blazing return fire from the turret. Stuart completed the maneuver and started elevating the ship again.

"Missile still closing in," he stated. "We may have to eject and use the autopilot to lure the missile away."

"Yeah...eject...in the middle of all this? With no ship to get out? Yeah, it might just be easier to let the missile just hit us," Firebird said.

"You may get that wish, sir," Stuart said. The alarms flashed. *Proximity alert!* The missile was three hundred feet away and closing in fast. "Fifteen seconds to impact."

Firebird thought fast. An idea came to mind. It would take precise timing and a little bit of luck. As of right now, it was all they had.

"Put all power to reverse thrusters!"

"That would put us right into the missile," Stuart said.

"Not if we sidewind with the port elevator," Firebird said.

"Sir, the odds of this working are two-thousand..."

"Never tell me the odds!"

Stuart killed the main thrusters and put the ship in reverse. The Prime Eagle shot backwards, instantly closing the distance between it and the missile. He put the port elevator into full spin, causing the ship to flip to the side. They could hear the echo of the hull grazing the side of the rocket as it passed by.

They killed the reverse thrusters and steadied the ship, watching the missile curving high above them as it attempted to correct course.

Firebird targeted the warhead with the machine gun and fired. Plasma streaked high into the sky, punching through the tip of the missile. A tremendous *boom* echoed across the sky, sending hot hurricane-force winds blowing in all directions. Glass shattered and men on both sides of the complex held on for dear life.

Saegusa fell to her knees as the downward shockwave hit the complex like a hammer. She looked up, squinting at the sight of the huge blast. Though it was hundreds of feet above her, its effects were still devastating. The sky had been blanketed by a layer of fire. Beneath that fire, several Target-Seekers spiraled down and crashed, having been too close to the blast radius. She ducked and turned away as one of them crashed down near the Center Station, its bow punching through the ground into the tunnels below.

Smoke and ash rained down all over the complex, scattering the remaining forces. Daunhauer stopped then backtracked as a tsunami of ash engulfed him and the several ground forces that pursued the doctor.

Saegusa covered her human eye. Another downdraft hit, blowing some of the ash away. She looked up again.

At first, all she could see was spiraling flame and destruction circling like a hellish cyclone. Then, in the middle of it all, a shape took form. She saw wings descending from the cloud of fire. They were burning, yet solid. The shape grew larger as it descended upon the complex. It moved with a bliss within a world of hell.

Like a firebird.

Stuart engaged the landing gears and set the Prime Eagle down in the center of the Complex. Rebels, at least six of them, converged on the vehicle, firing plasma rifles into the hull. The fuselage door opened and Firebird leapt into the battleground.

A spray of gunfire immediately punched through two of the rebels, forcing the others to scatter. The mercenary ran left, putting another burst into the center mass of a third.

Hot energy zipped by his head, forcing him to duck low. He pivoted on his knee with his rifle aimed. He placed the shooter in the center of his scope and squeezed the trigger, watching the rebel's head burst as a result. He could hear the other two rebels shouting, drawing the attention of a few others. What had been reduced to two had now elevated to eight.

"That's all?" he quipped.

He grabbed the rifle from a dead rebel and zigzagged between large chunks of smoldering rubble, quickly disappearing within the plumes of smoke. He could hear the group of rebels branching out to converge on him. One of them was already unlucky enough to stumble upon his place of cover.

Both rifles tore his chest and stomach to charred bits, driving his body to the ground. Up ahead was the busted fuselage of another crashed Target-Seeker. Two of his comrades stepped around the back and opened fire. Their shots went wide, mostly due to the impact-vibration from being shot by Firebird's rifles. After putting a dozen blasts into both of them, he moved up and to the right.

Another rebel popped out from around the tail of the ship, only to be shot in the face point-blank by Firebird. Several feet to his right, two other rebels moved to cover behind a guard post. They peeked out around the corners and fired a few wild shots in his direction.

Firebird moved around the Target-Seeker. Several energy rounds whipped past him, forcing him to stay behind cover. A few additional moments passed and the barrage of plasma never subsided. The line of sight was relatively clear between the ship and their place of cover.

Either these idiots are desperate or…

He turned around in time to see the seventh rebel stepping around the front of the aircraft. Firebird pointed his rifles and fired. The numerous impacts put the rebel into a dance until one of them struck a grenade on his belt, blowing his body to pieces.

"Hmm, that gives me an idea," Firebird said to himself. He found the fuselage door to the Target-Seeker and pulled it open. Metal groaned as the door slid against the indentation that jammed it. He overpowered it enough to squeeze inside and inspect the armory. "Ah, here we go." He picked up an I.N.T. launcher and opened the door on the opposite side. The rebels were still firing from behind the shack.

Firebird charged up a blast and released the trigger. A ball of energy struck the guard post, blowing it to pieces. The blast launched both rebels several yards back, their bodies crashing into the rubble behind them.

Firebird discarded the launcher and stepped out of the fuselage. At his ten-o'clock, a human figure emerged within the cloud of smoke. It was the eighth rebel of the group. He shouldered his rifle and aimed at Firebird, who in turn aimed to shoot back.

Another figure emerged from behind.

Saegusa grabbed the rebel by the back of the head and pressed her other hand to his chin, then twisted hard. His neck broke with a large *pop*. She took a breath and ran toward Firebird, who rushed to join her.

There was a sense of awe in her eye, as though she had seen an angel.

"Firebird? You…you came back. I can't believe you came back."

The mercenary casually shrugged. "Eh. I forgot my wallet."

Another explosion drew their attention to the main gate. Blue flames swirled about as the door breached. Huge pieces of metal roared inward as another cannon blast hit the door again, widening the cracks.

"A couple more of those then they'll be swarming this place," Firebird said. He looked up to the walls. It was like a siege from medieval times. The few rebels that were still alive were locked in combat with hordes of Strikers who were climbing up from the outside. Uniformed soldiers with bayonets clashed in hand-to-hand combat with rebels who used their rifles as clubs. "Let's get the hell out of here."

Firebird and Saegusa darted for the Prime Eagle. The turbines were already humming, the elevators kicking up dust. Stuart had the thing primed and ready to go.

"Go, go, go," Firebird said, goading Saegusa up into the fuselage. She stepped in and took a seat. She looked back at Firebird, who had stepped up. Another figure was approaching from behind him.

"BEHIND YOU!"

Firebird turned. His eye caught a brief glimpse of the knife as it hurtled through the air. He yelled as it struck deep into his left shoulder, almost directly at the point where his robotic arm connected to his body.

Daunhauer growled. He had intended for the blade to go through Firebird's heart, but the damn mercenary moved at the last second.

The ship was starting to lift off, the wounded mercenary stepping deeper into the fuselage. It was now or never. Daunhauer charged and jumped as high as he could. The toes of his boots touched down on the edge of the open fuselage. He grabbed at Firebird, wrapping his arms around his neck.

Unable to hold on, the mercenary fell back, landing on Daunhauer as they fell back to the ground as the Prime Eagle lifted off.

He threw his head back, striking the Lieutenant in the nose and loosening his grip. He rolled away and made some distance. He struggled to move his robotic arm. The knife had likely severed the nerves connecting the cybernetics to his biological system. He tried to extend the arm and move his fingers, but it wouldn't respond.

Daunhauer got up and ran at Firebird, kicking down into the wound in his left leg. His nerves lit up, causing Firebird to drop to one knee. Daunhauer struck with a right hook to the jaw, knocking him to his stomach.

Firebird pushed up onto his hands and knees. Daunhauer, his face red with infected flesh, lunged forward and kicked him in the ribs as though punting a football. The blow rolled Firebird onto his back, a pained grunt gusting from his lungs. He opened his eye, seeing the rebel throwing himself down on him, driving his knee into his chest. He grabbed the knife and twisted it from its embedment in Firebird's shoulder.

The mercenary yelled out as Daunhauer pulled the knife free then. The Lieutenant reared the blade back high, then drove it down to stab Firebird in the heart. Firebird threw his right hand up and caught him by the wrist, stopping the tip within an inch from his chest. The two struggled on the ground. Daunhauer pressed both hands down against the knife, slowly sinking the tip toward Firebird's heart.

Saegusa watched from the side window as the two men struggled below. She raced into the cockpit and took the seat next to Stuart.

"We have to help him," she said.

"I can't shoot him from here," the droid said. "If we fire, we'll kill Firebird." Another large explosion drew their attention to the gate. Large chunks of metal burst into the interior of the fort as the tanks finally breached the complex. Within moments, a swarm of soldiers invaded through the entrance and spread, killing any stray rebels that remained on the ground level.

Firebird could feel the tip of the knife poking through the slit in his vest. With only one arm, he could not outmuscle the scarred maniac. Firebird propped his left foot into the ground, twisted his body to the right, balancing on his shoulder. The move shifted Daunhauer's weight, allowing Firebird to lift his foot and press it into the Lieutenant's chest, pushing him back. Both men quickly rose back to their feet. Without hesitating, Daunhauer ran at him again, slashing the weapon at all kinds of angles.

Firebird backed up, evading the attacks. His back hit a wall of hot metal. He had backed into the side of the Central Station. He spun to the side as Daunhauer lunged again. The knife struck the wall, generating sparks.

A kick from Firebird knocked the knife from his hand.

Disarmed, Daunhauer shook with rage. He deflected a punch from Firebird and grabbed him by the throat. Charging like a bull, he drove him against the wall, slamming him hard. Daunhauer raised a knee into his stomach, then took advantage of his lack of defense on his left side. He threw a sharp haymaker over Firebird's robotic shoulder, striking him hard in the jaw. A series of punches followed, hitting Firebird in the face and stomach.

The mercenary jolted left and right as the punches connected. It was like being attacked from an enraged beast. Finally, the Lieutenant ended the barrage with a kick to the groin. Firebird fell to his knees, his mouth gaping wide.

"That...was cheap," he groaned. He looked up, gasped, then threw himself to the side. The Lieutenant thrust a kick, missing his head and instead hitting the wall. Firebird stood up, dazed and off balance. He circled the Rebel, while trying to catch his breath and overcome the pain throughout his body. Daunhauer faced him, his back now turned to the station.

Firebird went in for the attack. He threw a kick to Daunhauer's midsection, which was blocked and parried in a sweeping motion of the rebel's left arm. Off balance, Firebird threw a desperate knife-hand strike at his neck. Again, his attack was deflected and parried. Daunhauer turned with his opponent's momentum, twisting his wrist and elbow, countering with a knee to the ribs, then grabbed the mercenary with both hands. Firebird felt the brief sensation of weightlessness as Daunhauer threw him headfirst into the building.

Glass grazed his body as he soared through the busted window. He hit the computer console and rolled forward until landing on the floor. His shoulder throbbed and bled profusely, forcing him to treat it quickly before Daunhauer followed him in. He could see the rebel moving back. He looked around in search of his knife, quickly finding it and picking it up. Holding it at his side like a deranged psychopath, he marched toward the station.

With a shaky hand, Firebird dug for a stapler. He took the vest off to allow himself better access, then tore at the hole in his shirt, revealing the wound. He punched a few staples into the slit, groaning with each one.

Daunhauer was nearing the door.

Firebird grabbed his metal arm by the wrist, desperately trying to get it to respond. It was like a statue, frozen, with the elbow bent at his ribcage.

Daunhauer kicked the door down and raised his knife. Firebird sidestepped and grabbed at a chair and raised it as a shield. Dauhauer followed him and thrust the knife, lodging the blade in the seat. Daunhauer grabbed the chair with his other hand and yanked it away. He struck Firebird with a hard kick to the chest, driving him back through the stairwell. Firebird reeled backward down the steps and hit the guardrail. Before he could find his footing, Daunhauer came at him and slashed.

Firebird evaded as best he could, twisting himself until his body fell over the rail down onto the second level of steps. His leg injury flared as he touched down, causing him to sprawl onto his stomach. His leg throbbed intensely where he had been shot, matching the pain in his shoulder. Unable to stand, Firebird started to crawl toward the underground corridor entrance.

Daunhauer descended the flight of stairs and turned the corner. He chuckled as he watched the mercenary crawl through the open doorway.

"I'll give you an 'A' for effort," he said as he passed the few remaining stairs. "Pulling a stunt like this, with two factions wanting you dead, you lasted longer than you should have." Daunhauer tossed his knife in the air, letting it flip over end before catching it by the handle. He pointed the blade down. "Luckily, I'm the one who gets the pleasure of killing you. Only an IDIOT would think he had a chance of getting out of here alive!"

Firebird rolled onto his back. He reached past the edge of the frame, beyond Daunhauer's line of sight. A pained smile creased his face.

"That's rich. Especially coming from the moron, who literally brought a knife..." he retracted his arm, a Model 10 revolver in his hand "...to a gunfight."

Daunhauer hesitated, seeing the gun he had knocked from Saegusa's hand pointing at his face. It was the last thing he would see before a .38 caliber bullet punched through his infected eye.

CHAPTER 27

Smoke and fire swirled throughout the complex. Screams of despair filled the air as the rebel defenses were overpowered by the horde of Strikers. The wall perimeter had been overtaken, its remaining defenders impaled by bayonets. Strikers flooded in through the gates, while others descended from the wall ladders, filling the interior of the complex.

Beretta passed through a short corridor and kicked open a door leading into the stairwell leading to the Center Station's surface structure. She moved around the stairs, immediately seeing a body lying near the tunnel entrance. She immediately recognized Daunhauer's ravaged face, now with a bullet wound through the eye.

She fell to her knees and squeezed her eyes shut to suppress a few tears. The Lieutenant had been loyal to her during the whole war. No matter how difficult the mission or controversial the decision, he always supported her leadership.

Shockwaves from explosions shook the tunnels, spilling dust from the ceilings. She opened her eyes and watched the world crumbling around her. Her mission had failed catastrophically. There was little comfort in knowing they had bled the enemy army drastically. The soldiers she killed would soon be replaced, and the Sovereignty would continue to run supreme. Her son's death had truly been for nothing. All that was left was to kill Zolnar...and those responsible for betraying her cause.

She heard rummaging from above. Somebody was upstairs.

"The mercenary!"

She turned and raced up the stairs.

Firebird pushed himself through the debris in the station, limping on his left leg as he found his way out. The wind blew hot air across the complex, kicking up dust, ash, and debris.

He was only two steps out of the doorway when he had been spotted by several Strikers.

"Kill him!" one yelled.

He aimed his revolver and fired, putting a round through the facemask of the one alerting the squad. Several more converged on him, firing Plasma Rifles. He fired again, killing another, then retreated. He only gained a few yards before his leg was ready to give out again.

A group of at least twenty Strikers were converging on his location. He fired back again, splattering another soldier's brains through his helmet. Another shot struck the next Striker in the left-center of his chest, causing him to spin with his rifle blazing, his stray plasma blasts inadvertently killing a couple of his comrades.

The group closed in, with several more advancing behind them. Firebird squeezed the trigger once more, only hearing that dreaded *click* of an empty weapon.

"I do *not* feel lucky..." he grumbled to himself.

He jumped back, feeling the heat of hot plasma raining down from above. They struck the squad, blasting the Strikers into blazing pulp. A shadow encompassed him, accompanied by a downdraft.

The Prime Eagle descended, its turret slicing through each Striker. It touched down quick and hard, its fuselage door open. A moment later, Saegusa peeked from around the corner.

"Come with me if you want to live!" she called out.

"Funny!" Firebird raced as fast as he could and dove into the Prime Eagle. As he hit the floor, rifle fire suddenly bombarded the ship.

Beretta charged the ship, having acquired a dead soldier's rifle. She ran through the heap of dead Strikers toward the ship. Saegusa dove down as several energy blasts struck the inside of the ship.

Firebird leaned to grab the fuselage door but was forced back as a few blasts exploded near the frame.

"Punch it, Stuart," he said.

The turbines whined and the elevators kicked up dust, lifting the ship several feet off the ground. Desperate, Beretta charged the ship, letting the rifle hang from its sling. She jumped with all of her might and caught the edge of the door frame.

Firebird stood up and tried to slide the door shut.

An alarm flashed. *Safety alert.* The electronic system detected her hands in the way and would not close. Beretta dangled from the ship and smiled up at the mercenary. She reached down at her belt and pulled a thermal detonator.

She was truly on a suicide mission. The blast would not only destroy the ship, but also rupture the chemical and kill Zolnar and every Striker in the battalion. As a bonus, she would have the pleasure of killing Saegusa and the mercenary.

Both of them were at the edge of the fuselage, gazing down at the fanatical General.

"This is what you deserve!" she yelled up at Firebird. "I paid you money! That's what matters to you, right?! And *this* is what I get in return?!" She armed the five-second timer on the detonator. As she prepared to throw it into the ship, she noticed Firebird holding the heavy bag of gold.

"Don't worry! I have your refund right here," he said. He let go of the straps. The heavy bag landed on her face, knocking her off the ship. She flailed in anger, her last thoughts being nothing but a whirlwind of rage. The detonator exploded in her hand, blowing her apart in midair.

Zolnar watched from the ground as the Prime Eagle elevated high into the air. It turned north, putting the fuselage into view. His stomach tightened as he recognized the doctor standing at the open doorway. The facial recognition in his visor confirmed her identity.

That rare feeling of genuine fear struck as the afterburners kicked in. After a few moments, the ship had disappeared into the horizon.

Zolnar stood silent while several mobile units gathered around him. A radio truck was nearby. Standing beside it was a nervous radio technician, holding a transmitter in his hand. The Commander swallowed hard.

"It's Cornelius, sir. He's asking for an update…"

Zolnar held the transmitter in his hand but couldn't bring himself to press the button. His mind raced for a lie. Any lie. But there was nothing. The Commander trembled in front of all of his troops as the voice boomed from the radio.

"Commander! Report!"

The door slid shut and Firebird collapsed into the passenger seat, exhausted. Saegusa rushed to his side and began to assess his many injuries. He was in rough shape but it was nothing the doctors back home couldn't take care of.

"You look like hell," she said.

"You too," he replied. He glanced out the window, admiring the distant view of the Sovereign military. Even this far out from the complex, the country was full of foot soldiers and ground vehicles. The Rebellion was over, and the Sovereignty reigned supreme.

"We really caused a stir," Saegusa commented.

"It was happening long before we set foot here," Firebird said. He noticed the container filled with the pressurized acid gas. "You actually made that?"

"I was stalling," she said. She looked at him and smiled. Strangely, he felt a sense of genuine peace looking back at her.

"Stalling?" Firebird said. She was alone in the Sovereignty, caught between two factions that wanted to utilize her skills. "Stalling for what?"

"I guess there was some inkling of hope in my heart. Turns out there there's more to you than I thought," she said. The two shared a long stare. Finally, Saegusa leaned in close to embrace him.

Stuart's voice boomed over the intercom.

"He only came back because I made him!"

There was a pause between the two cyborgs. Saegusa laughed then threw her arms around the mercenary.

CHAPTER 28

Espinosa was a country like no other. Firebird had seen it a long time ago but had forgotten the beauty of the vast gardens and peaceful neighborhoods. It was as if this region had never even been touched by the war. Even under the flickering atmosphere, the Territory was a place of beauty. The Governor welcomed the Prime Eagle with open arms and was quick to embrace Saegusa. From there, she and Firebird were transferred to the medical facility and given treatment for their injuries.

"This thing works pretty good now," Firebird said, extending his metal arm. The engineers and doctors had done some tweaking to it and helped to replace some broken interior mechanics.

Stuart stood by his hospital bed, waiting for his master to step up. He too had received treatment for his damaged components and was back to normal.

"I see they even replaced the blade," he stated. Firebird held up his metal fist and protruded the blade from the gauntlet.

"I can thank Ms. Saegusa for that. It's even better than last time," he said. "They actually hooked up the nerve endings properly, so now it just receives the signals from my brain. It's as easy as peeing." He retracted the blade. "Not that you'd understand that."

"I was a medical droid," Stuart said. "Of course I understand."

Firebird leaned on his left leg. The treatment had worked wonderfully. Another week or so, he'd be back to normal. He exited the room and continued to the lower levels, passing numerous patients suffering from radiation cancer.

He passed through a long hall and found a room. There, Saegusa laid in a bed, sound asleep. She smelled fresh, appearing as though she was in a peaceful bliss. The image was completed by a bright smile that she wore in her sleep.

The mercenary glanced across the room and saw all sorts of chemistry equipment. They had designed this special residency for physicians to follow her instructions on creating the cancer-eating formula. Doctors and nurses were monitoring her vitals, while ignoring the presence of the visitors.

"So? How's that formula working?" Firebird asked. One of the nurses reached over and handed him a long sheet of paper. It displayed x-rays of her stomach region. Firebird shook his head and shrugged. "Not sure what any of this means."

Stuart leaned up and gave it a look. "The cancer mass is depleting. Congratulations, Doctor. You've done it," he told Saegusa, as though she were awake.

"I suppose you're leaving?" one of the doctors said.

"Yeeeeep," Firebird said. "I'm broke. Gotta make that money."

"I see. Well...thank you for all of your help."

Firebird nodded and exited the building with Stuart.

They walked to the center of town where the Governor waited by their ship.

"Thank you so much. Are you sure you won't accept any payment?" he asked.

Firebird opened the cabin door.

"No," he answered, his voice somewhat drawn out. The selfish part of him wanted to change his mind but he suppressed it.

"Well, I wish you good health," the Governor said. "Godspeed."

"You as well. And keep that poison crap in the right hands," Firebird warned. It was a true warning. The Governor nodded and walked away with his staff.

Stuart started the engines. The turbines gradually rotated, generating enough energy to lift the ship up.

"WAIT!" somebody shouted. Stuart killed the engines and looked out. Firebird opened the cockpit door, seeing Saegusa running toward him. Two medical doctors followed her out. She ignored their protests about her being out of bed as she approached the mercenary.

"What are you doing?!" she said, angrily.

"Oh shit. Is this our *Shane, come back* moment?"

"You were seriously going to leave without saying goodbye?!" she said.

"You were asleep!" Firebird said. "You were recovering from a cancer treatment. WHICH, by the way, is still ongoing."

"And where are you going?" she asked.

"Gotta make some money somewhere, Doc," he said. "I may be a lot of things, but I'm no thief. I pay to put food in my belly. And to pay, I need doe. And you need rest."

Saegusa grabbed him by the collar and pulled him close. Her face was stern at first. Firebird anticipated a smack across the face.

Then, slowly, a smile took form.

"While you're in-between adventures, you plan to come back?"

Firebird stared silently.

"Well, I don't know. I suppose if business is slow, I might..." She cut him off by pressing her lips to his. Firebird stood dumbfounded. The feeling was intensified by her angelic gaze. "Yeah. I'll come back. I'll even bring flowers."

"Or you could bring some more of that Radialem," one of the doctors said. "We need more of it. If you're willing, that is..."

"We'll take care of it," Stuart said.

Saegusa gave Firebird another hug and kiss.

"Stay out of trouble," she said.

"Me? In trouble? Don't know how you could suspect such a thing," he quipped. The doctors took Saegusa by the arm and led her back to the hospital. Firebird sat in the cockpit and watched quietly as she walked away, glancing back every so often at him.

"Okay boss," Stuart said, snapping him back to reality. "Where to?"

Firebird took a breath.

"Well, I heard a doctor say some of that flower might be over in the west. Why don't we head on over there?"

"You think we'll find any work along the way?"

"There's always someone on this continent looking for a hired gun," Firebird said.

Stuart fired up the engines and initiated liftoff.

"Any tunes, sir?"

Firebird grinned. He looked back to the ground, watching Saegusa enter the hospital.

"Surprise me," he said.

They lifted up into the air and flew far into the horizon, blasting classic rock the entire way.

THE END

FIREBIRD WILL RETURN...

CHECK OUT OTHER GREAT
SCIENCE FICTION BOOKS

WARNING: THIS NOVEL HAS GRATUITOUS VIOLENCE, SEX, FOUL LANGUAGE, AND A LOT OF BAD JOKES! YOU MAY FIND YOURSELF ENJOYING HIGHLY INAPPROPRIATE PROSE! YOU HAVE BEEN WARNED!

MAX RAGE
by Jake Bible

Genetically Engineered. Physically enhanced. Mentally conditioned.

Master Chief Sergeant Major Max Rage was the top dog in an elite fighting force that no one in the galaxy could stop. Until, one day, someone did.

The lone survivor, Rage was blamed for the mission failure and court-martialed.

With a serious chip on his shoulder, Rage finds himself as a bouncer at the top dive bar in Greenville, South Carolina. And, man, is he bored with his job.

At least until he gets a job offer he can't refuse. Now, Rage is headed halfway across the galaxy to the den of corruption known as Horloc Station.

With this job, Max Rage may have a chance to get back to what he was: an unstoppable Intergalactic Badass!

RECON ELITE
by Viktor Zarkov

With Earth no longer inhabitable, Recon Six Elite are sent across space to scout promising new planets for colonization.

The five talented and determined space marines are led by hard-nosed commander Sam Boggs. Earth's last best hope, these men and women are the "tip of the spear". Armed with a wide array of deadly weapons and forensics, Boggs and Recon Elite Six must clear the planet Mawholla of hostile species.

But Recon Elite are about to find out how hostile Mawholla truly is.

CHECK OUT OTHER GREAT SCIENCE FICTION BOOKS

AGENT PRIME
by **Jake Bible**

Denman Sno is Agent Prime!

The best of the Fleet Intelligence Service's elite Special Service Division, Denman Sno will need to use all of his skills and resources to stop the galaxy from plunging into another War with the alien menace known as the Skrang Alliance.

Sno's assignment: protect and deliver Pol Hammon, the galaxy's greatest dark tech hacker, to Galactic Fleet headquarters.

Hammon is in possession of new technology that can and will change the landscape of galactic life. The Galactic Fleet will do anything to keep that technology out of the hands of the Skrang Alliance even it it means sacrificing their best agent.

Even if it means sacrificing Agent Prime!

GALACTIC TROOPERS
by **Ian Woodhead**

For three thousand years, the Terran Empire has ruled the Galactic Expanse with an iron fist, conquering any alien civilisation who dared to oppose the might of their new human masters.

Their grip is about to be shaken apart when an unknown invasion force starts to strip whole planetary populations.

Now humans and aliens must find a way to work together to prevent the Empire and the invaders turning the Galactic Expanse into a graveyard.

www.ingramcontent.com/pod-product-compliance
Lightning Source LLC
Chambersburg PA
CBHW022215170626
46807CB00005B/2374